Will sh

When Mike turne
she popped the pen
skittered across her c
She stood up quickly to retrieve it and felt the
uncomfortable hemline dust her legs above the
kneecap. Torn between slipping back behind her
desk or getting her pen cap, Jennie watched as Mike
strode across the room and scooped it up.

As he stood, offering her the cap, his eyes,
brilliant green and somehow all-knowing, traveled
up her legs to the blouse with its deep "V" neck,
before settling on her face.

A slow blush crept up her cheeks as she took the
cap from him.

"Nice outfit."

Jennie gritted her teeth and plopped unladylike
into her chair, words leaping unheeded from her
mouth. "It was on the clearance rack," she said,
irritated at the compliment. It meant Mae was right
again. "Probably because no one wanted such a short
skirt." She would have sworn he was laughing at
her. She needed to stop acting like one of her
students.

"What brings the school's most winning baseball
coach into my classroom?" she managed to say
lightly.

"Business. Someone told me you run your own
historical research company?"

Jennie nodded, dismissing the slight twinge of
disappointment that the faculty's most eligible
bachelor sought her for work purposes. "I don't do
much during the school year. Are you wanting some
research done this summer?"

"Actually, I need your help sooner."

A Family
to
Die For

by

AJ Brower

A Family to Die For

Cover Art by *Kim Mendoza*

The Wild Rose Press
PO Box 706
Adams Basin, NY 14410-0706
Visit us at www.thewildrosepress.com

Publishing History
First Crimson Rose Edition, 2009
Print ISBN 1-60154-612-2

Published in the United States of America

Dedication

Thanks to Sloan McBride and Melanie Carroll,
my Sassy Scribes,
who provided the wisdom and encouragement
to write till the end.

Chapter 1

Jennie Foster barely noticed the two teenagers tossing a skull back and forth. She was far too focused on stretching the length of her skirt to cover a bit more bare leg. Unfortunately, the unyielding waistband would not go any lower on her hips and what little stretch she could pull out of the length bounced back when she let go. Though her students wouldn't bat an eye at the new skirt, Jennie preferred a length that reached the floor and was more like pants. Whatever had possessed her to wear a skirt to school?

Giving up on the fruitless task, she turned her frustration on Josh and Adam and frowned at them.

"Enough already. Put Sir Isaac's head back on his body and get to your own classes."

Josh, one thumb in the plastic head's eye socket, pranced over to Jennie's desk, where she had retreated to hide her bare legs. The odd half walk, half dance made his skinny six-foot frame comical.

"First bell hasn't rung yet. Besides, your class is so much more fun than Mrs. Whitmore's. She makes us be quiet until class begins. Better to be tardy than be tortured like that."

Jennie eased herself down in her chair, tugging at the skirt as she crossed her legs. "Instead, you torture me."

"Ahhhh, Dr. Foster." Adam joined his best friend in towering over the teacher's desk. He angled his chin down and stuck out his bottom lip in imitation of a sad child. "You know you're our favorite teacher forever and ever. We would never torture you. Can I

1

borrow this?" He grabbed a new pen off her desk, a nice one Jennie had managed to snag from the school supply room before they all disappeared.

She sighed, holding out her hand for the pen. "No. And, if you're going to stay, make yourself useful." She handed them each a stack of papers and reclaimed her pen. "Sort these alphabetically. That'll make it easier to put the grades in the computer. And go far away from me."

The two students each took a pile and immediately began to laugh at the junior students' bad answers on the causes of the Cold War. Jennie smiled at their comments because they were right. In her U.S. History class last year, Josh and Adam had been stellar students. They were the exception among their peers in the required class, enjoying it thoroughly. No surprise they were also in the Archeology Club she advised.

With fifteen minutes until her first period, Jennie turned to the remaining stack of papers and began the tedious task of putting grades into the computer. But before she could get more than a couple typed in, a large shadow filled her doorway. She looked up in surprise to see Mike Garretson, one of Swansea High School's chemistry teachers. Hard to miss at six-foot-two and dressed in a suit and tie, the former semi-pro baseball player and current school baseball coach eyed her classroom warily, as if he expected the skeleton to walk over and shake his hand.

Jennie picked up the pen recently retrieved from Adam, repeatedly snapping off the top with her thumb and clicking it back into place. Mike had never been in her room. In fact, they hadn't said a dozen words to each other in the two years he'd been at Swansea High School. Not that Jennie hadn't noticed him. Every female teacher instantly fell for his tall athletic looks. But when faced with his cool reception, they quickly lost interest.

Jennie was no exception. However, Mike was one of many men she'd dismissed as not worth the effort. At least that's what her best friend, Mae Jefferson, accused her of doing. But what was the point of having a boyfriend if he was going to dump you in the end? Her argument stemmed from her most recent relationship.

Mae had pointed out five years should be sufficient to get over anyone.

Wearing the skirt had been an acknowledgement Mae was right. Jennie's wardrobe was reminiscent of a grandmother's garage sale find, unlikely to attract any man's attention. At twenty-nine, Jennie knew she needed to look more feminine. But she suddenly wished for a pair of pants and comfortable flats, not the short skirt and heels she had on.

It was little consolation Mike seemed as uneasy, his broad shoulders filling the room's entrance. He might be a teacher, but he looked the part of a successful businessman with an unmistakable athlete's body stretching the suit in all the right places.

Josh called out a greeting. "Hey, Coach! Great game yesterday. Think we'll get to regionals this year?"

The slightest hint of smile crossed the coach's face. "That would be the plan. I think if our players are as dedicated as you two are as fans, then it's doable."

The two teens exchanged glances, grinned, and gave each other high-fives. Their reputation as avid Swansea High School Skyhawk baseball fans gave them a bit of prestige in the hallways, especially when they donned face paint and hair dye.

When Mike turned his attention back to Jennie, she popped the pen cap off again. This time it skittered across her desk and dropped to the floor. She stood up quickly to retrieve it and felt the uncomfortable hemline dust her legs above the kneecap. Torn between slipping back behind her desk or getting her pen cap, Jennie watched as Mike strode across the room and scooped it up.

As he stood, offering her the cap, his eyes, brilliant green and somehow all-knowing, traveled up her legs to the blouse with its deep "V" neck, before settling on her face.

A slow blush crept up her cheeks as she took the cap from him.

"Nice outfit."

Jennie gritted her teeth and plopped unladylike into her chair, words leaping unheeded from her mouth. "It was on the clearance rack," she said, irritated at the compliment. It meant Mae was right again. "Probably because no one wanted such a short skirt." She would have sworn he was laughing at her. She needed to stop acting like one of her students.

"What brings the school's most winning baseball coach into my classroom?" she managed to say lightly.

"Business. Someone told me you run your own historical research company?"

Jennie nodded, dismissing the slight twinge of disappointment that the faculty's most eligible bachelor sought her for work purposes. "I don't do much during the school year. Are you wanting some research done this summer?"

"Actually, I need your help sooner."

Great. The project from the hot teacher she'd have to turn down. "There's only a month of school left. Not an ideal time for me, not with end-of-semester projects due and final exams around the corner."

"I need you to find one thing, not a whole family

tree or anything." He glanced over his shoulder at Josh and Adam. Then he pulled one of the student desks closer to Jennie's desk and squeezed into it before leaning in conspiratorially.

"I have an odd inheritance involving an old house. I need an expert's help with some documents," he explained. "A lot of them have to do with family history. It's complicated." He paused, obviously considering his words carefully. Jennie expected him to hand her a secret message and request she eat it after reading it.

"Do you like old houses?" Mike asked.

She glanced at the pictures on her desk. Next to a photo of her father was another of her pride and joy, the 1920s home she'd spent more than two years refurbishing. She'd gotten her doctorate in history because she loved anything with the hint of age to it, but architecture topped her interests.

"Sure, I suppose I like old houses." After she said it, she realized Mike probably wouldn't catch the sarcasm.

He plowed on with his pitch. "I inherited a house that's at least a hundred years old. Well, sort of inherited. Without getting into the details, I need some help with the history associated with it." He shifted in his seat again, looking over his shoulder at the boys.

Even if he hadn't already caught Jennie's attention with the clandestine voice, he hooked her with the century-old house.

"Victorian?"

Mike stared at her blankly.

"The house. Is it Victorian? You know, before the turn-of-the-century?"

He shrugged. "I have no idea. I can make you a chemical concoction to blow it up though. Does that help?" He tilted his head, arching his left eyebrow.

"Touché," Jennie said and grinned. "Victorian is

best described as, well, fancy woodwork, often multi-colored, twelve-foot ceilings, brick chimneys, musty cellar, big attic."

Mike nodded. "Oh, yeah. It's got all that."

She leaned forward, clasping her hands together as she mentally rearranged her schedule. None of her clients were expecting anything right now, and her weekends were still open. "I'd have to see what you want done. When do you need results?"

"Uh...in a month?" At least he had the grace to look remorseful.

Jennie stared at him. "I don't do miracles. Why do you need this so soon? Are you doing it for a birthday or something?"

He hesitated. "Or something. Can you come by the house on Saturday? I'll explain everything then."

"Okay, but I can't promise much. Where's the house?"

The warning bell for class rang. Josh and Adam got up and handed the papers to Jennie.

Mike eyed the boys as they walked out of the room. "I'll email directions." He headed for the door, then stopped abruptly.

"Oh, one other thing. Do you have any family connections around here? I was told you were from Chicago."

"As I've said all my life, I'm not from anywhere. My dad was in the military, moving all the time. Chicago was my most recent home, only because I could teach and get my Ph.D. too."

Mike nodded, apparently pleased she wasn't local. Jennie pondered that odd reaction after he'd left.

****

She forgot about Mike's visit until her lunch hour, when Mae, who was the head librarian as well as her best friend, joined her in the teachers' lounge. Despite her student teaching advisor's recommendation to avoid "that den of gossip and misinformation," Jennie had always joined her fellow teachers in the lounge. It was a needed break from the teen drama in the classroom.

Mae leaned back, pursing her lips, as soon as Jennie set down her tray of lasagna. "Josh Kowalzski said Garretson was talking with you before class this morning."

"Geez. Can't two teachers meet privately anywhere?" Jennie rolled her eyes. "Yes, Mike came by my room. He wants to hire me to do some history research, but he was very secretive. Didn't really tell me much. He said it has something to do with a Victorian house. I'm supposed to meet him there Saturday morning."

"Very mysterious," Mae agreed. "What do you think he wants?"

"Who knows with him," she said, eating between comments. "I'm surprised he talked with me at all, considering how little he does with the rest of the faculty."

"He must have some social skills. First made it to the minor leagues in baseball, then he married Veronica Houseman, megawatt socialite." Mae absently poked at her reheated leftovers. "Newspaper photos always made them look amazing together. She always seemed a bit cold to me, though. Wonder why they divorced."

"Maybe you should go in my place this weekend and ask him."

"I'm happily married, thank you. You, on the other hand, could use a social outing. It's been years since you've had a decent relationship."

"There was that guy. What was his name? You know, the one who took me boating."

"My point exactly," Mae said. "Girl, you need to open up some. Let someone know you."

"It was a *fishing* boat."

"So? Maybe he knew how to cook fresh fish. That's not a bad thing. You got to open the door if you want to find a man."

Jennie gave her friend a half-smile and shook her head. "I get it, Mae. But I'm pretty sure meeting Mike Garretson at some old house does not count as a door."

"Darling, you'll never know if you don't answer."

Jennie stood to throw away the remains of her lunch, tugging on the skirt hem. If this was what she had to wear to get some guy to notice her, she'd stick to history. Maybe she'd find some nerdy guy like her who enjoyed a walk in a cemetery or admiring the crumbling façade of a historical building.

Mike Garretson was not that guy. Still, she knew she wouldn't trade this meeting with anyone. Her life consisted of school, research, and dinner at Mae's on Sunday. This meeting had the potential of being the most exciting event in her life since finishing her house.

Chapter 2

Mike sent the promised directions, which seemed obsessively detailed to Jennie. From his description, the place was only a few miles from the school by a crow's flight. She turned down his offer to lead her there, expecting the house couldn't be that hard to find.

Warm spring air wafting through her open car windows, Jennie wished for crow's wings after the third missed turn. Now she was grateful for his attention to detail. No question though, a crow had it a lot easier.

She finally spotted a chain across a gravel driveway Mike said would signal the house was near. She had to get out of the car to dial in the padlock code, tediously obeying Mike's instructions to make sure the chain was locked again once she drove across it.

Jennie was concentrating so hard on driving she almost missed the looming architecture in front of her. Her mouth hung open as she drove out of the woods, staring at the immense stone and brick building. The car rolled to a stop on the rutted lane.

Across a stretch of recently mowed lawn stood Mike's "old house," the mother of Victorian mansions. It was stunning with dark green shutters, red brick and peeling butter yellow paint, meshed in fairytale fantasy all the way up its four floors. Wrapped around the ground floor was a full porch with an impressive stone foundation and broad steps. The original owners had been wealthy enough to indulge someone's whimsy, though it was desperate for renovation.

When Jennie saw Mike standing on the porch watching her, she clamped her mouth shut. He waved and yelled at her to park behind his car. Though out of place under the old house's porte-cochere—car park in any modern century—his red sports car was a 1960s Mustang in superb condition. She gave her Saturn some gas to ease in behind Mike's car. Beautiful house, great car. What more could she ask for?

"I take it you like River Bluffs." He stepped down from the porch and opened Jennie's door.

Okay. A gentleman too. Now her day was perfect.

"River Bluffs?"

"That's the name of this place. My great, great grandfather built it in the late 1800s."

"River Bluffs," she said with a sigh. Mike offered her a hand to climb out of the car. Managing a façade of blandness, she tried to recall if any date had ever helped her out of a car. Not that this was a date. But she did notice he could wear a T-shirt and jeans as well as a suit and tie.

"It's nice," she said with reserve. "I don't think I've ever seen anything like it. You've even got three turrets. Yeah. It's really nice." She was impatient to see the home's interior, but kept to her detached business persona. "So, what's inside?"

"I think you'll find it interesting," he said, matching her tone of understatement.

An irritating series of yaps preceded a small dirty-white creature running from the back of the house. Mike turned toward the dog, and Jennie would have sworn a smile escaped his granite features as he reached down to pick up the bouncing and vibrating animal. Jennie thought he'd be more of a German shepherd type of guy.

"Zippy!" Mike said in a commanding voice. The

dog ignored him, desperately trying to lick Mike's face. "Calm down. Sorry, Jennie. Along with the house, I inherited Zippy. He's, uh, different. He grows on you."

She scrunched her nose at the distinct odor of wet dog. However, seeing the handsome, stoic Coach Garretson unable to control the little monster was one point in the dog's favor. She lost her reserve and laughed.

"Apparently he also rubs off on you," she said, as Zippy muddied Mike's T-shirt.

Mike scratched the dog on the head and, sniffing, made a face. "Zippy, you're filthy and you smell too. What have you been in? I'll throw him in the carriage house."

The dog pointed his face with its lolling tongue in her direction. "That's okay." Jennie shook her head reluctantly. She wasn't much for small dogs, but animals of all types were a definite weakness. She tentatively reached out her hand and half-heartedly scratched his head, one of the few places where he wasn't dirty. He whined and his tail, sticking out from under Mike's arm, wagged madly.

Mike set him down on the ground. The dog immediately raced around the yard to the front stairs in anticipation of them entering there.

Mike tilted his head. "Come on. If Zippy wants us to use the front door, then we will. It's more impressive than the parlor door or the kitchen entrance anyway."

They apparently weren't fast enough for Zippy, who dashed between Mike and Jennie and the front door several times. After unlocking the tall double doors, Mike pushed them open, revealing a wide foyer the size of an average bedroom and a staircase Jennie mentally dubbed the "Grand Staircase."

She let out a soft "ahhh" in spite of herself. The two-story entry was exquisitely tiled with green-grey marble, every piece of intricately carved wood dark and highly polished.

"Before we go upstairs, let me show you the downstairs."

Jennie happily trailed behind. Through parlor, kitchen and dining room, every detail amazed the historian in her. Until she reached the last room on the main floor, the library.

It was in complete disarray. A huge oak desk took up a large part of the room, covered with a computer, printer and piles of papers. Surrounding the desk were several boxes, some overflowing and others partially emptied. The mess clashed with the wall-to-wall bookcases and antique chairs with clawed feet.

Mike grunted. "This," he said, waving an arm toward the mess on the desk and floor, "would be the reason I need you. Along with the house, I inherited a mystery. And I'm running out of time to solve it."

Jennie waited expectantly, but he didn't elaborate.

"I should show you the rest of the house first."

The grand staircase beckoned. At the landing was an enormous painting of River Bluffs, a family having a picnic on the grounds in front of the house. Jennie wanted to study the painting, but Mike had followed the hyper dog and was waiting at the top of the stairs.

He pointed out a warped board to the side of the faded and dusty carpet. "Watch this," he warned. "I meant to nail it down, but I haven't gotten to it. I've been making so many repairs on this place, I can't get to all of them."

The floor had six bedrooms, which Mike breezed through, including the last one.

"Here's where I sleep on weekends." He gestured to a large corner bedroom with a round sitting area. She guessed it was the small turret she'd seen outside. Jennie took a cursory look at the room with its more modern bed coverings and flushed as a completely errant thought about Mike in that bed crossed her mind.

With the warmth of Mike's body beside her, the bedroom's door frame was suddenly too confining for Jennie's thoughts and two people. She quickly moved around him, taking the lead up a set of narrow stairs coming from the kitchen since the grand staircase did not proceed up to the servants' quarters on the third floor.

Jennie stopped, eyeing the closed door at the top of another flight of stairs leading to the attic. She felt Mike's presence behind her.

"That's the attic. There's nothing but junk up there."

Jennie turned, finding herself face to face with him. She was so close she could smell his scent, an earthy smell that reminded her of the outdoors. For an awkward moment, neither said anything. She broke the silence by clumsily stepping backwards onto the bottom step.

"One man's junk is another man's treasure," she murmured. "I'll take a peek up here."

Zippy accompanied her up the steps, which were even steeper and narrower than the last flight of stairs, complete with darkness at the top. She opened the creaking door and fumbled for the string of the single light bulb dangling from the ceiling. From a lone grimy window on one end of the enormous room to a matching window at the distant end, dust danced in the small light where cobwebs held reign over the forgotten items. It was as exactly as old attics should be: broken furniture, trunks, discarded paintings, lamps with antiquated shades.

"Man, I wish my family had an attic like this." She sighed, then wrangled a heavy, gilt-framed picture into the light. She set down the frame and wandered partly down a narrow aisle, itching to open a box or trunk.

Mike raised a questioning eyebrow from the attic doorway.

"I was an Army brat," Jennie replied to his unasked question. "You should try living without a permanent home. Everything gets thrown out before a move, so there aren't any family treasures. Some of this stuff has probably been here as long as the house."

Mike shrugged. "You're probably right, but it still looks like junk to me."

"Then you'll just have to dig through it with me."

Mike gave that small smile again as Jennie realized belatedly she had given him reason to believe she had decided to help him.

"That is, if I take on your research," she added hastily.

"I have one last place to show you." Mike headed downstairs again, leaving Jennie to call a reluctant Zippy out of the unexplored territory.

Mike's muscular legs had eaten up half the hallway before Jennie reached the third floor. At the far end of the hallway, he pushed open a pair of doors leading out to a balcony, standing to one side as Jennie gazed, awestruck, at the scene.

Despite the overgrowth of trees on the bluff the house was built on, she could see St. Louis. The Mighty Mississippi was as iridescent as the shiny steel arch welcoming visitors to the West. Between the house and the city were miles of flat flood lands, the winding I-64 highway, and the crumbling community of East St. Louis. Much of the land was still being farmed, the fields a bright spring green. The whole scene was like a museum diorama.

"Oh, man," Jennie breathed. "No wonder they call this River Bluffs."

She wanted this view, this house. Mike's research project had better be good, because she was set on seeing more of this mansion.

Jennie turned back from the view. "So, Mike. What Herculean task do you want me to accomplish in one month? And I hope I get to hang out here."

She was startled when he laughed heartily.

"You don't know how much I needed to hear you say that. Let's go back to the library. I have a tale to tell you. And I'm afraid you're not going to be able to repeat it for a while."

Chapter 3

Mike had to control his desire to leap the stairs three at a time. He couldn't believe he'd gotten this far. He had thought asking her to do a research project in a month would have turned her off. It didn't. He had thought when she saw this rundown house she would have left fifteen minutes after she got here. She hadn't. Though he was still wondering why anyone would want to dig through another family's bizarre life, she was still here and wanted to know more. True, she hadn't taken the job yet, but there was definitely more to this history teacher than he'd expected. Sort of like seeing her legs the other day. If you ignored the dated clothes she usually wore, there appeared to be intriguing hidden parts to her.

He hoped she could make sense of his twisted family relationship. Thinking about his family tree made him want to hit something. Who gave a crap about people who had died decades ago? At thirty-two, he was no spring chicken, but a lot of people tied up in this mystery were dead long before he was born. However, his inheritance was all about the family. His dilemma was that River Bluffs wasn't really his until he figured out who some guy named Fred Houseman really was. All Mike had to do was prove someone had stolen the real Fred's identity and shown up at River Bluffs claiming to be the original.

Sure, no problem. Except he couldn't. Not that he hadn't tried. The mess in the library was testament to his efforts. Every time Mike looked at a document or pedigree chart, he had to run off his frustration. He was doing upward of ten miles a day now. Soon, he wouldn't want the house because he'd never be here. He'd be running the entire day, completely frustrated.

But his great uncle had thankfully left a loophole in his will. Mike didn't have to do this by himself. He could hire someone from outside the area. That's where Dr. Jennie Foster could save his ass. She'd already told him she wasn't local. All he had to do was convince her to do the research, find the document proving Fred Houseman was no Houseman, and he was in the clear.

Concern nibbling at the edges of his control, he waved Jennie to a seat in the library. Jennie wasn't committed yet. The hard part was still ahead of him.

Zippy, as usual, curled up on his pillow as soon as they returned to the library and fell asleep. While Jennie gingerly sat in a hand-embroidered antique chair, Mike balanced on the edge of the desk, his legs stretched out and crossed at the ankles.

"First off, sorry for all the secrecy. Less than a year ago I got a call from a lawyer who said I was the primary beneficiary of the will of Paul Garretson, my great uncle. I must've met him at one of our many family reunions, but I confess I've never had much desire to talk with anyone fifty years my senior. So I don't remember him and I'm still a little baffled why he picked me as his heir. Unfortunately, there are strange stipulations in the will that essentially disinherit me if I fail to follow them." He opened a folder and handed a copy to Jennie.

She read silently, flipping quickly through the pages. "According to this," she said, looking up, "you have one year to disprove a family lineage connection, or the house and property is to be sold off and the money given to charity. Disproving a family connection is a bit odd. But otherwise, this doesn't sound mysterious at all."

"The mystery is outlined here," he said, passing Jennie a personal letter. He resisted the urge to hold his breath.

Michael,

I'm certain you don't remember me from the Houseman-Garretson family reunion years ago. You were more interested in getting a game of baseball going than talking with an old man. That's okay. I spoke with your parents and have learned much about you and your family. I knew I had to pass this house onto a Garretson descendant. And since I have no children of my own, you are my chosen heir. I know enough about you to know you're probably already suspicious of this inheritance, as well you should be. Let me explain why secrecy is absolutely necessary.

My mother, Caroline Garretson—who is also your great grandmother—was working on the Houseman family history before she died. Her father was Josef Houseman, the founder of Houseman Pharmaceuticals and the builder of River Bluffs. She was very interested in a family story that Fred Houseman, a previous president of HP and Josef's nephew, was an imposter. The week before she died, she was certain she had found solid evidence proving Fred wasn't who he said he was. The proof was something she ordered from the National Archives. The night she died though, she called me, scared to death because she thought someone was in the house. I raced over there. By the time I arrived, she was unconscious. She died a couple of days later. There was no evidence of a break-in, no fingerprints, no sign anyone had been there at all. The inquest ruled her death accidental from an overdose of her medication.

I led my family to believe I agreed with that assessment. After all, she was seventy-six at the time of her death. But I continued to search for what she had found. When she died in 1991, my mother had been researching the family history for more than twenty years. My wife's terminal illness prevented me from thoroughly looking into the mystery until after the new millennium. Unfortunately, I am a retired general contractor, not a genealogist, and I did not grow up using computers. The learning curve has proven to be too much for me.

I believe whoever hurried my mother's death—or should I say "killed"?—is closely tied to the Houseman family. There are many innocent people involved in this family secret. But I'm just as certain there is one who carries guilt, and I'm not certain they won't act again.

Therefore, I leave you access to this house and its secrets and all my wealth to help you solve the mystery. But for your own safety, I place the same restrictions I placed on myself.

You may not tell anyone from the local area you even know this house exists until proof is presented to my attorney.

You may not ask anyone from the local area to help you solve this mystery. They might be related to or know one of the Houseman descendants, a chance you shouldn't take.

Finally, to make certain this doesn't go on forever, you have one year from the date of notification to determine what the family secret is. At this time, my attorney will formally file the will and start probate proceedings.

My attorney, Richard Boston, was new to the area when I wrote this will. I admit the guidelines I have given him are quite vague, but I hope what you find is as certain as my mother thought it was. He is a dedicated lawyer who spent many hours ensuring my will would meet all legal requirements. It is in his best interest to help you as he will receive an additional five percent of my estate if you successfully solve this mystery.

One other thing. I have given you my dog, Zippy. It is presumptuous of me to assume my great grandnephew would want my silly dog. But I ask this of you: please keep him for the year and should you fail to solve this mystery, find him a good home, yours or someone else's. He has been a Godsend in this giant house I often feel so alone in, though it was my childhood home.

Some people say skeletons in the closet should stay there. I'm not one of them. Michael, I wish you the best of luck in your search. May you lay this chapter of the Houseman history to rest, one way or another.

With kindest thoughts,

Your Great Uncle Paul Garretson

Mike watched worriedly as Jennie's chocolate brown eyes flicked over the document a second time. When she finished reading, she raised her eyebrows in surprise.

"Okay." She dragged out the word so it sounded almost like three syllables. "That's weird."

Mike nodded, pacing to the room's large window. "Truthfully, when I first saw River Bluffs, I thought it was a huge white elephant and selling it would be the best thing. I guess I changed my mind. Unfortunately, with time running out, now I don't know if I can keep it."

"When did you get notified of your inheritance— or whatever you call it?"

"May 20th last year," he said, feeling a bit defensive. "I know. Just a little over three weeks left. When Rick Boston showed me this place, I didn't do anything at first. The whole inheritance sounded too odd. I looked through these papers, checked out Paul's computer, but I didn't really care about the house or what Paul wanted me to do. Things changed. Maybe it was the house, or Zippy. Who knows? Now I want to keep the house."

He stared out the window overlooking the expansive lawn in front of River Bluffs. He knew what had changed. He had changed. A year ago, his marriage in the toilet, his short-lived baseball career a fading memory, and his career as a chemical scientist a nightmare from his past, he had been struggling to make a go of being a chemistry teacher. If it weren't for the baseball coaching and River Bluffs, he would long ago have packed up and moved to some remote location like South America.

The house and its peaceful woods had become an ideal escape, and not being able to tell his family about the house turned out to be a boon. Just him and Paul's crazy dog, Zippy. Somewhere along the line, he'd quit pining over his failed marriage, the mention of HP stopped making him cringe, and the old house became more like an old friend. How could he explain River Bluffs was giving him peace of mind like nothing else could?

Mike refocused his eyes and could see Jennie reflected in the window. He stilled, watching the brunette. She was looking at the ceiling, her lips pressed together in concentration. Her face, while not classically beautiful like his ex-wife's, was easy to look at. He couldn't tell if she had on makeup, but her coloring was neither pale nor tanned to that fakeness which looked peculiar so early in spring. Her auburn hair was pulled back in a pony tail, thick curls barely constrained by the band. He couldn't recall seeing her with it down and had an urge to pull out the binder. He blinked, his thoughts startling him.

She turned toward him and addressed his back. "So, do you think Paul's mother was actually murdered?"

"I don't know." Mike shook his head to bring

himself back to the business proposal. Dropping heavily into another of the embroidered antique chairs, he hesitated before his next comment, but decided Jennie had to take the job without doubts. "If she was, that would mean any work you do on this research project might be discovered. I don't know how desperate someone is to protect this family secret. In other words, if someone murdered once, then your research might give them the motive to murder again."

Absently rubbing a finger across her lips, Jennie didn't appear to have heard him. Perhaps he needed to be clearer.

"So, knowing there might be a murderer out there, are you interested in finding proof Fred Houseman is a fraud?"

She looked at him with startled raised eyebrows. "Of course! Wouldn't miss this project for the world. Seems to me if someone knew about this inheritance, they would have given you some idea they were watching you. I presume you've followed Paul Garretson's request to tell no one else?"

Mike felt a knot inside him ease. Her distant look wasn't indecision about taking the project, it was because she was already working on it!

"As far as I know, there are exactly three people who know about this house: Paul's attorney, Rick Boston, me, and now you. I haven't even told my own parents. Don't blow off Paul's warning. If there's a murderer on the loose..."

"Oh, I agree. Believe me, the first time I think this project isn't worth it, I'm outta here." She grinned. "So let's talk limitations. You're only giving me three weeks to figure this out. I might fail, but you'd still have to pay me for my time."

"I wouldn't have asked you if I didn't accept that up front."

"It's not much time," she pointed out, sifting

through a pile of papers on the desk. "But if Caroline Garretson ordered copies from the National Archives before her death in 1991, that would limit what she might have ordered. Few of the Archives' records were indexed then. She also would not have had the luxury of the Internet. And though the National Archives is the repository of the federal government's historical documents, those records are notoriously difficult to research without lots of time. So, the item she was looking for must already have been indexed or alphabetized, and she already knew precisely what she was getting. A very specific individual or family document. Something easy to order copies of. Federal census, land records, military service. It could be anything. I need to see what information she had to figure out what she ordered."

Mike listened to her in mild amazement. She was speaking a foreign language, but he appreciated the knowledge she had. In the few minutes she'd been thinking about finding the evidence, she'd gotten further than he had.

Her slender index finger was tracing a line on a piece of paper on the desk. He craned his neck to see. It was one of those charts showing relationships to parents, grandparents, etc. She had found Fred Houseman, traced his ancestral relationship up to the top of the page. Then she followed another relationship down to the bottom, stopping at Mike's name. As her finger rolled over his name, he felt unexpected heat creep through his loins. When she turned around, he crossed his legs, hoping to hide the ridiculous response he was having to watching her.

"So now it's my turn. If I'm going to do this, I'm going to need your help. Two pairs of eyes will get through this research faster than one set. We need to look for primary sources, original documentation," she said, indicating the disordered room. "That's what Paul's lawyer will be expecting: some legal evidence that would hold up in court. Also, we'll need to thoroughly shake this house down. If both Caroline and Paul grew up in this house, then they probably didn't appreciate the family history sources they had staring at them, like photos with names and dates, diaries or letters. I'll bet there's stuff up in that attic that hasn't been looked at in decades. Are you prepared to do your part?"

Mike closed his eyes, running his fingers through his hair. Excitement slid through his veins. Surely not for looking through tons of old papers?

Ah, but looking through them with Jennie Foster?

"Yeah," he said, opening his eyes and giving her a rare smile. "Let's get to it. But first, would you like some lunch? I make a mean ham and Swiss on rye."

****

While Mike cleaned up the kitchen from their lunch, Jennie began to cull through the pages of notes and documents in the library. She sat cross-legged on the floor, stacking papers into three separate piles: good stuff, garbage, and not certain. When Mike came in, she pointed him toward the computer, showing him how to print out the various charts she needed from Paul's genealogy program.

Mike finished his immediate task, including making a CD of the files for Jennie, and yawned. "You do this for a living?" he asked, as she read her umpteenth document.

She looked up from the paper she was examining. "I'm trying to save your house, if you've already forgotten. Besides, I have to justify all those years of getting degrees some way. 'Collecting dead relatives'—as my father likes to call it—is much easier for him to explain now that I have my own business. A lot of people with doctorates in history end up unemployed or doing something completely unrelated to their degree. He's happy I'm not living at home."

Mike grunted. "Let me get this straight. You've got a doctorate. So why aren't you teaching at a university? At the very least you should be a school principal or superintendent."

She had assembled a fairly large pile of papers, but had also tossed aside another box full of notes she didn't have any use for. She craned her neck to see Mike sitting at the desk behind her, then scooted around to see him better.

"That's exactly what my dad says every time I visit." Her father was proud of her, but couldn't understand why she had spent so much time and money getting a doctorate to become a teacher with a starting salary in what he considered poverty range.

"I really like teaching teenagers. They're the most fascinating people on the planet. They're so dramatic, funny, full of angst, and they think they own the world. High schoolers beat reality TV by a mile. You should know," she added. "You went from what I guess was a well-paid position as a chemist to become a science teacher."

Jennie's comment went right to the heart of a subject Mike wanted to avoid. "I went into teaching for the coaching," he said, turning the conversation in a different direction. "My mom's a teacher. She convinced me to try it out. Baseball, however, is my first love and almost worth trying to beat chemistry into the heads of some of these kids."

"So you left Houseman Pharmaceuticals to coach? Couldn't you have coached without leaving such a great job?"

Mike squirmed internally. He didn't want to explain the betrayal that had made him leave a job he loved. He sighed. Unfortunately, the reality of the situation was she couldn't look at the Housemans without connecting to HP.

Jennie's gold-flecked brown eyes were soft and naive. Could he trust her? Did it matter? He'd told her about his inheritance and the possibility of a murderer willing to kill to keep the family secret. He rubbed his eyes and let out a breath of air. If he was going to be an idiot, he would at least keep the details fuzzy.

"No, coaching was not enough to make me leave my job. That was because something was...not right." Mike got up and started to pace. "My wife—my ex-wife now—and I used to argue about what was going on." He hesitated, unsure of what to tell her. "We disagreed about how the company was run. I saw things that seemed unethical, if not outright illegal. Eventually I had it with both the company and Veronica telling me everything was fine." That had been the moment the last of his dreams had crumbled. "So I quit."

"Is that why you divorced? The arguing?"

Mike focused on her sharply. "This isn't relevant."

"No—wait." Jennie hesitated, catching her lower lip between her teeth and looking at him hard. "Yes, it is. Isn't Veronica a Houseman? How close are you two related?"

Mike glared and dropped heavily into the chair behind the desk. "What is this? Twenty questions?"

"It could be important. She's a Houseman. One of *the* Housemans, isn't she?" She stood, rolling her neck.

Mike was distracted from the question when Jennie clasped her hands together behind her back, stretching her arm muscles and subsequently pulling her shirt tight across her breasts. With alarm, he realized his groin was responding to her. He blinked, trying to remember her last comment.

"I didn't even know she was a cousin until we'd been dating for some time. We're really distant." He shifted uncomfortably, trying to ignore Jennie's movements. "My mother looked it up and said we were fourth cousins. She even went so far as to make sure we were legally allowed to marry."

"Didn't you know each other growing up? Paul Garretson mentioned Houseman-Garretson family reunions."

"Actually, no. Veronica didn't come to the reunions after her parents divorced. Her mother had primary custody. We met after I started working at HP."

"I guess if she was a Houseman heir that would make it uncomfortable to continue working there, especially if you were having marital problems."

Mike ignored the comment about his marriage. "Technically she's not an heir since both her father and her grandfather are still alive. Besides, I think the family's share in HP has been divided so no one owns a majority. The chairman of the board is George Houseman, Veronica's great uncle. Her grandfather, Joe, is also on the board of directors. Because she insisted on a pre-nuptial agreement, I never knew much about her financial status."

Jennie had completed her stretching and flopped into a chair. Mike swallowed hard, shifting uncomfortably in his seat. He needed to stretch too, but wasn't about to stand now.

Jennie switched the subject, brow furrowed. "Let's assume Paul Garretson is right, someone murdered Caroline to keep the family secret. Can you find out who has shares and how much in the company? The obvious question to all this is someone wants to maintain the status quo, and they know there's a question about the family's lineage."

"I see where you're going. The only people meeting those conditions would be those that already own a chunk of the company."

"Or...if they might inherit. Does Veronica have siblings?"

"No. Her father is Congressman Geoffrey Houseman and she's his sole heir. But Houseman Pharmaceutical's president Robert Houseman will inherit from his father George. He has a big interest. But he has siblings who would inherit too. Maybe Rick, Paul's attorney, could find out. I'll call him Monday."

The good part about talking about potential murderers was the chilling effect it had on the nether regions. Mike was able to stand and pick up the pages he'd printed from the computer. He handed them to Jennie.

"You know, it's strange to think about my relatives as potential murderers. It was much easier when I was hiring you for history research, not a homicide investigation."

Jennie shrugged her shoulders. "If it's any comfort, it doesn't look any different to me than a regular research assignment. However, I like Paul's idea of keeping the whole project under wraps. Makes me feel like we're out of the eyes of anyone with motive."

While Jennie grabbed another box of papers, Mike took on the task of searching through the books on the walls. He was supposed to be looking for anything that might have something personal about the family in it. After about a hundred dusty books that didn't look like anyone had opened them since the day they were bought, he was relieved when Jennie asked him about his own family genealogy.

"My father is the Houseman descendant," he explained, stuffing a book back in the bookcase. He leaned back against the shelves, trying to recall his lineage. "Caroline was my dad's grandmother and

Paul was his uncle. Caroline was born a Houseman. That's my family tree knowledge in short."

"What about your family?"

He shrugged. "Two sisters, mother and father still living. One sister married and the other a travel photographer. And I have two nephews."

"And you really haven't told them about River Bluffs? I don't think I could keep anything this big from my father."

"I have motivation in the inheritance." He also got a place to disappear from the family for a while. It made his life much easier when his mother and sister weren't constantly calling him, as if the failure of his marriage had been their fault. He was missing his nephews, but it was the price he had to pay to avoid his sister and her concerned questions.

"Do you suppose someone knows about this house and might want it? Maybe thought they should be Caroline's heirs?"

"No. I'm certain this is about ownership of HP. After all, it's probably worth half a billion, give or take a hundred-million dollars."

Jennie's eyes widened. "I knew it was big, but that's obscene."

"Enough to murder someone over," he admitted.

With Jennie finally focusing on her piles of papers, Mike returned to the books on the shelves. Despite her insistence that there could be clues hidden in this library, he had found nothing but some potential first editions that would make good auction material. He found himself envying his dog, who chose that moment to come back into the library clutching a bone he'd unearthed somewhere. Zippy dropped on his dog bed, thumping his tail enthusiastically on the floor. The bone was not quite as dirty as the dog.

The cell phone at Mike's belt vibrated. The search through the books was so desperately boring he decided even talking to his mother would be less painful. He pulled it out and looked at the caller ID.

Veronica Houseman.

Mike looked at Jennie, puzzled, as he flipped open the phone. "Uh, hello. Whoa! Slow down. What are you saying? Oh, come on. Why would someone try to kill you? Okay, okay. I'll come out. Where are you? Yes, I know the place. Stay there. I'll be there as fast as I can."

Jennie stared at him. "Who was that?"

"Veronica," he said, almost under his breath, hardly able to believe she'd called him. "She's at the BMW dealer. Apparently she was in an accident and the mechanic told her someone cut her brake line."

"Is she hurt?"

"I forgot to ask. I guess she must be okay if she's at the garage. Listen, you can stay here and finish going through those papers. Just lock up when you leave, not that anyone ever comes out here. I'll be back when I'm done."

"What about the dog?" They both turned to stare at the mutt chewing on the bone, some long thing from a deer or something.

"Would you feed him? Food's in the kitchen, in the pantry."

Chapter 4

Veronica calling *him*? Mike navigated the Illinois roads, rolling this thought around in his head. She hadn't tried to contact him in the two years since they'd divorced. The divorce had been handled without malice between their lawyers, except for a couple of necessary meetings to divide up belongings. It was as if the marriage had deflated, like a helium balloon left to its own. Mike had ended up with a stretched out shell that had none of the appeal the relationship had held for him at the beginning.

He dreaded seeing her again. That sort of summed up the final days of their marriage too. Toward the end, he had stayed at work later and later, found excuses not to go to events with Veronica, and spent any remaining time restoring his 1966 Shelby Mustang. The car was the one good thing left from his marriage. At least it ran like a dream.

As he drove into the BMW dealership, he reined in his tangled emotions. Veronica was history. This was support for an old friend, nothing more.

Almost before Mike had the car in park, Veronica was pulling open the door. She appeared to be unhurt. She wore well-fitted khakis and a lacy top inviting men to check her out. To Mike's surprise, he felt nothing at the sight of her. No anger, joy, or even lust. Instead, an unexpected image of Jennie stretching in the library left him trying to douse the heat creeping through his body. Fortunately, Veronica's perfectly manicured hand had wrapped around his wrist and was pulling him out of his car.

Her touch had an instant cooling effect.

"Thank God you came, Mike," she said, a hint of panic in her voice. She wrapped her arms around his waist and leaned in, resting her cheek against his chest. "I didn't know who to call."

Mike awkwardly patted her back. Veronica was not the type to need comforting. In spite of their history, he couldn't recall having done it before.

"What happened? Are you okay?" He eased her away, looking into her eyes. A tear was sliding down her cheek. Instead of wiping it away, he stared at the track it made in her makeup. When she tried to slip back into his arms, he shifted and walked toward the garage, steering her by the elbow.

"I'm fine, just scared. I thought I lost control of my car going down a hill. The brakes were sluggish. Fortunately, the hill wasn't steep and I was able to stop by running into some bushes. After I had it towed here to be checked out, the mechanic told me the brake line had been cut. Not damaged, but intentionally cut!" She choked back what sounded like a sob.

Brushing away fresh tears, Veronica looked more disheveled than he'd ever seen her. Even during their early dating when it was all about the sex, she hadn't looked this bad after a randy bout. She was a stickler for looking perfect.

"Why would anyone cut your brake line?" he asked, once again trying to head into the service department and keep some distance between them.

"I think it has to do with HP." She looked around anxiously. "You were right, Mike. There's something strange going on at the company and I think I'm the next target."

This time Mike stopped in his tracks, turning to stare at Veronica. "You mean you actually believe I was targeted when I worked there?"

"Yes. Yes, I do now. And now I'm the troublemaker."

She grabbed his arm and pulled him to the wall, pressing him against it. Trapped, Mike was unable to avoid her hands, which continued to caress first his arms, his shoulders, and then his chest. If she wasn't so distraught, he'd swear she was trying to seduce him.

"You know how long we've been working on the melanoma vaccine. I've been pressing our department head to try a different direction because I was certain our results were less than ideal. But when our recent testing results were compiled, they showed the vaccine is actually working. I complained. Someone's been messing with the test data. There's no way the data should look this good. And next thing I know, I'm skidding down a hill with no brakes."

"You think someone intentionally sabotaged your car? Why?"

With wide eyes, she glanced over her shoulder, as if she might be overheard. "To kill me. Someone wants me out of the way. It's got to be someone at the executive level. Maybe even Rob."

"Robert Houseman? The president?" Mike didn't like Robert, even suspected him of being behind Mike's own disastrous exit from the company. But murder did not seem to be in his character. "He's your cousin, for God's sake. It couldn't be him."

"But you believe me? That someone's after me?" Veronica's face showed hope. "Grandfather thought I was imagining things. I didn't know who else to turn to." She laid her head against his chest, her blonde hair tickling his nose. He reluctantly patted her back with one hand, the other balled in a fist at his side.

"I can't really help you, Veronica. I don't work at HP, and my departure was not exactly under the best of conditions."

"I know," she said, lifting her head from his chest and pressing her breasts against his body.

Her behavior was having an effect. He might not be interested in Veronica, but his body could only withstand so much flirtation from any woman. He took her by the shoulders and put some breathing space between them. If she was aware she was getting a response out of him, she hid it well.

"I'll take you home, where you can get something to help you sleep. You're just going to have to be careful who you talk to and what you say at work." He had intended to talk to the mechanic, but Veronica's clinginess was making him want to get this spectacle over with.

"Thank you. I appreciate it." Before she could show her gratitude in a way requiring physical contact again, he opened the passenger door, keeping it between them.

The drive to Veronica's house was excruciatingly long, with her hand continually drifting over to his thigh. Mike had the rare desire to exchange his sports car for something like a Hummer, to put a little space between the driver and passenger.

Dropping her at her house was an equal chore, and by the time he had her tucked into bed, there was little question she wanted him in it with her. A lame excuse about his parents holding dinner for him was the best he could do to get out of the situation.

As he left Veronica's modern ranch home late that evening, Mike was wondering how much more bizarre his life could get.

First he'd spent the day talking about which family members might be murder suspects. Then his ex-wife had called out of the blue and tried to bed him. Now it looked like there was either another murderer, or someone was expanding their victim list.

He could only hope Jennie wouldn't fold on the research when she heard about this latest development.

Chapter 5

Mike was disappointed when he saw the nearly dark River Bluffs. He wanted to talk with Jennie about what had happened to Veronica. Instead, he was greeted by Zippy, who though obviously delighted to see Mike, did not fill in the unusual emptiness he felt at coming home to River Bluffs. She'd left a light on in the kitchen, where he also discovered a short note with her even, flowing handwriting.

Mike—Leaving at 8:30. Hope all went well. This project is great! Attic tomorrow. See you around lunchtime.—Jennie

With the note in hand, he wandered out onto the porch. The sun had long since set and St. Louis glowed in the night sky, but it was still too early for bed. Exhausted, he carefully lowered himself onto an old vinyl and aluminum lounge chair on the front porch. With her constant need to be the center of attention, he had forgotten how draining Veronica could be.

Dr. Jennie Foster, on the other hand, had been nothing like he'd expected. He studied the note again, liking the fact that even though it was brief, her writing wasn't sloppy or hurried. Veronica's scrawl was often illegible, resulting in communication misunderstandings with her coworkers and her former husband.

Perhaps his sister was right about him judging people too quickly. Of course, Sara had no idea at this moment he was stretched out in front of a Victorian mansion and had hired a historian to help him solve a family mystery.

Zippy raced up the porch with a half chewed-up toy of some sort and dropped it near Mike. Tail wagging madly, the dirty white dog tilted his head and gave Mike eyes that would melt the devil himself. Mike resignedly picked up the ratty toy and threw it out into the yard. In seconds, Zippy was back with it. The thing would get wetter with each return if he continued throwing it. Instead, he picked up the dog, flipped him on his back, and gave him a belly rub that had the mutt's left leg twitching in the air.

"So, what did you think of her, Zippy?" Mike asked the dog. Zippy had closed his eyes in ecstasy. "Not at all what we expected," Mike murmured, remembering her hair. He wondered what she would do if he pulled off the binder holding the thick mass of red-brown curls.

Better yet, what if it had been Jennie seducing him at the garage?

Mike shook his head in irritation. What was he thinking? He wasn't ready for another relationship. Maybe a brief fling, but Jennie didn't strike him as the one-night-stand type. And if he *were* looking, he'd want sophistication, someone who would really make other people take a second look.

Like Veronica.

No, not like Veronica. Their meeting today had been terrible, verging on creepy. She could turn a head among the most glamorous crowds, but today he hadn't felt any attraction at all. In fact, he had almost pitied her.

Jennie was no Veronica. In his life, there were no Jennies. She didn't dress to attract, that was certain. But if she let her hair down it would be wonderful to run his hands through it. Under her baggy clothes was apparently a very shapely body. And her legs. That skirt she'd had on the other day was not too short for legs like Jennie's. They could wrap around a man's waist...

His cell phone started vibrating, interrupting his musings.

"Hello, Mom," he said, giving Zippy a gentle nudge off his lap as he sat up. Then Mike picked up the slobbery toy and flung it as far out in the yard as he could.

"Mike. You finally answered your phone," his mother said peevishly. "I've been calling all day. What's so important you couldn't call your mother back?"

"Sorry. I was working. Stuff I have to get done and I didn't want to be interrupted." He couldn't talk about Jennie and her research, and he didn't want to mention Veronica's call. That would be asking for the inquisition.

He heard a harrumph. "You're the only person I know who has a cell phone, but rarely uses it."

Mike rolled his eyes. "So, Mom. Glad you called. I'll talk to you again soon. Wish we had more time." He made no move to hang up the phone, but waited for his mother to take the bait.

"Don't you hang up! I wanted to make sure you were still coming to the reunion next week at Uncle George's house. Tori is asking for numbers so they can cater for the appropriate amount. You're still planning on being there, aren't you? You're not skipping out again this year? It's bad manners."

Hanging around his ex-wife's family wasn't his idea of a good time, but somehow his mother had squeezed an agreement out of him. Maybe Veronica wouldn't be there. Maybe everyone would forget he'd worked at HP. Maybe the moon was made of cheese.

"Of course, Mom. It's the Houseman social event of the year. Wouldn't miss it for the world."

"Are you bringing anyone?"

Mike winced. He should have known this was

coming. An image of Jennie Foster flashed in his head and before he thought it through, he blurted out, "I'll have a friend from school with me."

"You will? Who?"

"Uh...just someone who's interested in local history. You know the Housemans pretty well define local history."

"Excellent! I'll look forward to meeting him...her?"

"Her. Dr. Jennie Foster. She's a history teacher." He imagined his mother was practically salivating at the thought of meeting someone from school. Admittedly he'd given her reason enough, since he had been rather unavailable to his family for the last couple of years.

"Well, good." His mother hesitated, and Mike knew she had more on her agenda. "Mike, will you please do me one favor?"

"What?" he asked warily. Nothing was easy with his mother. It didn't matter he hadn't lived at home since his junior year of college.

"Would you please talk to your cousin Rob?"

"Mom, we've been through this before." He tried to keep his voice even. She'd been asking him for almost two years to talk to Robert. He admired her tenacity, if not the request. "There's nothing Robert could say to me I want to hear."

"Mike, he's family. His children grew up with you. I don't understand why you won't talk with him."

Mike wasn't about to enlighten her, but he recalled the note he'd found on his desk the day he'd quit Houseman Pharmaceuticals. The words were practically engraved on his brain: *"Someone in senior management wants you disgraced. The department's missing funds can be traced to your account name. Check your friends to make sure they're not your enemies."*

He'd never told anyone in his family about why he'd left. It hadn't taken much to see the missing department funds had been moved by someone with access to his company account. There were only five people who could have done that, three of them trusted members of his department. Another was in the finance office. And the last was company president, Robert Houseman. With Veronica's accident, he was convinced Robert Houseman knew something.

The short list became shorter when motivation was added as a factor. Robert had actually tried to talk Mike out of marrying Veronica. After his marriage, Robert had practically shut Mike out. Robert's anger had faded after a while, but apparently he hadn't gotten over the pair's happiness. Only since the divorce had Robert tried to contact Mike again.

"I know you mean well, Mom, but there's nothing he could say that would interest me. If I speak with him at the reunion, it will be out of courtesy. I won't embarrass you, but I also won't give him any of my time."

"I don't understand what is going through that head of yours," his mother said, her tone resigned. "Whatever upset you while you were at HP is over and done with. You really need to move on."

"I know. I'm working on it."

"All right, then." His mother probably wasn't fooled, but she also wasn't going to nag him incessantly, at least not on the phone. "Don't be a stranger. Call your father and me. Take care, sweetie."

"You, too."

He shut his phone. Maybe this reunion wouldn't be the big mistake he thought it was. He might have to face both Robert and Veronica after avoiding these reunions for the last two years, but he would have Jennie with him. He was certain she would come, since he would pay her. Having her there would take the pressure off him as she would be fresh meat for his mother and sister to gnaw on. Even better, her interest in local history would be real since she'd be meeting the progeny of Fred Houseman.

His mind eventually found its way back to the search in the library. Even though looking through all those books for potentially nonexistent clues to an ancestor's heritage did not seem like the best way to spend his evening, it would beat out next week's reunion by a long shot. He shoved himself out of the lounge chair and headed into River Bluffs.

Chapter 6

Jennie groaned at the voice on the radio. Somewhere behind her scratchy eyes she realized her radio was announcing it was nine, much later than she usually got up. But the Houseman genealogy had had her up until two in the morning. Sleep and food were her most reliable companions, but today there was something she wanted more than both.

She and Mike hadn't agreed on a start time at River Bluffs for today, but she had some very specific plans. Besides research, she had an urge to experiment with cooking on those old kitchen appliances. Though her desire was slightly on the side of the deranged, she really wanted to experience what life was like at River Bluffs, even if the stove only took her back to the 1950s. After the cooking, her plan was to investigate the attic. There were old trunks up there begging to be opened.

As Jennie went through her morning routine, her mind analyzed her research efforts from the night before. The box of documents she had brought back from River Bluffs had to be translated into source documentation for every birth, marriage and death in the Houseman family. Fortunately, Caroline had been thorough in her efforts, probably spending hours at the local county courthouse. With her genealogy software providing the framework, Jennie now had a picture of the family tree. Caroline had found most of the essentials prior to her death in 1991, all the way back to her grandfather Josef Houseman, the ancestor who had founded

Houseman Pharmaceuticals.

While it wasn't relevant to the research problem, Jennie found it hard to ignore details relating in particular to Mike Garretson. Having moved nine times before high school graduation herself, Jennie could barely imagine not only growing up and living in the same area for her entire life, but her ancestors as well. That was Mike's life. What would it be like to have family living nearby? Her mother dead by the time she was four, she now saw her father only about once a year. It was enough to catch up on what he'd done with his Army buddies, and what research or education she was involved in. He was happy in Texas, and if she wanted to keep tenure as a teacher—and the salary that came with that experience—she was staying put in Illinois.

Jennie's life travels had covered the world. But Mike's family events could be plotted on a small square of a map. Those local connections made researching the Houseman family easier than a lot of her research. Of course, she still had to find what Caroline had found in the National Archives, but she was certain she could figure it out.

Her wet hair curling at her shoulders, Jennie decided she had time to do some quick Internet research on the Houseman name in general. If they were as big a name in the local area as Mike said they were, then maybe something about Josef or Fred Houseman would show up online.

She typed in <Houseman "River Bluffs"> in the search engine query box. She drew nothing about a house named River Bluffs, though the Mississippi area had a lot of places bearing that name. Caroline and Paul had done a good job keeping River Bluffs a secret in the last couple of decades. She would have to check non-digitized newspaper archives as well, though. The Internet was the beginning of research, contrary to what Jennie's students thought.

Next she tried <Josef Houseman Illinois>, which yielded her a couple hundred hits. The first page was HP's website history page. It had a photo of Josef and a short story about how he'd used his grandmother's homemade remedies to start a drug store back in the 1800s that later became the drug company of Houseman Pharmaceuticals. The majority of the search results were genealogical in nature. She clicked on a likely candidate.

Jennie was rewarded with an entry on RootsWeb, one of the original genealogical web collecting sights. The vital statistics matched up with Mike's Josef Houseman. Though the information was sketchy, as websites tended to be, there was more information on Josef's parents, Johan and Anna Hausmann, natives of Germany, and their other two children, William, and Katrina. The supposed imposter, Fred Houseman, was listed as William's son. The information included the submitter's email, *jjh1910@danvers.net.* Jennie copied it down and sent a quick note to the address:

Hello,

I am searching for information on the Johan Hausmann family and saw your information on RootsWeb. Would you be willing to share information?

Thank you.

She intentionally left off her name, remembering what Mike had said about contacting people in the local area. It was bad netiquette, but she wanted to know who she was talking to before revealing her identity.

After visiting several other sites that appeared to be duplicates of the RootsWeb site, she sent a couple more emails before realizing it was ten-thirty. She backed up her files and shut down her computer, then hit the bathroom to finish drying her hair. A hint of makeup and some lipstick, and she was heading out the door, ready to take on River Bluffs and its current occupant.

****

As Jennie made her second trip through the winding back roads of Caseyville, a gray sky threatened from the west over St. Louis. She studied the gravel road and hoped it did not become so muddy she wouldn't be able to get her Saturn through it.

Zippy was at her door right after she pulled in behind Mike's car, barking and bouncing like a Mexican jumping bean on steroids. Once she gave him a good petting—which she was willing to do since he was clean of mud—and one of the promised treats she'd bought at the store, he raced up the porch stairs and waited for her. With her laptop and plastic bags of food slung across both arms, she stumbled up the stairs and tried the French doors leading into the parlor. They were unlocked.

"Hello!" she called, as if Mike hadn't heard Zippy yapping his head off. "I'm a murderer and you left your door open for me to just walk in."

"In the kitchen!" he bellowed.

Jennie followed the scruffy dog into the kitchen. Mike was balanced on a barstool at the large metal table, papers neatly stacked in piles, paperclips and binder clips separating them into groups. He held the teacher's favorite colored pen, red, and was using it to tick off errors on a student's paper.

Jennie groaned sympathetically. "I have a pile at home too. I try to avoid giving homework on weekends, but that means I almost always have homework to grade from Friday."

Mike looked up, shaking his head. "I don't have that luxury. If we've got labs during the week, they're going to get homework on Friday. And with chemistry, you want to make sure they understand

45

the homework before they start mixing chemicals together."

Jennie set the groceries and laptop on the clear end of the metal table. Mike looked at her plastic bags questioningly.

"I thought it would be a challenge to use this antique to cook on," she said, waving at the behemoth stove. "I used to be fairly good outdoor cook when I was growing up. How much different can this be?"

"It's gas, not wood," he pointed out. "It doesn't have an auto-light, though. Use the lighter on the counter next to the stove."

She picked it up, flicked it on, turned the stove dial, and had fire as quickly as her gas stove at home. She turned it back off.

"That wasn't much of a challenge," she said, frowning slightly. "So, are you up for a little spaghetti? You apparently do not have any Italian in your roots, not at least on your father's side, and as I don't either, I guess neither of us will be offended by my not-so-amazing sauce in a jar."

"I wouldn't be offended by sauce that wasn't previously frozen," he said. He showed her where the pots, pans and utensils were. Then together they figured out how to turn on the oven to heat some breadsticks. "Do you mind if I keep grading? I want to tell you about Veronica's call and I have stuff to show you when we're done. But I need to finish these papers."

"Not a problem. This is beginner cooking anyway."

As she chopped onions and garlic to add to the sauce, she had the chance to observe Mike's thick, dark hair and strong hands, hands that looked very capable of keeping her interest. A trip to the pantry let her eye his derriere perched on the bar stool. Tight and muscular, just like the whole package.

Zippy was stationed in her path, ready to clean the floor up if she needed help in that direction. She tossed a bit of hamburger his way. The dog snapped it in mid air. Amused by his appetite, she tried various other parts of the meal. Only the onion remained disdainfully ignored where he dropped it.

Mike dropped his pen with a sigh. "Finished."

"Good. Lunch is about ready. I always wanted to do living history. Cooking in a nineteenth century house with 1950s bakeware. I can die happy now."

"So can I," Mike said, chomping on a breadstick warm out of the oven. His reserve obviously did not extend to food. "Best meal I've had in this house, even better than the cold leftovers from the BBQ Shack."

"Hope you don't mind if I serve in the pans. Less clean up," she said, shifting the pans of spaghetti and sauce to hand towels she'd placed on the table. Mike pulled out another barstool from a corner and pulled it up to the table.

While they ate, Mike told Jennie about the visit with Veronica, leaving out the parts he wished he could have avoided.

"I don't know if what's going on at the company has anything to do with the Houseman's supposed family imposter," he concluded. "But if there is a murderer covering up a wrongful inheritance, it's not hard to believe that same person might be messing around at the company, trying to increase its value."

"How would faking test results increase the company's value? I mean, wouldn't someone eventually discover the drug wasn't doing what it was supposed to and then the company would be subject to lawsuits?"

Mike frowned. "You're right. But let's suppose someone wanted to sell out their share of the company. With information indicating HP was about to make a major breakthrough on a cancer drug, the value of the company would theoretically increase, at least for a short time. Anyone buying from another stockholder would subsequently pay more."

"I thought the company was privately owned."

"It is. But I remember while I was working there George Houseman bought out one of the family members. Veronica was furious because it apparently gave George a majority holding."

"So, family can still buy out each other. Interesting." Jennie pulled out the family tree charts in her laptop case, studying the information she had. "What happens if a branch of the family ends?"

"Ends? You mean if there aren't any descendants to inherit? There aren't any branches like that." Then he cursed softly. "Ah. What happens if Veronica dies?"

Jennie nodded, leaning forward on her elbows. "Maybe the accident wasn't to scare her. Maybe it was to permanently remove a claimant to the company. But wouldn't it be easier to buy out her father?"

Mike snorted. "Grandfather, actually. That's Joe Houseman, the most stubborn man alive. Uncle Joe would sooner cut off his right arm than give up HP. It's his life."

She flipped through the charts, settling on a family group sheet that had Joe Houseman's immediate family on it. "Joe is eighty years old. He probably doesn't have a lot of time left. But his only son, Geoffrey, is also still alive. Why bother killing Veronica if her father is still around to inherit?"

Mike sighed, rubbing his forehead. "This is giving me a headache. We don't have to find a murderer. We just have to find proof of ancient identity theft."

"Sorry. I get carried away sometimes. In any case, that's what I worked on last night while you were rescuing your ex."

Mike picked up his fourth breadstick, and waved at her to continue.

"Nothing amazing found yet. I stayed up way too late last night getting a feel for the research. Your great grandmother Caroline did a pretty good job of collecting the basic vital statistics. She had everything back to Josef, who immigrated here as a child with his family from Germany. She didn't have much on his father, Johan or John, but she did know Josef had a brother, William, and a sister, Katrina. She had nothing on Katrina, but tons on William, who, by the way, would be your ex-wife's great grandfather—*if* Fred is not a fake."

"Of course. It would have to be Veronica's line that was suspect, since my family, through Caroline Houseman, didn't inherit any part of the company."

"You know how you and your ex are fourth cousins? Johan Hausmann—that's spelled H-A-U-S-M-A-N-N—the original German immigrant, is the ancestor you have in common with her. The name's been Americanized to its current spelling," she explained. "Do you know anything about him?"

"No, just Josef. I guess the lack of a son was a disappointment to Josef. He was in his fifties when Caroline was in her teens, so he apparently decided to invite his nephew, his brother's oldest son Fred, to come out from California. Fred ends up running the company, which he ultimately inherits. Caroline gets the house, but no part in the company. It's a common theme on my side of the family that Caroline got the short end of the deal by being excluded from the company, but I think that's because no one, at least nowadays, knows about this house and the land."

"Hmm. I didn't see a will or probate proceedings from Josef Houseman in Caroline's materials," she said after a moment of thought. "If there was some animosity about how Josef's estate was divided, that might give us some motivation for murder, especially if we're talking about something as big as HP. I'll need to visit the county courthouse to see if a copy of the will was filed there and if anyone sued over it."

They finished the meal, but Mike insisted on leaving the dishes for now as Jennie was billing him for her time.

"You're not charging me for lunch preparation time, are you?" he asked with mock suspicion.

Jennie grinned. "No. But you're going to have to provide dinner in the future."

"What about the sandwiches yesterday? That was a meal."

"Sandwiches? Didn't count. You've got to make it," she retorted and laughed as they returned to the library.

Mike headed straight for a stack of slim books sitting on a chair. "I kept searching through the books yesterday, but most of them haven't been used. I did find these journals by Caroline. They start shortly after she was married and go all the way through to the year before her death. Of course I checked out her last volume to see if she mentioned what she requested from the National Archives. Unfortunately, the journal from 1991 is missing. I'd guess she kept it somewhere near where she wrote in it and it didn't get put here with the others."

"Then it could be somewhere in the house," Jennie said, juggling several volumes he handed her. "Another reason for searching everywhere." She sat down, flipping open the first one. It was dated June 14, 1929.

My first day of married life and I have this wonderful blank book to fill with my thoughts. We have returned from our honeymoon, a perfect week in Chicago. Dr. and Mrs. Franklin Martin Garretson: it sounds sophisticated. Frank is wonderful and I could not have asked for a better start to our new life together.

We will live at River Bluffs with Father, as Father has asked me to continue in my role as the household manager. There are always people coming and going, social events, and family visiting. The staff works for me. It is so exciting. I love it! I even get to plan parties and such. Of course Frank will continue his medical practice in Caseyville, and Cousin Fred is always visiting if he's not at the company with Father. I am glad Fred will not be living here any longer. His wife, Betsy, always makes me feel uncomfortable. She's never anything but polite, so I do not really know why I feel this way. She is still a stranger to me, even though she has been here almost since the end of the Great War. After Mother's death last year, she tried to run the household as Father wanted, but she was not able to—which is good for me. Now that I am married, Father thinks I can manage. I am the same person I was last week, a nineteen-year-old woman, but with this ring on my finger, all of the sudden he thinks I am capable of the job. I always helped Mother when she was ill, so it is old hat to me.

I cannot spend all my time writing. I must go meet with the cook to see what we will be eating for the next few days.

The entry was immediately followed by the next day's thoughts. Jennie flipped quickly through a few pages. "Not very exciting, is it?" she asked Mike rhetorically. "How much did you read?"

"Sorry." He grimaced. "I have way too much testosterone to read more than a few pages without wanting to run outside and give off a loud Tarzan yell."

Jennie chuckled at the image. "Unless you want me to spend my precious time reading journals with mostly irrelevant material, you need to find your feminine side and read your great grandmother's journals."

"Fine. I'll read them," he said grudgingly. "Nobody will hear Tarzan yells out here anyway."

Jennie shook her head in surprise. Who knew Mike Garretson had a sense of humor?

She knew precisely what room they had to go to now. "Since I've got the papers I need from here and you've canvassed the books, we need to hit the attic."

"I don't suppose you think there's anything in the carriage house out back that needs searching, do you?"

Jennie gave the question serious consideration. Mike raised a hopeful eyebrow when she didn't shoot his idea down right away.

"Maybe, but it's not going to be key documents or photos, and if it was, they would likely be decaying or moldy. I'll let you take that on by yourself, once you get the feel for what we're looking for."

They climbed up the grand staircase. Jennie lagged behind, checking out the picture at the landing. It needed cleaning, the colors faded under an obvious layer of grime. As she was about to follow Mike up the rest of the stairs, one of the figures in the painting caught her eye. Startling green eyes, like Mike's, glimmered through the grime.

"Mike!" she yelped, immediately drawing a surprised grunt from upstairs.

He thumped back down the stairs. "What?"

"Look at this guy here," she said pointing to the noble face of an older man. "Do you know who this is? Commissioned artwork sometimes contains family members. Maybe this is family?"

Mike studied it closely and shrugged. "Sorry, he has the Garretson eyes, but beyond that, I don't recognize him. Dad might, but I can't bring him out here."

"Garretson eyes?" she echoed. "What do you

mean?"

"Almost a third of my family has green eyes, though if this is Josef Houseman, which we might guess it is, Veronica's branch apparently missed the trait. They have mostly brown eyes."

"Interesting," she said, half to herself. Among the dozen or so people in the painting, three others had the same green eyes. "We need to find a photo album. Do you know where there might be one?" Mike shook his head as Jennie continued, "Then let's hope your efficient, organized great grandmother put some together, wrote names in it, and left it somewhere easy to find."

At the top of the stairs, Mike caught his foot on the loose board he'd warned Jennie about. "I really should nail that down," he said, barely catching himself from falling.

Faced with the enormous amount of attic accumulation—which Mike insisted was junk—they decided to clear out one end of the attic so there would be a place to shift items they'd examined. It was a challenge since the area nearest the stairs was the thickest with cast-offs. Apparently as the attic filled up, less effort was made to move items away from the stairs.

After less than an hour, they were both sweating and covered in dust. Mike cracked open the windows to let in air. They needed the spring air blowing through the attic to clear it out.

Jennie pushed loose strands of her hair out of her eyes and sucked on a bottle of water during a break. "Meeting your will's requirement in three weeks is definitely the biggest challenge I've had," she said.

Mike paused from shifting a trunk, and wiped the sweat on his forehead against his sleeve. "You seem to know what you're doing," he said, and sat on the trunk. "You're better than the last guy I had doing the work."

For a moment, Jennie thought he'd previously hired somebody else.

"Me," he said, rolling his eyes.

"Ah. Dust in my brain cells. It must be fogging my thinking."

Mike picked up another water bottle, while Jennie, her back to Mike, dropped to her knees next to a cardboard box. Deciding the box of receipts from Caroline's later years might be worthwhile, she closed the lid and turned around. Mike, his shirt wadded in one hand and a water bottle in the other, was examining a small porcelain statue. Jennie felt as if the air was suddenly sucked out of the attic, because she couldn't get any to her lungs. Eyes wide, she stared at Mike's tanned chest. When he looked up, heat filled her face and she desperately searched for something else to look at.

She flipped the lid back off the box, and shuffled through the pages she'd already gone through. Nobody could have been more surprised than she was by her reaction to Mike. The last time she'd reacted to a man like this was in college, years ago.

Appalled at her thoughts, she abruptly shut the box and stood. She grabbed and wrested it upward. A muscle in her back twisted and Jennie gasped.

"What's wrong?" Mike reacted instantly, took the box from her and motioned for her to sit down. "What'd you do? You shouldn't lift that way."

"Right. Don't know what I was thinking."

After that, Jennie's concentration was spotty at best. Digging through an attic was like a treasure hunt, but watching Mike was even better. However, the search did go faster when she wasn't trying to check him out every ten seconds.

"So why do you like doing this? It's not particularly exciting," Mike asked during another break.

"My grandmother got me interested in my family's history. I was her only grandchild, so I think she figured I was the family's last hope. I fell in love with old stuff. Of course I was an old soul anyway, hanging around her and my dad. We moved so often, they were the only steady people in my life."

"You had friends your own age, didn't you?"

She sat in a broken chair, trying not to stare at Mike's chest.

"Of course. But they moved or we moved. Being an Army brat isn't good for long term friendships." That was an understatement. Her oldest friend she still kept in contact with she'd known only since high school. Even though she didn't have many old friendships, she had developed the ability to meet people easily. She knew lots of people now after three years at Swansea High. Except for Mae though, none of them counted as best friends. Mae kept encouraging her to get out and make more friends. Easy for her to say. She'd lived in the area her entire life. She knew everyone.

"You've done all right in the Metro East area," Mike said, interrupting her thoughts. "I asked three people I know about researchers and two of them recommended you."

"Really?" She knew she had a steady business, even during the school year. Still it was an ego boost to hear Mike's comment. "Two out of three? Who didn't know me? I'll go give them a card."

An easy rapport developed over the afternoon as they culled through the debris of decades for items of value. Their conversation about school, sports and current events was interrupted occasionally by a "look at this," then a debate over what some of the stuff might have been used for. Furniture, odd tools, a variety of clothes, a baby carriage, forgotten paintings, and an antique sewing machine were some of the material they sorted through. Boxes, crates or trunks that looked like they needed more searching, they set near the door for picking through later.

The shadows in the attic were growing toward late afternoon when the cell phone at Mike's hip rang. He pulled it out of its case, checking the caller ID.

"Hello, Veronica," he said.

Jennie surreptitiously strained to hear what they were saying, losing interest in the box of broken items she was examining.

"Just doing a bit of cleaning. How are you feeling?" His voice was coolly neutral. "No, that wouldn't be convenient. I've got a lot of work yet to do and another school week begins tomorrow morning." He sighed as his ex-wife apparently gave him an earful.

"Veronica, I shouldn't need to remind you we aren't married anymore," he said, turning his back to Jennie. He walked down the stairs a couple of steps. His back still turned, he rubbed his face with his free hand.

"I really can't help you. If your grandfather or Robert won't help, go to the police, or talk to your father or Uncle George. If you still need me, I'll meet you after baseball practice on Thursday. That's the soonest I can make it."

As he signed off with Veronica, Jennie returned her attention to the box she had been searching through.

"That was Veronica," he said.

"I heard."

"She's freaking out again about the car accident. I don't know what she expects me to do."

Mike had been a bit harsh with Veronica if that was what she was calling about. "Does she think Robert's behind it? Why won't she talk to him?"

"There's always been a bit of rivalry between

George's family and her grandfather's family. She doesn't think she'll get help in that direction."

"Well, can't you talk to them? You're a Houseman descendant, and you used to work there too."

Mike's reaction was unexpected. His eyes narrowed and even in the growing darkness, Jennie sensed anger. "I have no influence at HP," he said flatly.

The awkward silence that fell between them abruptly ended when Zippy gave a loud yip as the distinctive sounds of a thunderstorm rumbled the eaves. The gray sky had turned black. Jennie negotiated her way through the piles to one of the small arched windows.

"Whoa," she said, spying the roiling black clouds outside. "It looks like a whopper. We'd better get downstairs and listen to the radio for the weather report. This looks like it could spawn tornadoes." They closed the windows and, each grabbing one of the boxes they'd set aside, humans and dog stumbled hurriedly down the three flights of stairs.

After setting the boxes on the kitchen table, Mike turned on the radio. He adjusted the antenna to see if he could pick up any better reception. The weatherman's voice urgently catalogued a list of thunderstorm warnings and tornado watches around the area.

"Better get out the candles," Mike said, walking to the shelves holding all sorts of stuff, including the emergency candles and two large flashlights. "Electricity in this house during a storm is dicey at best." He lit several fat candles on plates. They were all different colors and it wasn't long before Jennie realized they had different aromas as well.

"You couldn't have bought candles with the same fragrance?" she asked, wrinkling her nose.

"Candles shouldn't smell," he grumbled. At that

point the lights flickered and went out, along with the radio's weather status. Mike grunted. "Fragrance is irrelevant when your primary goal is light."

"So, should I head home?" she asked, disappointed the evening would end like this.

Mike shook his head. "You can't go anywhere with this kind of storm, branches and trees flying around. Wait it out. You know Midwestern storms are fierce, but short."

"Guess I'm still on the clock then, eh?"

"In that case, come with me." He took a flashlight and headed up the back stairs to the third floor, grabbing her hand at the top of the stairs and leading her through the dark hall to the balcony. The heat of his hand caused a reaction in her body like that of the storm building tension outside. Mike flicked off the flashlight as he led her out on the windswept balcony, then—to Jennie's disappointment—dropped her hand as the strong smell of ozone accosted her nose.

Above most of the furiously waving tree tops and overlooking the Mississippi flood plain, she had a bird's eye view of the storm. Lightning stabbed through the angry black sky, followed quickly by rumbling thunder. Sheets of rain were visible moving across the fields in front of them, obscuring St. Louis completely. The front of the storm had not yet reached them, and she inched near the balcony railing, leaning slightly out to get the full effect of the mad wind.

Suddenly Mike grabbed her wrist and yelled in her ear, "Are you nuts? This railing is more than a hundred years old!" He jerked her back against his chest and she unexpectedly found herself face to face with him, his hand still wrapped around her wrist. Her heart thudded loudly, and for a brief moment, she imagined him passionately kissing her. His deep green eyes locked on her mouth, and he made a slight move toward her, but then, abruptly, he was setting her away from him.

"Watch the rail," he muttered in a surprisingly deep voice and stepped away.

Jennie nodded blindly, heart pounding. She watched the fury march toward River Bluffs, and tried to sort through the emotions roiling inside her. She had wanted to kiss Mike, and she was reasonably sure Mike had wanted to kiss her too.

She could feel him behind her as they watched the rain travel closer, then heard the telltale thumps of hail pelting the roof and slipping under the balcony's fancy gingerbread woodwork. She held out her hand to try to catch some, drawing it back with three small beads of ice. The air was still warm, but she shivered, partially in excitement, wrapping her hands around her arms.

"Are you cold?" Mike asked, his voice surprisingly close to her.

She shook her head. "No, I love a Midwestern storm."

"Then let's enjoy the show."

The hail turned to rain as Mike pulled up two wooden chairs, worn of their paint, but still solid. They sat down and watched the rest of the storm in silence, an occasional spray penetrating under the gingerbread carvings. It was another twenty minutes before the worst of the weather passed and the rain fell into a steady stream.

"I think we're done here for the night," Mike finally said, breaking the silence. "The power probably won't come back on for a while. I'll follow you out of here so you don't get stuck somewhere. Do you want to take the things we've found in the attic with you?"

"I'm not going to get through them anytime soon. They either stay here till next weekend, or you can take them with you and see if you find anything of value," Jennie said. "I'll have enough on my hands sorting out the family ties and going to the courthouse. Caroline was a good genealogist, but she didn't have access to the material we have today. There's a lot more out there that may help us. And, of course, I still have to find what she found, which is probably not in any of those boxes."

They carried Caroline's journals to Mike's car after voting to leave the boxes for next weekend due to their schedules. The porte-cochere kept Jennie and Mike dry, the rain still steady. Zippy jumped into Mike's car, ready to go for a ride anywhere.

In the pouring rain with Jennie following closely behind, Mike led the trek back to civilization.

Chapter 7

Jennie opened her classroom door as a slightly plump Mae hurried down the hallway.

"Hey, girl," Mae called, stopping to hold the door with fingers sporting burgundy nails with white starbursts. "So, what's up with the reclusive coach? What interesting stuff did you learn about him?"

"Nice manicure," Jennie offered, stalling for an answer.

She had become friends with the librarian when Mae had asked Jennie to help trace her African-American roots. Since Jennie did not have expertise in that area, she had offered to assist so she could learn as well. Tracing family history is personal, and doing it together had made the two close friends, in spite of a twenty-five year age difference. Jennie had become another one of Mae's five children, an honor that regularly humbled Jennie. Mae had taken on Jennie, providing both sisterly advice and motherly support as needed.

It was that bond giving Jennie problems. How was she supposed to honor Mike's request for secrecy without keeping secrets from her best friend?

"Okay, Mae. I'm going to tell you right up front I can't tell you what you want to know," she blurted out.

Mae pulled back in surprise, crossing her arms. "What? I don't understand."

"Mike's hired me for a job, but I can't talk about it."

A good five inches shorter than Jennie, Mae had the amazing ability to make Jennie feel small. Her black eyes bored holes into Jennie's resolve.

"Don't look at me like that! I promise I'll tell you everything on May 20."

"You meet the most mysterious man in school at some old house. You get hired for some secret project. And you want me to wait three weeks to tell me what you're doing?"

"Yes." Jennie shrugged apologetically.

Mae snorted in disgust. "All weekend I fantasized on your behalf about what your meeting would have been like. After all, it's the closest thing to a date you've had in forever. Did Mike at least try to make out with you?"

"Yeah, right, Mae. And then I agreed to bear his child. What do I, a bookworm with tendencies toward the archives, and a chemist with tendencies toward World Series tickets, possibly have in common?"

"You're both single. And don't sell yourself short, sweetie," Mae said, patting Jennie's shoulder. "You're shapely, you're funny, and your hair is naturally curly. Everything a man needs. My poor hubby only got the funny part."

"Ah, but how many men get the female half of Krusty the Clown?" Jennie said, dropping her work on the desk and leaning over to turn on the computer. She smiled at Mae.

"Gee, thanks. I'll remember that when I pour arsenic on your lunch today. I will be expecting a call at one minute past midnight on May 20." She dramatically turned around with a swing of her ample hips and stomped out of the room.

Jennie was relieved Mae had not pressed her. It was the kind of friendship they had. But born and raised in the area, Mae definitely fell into Paul Garretson's category of someone Jennie couldn't talk to.

She opened her email and scrolled through the

usual set of announcements and reminders always appearing after a weekend. Then one caught her eye.

Jennie, Thanks for the help this weekend. Talk to you soon.—Mike

She smiled. It was a simple note, but it made her feel warm. She was still smiling when her first class arrived.

****

Monday evening was a wash for looking into Mike's problem. Jennie had put off more schoolwork than she should have over the weekend. Payback meant working until dinner at the school, and dragging more work home with her.

By Tuesday, the urge to see Josef Houseman's will was overwhelming, in spite of a pile of reports threatening to take over her bag. Since the county courthouse wasn't open in the evening, she rushed to downtown Belleville immediately after school.

The St. Clair County courthouse did not have any of the charm of most Midwestern towns. However, because it was a modern building, it did have the advantage of being easy to get into, find what she needed and get out in a relatively short period of time. With minutes to spare, Jennie had a copy of Josef's will in her hands, and she had the location of both Caroline and Fred's wills as well. They would have to wait for a second visit though, as the desk clerk, a tense woman whose eyes kept straying toward the clock, was impatiently tapping fingers on the desk.

Trying to keep one eye on the sidewalk as she walked to her car, Jennie read the will. It was pretty standard, the company going to Fred, the house and lands to Caroline. But she stopped in the middle of the parking lot when she read:

Evidence proving an illegitimate claim on the company should be submitted for legal examination. If such evidence proves the claim is true, then the company should be equally divided, one-third to each branch, to the heirs of my father Johan Houseman, including myself, my brother William and my sister Katrina, if she or her descendants can be found. If Katrina cannot be found, the company should be equally divided in half between William and my heirs. This provision will survive in perpetuity and cannot be dissolved.

Jennie reread the paragraph. Did Josef suspect Fred was an imposter? Why else would he put such a weird clause in his will? In addition, if Fred Houseman was not who he said he was, then the will very clearly indicated his heirs would not inherit.

The will gave Caroline a major motive for proving Fred Houseman was a fake. Potentially she would have inherited at least a third of the company. Caroline, however, could not be a suspect in her own murder, even if this inheritance clause gave her motive. In fact, the will gave her all the motivation she needed to pursue proving Fred was fake, and all the reason for Fred or his heirs to ensure no one else proved otherwise.

Jennie climbed in her car and read the remainder of the will with Josef Houseman's stern slanted signature at the bottom. Too excited to wait longer, she called Mike at the cell phone number he'd given her.

Mike picked up his phone, sounding like he might still be in the locker room.

"Did I catch you at a bad time?"

"Practice is over. The team's changing. What's up?"

"I found Josef Houseman's will. It's very interesting."

"Yeah?" The noise level in the background dropped after the distinctive sound of a door closing. "What'd you find?"

Jennie told him about the Josef's obvious doubt

about Fred Houseman. "Why would Josef leave the family business to someone he wasn't sure was even a relation? I understand he didn't want to will his business to Caroline, since women weren't expected to have that kind of role. But why not her husband?"

"Maybe Caroline's husband was an idiot, and Josef didn't trust him."

"Yet he let him live at River Bluffs? I don't think so. Besides, he was a doctor. Why wouldn't he be smart enough to run the company?"

"I don't suppose we'll ever know the answer to that question." After a brief pause, he said, "I'd like to see that will. And I have some journal entries I think you'll find interesting. Have you eaten?"

"No, I'm still sitting in the courthouse parking lot."

"Then meet me for dinner."

"I've got test essays to read, so it has to be somewhere quick," Jennie said reluctantly. She would have liked to have a nice, relaxed dinner where she could have learned a bit more about her client. Instead, they settled on a buffet halfway between Swansea High School and the courthouse. It wasn't anywhere special, but Jennie was happy to have an excuse of any sort to see those intriguing green eyes again.

****

Jennie spotted Mike's classic red sports car as soon as he drove into the parking lot. Carrying four of Caroline's journals with him, he greeted her by sliding his hand down the back of her arm. Heat floated through regions of her body that were unused to a man's touch. She gritted her teeth and managed a friendly, but not too friendly, smile.

Mike offered to pay for dinner as reciprocation for her cooking lunch over the weekend. She could have paid and turned around and billed the dinner as expenses. But she got the feeling he would have offered to buy any woman dinner he was meeting. It was kind of sweet. Sort of like a date.

She really had to get a life after this job.

They found an isolated corner table. Mike silently read the will Jennie handed him. "Does this mean what I think it does? I don't have much experience with wills. First one I ever saw was Paul Garretson's, and I'm still trying to figure that one out."

"I'm not a lawyer, but I think it's pretty obvious Josef was having doubts about Fred."

"This question probably sounds self-serving, but what happens if you prove Fred's an imposter? Would the will still be upheld in court today?"

"I don't know. 'Perpetuity' is a long time to normal people. But lawyers aren't normal. Speaking of which, have you talked with your lawyer yet?"

"No, left a message, he returned my message. It's back in my court, but my hours and his are not compatible."

"Ask him what he thinks," Jennie suggested. "What a mess. Can you imagine how this would affect your family? The question is: what happens to the Housemans who have run the business for years if their ancestor is a fraud?"

Mike shook his head. "Interesting question. Just because it happened decades ago, it would still be identity theft. Last time I checked, that was a crime. But I'll talk to Rick about it and see what he says." Mike handed the pages back to Jennie and tapped the journals. "I suggest we get some food before you start reading these."

Leaving the journals unattended didn't seem like a good idea, so Jennie went for a salad first. She began reading while Mike gathered a plate of food. He had marked every significant event with a sticky note so she wouldn't have to read the whole journal. The first journal was full of Caroline and Frank's new life together. But Mike had found more than a few entries that were far more interesting.

October 14, 1929—Father brought Fred home drunk last night. He was as bad as I've ever seen him, and Father was not happy. To make the night worse, as we were helping Fred up the stairs to bed, he lost his balance on the upper flight and fell backward. To catch himself, Fred grabbed a vase of flowers on a pedestal on the landing and somehow managed to fall into the painting. The vase shattered and not only tore the painting, but soaked it as well. Father was furious. He was up half the night smoking his pipe and examining the damage. This morning he announced the painting was ruined and would need to be replaced.

October 17, 1929—Father has found an excellent painter in the local area. He is going to have him paint River Bluffs and all of us into the new painting that will hang on the stairs! The painter is even going to design the painting so any future children born to Fred and Betsy, or to Frank and me, can be added to the painting. I am so excited! I have never had my painting done. Betsy is pregnant now and I think that is why Father wanted to make sure future children could be added.

December 28, 1929—Marcus Laramie, our artist, revealed the new painting today. It is absolutely marvelous! And we are all in it: Father, looking commanding—even without his pipe—then Frank and I, and Fred, Betsy and their boys, George and Little Joe. I think it is a huge improvement over the last stuffy painting and will be quite the conversation piece. Marcus left space to paint the baby Betsy is carrying and any future children, as Father requested. Here is a drawing of who everyone is.

Caroline had sketched a small version of the painting, with little heads indicating the people in the painting. She carefully labeled them all in tiny print. "Great," Jennie said. "Now we can identify everyone on the wall."

"Except I don't think she added future babies to her sketch," Mike said. "There are fewer faces on her sketch than on the painting. But it wouldn't matter anyway. We can't identify an adult today from a baby's portrait anyway."

In the second journal, Caroline's newsy writing carried more substance:

April 6, 1930—Betsy gave birth to their third little boy today. They named him John Francis Houseman, John after Grandpa John Houseman, the first Houseman from Germany. George is not too happy to have another baby in the house, especially since he is ten and wants his father's attention so much. He came to me to talk, which I let him do as much as he wants. I tried to help him with his feelings, something Betsy is not very good at, especially as she has demanding Little Joe at home as well. Fortunately, I have lots of time on my hands with my own baby not due until August.

George told me his parents have been arguing again. We all know they argue, though we are supposed to pretend we do not notice. Father smokes his pipe and goes outside on the piazza when they argue at our house.

On the sticky note on the next entry, Mike wrote: *This is my grandfather.*

August 25, 1930—Today I am a mother! I gave birth to a beautiful little boy, Henry Otto Garretson, right here at River Bluffs. His papa and I are the proudest parents around. Everyone has been coming to the manor to see us and give us congratulations. I am very tired, of course, but my loving sweet son is worth all the effort. I swear I can see the Houseman green eyes already, even though they say eye color doesn't show up until the baby is older. Father says both his parents had green eyes and that's why they keep showing up in the family. Fred doesn't have them, though, and neither do any of his boys. Ah, well, I guess the Garretsons will have to carry on the Houseman eyes.

Mike came back with a second full plate. "So, what do you think so far?" he asked, taking up a forkful of food.

"I like knowing the history behind that painting. We don't have to find a photo album to know who's in it. And that stuff about the eyes is fascinating. It's not often you find who you inherited something from."

"Definitely interesting. Especially when you read the next journal. And it involves eyes again." Mike outlined Caroline's comments on the family's plan for a get-together with the Housemans that lived in California. Caroline had the idea to invite Fred's brother and sisters, especially when she'd learned he had never gone back to California after World War I. Only Jacob, his younger brother, had taken up the invitation, but that was enough to get Caroline excited.

March 12, 1932—We received a letter from Cousin Jacob this morning and I immediately went to the company to tell Father the news. Father has never met any of his nieces or nephews, except Fred. He was quite excited to hear Jacob would be here for the family reunion. Unfortunately, Fred and Jacob's sisters cannot come as they all have children and too much happening with their orange crops.

Fred came into Father's office while we were talking and when I told him the news, I would swear he looked positively ill. Jacob was only seven the last time he saw Fred, before he went off to the Great War. He says Betsy doesn't like to travel, and he would never leave her alone for such a long time, so that's why he's never been back. I do not understand why he isn't excited about seeing his little brother. Perhaps he was a horrid older brother who played too many tricks. I, for one, am very interested in learning more about Fred's childhood. He doesn't talk much about his early life. Perhaps his war injuries changed him greatly and he does not think much about the past.

It will be a very interesting family reunion!

"Well, that's a very interesting entry," Jennie said, repeating Caroline's words unintentionally. She finished reading the entry and eating her salad simultaneously. She barely noticed Mike, she was so deep in thought. He had already finished his food and was watching her expectantly.

"Yes?" he said, eventually interrupting the silence.

"Oh, I'm trying to determine what sources there are with Fred having been in World War I. Some military service records were destroyed in a fire at the St. Louis records depository. But I think the draft registration cards men were required to fill out might show us something. I'll have to check online to see if Fred's name comes up in the index. If it does, we can get a copy of the draft record."

"What would that show us?"

"Residency, age, birthplace, a short physical description. There were three types of draft cards and the information varies on them."

"That's sounds promising," Mike said neutrally. He stood, taking a clean plate with him. "The next entry gets better," he said. "While you're reading, I'm going back for more food. Do you want to go first?"

She waved him off. The food was not nearly as fascinating as the reading.

April 25, 1932—Father, Frank and I met the train today with Jacob on it. Fred said he would meet us at the house at dinner with Betsy and the boys because he was too busy at work. I do not see how Fred can be busier than Father, but Father seemed pleased, rather than annoyed.

Jacob and I, it turns out, are the same age! Of course I am getting large with my second baby and could hardly keep that a secret, but Jacob was very sweet to me. Very much a gentleman. I do not know why he is not married, though he confessed to having a sweetheart at home. He is working with his brothers-in-law on the orange farm and feels he will soon be running his own farm. He told us he had pretty much been raised by his oldest sister after his mother died, she being twenty years older than Jacob. Though I know it is not uncommon, I cannot imagine having children twenty years apart!

Dinner was most remarkable. I know Fred and Jacob have not seen each other since 1917, but they did not even act like they were family. Jacob kept staring at Fred as if he were a stranger. Fred kept talking nonstop, something he never does. Betsy was even less social than normal. Father asked a lot of questions about California, and Jacob would turn to Fred and say, "But surely you must have told him about that?" or "Tell him all about that, Fred." Fred would defer to Jacob to tell the story.

Fred and Betsy are staying the night, as is Jacob, of course. We will go to church tomorrow and then have a picnic outside afterward. If Fred and Jacob continue to act this way, I think Father will smoke his pipe into nothingness.

***April 26, 1932**—Oh, my! What a day it has been. Betsy is missing. Fred says she was so angry at him today she told him to stop the car and let her out. He tried to talk her back into the car, but she would not come. She said she would walk home. When she didn't show up, Fred called us to see if she had come here. This happened after a day that would have been unusual on the earlier events alone.*

We had the picnic today as planned. It was a perfect day, and the children were all dressed in their play clothes and behaving so wonderfully. The cook prepared a meal and it was all set up outside so we could talk and play. But the odd dinner conversation from last night continued. Jacob seemed to egg Fred on about California, with Fred not talking about it at all. Betsy did not know anything about California, as she was born in Pennsylvania, and she chose to be a particularly attentive mother today to avoid making conversation with the brother-in-law she had never met.

Then I saw Fred inside River Bluffs. He had escaped Jacob's constant questions, and was talking with Mattie, our housemaid. She was giggling quite unaccountably. Then who should come up behind me to see the same scene? Betsy. I think she was breathing fire when she called Fred's name. He turned bright red, though surely it was nothing. I quickly made my exit.

Later I was playing with baby Henry outside, and talking with Jacob. He said he would swear that before Fred left for the war he had green eyes like mine. But now they were brown, like Jacob's. He was quite frustrated Fred had never been to visit his childhood home in all the years since the war. Then, he actually confronted Fred about his eye color! It would have been quite funny if it wasn't so horribly embarrassing. Fred denied having green eyes ever and that Jacob must have been mistaken. Father even suggested that maybe the war experience changed Fred's eyes.

About that time Betsy came out of the house with their boys and said it was time to go home. Fred looked quite appalled, or maybe relieved. He certainly was not himself today. They all left in Fred's new car.

Shortly after that we heard a gunshot. Father got

Frank and the gardener to see if they could catch the trespassing hunters. With as much land as we have, it's quite common to find poachers. Jacob stayed with me in case the shooter came near—as if with four servants in the house I am ever alone! They didn't find anyone, and soon we got the call from Fred saying Betsy is missing.

I am quite exhausted and my husband is insisting I rest. I will follow his orders, mostly because he is right.

Jennie had uncharacteristically forgotten about eating. When she finished the entry, she gasped for breath, since she had apparently been unconsciously holding it. "What a family!" she said with wide eyes. "No wonder you have a mystery."

"I remembered my grandfather talking about this incident," Mike said, leaning forward. "Betsy was never found. To this day, they don't know what happened to her, though most suspect the hunters and Betsy may have had a run-in. I didn't remember the family legend until I read it in Caroline's notes, but the story about her disappearance is well-known among the family. Fred had to raise his three sons alone after that. He never remarried, and he had a nanny raise the kids with a lot of help from Caroline.

"Now would be a good time for you to get some real food." He waved his fork at Jennie's empty salad plate.

She picked a few items off the buffet bar and hurried back to the table, her mind in a whirl. "So, Fred's wife Betsy disappears after she catches him flirting with a maid," she summarized while half-heartedly eating popcorn shrimp. "Fred is visibly upset by the appearance of a brother. And Josef smokes a pipe a lot when he's stressed." Jennie abruptly sat up, mouth open. *"The eyes!"* she said breathlessly. "Mike! It's the eyes!"

"What?" he said, baffled by her comment.

"Jacob said Fred's eyes were green. Caroline said they were brown. The National Archives has the World War I draft cards and they have *eye color* on them! Fred would have filled one out before the war started."

Mike's own eyes opened wide in understanding. He looked around and leaned in close. "Do you think this is what Caroline ordered and was waiting for?"

"I hope so," she said just as quietly. "Caroline wouldn't have had the advantage of an online index, but I do."

"Then you need to go home and prove this," Mike ordered. "That's the last of the best entries in 1932 except that Paul Garretson is born in December."

"Don't I get dessert?" she said, playing with his anticipation. With anyone she knew better, she would have excused herself already to get to her computer.

"I don't suppose you can prove it tonight anyway," he said, shrugging.

Jennie shoved the journals across the table. "Fine," she sighed dramatically. "For the sake of the pay, I'll give up my dessert."

Mike didn't try too hard to hide the self-satisfied smirk on his face.

"Before you go. You're on for a family reunion this weekend."

"What? I don't think so."

"Sure you will. It's the Houseman/Garretson reunion this weekend, which we have learned was a tradition started back in 1932. You get to meet all the suspects in one location. And you get paid."

Jennie's heart skipped a beat and then returned to practicality. It wasn't a date, just a chance to meet the family. "Won't that be inviting a bit of suspicion? 'I'd like to introduce the historian I've hired to determine if some of you are illegitimate heirs?'"

"You'll go disguised as a friend of mine from work. The description will drive my mother and sister nuts. They love these events, partly because they're at George Houseman's house."

"Which one is he again?" Jennie asked.

"The multi-millionaire senior patriarch of the Houseman family and chairman of the board of directors of HP. You'll love his house, even though it's not Victorian."

Jennie agreed, but her apprehension was plain. She would be meeting Mike's extended family under the pretense of being his friend. She'd only known Mike a week. She hoped she could do better than Fred had when Jacob showed up at their reunion.

Chapter 8

Jennie's computer wasn't very old and she'd thought it was pretty fast for its age. But this evening as she tried to get her computer up, it wouldn't boot fast enough. She kicked off her shoes and got a bottle of water before the screen finally booted fully. Then, calling up a search page, she quickly found a World War I draft card registration index.

It was almost too easy. There it was: Frederick Houseman, born California, 1897. She copied the rest of the index entry. She would need it to get the actual record. Instead of ordering it from the National Archives, which could take weeks considering the budget constraints they had, she picked up the phone and called a researcher in Atlanta. She lived near the National Archives' Southeast Region center where all original World War I draft registrations were kept.

Sheila Armstrong answered the phone in her deep southern accent. "You never call to chat, so y'all must have something you need. I'm right, aren't I?"

"You bet, Sheila. And I need it fast. A copy of a World War I draft card. Do you have time to stop by the Archives branch in the next couple of days? I'll pay the usual rate." Jennie could practically hear Sheila's doubts melt away. Like doctors hate being asked to diagnose friends, nothing bugs a professional genealogist more than someone wanting research for free.

"For you—and the usual rate—I can swing by there tomorrow, after the morning rush hour is over.

Shall I scan the copy and email it to you?"

Jennie agreed and gave her Fred's details from the index listing. Now, all she had to do was sit back and wait for this project to finish. But then she wouldn't be the perfectionist her father had trained her to be. Besides, more evidence was always better.

She logged onto email and saw she'd received a message back from *jjh1910@danvers.net*. It read:

Hello,

This is my great grandfather's email address. He's under the weather right now but asked me to check his email. He's the one looking for Housemans or Hausmanns, descended from his father Johan Hausmann/John Houseman of California, born in Germany in 1840. If this is the family you are looking for, I'm sure he would love to exchange information with you.

My great grandfather is Jacob Houseman, and I'm Rachel McGregor. Hope we hear from you again!

Rachel

Jacob? Could she mean the same Jacob that had visited Illinois in the 1930s? Jennie opened her genealogical software and checked the name. There was only one Jacob, and he was born in 1910. Stunned, she picked up the phone again and called Mike.

"I got an email from Jacob Houseman's great granddaughter," she said, unable to contain her excitement. "I think it's the same Jacob Caroline said came out from California in 1932."

"How's that possible? Shouldn't he be dead?"

"Nearly so. He'd be ninety-seven years old, but it was his email account I wrote to. What's the rule on me telling him or his great granddaughter I'm researching Houseman family history? She's in California, not local."

"I don't know. Let me check with Rick tomorrow when I'm asking about the inheritance stuff. If you talk to Jacob, what would he tell you?"

"Hopefully he can confirm the story about the eyes, maybe put his spin on it. It's not often you get a relative that old. He probably has some stories that will clear up—or cloud up—what we've already learned. Also, I have a fellow researcher heading over to the Atlanta branch of the National Archives to get a copy of Fred's draft record."

"This can't be that easy," Mike said, his voice laced with doubt.

Jennie hoped this would be Mike's lucky day. "It can," she said. "But I wouldn't count on it. I like to expect the worst, then I can always be pleasantly surprised when things go right."

"Thanks for the update." He paused and added, "I thought you had tests to grade. Quit running up my bill."

"Reality bites," she said, sighing. "An essay about the Soviet Union just doesn't hold a candle to Fred Houseman and company."

She hung up the phone staring at the receiver. It occurred to her that if Sheila came through, this project would be over. A professional coup, but one that would end an enjoyable working relationship with Mike. She sighed, not certain whether to cheer for her professional side or her personal life. Putting aside her research, she picked up the stack of tests.

Chapter 9

Jennie's news about Jacob Houseman's email still on his mind, Mike stared blankly at the sheaves of ungraded homework in front of him. His townhouse dining room, which was also the living/family room, was decorated in a style he'd stolen from a furniture store. It rarely distracted him from his work.

Jennie, however, was another matter. He wouldn't mind having her sitting across the table from him, discussing the latest twists to her research, or whatever it was she was doing in her classes. After two years of avoiding people, it appeared he'd found someone he didn't mind being around. Of course, it was probably because of what she was doing. This family history stuff was far more interesting than he'd thought it would be.

His visions of her curly hair and long legs were abruptly interrupted by the doorbell. Zippy, curled up on a dog bed, dashed to the door and yapped furiously. Mike automatically looked at his watch, the digital face glowing eight-forty-seven. He peered through the peephole. Veronica stood outside, impatiently examining her nails.

"Veronica?" Mike said, opening the door. "What are you doing here?" His voice registered his displeasure.

The dog sniffed curiously at Veronica's ankles. She gave him one disdainful look and nudged him away. Zippy backed away, yipped once more, and retreated to his bed. He kept a steady eye on the woman.

"Mike," she said breathily, wrapping her arms around his neck. "I had to see you. You don't answer your cell phone messages. You need to know what happened at work. Jack Elliott died. I think he was murdered."

"What do you mean, murdered?" Mike disentangled himself from Veronica's arms and stepped away from her. A tight top, which dipped dangerously low on her chest, was plastered to her curves. A short skirt completed an outfit more appropriate for a night on the town.

She brushed past him and gracefully lowered herself onto the couch. Patting the seat next to her, she eyed Mike hopefully. He promptly dropped into the one armchair in the room.

Frowning, she leaned toward him, placing an elegant hand on his knee. "Jack was found dead this morning. A simple safety precaution he overlooked: one of the valves on a CO_2 tank was leaking and he didn't catch it. The lack of oxygen killed him."

Mike shook his head in disbelief. "You're right. I know Jack. He's too good to do that. Is Robert investigating?"

"Of course there's a standard company investigation. But whoever killed Jack knew what he was doing. It'll be ruled an accident." She was sliding her hand against the soft cotton of Mike's jeans, an action that at one time would have encouraged him to drag her onto his lap. Now it was irritating. He stood, forcing Veronica to withdraw her hand.

"There's nothing I can do," Mike said, intentionally walking back toward the door. "Just because I have Houseman blood running in my veins does not give me influence at the company. I think that was aptly proven once already. You have more influence than I do."

She stood, gracefully closing the space between

them. Her three-inch heels put her eyes at his chin. Mike realized they were milk chocolate, much like Jennie's, but they lacked warmth and the gold sparkle that was obvious when Jennie was excited about something. He grabbed Veronica's hand to keep it from sliding against his cheek.

"I'm sorry, Mike." Her voice was a husky whisper. "I know you can't do anything. I...I needed someone to talk to. We were friends once. I thought we still were."

He sighed. "I can listen, Veronica. I just can't help you. That will have to be enough."

She bent her head, silky blonde hair sliding forward. "I called you three times this afternoon. Where were you?"

"I told you on Sunday I'm busy. I have both my job and my coaching." He waved at the table full of papers.

Veronica sighed. "You're a great chemist, Mike. Why would you trade a high-paying salary for teaching?"

Mike thought of several rebuttals, but his ex had heard them all. She would ignore them now too. Instead, he crossed his arms and kept his face as neutral as possible. "I need to get back to my grading."

"Okay. Thanks. I...I'll be going now." She looked at him, eyes warm and misty with unshed tears. "Mike, you know I still love you. If you'd give us another chance..."

Mike felt a crack in his armor. He would have liked more than anything else to fix his marriage. But neither he nor Veronica was willing to bend to the other's expectations. More significantly, Veronica Houseman did not have what he was looking for, whatever that was. He awkwardly patted her arm. She entwined her hand in his.

He shook his head, pulling away. "No, Veronica.

We aren't good together." Mike didn't want to offer anymore than his friendship, certain even that was too much.

Veronica nodded, pushing her hair back from her face. "I don't agree. But I'll go. Anyway, thanks for listening." She threw a sad look over her shoulder as she walked out the door.

Mike closed the door, locking it to ensure she didn't burst back in again, a dramatic action he knew she might consider. He closed his eyes and breathed in deeply. Zippy was sitting at his feet when he reopened them, tail wagging expectantly.

Scooping up the white mutt and ruffling his fur, Mike strode into his small kitchen and found himself some ibuprofen for a sudden headache. Unfortunately, that was one reaction to Veronica that remained the same.

Chapter 10

Jennie was in the teachers' mail room after school on Wednesday when Mike tracked her down. Since there were several other teachers talking and copying papers, he crooked a finger at her to join him in the hallway.

Once in the hallway, he leaned against the lockers, his gaze scanning the mostly empty corridor. "I've got to get out to the field. We've got a game," he explained unnecessarily since he was already dressed in his coach's uniform.

Jennie had been thinking about sneaking out and watching the game. Sneaking was the ideal term. If Mae thought for an instant her library-addicted friend would want to watch a sports game, she would be as suspicious as a cop behind a weaving driver.

Mike continued. "I talked with Rick today. He gave me his interpretation of the will. Also, he told me what he knows about HP's ownership. Oh, and Veronica thinks one of the company's scientists was murdered Monday night."

"What?" Jennie asked, her mouth dropping open.

"We can't talk here. Can we meet after the game?"

"I was going home to do some research when I'm done here."

"Great. I'll meet you there."

Jennie started in surprise. Mike, at her house? So much for the game. She mentally dashed through her house to see if it was acceptable to a visitor. She was so engrossed in making a clean-up checklist she missed Mike's question.

He waved a hand in front of her face. "Jennie? I asked you where you live. Unless my stopping by would be inconvenient?"

"No! Of course not," she replied, somewhat over-enthusiastically. "How about I throw some dinner together too? You'll be hungry after your game."

Mike was raising a questioning eyebrow. "I wouldn't want to be a problem."

"I was planning on cooking anyway," she lied. She tried to recall what was in her refrigerator that wasn't microwaveable. "What time will you be done?"

"It varies. I'll call you when the game's over, somewhere around seven. I should be at your house about thirty to forty-five minutes after that."

She scribbled her address on the bottom of a flyer she'd picked up out of her mailbox and handed it to him.

He read the address and nodded. "I know where that is. See you later."

****

As he rounded the corner, Mike nearly ran into school matriarch, Mae Jefferson. He put on his best poker face. Mae knew everyone and everything. Though not the oldest faculty member, she was the one everyone went to when they had a problem they couldn't solve. Even the tech guys running the school's network sometimes sought her out. However, the most worrisome thing about Mae was that she was Jennie Foster's best friend.

"Mike Garretson," she said, eyebrows raised. "Looks like you should be at a game."

Mike was wary. Why did he feel like she knew more than she should? "The assistant coaches are doing the warm-ups."

"So, I guess you hired Jennie for a history

project."

"Uh. Yes. Jennie Foster." His brain felt slow. Mae was practically an icon in the area. If his family had roots, so did the Jeffersons. "Just a little project."

"Hmmm. You be careful, you hear? I don't want Jennie getting hurt."

Hurt? He tried to keep any expression off his face as he examined Mae's cryptic comment. Jennie was just looking for papers, very dry and boring documents. Mike didn't really put much credit in the story about some supposed murderer killing people who knew about the family lineage. So how could Jennie get hurt?

Unless Mae thought *he* was going to hurt Jennie? He opened his mouth to protest, and was startled all over again when Mae smiled broadly and wished him luck in the game. She disappeared around the corner. Oddly, the smile was more disturbing than her comments.

What conclusion had Mae just reached?

****

Jennie rushed through her school work, finally sliding into her car after five. She immediately turned on her cell phone.

Sheila Armstrong had called from Atlanta. "Bad news, honey," she announced when Jennie called her back. "I went to the archives today, and spent a lot of time looking for Frederick Houseman's draft registration, but it's not there."

"Please tell me you're kidding," Jennie said hopefully.

"Wish I were. You know the draft cards sit in boxes down here," she continued. "You can only take them out one box of registrations at a time, and you sit in a room with an archivist. Still, if the card was there—and it must have been at one time to get in the index—someone with low ethics could simply have walked out with it years ago."

"I take it you searched the box thoroughly?"

"Of course, honey. Spent hours reading the handwriting to ensure that's why I was missing it. There's nothing there to find."

Jennie sighed. "It figures this was too easy. Thanks, Sheila. Send me a bill."

Jennie was certain Caroline's secret find had been a copy of the draft card. It made the most sense and certainly would have proven Fred's eye color. The question was whether someone had taken it before or after Caroline ordered the copy.

She decided not to call Mike with the bad news. She didn't think it would help the game he was coaching. Besides, there were other angles to pursue. She mulled them over while making dinner and cleaning the house.

****

The doorbell rang barely thirty minutes after Mike called from his winning game. Sliding her feet into sandals, Jennie let him in. He stopped just inside the door, the pleasant smell of soap reaching her nose. He had somehow managed to shower and change.

Jennie curiously watched Mike, who had paused and was examining the living room with its built-in shelves and mix of period and modern furnishings. She'd bought the 1920s home cheap after moving to southern Illinois. The house had been a dive: missing shutters, rotted wood, ancient plumbing, and molding carpet. The summer before she'd started teaching at Swansea High School, she'd ripped out carpet and pulled down bad wallpaper while researching client histories. Later, adjusting to a full work load of teaching, she'd sanded hardwood floors, replaced windows, and refinished the kitchen and bathroom.

It had taken two years of blood, sweat and

money, but last year, after school started, she'd celebrated with a few teachers she got along with, the Jeffersons and her father at a housewarming party. The house was her baby, so everyone who came to her house was subject to the same scrutiny. As far as Jennie was concerned, the worst thing a visitor could do was not notice the house—for better or worse.

Unaware she had been holding her breath, she exhaled forcefully when he finally asked, "Did you do this?"

"This? What do you mean?"

He turned and studied her as if he'd never seen her. "I mean, did you refurbish this house?"

"Of course, I had to," she said, giving up on trying to beat him at his own game of reticence. "When I moved here, pretty much everything I had went to pay for my education. This house was a derelict, a fixer-upper of the worst kind. I got it for practically nothing. But there was quality under the mess, 'good bones' as my grandmother would say."

Then he did something totally unexpected. He walked over to a wall and reached an arm up to run his hand over the carved moldings at the ceiling's edge, something he could do because he was so tall and the ceiling only eight feet high. Then he gently picked up a Depression-era colored glass piece from a shelf nearby, feeling the smooth sides with his free hand. Jennie's mouth gaped open in disbelief as he wandered around the living room, dining room and kitchen, silently perusing their contents. No one had ever reacted to her house like this.

Mike finished his examination. "You did an excellent job. I'd like to see the rest of the house."

Jennie was horrified to realize she was blushing. "Th-thanks," she stammered, failing to recover from her pleasure at his compliment. "There's not much more. Just the two bedrooms and a bathroom."

The first bedroom served as her office, and it didn't look much better organized than River Bluffs' library.

"The mess is a good sign," she offered as an excuse. "It means I'm hot on your case."

She caught Mike's gaze, a smile at the corner of his mouth, and realized the double meaning in her words too late. She tried to cover up by twisting around in the small hallway to show him her bedroom.

"And this is my bed, uh, bedroom." She winced at her word choice again, but this time, Mike didn't look her way. Instead, heat sizzled along her skin as she watched his eyes study the antique quilt on her bed with unusual interest.

He turned his gaze on her. If she hadn't been leaning against the doorframe, she was certain she might have turned into a puddle on the floor.

"I like what you did with this house. You'll have to advise me when it comes time to fix up River Bluffs."

She managed to loosen her tongue before the silence became uncomfortable and replied, "I'd love to help. It's a beautiful home. It's definitely got 'good bones.'"

Mike smiled. Not one of those that just played at the corner of his lips, but a real, full-fledged smile. "Yeah, I guess it does."

Jennie covered her continued amazement by heading into the kitchen to pull out the chicken casserole she'd put in the oven earlier. Being a hostess was an easier job than being recipient to Mike's compliments. He was not known for his praise. His baseball players often remarked they had no idea whether their coach thought they were playing well or not. Generally, it wasn't until they were cut from the team, or moved up to start, that they knew how they were doing. Being on Mike's starting team felt pretty damn good, Jennie thought.

She offered him a beer and finished the dinner preparations, breaking the news to him about the draft card.

Mike was quiet, leaving Jennie to wonder how he was taking the information. Sitting at the dinner table, he idly turned his beer bottle back and forth. He closed his eyes momentarily, and she felt obliged to fill the silence. "I'm sorry, Mike. I think I led you to believe this would go quickly because I thought it would be so easy."

His frustration abruptly boiled over. "The government should control access to records better. Shouldn't they digitize them or something?"

"The National Archives would love to digitize all their records, but Congress doesn't fund for that kind of work. Besides, the draft cards really have little value except to genealogists. I hate to even suggest this, but it's possible Caroline did order a copy of the card. If she was murdered, the murderer knew about the registration from Caroline, and made sure the original disappeared forever."

"That's possible?" he asked.

"Sadly, it is. Historical documents are being taken care of better than ever, but that doesn't mean someone didn't walk with the card years ago. Someone could have slipped the original in a pocket and that would be the end of it."

"I wasn't ready to believe Caroline was murdered over this, but now I'm wondering if River Bluffs is worth it. If someone killed her over a piece of paper..."

"Don't give up yet," Jennie urged, panicked Mike might give up before she'd really had a chance at solving the problem. "We've barely scratched the surface on what records are available. And we still might be able to talk to Jacob."

He sighed. "No wonder I couldn't do this by

myself. It'd take someone with a doctorate to figure it out."

"Not really." She grinned, relieved at his change of mood. "But fortunately, you got one. There's more evidence out there. We'll find it."

While they ate, he told Jennie what he'd learned from Paul Garretson's lawyer during a lunchtime conversation.

"He wanted to see the will, which I faxed to him," he said between mouthfuls, eating quickly as teachers are wont to do. "Essentially, he agrees with you. If Fred is proved an imposter, he and his heirs are out, and Caroline and her heirs are in, as well as any other descendant of Josef's brother and sister. He even said the 'perpetuity' clause basically means as long as HP exists, the company can be taken away from the descendants of Fred Houseman. He was curious to know how many descendants you had in your genealogy program."

"I can check, but I haven't really started looking for Josef's sister Katrina yet. And my information on Jacob is limited to him and his siblings. I'll work on them as soon as I have Rick's blessing to talk with Jacob Houseman or his great granddaughter, Rachel McGregor. I assume they will fill me in about that side of the family."

"You got it. He said it was okay to talk to the California Housemans, but not to mention why. He said you should say you've been hired by the family to research the family tree."

"Can I at least indicate it's your side of the family that hired me? I'm guessing Jacob is not going to want to talk to anyone hired by Fred's descendants, since Caroline indicated Jacob didn't believe he was Fred."

"I didn't ask Rick, but it makes sense to me," Mike agreed.

"Good. I'll email Jacob and give him my tale."

"As for ownership of HP, it seems Rick knows a bit about this subject because Paul had him check out the family ownership as well, primarily because he too was looking for potential murderers.

"After Fred died in 1978, the company was inherited in equal shares by Fred's sons, George, Joe, and John. Do you have one of your family tree charts? It's easier if I can show you."

Jennie went to her office and brought one back. He examined the chart and pointed to George. "Of course, George is still alive. He owns fifty percent of the company. In addition to Robert, the company president, George has two daughters, whom I suppose are also in line to inherit.

"Next is Joe. He turned eighty recently. His only son Geoff is a Congressional rep, and you know about his one granddaughter, Veronica. His percentage is one-third.

"The last line is John's. He died in 1986. He had three children, one of whom died in Vietnam. Richard and Charlotte split the inheritance, but it was Richard who recently sold out to George. Charlotte's on the board of the company, but her share is one-sixth."

"So our primary suspect list consists of two octogenarians and a woman who has the least to lose if a fraudulent inheritance is proved."

Mike leaned back in his chair, locking his hands behind his head. "Not so. Look at George's heirs as opposed to Joe's."

Jennie followed the relationship lines. The game could get tricky depending on how George wrote his will. When he died, his shares could be split among his three children. However, when Joe died, he had only one heir, Geoff.

"All of George's children are in their fifties, still relatively young, as is Geoff," she noted, examining the birth years. "George and Joe, however, are both in their eighties. I guess that means there's going to be a scramble for control of the company when they die, which statistically isn't far away."

"Bingo," Mike said, nodding his head. "Charlotte, if she can be convinced to sell, is sitting on a gold mine."

"But, of course, if we prove Fred was an imposter..." Jennie trailed off, the implications hitting her. All the current owners would be disinherited and Mike would be an heir.

Mike leaned forward, resting a hand on top of Jennie's. "This isn't what you signed up for, Jennie. If Caroline and Jack Elliott were murdered, and if someone did try to kill Veronica, someone's not playing around. This is big money. People get nasty when even small amounts of money are involved. If you want to bow out now, I wouldn't fault you for it."

She stared at her plate and surreptitiously at his hand on top of hers. His touch sent sparks radiating up her arm. It wasn't enough that projects like this came her way only rarely. But who could think about danger when a touch from this man short-circuited her rational thinking?

She grabbed at a reasonable argument. "That's a lot of 'ifs.' I don't feel like I'm in any danger. I mean, even if we assume someone has found out you have River Bluffs, for what reason would they think you are trying to prove Fred was a fake?"

"I don't necessarily agree with you," Mike said, pushing back from the table. "But until we know otherwise, we'll have to be extra careful. And the instant I think you're in danger, I'm firing you."

She raised her eyebrows. "Thanks. I appreciate the thoughtfulness." For the second time that night, he gave her a disarming smile. Her stomach muscles tightened. She managed to return the smile without slobbering.

As he helped her clear the table, they talked a

bit more about Caroline's journals, which Mike had managed to read to the 1950s. For the most part, the information was irrelevant. Caroline made reference to the "new" bathrooms, which they were having trouble with ten years after they were put in, and she did a lot of speculating about Betsy's disappearance and the boys' sadness at the loss of their mother. The most major item he'd read was about Josef's death in 1939 and the fact Caroline was delighted the house became hers.

"She didn't even mention being disappointed about the company," Mike noted. "I don't think she cared about it at all."

"It's just as well, because she would make a lousy murder suspect," Jennie said, setting the last dish on the counter. "How many Tarzan yells have you made reading Caroline's journals?"

"It wasn't all boring. It's kind of interesting to see how my ancestors lived before TV, cell phones and the Internet."

She gave him a lopsided smile. "Mike Garretson, interested in history? Don't let that get out or your reputation is shot."

"Then I'm safe, thanks to Paul Garretson's will."

He offered to help wash the dishes, once again surprising Jennie. When her father visited, he never did dishes, a carryover from the days when Jennie's grandmother lived with them. Despite Grandma's age, she never let her son do anything around the house and retirement had not improved his capabilities in the kitchen. Mike's offer was another indication Coach Garretson was anything but a jock.

"I'll do the dishes," she said. "You probably have other things to do since your practice takes up all your free time."

"It does, but I got dinner. Seems to me I should give something back."

His green eyes locked on hers and for the first

time in her life, doing dishes became a turn-on.

"I'm good. Go take care of your dog."

"Thanks. Zippy will be happy to see me. He has a dog door, but that means he stores up all his energy for when I get home."

She followed him out to his car in the driveway.

"Unless something else comes up, it's the reunion on Saturday. Dress casual, but bring a swimming suit. George has a huge pool in his back forty."

Jennie snorted. "No swimsuit. I am not going to your family reunion and totally expose my body to a bunch of strangers."

"Too bad. I would have enjoyed it," he said as he backed out of the driveway.

Chapter 11

Unable to think of a thing to say, Jennie was left watching the red car disappear down the street in stunned silence. Heat flamed in her cheeks. She must be desperate if a little flirtation affected her like this.

Once upon a time she could have handled an off-handed comment like Mike's. Years of half-formed friendships that ended before they fully blossomed had made her an expert in deflecting people getting close to her with trite lines. She didn't get what was different about this. He was just another guy with a line. Wasn't he?

As she was about to head inside, she caught sight of a strange car with the driver sitting in it across the street. Since the neighborhood was older, it wasn't unusual for people to park in the street. However, the car was not one she'd seen before and the man didn't appear to be going anywhere. Deciding it wasn't her business, she headed for her office.

She checked email, hoping for good news. There was nothing from Rachel McGregor or Jacob Houseman. She then pulled out the pile of papers she'd taken from River Bluffs' library and started going through it again. If the draft registration was not an option, then she had to take another tack.

Half an hour of taking notes and writing down possible leads elsewhere, she came across a copy of Fred and Betsy Houseman's 1920 marriage certificate from New York City. Now here was a thought: what if Betsy's disappearance was not an accident? Who was Betsy anyway? The certificate listed her parents' names as Charles Borders and Kate Daniels Borders, and Betsy's birthplace as Washington County, Pennsylvania. Caroline's research had nothing in this direction.

Jennie rolled her chair over to the computer to check the 1920 Federal census records for the Borders family. These constitutionally required surveys of the American population were pure gold to family history researchers. In the Housemans' case, if Betsy was married to Fred in February 1920, she might be with her family or with Fred.

She opened a genealogical website and searched for the Borders in rural Pennsylvania, an easier task than looking for Fred in New York City. There was only one family with those names in the index. She clicked on the icon to bring up the digitized page. When the page finally loaded she saw Betsy's parents, Charles and Kate Borders, were living with Robert and Margaret Daniels. Charles and Kate were listed by their relationship to Robert as "stepfather-in-law" and "mother-in-law." Translation: Kate was Robert's mother and on her second marriage. She'd had the last name of Daniels on her first marriage. Another family line Jennie could pursue. Unfortunately, there was no Betsy in these census records.

Researching New York City's census records was more difficult, and it was getting late before Jennie finally found a Fred Houseman, misspelled as "Housman." She was surprised to see Betsy with him, not with her maiden name of Borders, but as a wife! She grabbed their marriage certificate again and checked the date: February 12, 1920. The enumeration date—the date the census was taken— was January 2, 1920. Had the census taker made a mistake? Or was there something more going on here?

Jennie rubbed her eyes after hitting the print button. People didn't live together before marriage back in those days. She was certain there was more, but her brain was getting muddled. She yawned, looked at the clock on her computer screen and groaned. It was already past eleven and she needed sleep. Reluctantly, she shut down her computer.

Maybe Mike would give a different spin to it, she decided after lying awake for some time.

She'd never been in Mike's classroom. It was time to pay the lion a visit in his own den.

****

If it weren't for her odd fascination with the Houseman genealogy, Jennie was certain she would have dragged into school Thursday morning. She was losing too much sleep lately.

After she dropped her work in her classroom, she sought out Mike's room. He was pulling out lab equipment and nearly dropped a test tube at her greeting.

"You could give a guy a warning. No one comes in this early," he said, his eyebrows knitted together.

"Sorry. Just wanted to give you the latest. After the bad news about the draft registration, I went back through the material I have and decided Betsy Houseman might be a person of interest in this case." She told him about the oddity on the census records versus the marriage certificate.

"How's this going to help?"

"I don't know yet. I'm going to ask a Pennsylvania researcher to find everything they can on the Borders family. Someone in the area will be able to visit the courthouse, which will be faster than me ordering microfilm and cheaper than flying there to do the research myself. Also, Betsy's parents are living with a Daniels family in 1920. Even though her marriage certificate says Betsy's last name was Borders, I still want to find out about this

Daniels connection."

"That's sounds promising," Mike said, but his attention remained on his chemistry equipment. He gave her an apologetic look. "I'm sorry I can't talk, but I've got to have this demonstration ready before the students get here." He paused long enough to suggest he pick her up Saturday morning so they could drive to the reunion together, after doing some more searching in the attic.

"Sure," she replied, yawning. "However, I will be sleeping in late, so don't come too early."

Mike's eyes narrowed and then his left eyebrow rose. "Someone keeping you up late?"

She huffed out a breath of air. "Yeah, Mike. Your family is keeping me up at night. You make them leave me alone and quit prancing around in my head after I turn the lights out, and then I will get more sleep."

She turned to leave, but before she got out the door, he called out, "You're not charging me for hours you lay awake in bed, are you?" His eyes twinkled as they caught her gaze.

Shaking her head in mock disbelief, she let the door shut behind her without answering. As she contemplated beds and Housemans, however, she knew there was one descendant she definitely wouldn't mind keeping her awake at night.

Chapter 12

Every other Thursday afternoon Jennie met with her Archeology Club, a group of self-confessed history buffs who loved to get their hands dirty. A week from Saturday was their major field trip to Cahokia Mounds to help a real archeology team at work. But a message from the archeologist's assistant said he was in the hospital. When Jennie's prep period came, she called the assistant right away.

The archeologist had broken his hip over the weekend, and the dig had been cancelled. No one else could lead the project, and the assistant was not able to point her to another project.

Out of desperation, Jennie had a wild idea—if Mike would go for it. She got the meeting going first, telling Josh Kowalzski the problem with the field trip.

"But before you get upset, Josh," Jennie said, halting the words already forming on the club president's lips, "I have an idea. You get the meeting started. I need to go talk to another teacher."

Jennie found Mike in the coach's office next to the boys' locker room. If he'd been surprised to see her this morning, he was completely baffled to see her now. He had to leave his office to get away from his two curious assistant coaches.

"This is probably not the best place to come when we're trying to play it low key," he said brusquely.

"I know, but I need an answer quickly," she said without apology. "And don't be so touchy. Teachers are allowed to talk." He didn't quite glare, but it was close. Jennie plowed on.

"My Archeology Club field trip is in jeopardy because we don't have a place to dig. Can they dig at River Bluffs?"

"No!" His eyes nearly popped out of his head in horror.

If she wasn't so desperate, his reaction would have been funny. "Wait, hear me out. One of the best places to dig is where the privy used to be. Back when they had outdoor bathrooms, they also used the outhouse as a trash disposal. River Bluffs had to have one. And I'll tell the group I got permission from the homeowner to dig. They don't have to know it's you."

Mike crossed his arms, scowling some more. "How will you get them there? You can't bring a school bus out there."

"We aren't going by school bus. The kids are car pooling. I'll get them to come in three cars. There are only eleven of them anyway."

Mike was waffling. Jennie could see it.

"I wouldn't bill you for the time," Jennie said coaxingly.

He snorted. "They can't come in the house," he insisted. "And they need to bring whatever they need with them, food, water, whatever."

Jennie agreed again, pointing out they wouldn't have had much more at Cahokia Mounds.

He sighed. "I hope this is worth it. If this jeopardizes the stipulations of the will..."

"Check it out with Rick," Jennie said, confident even a lawyer couldn't turn down a worthy event like this one. "Tell him it's me asking. It might help to know it's someone on your side."

"Fine," Mike said, and when Jennie didn't leave, his eyebrows raised, alarmed.

"Can you call him now?" Jennie pleaded. If there

hadn't been students coming out of the locker room, she was sure Mike would have let her hear some colorful language. He went back into the office and told his assistant coaches he had to make an important call. After they left, he picked up the phone and dialed Rick's number.

"Okay," Mike said, sighing, when he hung up. "Don't provide anybody directions. Meet them here and you lead them out to the site. The less they remember about where the house is, the better off we are. Rick noted most helpfully I have two weeks left."

"Don't worry," she called over her shoulder as she dashed across the gym, "it's my job to solve your mystery before time's up."

****

The Archeology Club members were even more excited about digging up an outhouse than going to Cahokia Mounds. Though she had no idea where the privy might be located, searching for it might be fun too, even if all they turned up was a button or two. If she got the chance this weekend, she wanted to look for some architectural plans on River Bluffs. Maybe they would show the privy location.

The new arrangements made, she submitted corrected paperwork for approval to the school office. She hedged on the location of the field trip by using the address of the house nearest to River Bluffs.

The baseball players were finishing their practice as she left after five. She avoided waving at Mike as she left. Perhaps it didn't make up for barging into his office, but she thought it should count as sticking to his requirement of playing low key. She hoped he wasn't too irritated with her for bringing out the Archeology Club.

When she got home, she threw a frozen entrée into the microwave and flipped on her computer. She promised herself an early bedtime, after finding a

Pennsylvania researcher. She pulled out a directory of professional genealogists, failing to get an answer until the third call. Ken Capelli of "Pennsylvania Roots, Inc." answered the phone.

Jennie outlined what she needed and the timeframe. Though Ken's rusty baritone gave evidence he was older and he admitted he was semi-retired, Jennie's request for information from the early twentieth century was an easy one. He agreed to send her what he'd found in a week.

She opened her email and while the computer downloaded new messages, took her dinner out and grabbed a bottle of water. When she returned, one message stood out from junk mail: *jjh1910@danvers.net.*

Hello,

I understand you are researching the Houseman family genealogy. I'm Jacob Houseman and have a lot of information to exchange with you. Also, I would love to talk. Who are you related to?

Give me a call if you can.

Jacob Houseman

909-555-4356

She gave a little whoop of excitement. Though she'd been expecting him, it was exciting to know one of the old family members was still alive. After all, this was the same Jacob who had confronted Fred Houseman back in the 1930s. She typed a greeting and wrote:

I'm a professional genealogist working for a descendant of Caroline Houseman Garretson. I have a lot of information on the Illinois Housemans but little on the California Housemans. I especially would like to know what you have on William and Katrina Houseman.

If it would be convenient, my client and I would like to talk to you Saturday morning at 10 a.m. Central Time if that's not too early. If it is, our schedule is somewhat restrained and we would have to call later in the day.

I have attached a file with the information I have gathered so far. We look forward to talking with you.

Dr. Jennifer Foster

Before sending the message, she attached the genealogical file she had created on the family in GEDCOM, the international translation system that allowed different genealogical software programs to talk to each other. She was startled to receive a response almost immediately.

Great! I was waiting for you to respond. My great granddaughter helps me out with my computer stuff and she's here now. We're sending you what we have. I also have stories behind the data I want you to know. I'll be waiting for your call on Saturday morning.

Call me Jacob. I suspect you have a few too many Mr. Housemans around there I don't want to be confused with.

Jacob

She opened his file and studied it. Wilhelm, or William as he became known, had five children, Frederick being the second youngest and Jacob, the youngest. Jacob and his sisters had produced fifteen children among themselves, and the trend had continued. She counted more than fifty great grandchildren to William.

Fred's family page in the program was empty, except for his birth information. In fact, Jacob had placed a note in the death comments reading: *Probably died World War soon after June 1918. No letters received after this time.* So, Jacob had more than missing green eyes to indicate the Fred he knew before the war and after the war were not the same.

Jennie's files had tons of information on Fred, while Jacob had intentionally left out any descendant information. Ironically, she was out to prove Jacob had the right file and her information was wrong.

Though it was only a little after nine when she shut off her computer, she was ready for bed. She called Mike first. He answered a little sleepily.

"Mike?" she asked, not certain if she had the right number. "Are you in bed already?"

"No, Jennie," he said with a sigh. "I fell asleep reading through this pile of stuff you made me take home."

"Good deal," she said, wishing she'd been the one to read it. "Maybe this will wake you up a little: we have a date to talk to Jacob Houseman on Saturday morning at ten."

She could hear him shift the phone. "That's good news," he said.

"He also sent me his files and a picture of your three times great grandfather, Johan Hausmann, the original immigrant from Germany."

"I'd like to see that."

"All right. I'll bring it with me on Saturday. I'm sure you can wait that long." His enthusiasm was underwhelming. She didn't blame him though, as she yawned during her farewell. A murderer wouldn't need to kill her. Working two jobs would eventually do it.

****

Jennie didn't wait around after school on Friday. Only a few stalwart teachers ever did, and with the Houseman reunion looming tomorrow, she had a decision to make: what to wear to a casual family reunion at a millionaire's home with a man who wasn't her date. The situation rather narrowed down her choices. On the one hand, she wanted to remain in the background; on the other, she desperately wanted to impress Mike's family. It was silly; why did she care what his family thought of her?

The reason didn't matter as much as realizing Mae was right. Her clothes sucked. She picked up the phone.

"Mae, I need help," she announced when her friend answered. "I need Tanya."

"What's wrong? Can I help?" Mae asked, immediately assuming her role as super-mom.

"I need wardrobe advice."

"Oh." She paused, giving Jennie reason to expect a barrage of questions. "Why? What life-changing event has occurred?"

"Uh...Mike Garretson's research project. I have to go somewhere with some important people and I want to look good."

"And of course you can't tell me why or where or who."

"No," Jennie said apologetically. "After May 20."

"You know I could find out what you're doing—if I really wanted to."

Jennie had no doubt that was true. Mae knew things only God should know. Her children had grown up thinking she had spies everywhere. "Please don't, Mae. There are reasons I don't want anyone knowing what I'm doing."

"You're not doing something illegal, girl, are you?"

"Of course not! Dangerous maybe, but not illegal. Please let me talk to Tanya."

Mae sighed heavily, but put her youngest on the phone. At twenty-one, Tanya was one of Mae's two kids still living at home, and as a fashion design major and Jennie's size, she was Jennie's best bet for clothes advice. With a brief explanation of what type of event she needed clothes for, Tanya promised to assemble acceptable items and head right over to Jennie's.

Two hours later, Jennie had a slimming white camisole under a blue and yellow striped blouse and a yellow skirt. This skirt was shorter than the one she'd worn at work, but Tanya swore it was the perfect length for a pool party, especially with Jennie's long legs. Except for the shoes and underwear, Tanya provided everything else, including the jewelry.

"Thanks, Tanya. I couldn't have done this without you," Jennie said as Tanya picked up her purse.

"You know Mom's right. We need to go shopping."

"My budget..." Jennie said, using her oldest excuse.

"Your budget will work fine the way I shop. I could find a five dollar shirt on Fifth Avenue in New York."

Jennie nodded contritely. "When school is out, we'll make a date, okay?"

"Fine, and I'll make sure Mom will hold you to it."

As she shut the door, Jennie was relieved. The Jeffersons weren't the only people who thought her wardrobe needed an extreme makeover. It would be good to have professional help overhauling her closet.

Now it was time to focus on immediate concerns. It was still relatively early. But with a weekend already looking packed with Houseman research, she set her mind on completing her school work first.

It took all she had not to plunge back into Mike's project. She raced through the classwork, writing the last grade on top of the paper with a flourish. As she stuffed the reports into her school bag, her mind began to pick through her research, examining the pieces to a puzzle with too many parts missing yet.

She'd been through every item in the box she'd brought home from River Bluffs. But she remembered Jacob had written in his family history notes about June 1918 being the last time the family had a letter from Fred. The U.S. had not been in World War I very long at that point. A quick research revealed Jacob's date coincided with the Battle of Belleau Wood, which was fought June 6-26, 1918, in a small wooded area about fifty miles east of Paris.

Jennie wasn't surprised to find huge numbers of hits on the Internet for that particular battle, as war history was easy to find on the web. She scanned through several pages, picking up various bits of information. At Belleau Wood Fred Houseman had faced the bloodiest and deadliest battle the Americans would face during the Great War, and if he died there, he was one of almost two thousand. The Army 2nd Division, with Marines supporting, took a small piece of land six times in three weeks before claiming it from the Germans. She wondered as she looked at images of a small hill with trees poking into the skyline: Was this where Fred Houseman had died and had his identity stolen?

Checking cemeteries from World War I led Jennie to search the American Battle Monuments Commission website, which contained a searchable database of American cemeteries in Europe. There were two near Belleau Wood. Just to be sure the military hadn't made a mistake, she searched on the name Frederick Houseman, even trying variations. She drew a blank, again.

Leaning back in her chair, she rubbed her eyes and yawned. Squinting at the small numbers in the corner of her computer screen, she saw twelve-oh-four. She groaned. So much for early to bed. Mike would be here at nine tomorrow morning—correction: this morning. She folded away her laptop in preparation for morning, hoping for a dreamless night's rest.

Chapter 13

Mike was early. Her toothbrush in her mouth and feet bare, Jennie ran to the front door, unlocking it and running back to the bathroom without a word.

Her mouth clean, she yelled to Mike, "I'm almost ready!"

"No problem," he replied.

With the sun already heating up her bedroom, she tossed sunscreen into a bag of items she might need, her clothes for the reunion hanging neatly on a hanger. She would change before the reunion to be certain any work they did in the attic did not mess up her loaned outfit.

Putting on a tennis shoe, she bounced into the living room on one foot, looking for the other one. She'd had it last night, she thought, searching the floor. She was normally so organized. But every second of her free time was being dedicated to Mike's project.

He held up a shoe from where he was sitting on the couch. "Looking for this?"

"Yes, thank you," she said, taking it from him and sliding it onto her foot. She put her sports bag and purse over her shoulder and grabbed her briefcase with the computer. "There, I'm ready. Can you get that box of documents?"

"And ahead of schedule," Mike said, picking up the research material Jennie had completed. "I could get used to timeliness in a female."

"What do you mean?"

"Oh, you'll understand when you meet Veronica."

As she locked the door, she spotted the odd car she'd seen earlier in the week parked up the road a bit, nowhere near where he'd been before. Someone was definitely sitting in it too. She would try to get a look at him as they drove by.

Mike opened the trunk and set the box next to a pile of Caroline's journals in the trunk. Zippy was in the car, yapping and bouncing around like Jennie was his best bud. She patted him on the head. "Hello, Zippy. Yes, I have your treat, but you can't have it now. Behave yourself and I'll give it to you later."

She slid into the leather seat of Mike's car. "This is really nice," she said, squirming around in the seat to check out the car. "What a classic. It's a Shelby Mustang, isn't it? Someone took a lot of time refinishing it too."

"I did the rebuilding myself. Took a while, but it came out all right," he said self-depreciatively.

"One of my father's friends tried to rebuild one of these. He didn't do near the job you did. How long did it take you? What year is it?"

"Four years and 1966. I'm surprised you know anything about cars. Most women don't even know what they drive."

"I don't know anything about cars," she said, grinning. "I just happen to know something about this type of car. Come on—I drive a Saturn. What I know about cars could be stuck on the head of a pin. But I do appreciate someone who takes care of a classic. That I know lots about."

One eyebrow raised, Mike nodded appreciatively.

As they headed down Jennie's street, she remembered to look at the driver of that unknown car. Craning her head around to see, she missed his face as he appeared to be looking for something on the passenger seat as they went by.

"What are you looking at?" Mike asked.

"That car. It was parked closer to my house when you were here the other night and there was someone in it. It looks like he's back again."

"Who is it?"

She shrugged. "I couldn't tell."

"Maybe you're being stalked."

She snorted. "I think you have to have someone madly in love with you for that." And you have to have a love life, she added to herself. "Did you finish reading Caroline's journals?"

"No. When you called Thursday night, I'd fallen asleep reading 1954. It was pretty darn exciting, therefore I slept."

They talked over the possible information they might get from Jacob as they unloaded the car, including groceries Mike had bought. He admitted to feeling outdone in his own kitchen and wanted to do some of his own experimenting. It was still before ten when they finished, but they couldn't wait any longer to talk to Jacob Houseman. Jennie dialed his number from her cell phone.

Jacob picked up on the first ring. His voice, crusty with age, greeted them heartily. "Hello?" he said loudly, clear even on her tiny phone speaker.

"Hello, Jacob," she replied, leaning toward the phone on the table. "This is Jennie Foster. I'm here with my client, Mike Garretson, your first cousin, three times removed."

"What's that?" barked Jacob.

Mike answered. "I'm Caroline's great grandson. I think you met her back in 1932."

"Oh, yes. Caroline," he said enthusiastically. "She was a ball of fire. We exchanged letters a few times after that. I liked her very much, even though she didn't support me when I told her the man who said he was Fred Houseman was not Fred.

"You know that's why I posted all my genealogy

online," Jacob continued without pause. "I wanted to find family who would believe me. I was only seven when Fred left for the war, but I know he had green eyes when he left. No one can tell me that mustard gas or any of the other things that went on over in Europe can change eye color. But that's not all. That guy didn't come to Papa's funeral, he never wrote a letter after 1918, and he didn't know a damn thing about California. It was like he'd never been there. He sure looked like Fred, but he wasn't Fred. I'd swear that in court."

"Did you keep any of Fred's letters?" she asked, squeezing her question in while Jacob caught his breath. He was quite animated by the subject, obviously holding back a lot of anger over Fred Houseman.

"No," he said sharply. "They were to my sister, and she didn't believe me either. None of them did. They didn't care. They all had young families in the 1920s and then when the Depression hit, any possible concern they might have had over an imposter a couple thousand miles away was completely overcome. I got married too, and then even I was too busy to think about it.

"Of course when Caroline wrote her father had died and Fred had inherited that drug company, you know, Houseman Pharmaceuticals, I was angry. I wrote the lawyer and told him Fred was a phony. Nobody believed me. Said I was nuts. By that time, Fred Houseman was a pretty powerful man. I should have dropped it then, but no, I had to go and tell my children about it."

"Why should you have dropped it?" Mike asked.

"Because if I hadn't have told them, my daughter wouldn't have died."

"What?" both Mike and Jennie said simultaneously, exchanging startled glances.

"My daughter, Sue McGregor, was a reporter for

a local newspaper, the *Redlands Sun-Times*. She believed me when I said Fred Houseman was not my brother. In 1968, she traveled out to Illinois to prove he was a fake. She interviewed everyone who knew him, and by then, HP was a big deal and Fred was the president of the company.

"She phoned me the week she died." Jacob paused, his voice choked with emotion. "She said she did not have absolute proof, but she had enough circumstantial evidence she was going to publish what she had. She believed the story itself might bring out more evidence, since his wealth and standing would make the story go national. It was the last time I talked with her."

"She died here?" Mike asked.

Jacob's voice broke, cracking with pain. "They say she drove off a bridge over the Mississippi going into St. Louis. The police said she'd been drinking. Only one problem with that. Sue was a teetotaler, hadn't drank a drop since she was in college. I know she was murdered, and I'm certain that damn Fred was behind it." Jacob gasped as he tried to control the sobs.

"I'm sorry, Jacob," Mike said. "We're trying to prove you're right. Caroline did come around to your thinking. She was searching for proof when she died. Her son Paul thinks she might have been killed too. And now we think you're right."

"Oh, damn it all anyway," Jacob said, his voice resigned. "What difference would it make now anyway? Fred's dead. You can't put a dead man in jail."

"No, Jacob, we can't," Jennie said. "But we can prove Sue was right and that will make her death less pointless. We'll do our best."

Jacob's voice grew stronger as he gathered his years of wisdom around himself. He said, "Okay. It's good to have folks believe me. So many lost years..."

Jennie, afraid he was going to lose it again, switched the topic to Katrina, which Jacob was equally willing to talk about.

"Can you tell us what happened to your Aunt Katrina?" she asked.

"Not much," Jacob admitted. "Just what I was told. Apparently she got herself in the family way without being married. Grandpapa—that's John Houseman, the German immigrant—was humiliated, said she had ruined the family name. So she married the first man that would have her. Don't know if he was the father of her baby or not. They left for the East coast, and none of the family heard from her again."

"Do you know who she married?"

"No, before my time. Heck, I only learned about it by eavesdropping on some adults talking about it when I was a child myself."

"How about where she was married?"

"Well, California wasn't like it is today. Hardly anyone lived here in the late 1800s. I heard she was about eighteen, nineteen years old, when it happened. She must have gotten married locally because she wouldn't have had money to go anywhere else."

"Any chance you could look for a marriage record?" she pressed, not willing to let this lead die.

Jacob laughed, coughing toward the end. "Sorry, got myself a little cold. You're as eager as I was about the family. I like that. However, I don't get around much now. But I think Rachel might be willing to go. She's a college student and comes and visits me whenever she can. You know she's Sue's granddaughter, and I think she got Sue's spirit. I'll ask her."

"Thanks, I would appreciate that."

"Jacob," Mike said, his look speculative, "what do you think happened to Fred?"

"I have some strong ideas at that area, cousin," he said, chuckling at his name for Mike. "I think Fred died in World War I, never came home. He's buried in some grave under the name of a stranger that took his name. It's a shame the Army service records from that war were lost in a fire, because I'll bet we could have found out a lot more about what happened after Fred died."

"Belleau Wood," Jennie said abruptly.

"Yes, that's right. That was the battle I bet Fred died in." Jacob was quiet for a moment. Then he said, "I hope Susie didn't die for nothing. Mike, Jennie, you find out who did this for me, okay? I want some peace before I die."

Mike hesitated. "If it's possible, Jacob, I'll call you the moment we figure it out."

"Tell you what. I think I'll hang around this old earth a few more months to see you do it. I better let you go. Don't want to run up your phone bill."

The phone clicked and Jennie touched the end button, while covertly wiping away a tear in the corner of her eye.

****

Mike stood and paced the room while raking his hands through his hair. He had just spoken with the oldest Houseman living, a man whose daughter also might have been murdered.

All he wanted was to keep River Bluffs. Now they knew of three potential murder victims.

"Jennie, this is ridiculous," he said, shaking his head. "How can a murderer be working in 1968, 1991, and today? Can you get out those charts, the family charts?"

Jennie opened her briefcase and pulled out the requested papers. They showed birth and death dates, as well as relationships.

"Look," Mike said, pointing at Fred Houseman's name. "He died in 1978. So he could be behind Sue

McGregor's death, but not Caroline's. George and Joe were alive during all the 'alleged' murders, but they're ancient and I find it hard to believe they could be behind today's events. The next generation, Robert Houseman and Charlotte Wainwright, were both alive during those dates, but Robert was only eighteen and Charlotte fourteen at the time of Sue's death. And my generation, which includes Veronica, doesn't even start till the 1970s. There's no way Sue McGregor, Caroline Garretson, and Jack Elliott were all murdered by the same person."

Jennie was still perched on the bar stool, studying the charts. "Not the same person. More than one person?" Her chocolate brown eyes were reassuringly solid, not like this nightmare of a family.

Mike leaned against the table. He'd brought Jennie in to help him hold onto River Bluffs, not find a serial murderer. The house was wonderful, a dream, and he was really looking forward to fixing it up. But was it worth blowing apart his world?

"Let's presume for a moment you find our evidence and Fred Houseman is proven a fraud. What happens?"

Jennie shrugged, pushing back a loose strand of hair. "I'd guess the courts would get involved and there would be some major changes at HP."

"And my family?"

"They'd get a part of the company?" She looked at him questioningly. He knew she didn't have the answers, but he needed to hear someone else see this thing the way he was seeing it.

"I'd agree. But what about the Housemans, the current owners?"

"They'd be disowned, I presume. It wouldn't be their business anymore."

Mike rubbed his forehead. "Exactly. Damn. I just want the stupid house. I don't want some overblown scandal that hurts people I consider family."

"I understand. It's like my dad's Army buddies. They're his family. It's why he doesn't get here very often." She gazed at a distant point with solemn brown eyes. "Sometimes family isn't related by blood."

The sadness in her voice tugged at him. He was surrounded by people he called family, so much so that Paul Garretson had made talking to anyone around here part of his legacy. Yet all she had was her father. She probably really did understand proving Fred Houseman was a fraud wasn't about the money.

"Even ignoring the family part of it, we also have someone who thinks HP is so important they are willing to kill for it," he noted.

He paced around the metal table, Jennie silent. Zippy wandered into the room and began following eagerly behind his master. When Mike nearly stepped on him, he scooped up the dog, flipped him on his back, and rubbed his stomach. The dog's leg thumped against Mike's arm.

"Zippy's the only sure thing I know right now," he murmured, realizing no matter what happened, he got to keep the dog.

"What about Jacob?" Jennie asked. The question hung in the air.

Jacob, who wanted to know his daughter didn't die in vain. That his brother hadn't forgotten him after the war and maybe had died a hero's death.

Jennie was beside Mike suddenly, her hand gently touching his forearm. It had been so long since he'd let someone touch him like this that he almost pulled away. Only the heat of her fingertips stilled his normal reaction.

"Mike, no one said you have to tell the world if you find the evidence. Paul Garretson said you had to find it to keep the house. What you do with it after that is your choice."

Zippy squirmed and Mike let him slide to the floor. He caught Jennie's hand in his own.

"You're right," he said, caressing the back of her hand with his thumb. "Nobody but Rick Boston, you and I would ever have to know." He pulled Jennie against him, hugging her and spinning her around in relief. "You're a genius."

And then he kissed her.

He wasn't certain where the urge came from. His kisses were normally calculated, planned for a certain result, usually sexual. This kiss was because it was Jennie. Because she made him feel good, a feeling that had been missing in his life recently.

His lips tingled as she stood back, eyes locked on his. She tasted like wintergreen and her scent teased his nose. He wanted more. He couldn't stop himself as he pulled her against him, her body fitting finely against his.

He pressed his lips against hers again, this time letting her response guide his actions. When one of her hands snaked around his waist and another splayed against his chest, his kiss grew more urgent. He slid a hand up her back and into the hair pulled into a pony tail, loosening the binder until it caught in her hair.

The slapping of the dog door off the kitchen awakened the demon in the back of his head. He couldn't do this. Not to Jennie. She deserved better.

"Jennie," he whispered, wanting more and knowing this was not the time. "We shouldn't."

She nodded, gold-flecks in her eyes sparkling through half-hooded lids. She studied him a moment, her face a mask.

"Attic," she said huskily.

Mike chuckled, brushing his fingers along her cheek. "You're the best damned historian I could have hired. Always focused on the goal."

"You do still want River Bluffs, right?"

"River Bluffs, definitely. But let's hold the murders down to three and avoid HP like the plague, please."

****

As she toweled off her body from the quick shower she'd taken, Jennie's thoughts continued to stray in the wrong direction, where they'd been focused in the two hours since Mike had kissed her. The work they'd accomplished in the attic was all kind of a blur. She stood in the steamy bathroom with only a door between her thoughts and action, wondering how she was going to survive a family reunion with Mike. The drive alone was going to be torture if she couldn't get her libido in check.

She didn't get it. She'd known Mike for two years and had never reacted to him like this. Sure, he was great to look at—all the teachers acknowledged that. So it wasn't looks.

Working together had shown her he could be a gentleman, was willing to work hard for what he wanted, and cared about family. She swallowed hard on the last thought.

Her father *was* her family. There were some aunts and uncles out there, but the Army life didn't lend itself to close relationships with people hundreds and thousands of miles away. How many times had she wished for a brother or sister? Her dad had been a good parent, maybe a little short on the praise and often deployed, but he had done the best he could. Her grandmother had tried to fill the gap after Jennie's mother died. Jennie knew she was loved. But she was also desperately alone, especially after each of the nine moves they'd made.

What did she have now? Her grandmother was dead. Her father lived a twelve-hour drive away. Maybe she was drawn to people with big complicated families. Mae's family was like that. Mike had an enormous family too, all within minutes of each other. She was a historian, oriented toward people. Mike had people. That was all.

However, her theory didn't explain why she'd changed her hairstyle abruptly. Usually she pulled it back in a binder. She remembered Mike's hands in her hair, and on a whim, had pulled out the binder and brushed out the curls. She had a lot of hair, and always wore it back to keep it out of the way. But Mike's fingers sliding through it was a feeling she could get used to.

Family. Yeah, right.

She eyed her hair in the mirror. She smoothed down the skirt, tugged briefly on its hem, then pulled the camisole edge up to cover the excess cleavage. Deep breaths, she ordered herself. Tanya said she looked hot. That was a good thing, not bad. She could do this.

She'd replaced her tennis shoes with low heels and they clumped on the grand stairs as she went down them. Mike was waiting in the kitchen for his time in the shower. At the lift of his eyebrows, she felt herself flush.

He nodded approvingly. "You look good. You should wear your hair down more often."

Her stomach was tense with nervousness, but she wasn't about to show Mike. She went with indifference, and shrugged. "Thanks. Just thought your relatives deserved it."

"Works for me. Give me fifteen minutes and I'll be ready to go. And don't worry," he said, as he headed up the stairs. "My relatives aren't near as odd as the newspapers make them out to be. You'll have fun."

She wasn't hiding her nervousness well.

"Right," she muttered as his feet disappeared from view. "Like a rabbit in a pit of starving lions."

Chapter 14

Mike's sister Sara was a psychic. Or at least she could have been if she wasn't already a lawyer.

"So, you and Mike don't have a normal relationship, do you?" she asked the moment Mike left with her husband to get drink refills.

If Jennie hadn't already plastered a benign smile on her face after meeting several other relatives, she might have gasped, exclaimed something revealing, or run after Mike. Instead, she tilted her head, looking puzzled. "What do you mean?" she asked, hardly sweating at all.

"Well, Mike's never mentioned you and yet he's obviously infatuated with you."

Jennie laughed. "We're just friends. I'm only here to learn some local history."

"That may be what you think. But he definitely likes you." Sara leaned back in her chair, smirking. "You like Mike, too."

Absolutely nothing came to Jennie's mouth. She stared at Sara's deep green eyes, identical to Mike's, and mentally urged her to drop the subject.

"Mom says I'm too forward," Sara said with a sigh, getting the hint. "Sorry. Here I've known you for less than ten minutes and I've already made you uncomfortable. I'm really not like that."

Jennie knew she'd been given the opportunity to drop the subject, and yet she found herself asking, "What in the world would make you think Mike liked me?"

"The way he acts around you. He treats you so...protectively. Escorting you around, getting you drinks, making sure you're included in the conversations. You know what he usually does at these reunions? Grabs a beer, finds some other bored man and hides in the farthest corner talking about baseball, golf or some other sport."

"He didn't do that when he was married to Veronica, did he?"

Sara snorted. "Are you kidding? We named a table after him when he was dating her: Guys Group Therapy. It didn't stop after they married either."

Jennie didn't think Mike's sociability toward her had anything to do with liking her, but everything to do with their secret project. After all, she was on assignment, finding out as much about the Housemans as she could, and he was a part of that. Of course he would want to hang around with her and find out information too. Not that she was going to tell Sara.

"So why did they get married if they were so incompatible?"

"Veronica pressured him. At least that's what I think. I don't think she's even capable of loving anyone but herself. And Mike, he's a guy. Smart as he is, he was thinking with his pants. I love my brother, but when it comes to women, he's a bit slow. And now he's scared to death of women. Look at him. God, he should have a family."

One of Sara's kids had run up to Mike, wrapping skinny arms around his muscular leg and pulling him toward George Houseman's gigantic, artful swimming pool. Mike was protesting, obviously playing along with the game. Right at the edge, he scooped up the boy, dangling him over the water by his wrists. The boy laughed hysterically. When Mike finally dropped him in the pool, he immediately crawled out, demanding Mike do it again.

"My boys love their Uncle Mike." Sara sighed. "Sadly, he's hardly been around lately. Don't even know what he does with his time anymore."

Jennie felt a catch in her heart at Sara's sibling love. She might be the only person who had any idea what Mike was doing. How much hanging out at River Bluffs was because it needed work, and how much was because Mike needed to be alone?

"It's not me taking up his time and I don't know of any other woman in his life," Jennie reassured her. Sara painted such a different picture of Mike than the one Jennie was familiar with. She studied Mike playing with the boys, careful to school any telltale emotions from her face. She was well aware Sara was watching her, a fact that had Jennie gazing pointedly anywhere but toward Mike's sister.

Mike and Sara's parents joined them as Mike dragged himself away from the two boys. Jennie slid her chair back a little as the family used the opportunity of a new audience to tell stories about each other. There wasn't any family rivalry, except the give-and-take Jennie would have expected if she'd had siblings. Mike, so reticent around school, talked and laughed like she'd never seen him. Occasionally, he'd reach over to her, patting her hand or touching her shoulder, including her though she had no right to be included. An unfamiliar ache lodged in her chest. Family gatherings with her dad could never match up to Mike's family, but she felt a bit homesick nonetheless.

Sara was called to break up an argument over some pool toy, and while they watched her negotiate between her two sons, a middle-aged man with thinning hair and glasses strolled up to their table.

"Have the Garretsons decided to have their own party?" he asked, smiling. The men stood to shake hands, greeting him as Rob. Only Mike held back, grudgingly rising as well. Of average height and with a growing roll around his belly, Rob did not appear to be the powerful president of a multi-million dollar company. More like the mild-mannered manager of a small office.

"And who is this lovely lady?" he asked, moving around the table to take Jennie's hand in both of his.

Mike managed to wedge himself between Rob and Jennie, forcing the older man to drop his hold almost before the introductions were made.

"Robert, this is Dr. Jennie Foster, a colleague of mine. Jennie, this is Robert Houseman."

Her left thigh pressed up against the table, Jennie had to push back her chair to keep from falling over with Mike so close. She was finally meeting one of the primaries on their list of suspects and Mike was practically putting a wall between them.

"I hear you're interested in local history and the Housemans' place in it."

"I am. I'm a history teacher and I like to connect history locally. It's easier for the kids to grasp."

Jennie was baffled by Mike's abrupt change. His face was in complete contrast to a moment ago, his eyes narrowed slightly and his mouth set in a firm line. Rob, however, seemed determined to counter the coldness.

"Well, Mike, did you tell her about Richard Houseman? He died in one of the prison camps in Vietnam. And Fred Houseman, he served in World War I. Survived one of the worst battles the Americans fought in."

"Was that Belleau Wood in France?" Jennie asked, to test Rob's knowledge.

"I think it was," Rob said, nodding. He pushed up his glasses, looking so harmless Jennie was puzzled by Mike's physical stance. Clearly Mike was angry, but about what?

She glanced at Sara returning to the table. Sara shrugged, apparently as unable to fathom Mike's sudden mood change as Jennie. In fact, everyone at the table had gone silent listening to the exchange. Jennie was certain the subject was not what interested them, but the tension between Houseman Pharmaceutical's president and his former employee.

"You know who would be the best to talk to? My father and his brother. They would be able to tell you everything you would like to know about the family history. Why don't I introduce you?"

Before Jennie could respond, Mike interrupted. "I was going to do that." He slipped a hand under her elbow and led her away from Rob.

Jennie managed a "Nice meeting you," over her shoulder, before retrieving her arm from Mike's grasp.

"What was that all about?" she asked, glaring at Mike.

"Nothing. I just don't get along with him."

"You were rude and he seemed quite nice. He was trying to help me out."

"Trust me. You don't need his kind of help. In fact, if he ever tries to call you, don't answer the phone. Stay away from him." Mike's voice dropped as they neared George and Joe Houseman's table on the opposite side of the pool.

Aside from the embarrassment she felt at being used by Mike to get away from Robert, she was confused about Mike's motivation. In all their conversations, Mike had never indicated Robert Houseman might be guiltier than any other Houseman. Mike had said he'd left the company because things weren't "right." Whatever that meant. He'd also mentioned Robert had not liked Mike's marriage to Veronica. She knew she didn't have the whole story about that, but it seemed Mike was being obstinate. In her judgment, Rob had gone out of his way to ignore Mike's behavior. True, Robert was on the list of prime suspects, but talking to all the Housemans was the reason she was here. Why block her conversation with him, particularly if Mike suspected Rob?

Refocusing her attention, she smiled as they approached the three elderly people sitting at a table with a large umbrella shading them from the unusually warm spring day. Both George and Joe were showing the loose flesh of age, sporting wispy white hair, balding on top. At eighty-six to his brother's eighty, George was much heavier and healthier-looking than his brother, who looked as if he might blow away if the wind acted up. His wife Victoria sat at the table with them, all of them with fruity drinks sweating in the humid afternoon air.

"Mike, good to see you again," rumbled George, offering Jennie a firm grip. Joe struggled out of his seat to shake both Mike and Jennie's hand, while Tori, as George called her, offered a limp hold that made Jennie think of spaghetti.

As they took their seats at the table, Tori interrogated Jennie about her history knowledge, unimpressed by Jennie's doctorate.

"So you're interested in local history," she said, pursing her thin lips and eyeing Jennie through squinting lids. "I don't suppose you know anything about my family. It's older in the local area than the Housemans. My maiden name is Bauer."

Quickly glancing at Mike, who had warned her about the old battleaxe, Jennie frowned in mock concentration. "That's a fairly common name around here. A lot of Germans arrived in the Midwest during the nineteenth century. I suppose you might be one of the Bauers of East St. Louis, who established a fine entertainment business there during the city's heyday. But I believe they have moved on, both in location and business. So, I would guess you are Victoria Bauer, daughter of brewery icon Leonard Bauer and sister to Davis Bauer,

current CEO and chairman of same said company."
Jennie held up the Bauer brew she was nursing.

Tori's thin lips stretched into what might have
been a smile. "Mike told you."

Mike shook his head. "Just your name, not your
background."

Tori harrumphed, her husband patting her hand
as if she needed mollifying. George took over the
conversation.

"I hear you are particularly interested in the
Houseman history. What would you like to know
about the family?"

Jennie chose an easy question, hoping to get to
something more revealing later. "How about how the
Housemans came to Illinois?"

"Ahh. You want to start at the beginning. That
would be John Houseman," he said, settling back
into his chair. "He brought his wife Anna and two
boys, William and Josef, from Germany in 1878.
They moved to Illinois for a few years, long enough
to have a daughter, Katrina. When Josef was still
quite young, he started making medicines from his
mother's recipes and selling them. He had a real
knack for business and knew how to make a product
that would sell."

The younger brother, Joe, interrupted. "You
know I was named after our uncle. You should meet
my wife." He sat up a little in his chair and scanned
the pool and surroundings. "There she is. Over there
with Stanley Garretson." He pointed at a woman
that must have been fifty years younger than Joe.
"She's my third wife," Joe said, grinning at his own
manliness.

Shading her eyes, Jennie raised her eyebrows in
surprise at a slim woman in a bikini and bare feet,
who appeared to be flirting with the man she was
talking with. Mike, who didn't bother to look, gave
Jennie a small smile, his eyes twinkling at her

obvious thoughts. Joe's child-bride had not been mentioned in previous conversations.

Taking a long draw of her beer because Joe had left her uncertain what to say, Jennie moved the conversation back to George. "So Josef was the founder of Houseman Pharmaceuticals?"

"Oh, yes." George smiled, nodding. "He played around with various plants and their effects on people. Soon he had to hire a couple of workers and salesmen. By the 1920s, he had over a hundred employees, one of the biggest employers in the area, bigger than a lot of St. Louis businesses even."

"What happened to John and the rest of his family?"

"Oh, John and Anna decided to take a chance at farming in California, so they left Illinois about 1890. William and Katrina went with them, but Josef was reluctant to start his business again. So he stayed."

"So, Josef is your father? Or grandfather?" The game was on, Jennie thought, flicking her eyes toward Tori. Despite her age, Jennie had no doubt Tori was a pure-bred aristocrat, with all the snobbery that came with the title. She could have as much motive to murder as any of the Housemans since she bore their name. However, the older woman's attention had drifted and she seemed to be studying the activity in the pool.

"No, no, no," George leaned forward, waving his hands. "Josef and William were brothers. Josef was Fred's uncle and William was Fred's father. My father was Fred Houseman."

George's eyes briefly slid toward Joe as he spoke. Joe was still trying to get his wife's attention. In any other circumstance, Jennie wouldn't have given the odd glance a second thought because Joe was looking pretty silly, jumping up and down like a toddler. However, Jennie distinctly felt the hairs on the back of her neck stand up at George's sidelong glance, a premonition there was more here than she could fathom.

Mike had shifted his chair back to remain out of the conversation, appearing to be watching the children playing in the pool. Jennie could not see his expression without making an obvious turn toward him. The game was still hers.

"Wait. I'm confused. How are the descendants of William, not Josef, owners of the company Josef started? Didn't Josef have any children?"

George sighed. "Not that it's politically correct today, but Josef was a good old chauvinist. He had one daughter, and he didn't want a female to inherit his company. It wasn't proper. So he asked his brother's oldest son Fred to join the company, with the intent that if he was any good at it, he would inherit. The rest, as they say, is history. Except we do have women in the company now. Charlotte Wainwright is part owner, isn't she, Joe?"

Joe had returned to his seat, having given up on getting his wife's attention. At George's pointed question, he gave George a malevolent glare, pausing before he answered. "Yes, she is."

Though the answer might imply Joe disliked women in business, Jennie guessed Charlotte Wainwright was the target of the emotion, because George was looking slightly smug. These were two men who should be enjoying the fruits of their labor. Instead, they were siblings still battling it out to be king of the hill. Had one of them tried to buy out Charlotte to gain more shares in the drug company?

"Well, you both must be doing a fine job running HP because this is a beautiful home," she said truthfully, figuring she was due to suck up a bit. "I'm sure there's nothing in the St. Louis area that equals it, except maybe some of the mansions built in the 1800s."

Mike suddenly stood up, "accidentally" kicking her. "Jennie, I'd like you to meet Veronica. I think I told you she's my ex-wife?" he said, pulling her out of her seat and barely letting her thank the octogenarians for their time.

"You know, Mike," she said when they were out of earshot. "I'd get a lot more information if you'd quit dragging me away as I get the folks talking."

"That comment about 1800s mansions... You do realize George and Joe lived in River Bluffs? They know it's still there. I can't believe they don't know, or at least wonder, about its current ownership."

"I'm sure they must know who Caroline left it to. But could they know Paul willed it to you?"

"Rick Boston told me that until the will is submitted in court, no one knows what it says. He's filed something to indicate a will exists, but he's been using the legal system to drag out the probate process until the year is up."

"Then no one knows you're in current possession without having seen Paul's will. As far as we know, that's no one but Rick and you."

"And you. Here's Veronica," Mike said.

When Jennie saw Mike's ex-wife, she instantly understood what he'd meant when he said he could get used to a woman being on time. Veronica Houseman was immaculate in a way that said she would spend as much time and money as needed to achieve perfection. Her hair was absolutely straight, platinum blond. Her skin was superbly tanned and her face made up to a standard Jennie wouldn't have been able to achieve after a course on makeup. Well-toned muscles on a curvaceous body indicated a rigid workout schedule, maybe even a personal trainer. To finish off the masterpiece was an elegant bikini top that would never touch chlorine, paired with a lovely draping skirt and stiletto heels.

Jennie looked at Mike in awe. How had he had

the courage to divorce this woman?

Veronica showed a brilliant white set of teeth as she leaned into Mike, kissing him full on the lips, a little longer than necessary. One hand caressed his cheek and the other clutched his hand. Something bitter rose up in the back of Jennie's throat. She was unsure if she was going to throw up over the display or seize up with jealousy. If she hadn't known better, Jennie would never have guessed these two were married and divorced.

"Veronica, I want you to meet my friend, Dr. Jennifer Foster," Mike said. To his credit, he had taken both of Veronica's wandering hands in his and released them next to her own body. He then slid his hand behind Jennie's back, gently pulling her forward for the introduction.

Veronica's handshake was limp as Tori's. Maybe rich women were taught to shake hands like that.

"Dr. Foster?" she said questioningly. "Are you a medical doctor?"

If the ice princess hadn't already made her feel inferior, jumping to the least likely career didn't help Jennie's self-assurance. "Doctor of history," she replied and tried to deflect the awkwardness with a joke. "My residency was spent prying into dead people's lives, not their bodies."

"Oh," Veronica said. "How interesting." She turned to Mike, dismissing Jennie and her credentials, and ran her hand intimately up and down Mike's arm. "So, Mike. We need to talk." Though shorter than Jennie, Veronica clearly looked down her nose at Jennie. "Do you mind? We need some privacy."

Sara was right. The only thing about this woman that would attract a man was the sex. She oozed sexuality. Jennie wondered if women ran in fear of her, dragging their men with them. She couldn't help picturing a snake and all men as mice.

Holding a hand up to her face to hide a smile, Jennie made a barely audible excuse, and caught an apologetic look from Mike. Of one thing she was sure, Veronica had plans for her ex, whether Mike knew it or not. The thought worried Jennie more than it should.

The pair disappeared quickly into one of the more heavily treed areas. So much for his sister's estimate that he liked her. Jennie quelled the annoyance she felt, reminding herself that Mike and she were not a couple. He could go wherever he pleased. She didn't like being dumped at his family reunion, but years of moves had made her an expert at striking up conversations with strangers. She would not be a wall flower.

Without a specific destination in mind, Jennie wandered down the expansive lawn to a creek, where a few tables offered a shaded haven. A handful of adults had found this escape from the children playing in the pool. Jennie recognized Charlotte Wainwright, sitting alone and staring in the general direction of the pool.

"Hi. Can I join you?" Jennie asked, taking the opportunity while she had it.

Charlotte's salt-and-pepper graying hair trimmed in a short style and a face lined with wrinkles indicated she did not have Veronica's obsession with looks. When the older woman hesitated, apparently wanting time alone, Jennie offered an introduction.

"I'm Jennie Foster. I teach with Mike Garretson," she said, hoping his name would make her more welcome.

Charlotte's face lit up. "Wonderful!" she crowed, introducing herself. "Have a seat. I was hoping you weren't a close relation. These reunions can be so tiresome after a while. 'George said this,' or 'Joe wants that.' It's almost more than I can stand."

"I met George earlier. He mentioned you were HP's lone female owner."

"Hmmph. No news there. What else did he say?" For someone who didn't want to talk about her business partners, she didn't waste any time looking for information.

Jennie shook her head. "Nothing. I'm relatively new to the area, so I thought that was pretty interesting. I'd think you have an important job when you're one of three board members."

"My role is to keep those two antiques on their toes. I don't have enough shares to change anything on my own, so I enjoy being a pain in their rears," she said with a smirk. "I keep involved to entertain myself. I could care less about making drugs—except in relation to improving my own well-being."

"George and Joe seem harmless. Is there some reason I should avoid them?"

She eyed Jennie thoughtfully, and then shrugged. "Only that I think the two of them are capable of doing anything to get what they want."

"Even murder?" Jennie laughed, making a joke of the statement, once again pressing the limits of conversation.

Charlotte cocked her head to one side, raising an eyebrow as she studied the teacher.

"Funny you should ask that. I've wondered that myself. You've heard the old saying that blood is thicker than water? Their blood runs in that damn company. What would they do to keep the company in the family? Do you know I've pushed to go public several times, and they both refuse. I'm sure things will change when they die. I can win the age race. But I'm not certain if I want to wait around that long."

"HP is doing enormously well though, isn't it? It's not in any financial danger."

Charlotte snorted. "Right now. I hear Rob has

been putting a lot of money on research of a melanoma vaccine. If it fails, that's going to affect a lot of people. Might even be a little funny stuff being done to ensure the research looks good. I've got my spies. Your Mike over there probably got caught in the funny stuff. Certainly was suspicious how that happened."

Jennie held her breath. She kept her face bland, but once again, there was that reference to Mike and something strange going on at the company while he worked there. Before she could figure out a way to drag more information out of Charlotte, her daughter joined them and the subject veered into one about children. Jennie eventually excused herself to replace her long emptied beer.

The bartender's back was turned away from her when she reached the bar, but when he turned to face her, his eyes opened wide. "Jennie! What are you doing here?"

"Darius, I didn't know you were a bartender," she replied, avoiding the question. Darius was a good friend of Tanya Jefferson's, and Jennie knew him through the many visits they both made to the Jeffersons' open household.

"Part-time college job. These Housemans pay real nice. I've done this for a couple years through the catering company I work for. But you didn't answer me. How do you know the Housemans?"

It didn't matter what Jennie said, Mae would soon know Mike Garretson's secret project was tied up with the Housemans in some manner. Elusiveness was a wasted effort.

"I'm friends with one of the distant Houseman relatives," she said, sighing inwardly. "Just here to provide support."

Darius finished mixing several fruity drinks Jennie recognized as the beverage of choice of the elder Housemans. Handing her the water bottle she asked for, he apologized for not being able to talk and headed off to deliver the drinks and take more orders.

Jennie wasn't left alone for long. A small woman, dressed more appropriately for a cocktail hour, climbed on a stool next to her.

"Hi!" she said enthusiastically, panting a little with the effort of climbing on the chair. "I'm Paige Houseman. Darn, I missed the bartender." She shook the ice in her empty glass disappointedly. "I saw you talking to my stepdaughter, Veronica. You're here with Mike, aren't you?"

"Yes, I am," she replied. "Jennie Foster. I work with Mike."

"Oh, he's such a sweet boy. It's too bad the work at HP didn't suit him." Her chubby legs barely reached the bar for resting her feet on. One leg tended to swing loose as she perched on the stool seat.

"What do you mean?"

"Oh, I shouldn't be repeating gossip, should I?" she said rhetorically, since she had apparently already determined she would. "Well, you know, after he'd been working there for a while, he married Veronica. Some people think he must have felt like he had a personal right to the company, because soon after that, funds were found missing from his department. Of course he said he didn't have anything to do with it. I suppose he either quit because he got caught, or because he wasn't guilty at all but was being treated like it." She leaned in conspiratorially. "Personally, I think it was all a mistake. Mike's too nice to steal."

Mike left Houseman Pharmaceuticals over missing money? No wonder he didn't want to talk about it. Since Jennie was unable to think of anything appropriate to say, Paige willingly filled in the silence.

"I mean, I hear he makes an excellent teacher and he's got those boys playing baseball so good. Geoff—that's my husband—says Mike was a great athlete in school. And it's too bad he left the company. He's excellent with people, much better than its current president. Poor Rob will be the ruin of HP, though I'm sure he means well. Our dear Veronica might never even see an inheritance if he's left in charge."

"She's got a long wait to inherit, doesn't she? I mean your husband has a lot of years left on him. I've seen him on TV."

Paige was eyeballing the bottles of liquor behind the bar. "I suppose I could mix my own drink," she said, looking around for the bartender. She tottered behind the bar, pulling out bottles and studying the labels. Then she poured flavored vodka into a glass, plunked in some ice, and sipped it with a smacking sound. She wobbled back around to her chair, daintily placing her drink on a napkin.

"Now. What were you saying, hon'?"

Jennie smothered a grin. She had a drunken congressional wife on her hands. "Uh, we were talking about your husband's inheritance."

"Oh, right. Because Geoffrey is in Congress, he asked Joe to leave him out of inheriting any part of the company. You know that can be so awkward to have ties to a certain industry when you're in politics. Geoff has done so well on his own anyway; he hardly needs Joe's money. Of course I've got my own money too. I'm Geoff's second wife. But he's my third husband!" She tittered.

"So Veronica gets Joe's shares when he dies?"

"Oh, yes! Drives Rob crazy knowing that, too. I mean, how do you control one of your employees when she might be your boss some day?"

Jennie chewed on her lip, wondering about this bit of information. At least one thing was certain,

Paige was failing to make Jennie's list of murder suspects.

"Do you know George and Joe very well?"

"Oh, those two!" she said as if they were a nasty taste on her mouth. She frowned, leaning forward and nearly falling off her seat. Jennie caught her arm, helping her back into her chair. "I've known them forever. In fact, Joe introduced me to Geoff. Probably wouldn't have if he'd known I was going to be his daughter-in-law." She giggled, slapping the bar. "You know, if Joe wasn't Geoff's father I'd tell you a few things." She paused, glanced around briefly, and launched into a monologue.

"George and Joe put on a great show, but they are anything but friends. Did you know George bought Richard Houseman's share of the company? That really pissed off Joe. Gave George control of half the company, when before they had been equal partners. Joe's been trying to buy out Charlotte Wainwright ever since. She won't sell though. Her husband is an investment broker and he's told her not to sell—yet. He figures the offers will go through the roof once George dies.

"George'll probably go first," she plowed on, her hazy blue eyes staring into her drink. "That's not all, honey. He has three children, so that's going to be a problem when he dies. Only Rob helps at the company though, so I can't help wondering how George's will is written. If he doesn't will the company to Rob alone, then Veronica will have majority ownership, and even Charlotte will have more shares than each of George's children. It's killing Joe not to know what George is planning."

Charlotte's eyes narrowed and she peered around suspiciously. Her voice dropped to a whisper. "There's more, hon'. The wrangling especially goes on in the company. Rob plays favorites as president. Veronica's department often gets the good projects pulled as soon as they show potential. Poor dear. I know she works so hard. When Geoff is home, she unloads on him, and of course he has to go talk to Joe. It's a regular soap opera, I tell you.

"Oh, I've said too much. Don't tell anyone, okay?" she slurred, saluting Jennie with her drink and taking a big slurp. "Ah, finally. It looks like Mike has gotten himself free of Veronica's claws. She can be so needy around men, you know. Always has to be the center of attention."

Mike caught the last words. "Who needs to be the center of attention, Paige?" he asked, giving her a peck on the cheek.

"Any Houseman!" Paige tittered, nearly losing her balance on the barstool. "Except you, dear," she told Mike, patting him on the arm. "You are the paragon of aloofness."

"Where's Geoff?" he asked Paige, coming to the same conclusion Jennie had and holding onto her to make sure she didn't fall off her chair.

"Oh, honey, he's in D.C., of course. I came back for the reunion. You know how I love your family." Unbelievably, she seemed sincere.

"I think you should get out of the sun for a bit, Paige," he suggested. "You're looking a bit red."

"Oh, dear," she said, fanning her face. "That wouldn't be good at all. Veronica was telling us how their research on that melanoma vaccine is going and it sounds like it's going to be a real success. But it's not ready yet, so I can't be getting skin cancer now, can I?"

Jennie caught sight of Mike's arched eyebrow and shrugged, indicating she had heard the conflicting information as well.

Mike helped Paige down from the chair. Jennie and he supported her as they walked into the house. They found a couch and eased her onto it. Paige mumbled her gratitude and instantly dozed off.

"Well, have you had enough?" Mike asked, after placing Paige's limp arms on her chest.

Jennie was still reeling from Paige's download of information. She had so many questions to ask, but Mike might not want to answer them.

"I think I've had about as much of the Housemans as anyone could take," she said, nodding. "I like the Garretsons though, especially your sister Sara, who, by the way, is certain there is something going on between us."

Mike grunted. "Let her imagination go wild. Her kids are driving her nuts at home. She's a great lawyer, but not used to being a stay-at-home mom."

"We didn't get to talk about her career—since you dragged me away from the table."

"I dragged you away from a conversation with that...Robert, not with Sara," he said, censoring his own language.

"You dragged me away from George and Joe too. If you were going to stop me from talking to people, why did you bring me along?"

"You don't need to be around Robert."

"What is it with him? Just because he didn't want you to marry Veronica? You're divorced now. Couldn't you make amends?"

Mike's eyes were dark and stormy. "That's my business."

Thinking Mike had made it *her* business, she gritted her teeth, not wanting to argue as they walked back to the party. It wasn't hard to put the two topics Mike wouldn't talk about together: his distaste for Rob Houseman and his departure from HP. She wondered how closely related they were.

"Mom, Dad, we're going to get going now. I think I've subjected Jennie to enough of my family for a lifetime."

"So soon?" Linda Garretson reached out and hugged Jennie. "It was so nice to meet one of Mike's friends. I hope we'll see you again."

The motherly desire was barely veiled and Jennie had to suppress a smile. "I'm glad Mike brought me. I had a wonderful time."

Sara picked up her youngest son who burrowed his tired head into her shoulder. "Hey, you call me if you want to talk," she whispered, sliding Mike a sly glance as he said goodbye to his parents. "He's a good guy. He needs someone with a lot of patience though. But he catches on eventually."

Jennie received another hug, sparing her from responding to Sara's comment. She gave a last, wistful glance at the Garretsons and followed Mike to his car.

Chapter 15

Slamming his car into gear, Mike pulled out of the Housemans' driveway, relieved to put the reunion behind him. As expected, he could think of a dozen things he'd rather have been doing, but this gathering hadn't been as bad as usual. Having Jennie along had been a welcome relief. He'd made his rounds of family members, but was able to put the focus on her. Surprisingly, she was a great conversationalist. He'd assumed someone that was as interested in research as she was would be reticent in a crowd.

Veronica, on the other hand, had been the same as she'd been at the dealer's garage. She'd somehow managed to get him to a secluded location where she'd proceeded to try to seduce him. Then she'd accused him of avoiding her because he had taken Jennie as a lover.

That had pissed him off. He was quite willing to admit his conquests, but his ex-wife had no rights in that direction. Besides, he wasn't about to let Veronica say anything bad about a woman who was occupying his thoughts a lot lately. Oh, and that same woman was doing one helluva job on his research project.

After he'd chewed Veronica out, she'd apologized and managed to keep some distance between them while expressing her concerns about HP. She didn't have any new information, except it had been confirmed Jack Elliott appeared to have died accidentally by failing to follow safety procedures.

"That means they couldn't find any reason he

committed suicide or was murdered," Veronica had angrily claimed.

"So how did your conversation with Veronica go?" Jennie asked, pulling him back to the present.

He glanced over at her. "Contrary to what Paige said, Veronica did not say the vaccine was going well. She repeated someone appeared to be making it look good when there were definite research problems," he summarized, leaving out the seduction parts.

"Why would she tell her father and stepmother one thing and us another?" Jennie shook her head. "What does she expect you to do about it anyway?"

"She wanted to know if either George or Robert had tried to contact me for any reason. She wouldn't explain why she thought they would want to talk to me. When we were married, one of the reasons we argued was that I was certain there was someone corrupt within the company. Now she's agreeing with me. Maybe she thinks the problem is at the top."

"That goes with what Charlotte said. She seems to think something strange is going on too. Claims she has spies in the company. That sounded a bit suspicious in itself."

Mike grunted. "Interesting. But then again, what isn't in this weird search? What did Paige have to say?"

"What didn't she have to say," Jennie said with a snort. Mike listened silently about the inheritance issues Paige had brought up.

"I had no idea Veronica was Joe's sole heir," Mike remarked, turning over the new piece of information in his head. Funny Veronica had never mentioned that, especially as she was quite proud of her association with HP. "I'd really like to know what's in George's will. If Paige doesn't know though, I'm certain George isn't about to reveal it to us. That is one piece of family information we won't be able to use."

"Uh, Mike?" Jennie interrupted him. "You're heading to River Bluffs. Aren't you taking me home? It's already past five."

"I thought you might like to join me for dinner in the dining room tonight. I'm cooking." He smiled and patted her knee, sending heat up her thigh.

"Oh? Usually when you invite a girl to dinner, you ask her first."

"I'm sorry. Did you have other plans?"

She threw Mike a quick look. His green eyes caught hers and her lungs constricted when he winked.

Crap. Somewhere in this research, she'd let the lines blur on the client-professional relationship. She'd seen him with his family. He could be so much more than he was now, a father, a husband. But something was broken in him. Was it what happened at HP that did that to him?

"I'd love to see what you can cook," she replied. And she'd get him to open up to her.

****

Mike shooed Jennie away when she offered to help him cook, so she took one of the boxes from the study back up the stairs to the little round room on the third floor. With curved windows giving a nearly 270-degree view and built-in benches sporting hand-sewn cushions, it was the perfect reading room. Heat had built up in the tiny area because of its westward-facing windows. Struggling with old paint and warped wood, she finally managed to get two of the windows open to allow a cross flow of air. Then, tucking bare feet under her, she curled up in a position that let her look over the large green lawn, the box of papers ignored.

She could only see parts of St. Louis' skyline, mostly because the trees were too tall to see over from this position in the house. She could easily imagine a young Caroline holing up in this room with a book or a couple of friends. Maybe her mother had nursed her children while resting on this bench, or Fred Houseman's boys had hidden here when their parents argued.

Finally, she shook her head and came back to her task. The first piece of paper out of the box turned out to be some kind of household accounting document from the early twentieth century. She quickly scanned about half the box in disappointment. If she were looking for primary documents on the running of a home in the 1910s and 1920s, she would have a rich source of material.

But she wasn't.

Between the birds chirping and the distant drone of traffic numbing her thoughts, she nodded off.

****

"Hey, sleepyhead. Dinner's ready."

Jennie heard Mike's soft voice as if from a distance. When his fingers touched her face to move hair out of eyes, she almost didn't open her eyes. The warm touch sent molten heat sliding through her veins. Then her body made her painfully aware she'd fallen asleep in an awkward position.

She groaned, feeling drool on the left side of her mouth and a cramp in her arm. She blinked the sleep out of her eyes and tried to sit up, tight muscles protesting. "Ugh," she said, taking a swipe at the drool.

"Wow," Mike commented cheerfully. "You're a real beauty when you sleep."

"You try sleeping on an eighteen-inch wide bench. And these cushions could use some new stuffing."

He eyed the bench doubtfully and nodded. "No. I'm good. It's all yours, anytime you want to sleep."

He held out his hand and she wrapped her hands around his wrist, accepting the help standing, then groggily followed Mike down the narrow back stairs. Stumbling, she grabbed his shoulder to stop her fall. When he stopped, she laughed, resting her head against his back, the solid wall of muscles beneath her forehead.

"The dangers of too much rest," she mumbled into his shirt.

He put his hand on hers. "Or too little. Hold on. I will be your guide, O Sleepy One."

He led her through the butler's pantry into the dining room. When he stepped aside, giving her a full view of the room, she was stunned at the sight of the dining room.

"Oh," was all she could think to say. Her heart had migrated into her throat.

If she had thought Mike was detached, all thoughts of that vanished as she wandered into the room. An elegant, multi-tiered, silver candelabra sat between two place settings on the table. Mike had removed all but two chairs and brought out some of the beautiful antique china in the butler's pantry. He'd covered the long table with a tablecloth edged with fine lace and matching cloth napkins, and added silverware that shined from a fresh polish. Dinner was already on the table with wine poured in finely cut crystal goblets. A vase of flowers from River Bluffs' own overgrown gardens provided a final touch.

"Couldn't resist trying out the family china?" she teased, though she was absolutely charmed by his gesture. Mike, a romantic?

"Something like that," Mike said, pulling out one of the high-backed chairs for her. He took his own seat. "Unless there is some miracle waiting in all these papers you have us searching through, I'm not expecting to get to do this again. I thought you would appreciate it."

"Oh, I do," she said with sincerity. "This is even better than cooking on a 1950s stove."

Mike grinned, and the uncomfortable moment she'd felt not knowing what he was doing passed.

"Dinner," he said, "is Cornish game hens in a dill sauce, asparagus sautéed in oil and garlic, and rice pilaf." He paused a moment while she used tongs to place asparagus next to half a hen. "And crusty French bread all the way from the grocery store."

"You're making me regret my chicken casserole the other night. You didn't tell me you cooked."

"There are a lot of things I haven't told you."

The comments about the funds scandal flashed in her mind, but she wasn't ready to broach that subject quite yet. She accepted a glass of wine, and the conversation drifted to safer areas as Mike regaled Jennie with tales of his sisters. As Mike told it, he and his father were much maligned by the three women in the small house they grew up in. He was forced to fight for space in the shared bathroom that had gradually been overtaken by hair products and makeup.

The images he conjured were priceless. She countered with the challenges of moving every two or three years during her childhood years, with a very out-of-date grandmother to raise her during her father's deployments.

"I had to get my friend's mom to shop for a prom dress. Between my father and my grandmother, I was doomed to wear a potato sack to my senior prom." Her grandmother had died shortly after she'd started college, as if she'd hung around long enough to make sure her only grandchild made it through high school. "It was my dad's sole goal to ensure boys and I never came in contact."

"We could use him at Swansea High," Mike said,

grinning. "Keep some of those hormones in their place."

She grimaced. "Oh, he'd be the expert on that."

"It must've been tough growing up without a mother."

She shrugged. "I don't really know, since she died when I was young. But I will say, watching you with your family, I'm a bit jealous. Your family's fun."

"You must have had fun times with your dad."

"Yeah." She snorted. "For my twelfth birthday, he thought it was a good time to learn how to shoot. I forgot the safety after one lesson and shot out a tire on the car. Boy, was he pissed. It took a lot to get him to let me shoot again. Then, when I was learning to drive, he thought I'd be safer in a Humvee. So he took me out on a range and let me go. Until I ran over the 'Restricted Area' sign and the security police chased us down."

"You're kidding?" Mike gave up not laughing and chuckled.

She shook her head, smiling. "Nope. He was a colonel then, high enough to talk his way out of the mess I got him into."

"Not a normal childhood, I suppose."

"Now it's funny. Back then, you did not want my father angry at you. If he wasn't trying so hard to make up for me not having a mother, it would have been much worse. That and Grandma constantly reminding him how he'd been as a kid, illegal bottle rockets, playing on the train tracks. Boy stuff. Made me look like an angel."

"And I thought you were a stuffy history teacher."

"I *am* a stuffy history teacher—who can scale a ten-foot wall and fire an M-16 rifle." And would have traded her entire mint-condition Barbie doll collection for a sister or—some days—a stepmother.

"Wow. Maybe you should be coaching the baseball team."

"I didn't say I was good at any of these things. Besides, Dad says I throw like a girl. Hard as he tried, he wasn't able to turn me into a son. I was a lousy tomboy on top of it all."

The lazy smile didn't leave his face. Instead, running his fingers up and down the stem of his wine glass in such a way that Jennie's face heated, he said, "Some boys like girls who are just girls."

The temperature in the room climbed at least ten degrees, even though the sun was setting on the opposite side of the house.

"Good," she finally replied, searching for a way around the bottleneck in the conversation. "Find me one of those guys."

That wasn't the answer. She abruptly pushed back her chair, trying to look anywhere but the smile playing at the corners of Mike's lips. She was reading too much into his words and actions.

"I'll clean up since you cooked."

"I've got dessert. Just sit for a minute more while I get it."

By the time Mike brought out a cobbler with ice cream, the sky glowed with twilight. Patting her stomach as she finished, Jennie let out a long breath of air. "I could live like this forever, here at River Bluffs."

Mike's eyelids were half closed as he watched her. Jennie would have loved to know what was going on behind those green eyes, lit with the fires of the candles. Zippy, however, had other plans. He raced into the dining room with an excited yap, and shook next to Mike, water dancing in the air.

Mike leaped up and scolded the sodden dog. "Zippy!"

"I take it the rains are returning," she said. "His timing is perfect. I can't eat another bite. You are one fine chef, Mike. I'll hire you at my next catered event."

"I'm a chemist," he said, brushing his wet clothes. "What's cooking but changing the chemical nature of food with heat or cold?"

She laughed. "Good point. How about you find a towel to dry off that mutt of yours, and I'll clear the table?"

"Deal. I have old towels in the kitchen."

She stacked dishes on top of each other and carried them to the kitchen. Even a wet dog couldn't ruin the deliciously warm buzz from the wine, food and conversation running through her veins. Considering she'd gone to the family reunion of someone she barely knew, today had been well above average. When Mike joined her to help wash and dry the dishes, the hominess of it strung a chord inside her, like a Norman Rockwell painting.

She was getting sappy over washing dishes.

Enough.

As Mike snuffed out the candles on the table, she carefully returned the china and glassware to the butler's pantry. She turned around as he was passing through and they nearly collided. As he placed his hand on her hip to steady her, a prickle of heat rushed along her skin.

In the dimly lit butler's pantry, either could be accused of making the slight movement that brought what she wanted. Their lips touched ever so slightly. Jennie swallowed hard when he pulled back, then caught her breath as he slid one hand around her waist and wrapped his other hand into the hair at the base of her neck.

There was no mistaking what Mike wanted now. Throwing caution to the wind, she snaked her arms around his neck, dragging him back down for a second go.

Fire lit in her belly and her heart thumped in

her chest as Mike's mouth pressed against hers. Lips parting, she joined his crushing embrace, their bodies molding against one another. She pressed her right hand against his chest, hard with muscles, yet soft to touch. His hand on her waist slid down her back. She revised her opinion of the shortness of her loaned skirt when his hand slid under the hem and cupped her bottom.

At her groan, he pulled back. Looking up into his eyes, she wasn't ready to stop. But Mike had more restraint.

"Jennie," he said, brushing his knuckles against her cheek. "I'm sorry. I shouldn't have...I shouldn't have done that."

Her body screamed for more. "What? It's okay." Maybe he thought she wasn't interested.

"No, you don't understand. I want to. But I don't—I can't offer you what you deserve." He stepped back, just as the light rain turned into a roaring downpour and thunder rattled the windows.

Mike looked startled, then turned and dashed through the kitchen. "I left the car windows down!"

Jennie slumped against the counter in the butler's pantry, both frustrated and relieved. What did he mean by his last comment? What couldn't he offer her? She didn't even know if she *wanted* this man and his secrets. Her body knew exactly what she wanted from him, but Jennie Foster was not one to sleep with a man just for sex.

She sighed. It was good someone upstairs was watching out for her. If the storm hadn't hit when it had...

She shook her head, rubbing her eyes, then glanced at her watch. It was after nine. Mike was going to have to take her home in this downpour. She walked into the kitchen and started pulling out flashlights and candles.

He came back in soaked. "I thought you parked

the car under the porte-cochere?" she asked, tossing him one of the dog's unused towels left on the kitchen table.

"I did. The wind was blowing rain through the open windows. We're going to lose a few trees in this one," he explained, wiping the water off his face, arms and legs. "Oh, and the rain got inside the car." He scowled at that, having proven earlier he doted on his antique car. "I hope it didn't ruin anything."

"So, when are you taking me home?"

"Let's wait till this dies down a bit and then we'll make a go of it." He watched her light the candles. "Look at you. A week in this house and you're already an expert with its quirks."

"You did say the lights go out *every* time there's a storm. I'm assuming this weather qualifies."

"Absolutely."

She lit the last of the fat aromatic candles. Now was as good a time as any to broach the subject of the funds scandal. She half sat on a stool, sucking in a breath.

"Mike, Paige said something I want to ask you about and I'd like to hear your side of the story. You know how you told me you left the company because you weren't happy with some of the practices there?"

The room's temperature appeared to drop as Mike's face grew still. The smile that had been playing at the corner of his mouth for most of the evening was gone, and his eyes had narrowed.

"Paige said you were involved in some missing funds in your department. She said you left because you were either guilty, or because you weren't and were tired of the harassment. So what's the story?" She crossed her arms and met his glare head on. No backing down now.

Somewhere in the midst of her question the man she had just passionately kissed had been swallowed up. The cold shell left behind was the Mike she'd known two weeks ago.

Even so, she didn't wish she could take back her question.

"What difference does it make?" he asked flatly.

"It makes a lot of difference. You bring me here to solve a hundred-year-old mystery that's tied into a half-billion dollar company, but you don't give me all the background? What else aren't you telling me?"

He turned to walk away, and she caught his arm. She could see a muscle working in his jaw as his lips pressed together.

"All this talk of danger, Mike. Why would you hold back on me? How can I make rational decisions without all the information?"

"Do you think I did it?"

"That's irrelevant. The point is I work with facts. I should have all the facts, not just the ones you think are important."

His eyes bored into hers, but she held her own.

"So?" she challenged him.

"It's none of your business. It has nothing to do with the inheritance."

"Everything about HP has to do with this inheritance. If you think otherwise, then my work here is done."

"Fine."

Jennie gritted her teeth, matching his glare. "Fine," she said with finality. "I think I should go now."

"Yes. That would be a good idea."

He abruptly turned to leave. Her eyes widened at his back as it dawned on her what she'd just done. She'd quit.

Anger burning her cheeks, she grabbed her backpack, purse and computer briefcase, and followed him out the parlor doors. He commanded Zippy to stay, and climbed in the driver's seat.

"Wait," he ordered as she headed into the

spraying rain. She backtracked up the porch steps as Mike ran back in the house, and came out with a towel. She watched him soak up the water on the passenger seat.

Her heart flipped at his kindness and consideration. Had she really just quit working for this guy?

At his wave, she rounded the car, shoved her briefcase and backpack over the seat, and climbed in with her purse resolutely clasped on her lap. The whole time, Mike didn't say a word. Which hardly mattered for the voices in her head calling her an idiot for quitting on him.

They didn't get even fifty feet into the woods before Mike slammed on the brakes with a string of curses.

There, straddling the narrow road, was a foot-wide tree.

Chapter 16

Mike dumped the bed linens that smelled of mothballs on Jennie's chosen bed in a tiny third-floor bedroom, probably used by a servant back during grander times at River Bluffs. It gave him some satisfaction she would hate the mattress, since it was probably forty years old. Unfortunately, he was enough of a gentleman to wish she'd taken the offer of his bed, which was at least twenty years newer than this one.

Besides, it would have been easier to nurse his righteous fury at her if he couldn't sleep.

What was it with people that they had to know his personal business? He had handled HP sufficiently for his needs. The subject did not have to be rehashed with everyone that found out about it.

He clumped down the stairs to the kitchen, listening to the water running in River Bluffs' lone second-floor bath. He wondered what she would wear to bed, hoping it was nothing.

What was he thinking, letting his mind go in that direction? The further away he stayed from her, the better off she was.

While he was on the subject, what was the point of a romantic dinner with Jennie if he wasn't going to sleep with her? He sighed, staring at the ceiling.

Thanks a bunch, Veronica. Here he was, wooing a woman and then pushing her away. Hiring her for a job, and then letting her quit because he didn't want to face his past. All because Veronica had poked his ego full of holes. He wasn't even certain what a woman wanted anymore. And one like

Jennie...

She was unique. For some reason, he knew he couldn't just bed her, then tell her thanks, that was fun.

He haunted the first floor, moving from one room to another and listening first to the movements in the bathroom and finally the creaking of the stairs, indicating his unexpected guest was on her way to bed. Giving her reasonable time to make sure she wasn't coming down again, he headed up himself.

Little good it did. He glared at the clock two hours later, listening to Zippy's nails clicking on the wood floor. Then he sat up. Jennie was obviously coming down the stairs, her little flashlight barely cutting the thick blackness. Through his open door, he could see the light dancing on the stairs.

Not sure what he was doing, he crawled out of bed and slipped over to the door. He wanted to explain why he didn't think his time at HP mattered. Jennie might have a point: she should know everything, especially now that Veronica agreed something weird was going on. There was every chance he had been targeted by the same person or people that were now targeting his ex-wife. He definitely did not want Jennie to quit. He'd only offered that option earlier because he didn't want Jennie to blame him if something went wrong.

Jennie wore shorts and the shirt she'd worn Saturday morning, with one exception. She obviously had no bra on. The hardness in his groin was instant and unwanted.

Jennie gasped and flashed her light briefly at his face. Still warring with his own emotions, he doubted she'd wanted to see him in the middle of the night. Her eyes wide with alarm, she backed up, then hurried down the hall toward the bathroom, tripping over Zippy in her rush.

Mike shut his door, leaning up against it and rubbing his eyes. Jennie was trouble. His life had been under control, if not normal, before she'd entered it. He should look at this positively. Now that she'd quit, she wouldn't be a problem for him.

Maybe.

But who was going to help him find proof of an imposter? Did it even matter if he kept River Bluffs? Crawling back into bed, he pulled a pillow over his head and decided not to face the issue.

****

When dawn broke the next morning, Jennie felt gross. A gray sky did little but add to the extra heaviness of her headache. Without a toothbrush and having never showered off the previous day's sunscreen, she felt like someone's unwashed laundry. At least she had the clothes she was wearing yesterday morning. Unfortunately, that did not include a change of underwear, so she'd washed them out and hung them on a chair to dry.

Sleep had been elusive, which she tried to blame on her long nap, but knew was because she'd gone to bed mad at Mike. On top of her miserable sleeping accommodations, she'd awakened sometime after dozing off, needing to use the bathroom. After encountering Mike's eyes, glinting with the light from her flashlight, it had taken her a while to get her racing heart back to a speed that would allow sleep. Then she'd had a terrible nightmare where she was chasing Mike in a storm, yelling for him to come back and feeling a desperate sense of loss. A tall, shadowy man would turn toward her, his face a big pair of deep green eyes, and then start running in the opposite direction. She would have sworn she actually cried. Except when she opened her eyes, Zippy had jumped up beside her on the bed and was gently licking her face.

She'd patted him on the head, oddly grateful to

have someone there with her this morning. Now she reached across the dog and picked up her watch. It was only six. She dropped her head back into the smelly pillow and pretended she might go back to sleep.

When that didn't happen, she grabbed her slightly damp underwear, sandals and watch, and headed downstairs to the bathroom. Mike's door to his room was open and she peeked in. He was already up. She briefly wished he had slept as badly as she had. But then remorse struck, and instead she wished he had slept great and wanted her to keep working. The discussion she had imagined about the funds scandal had gone a lot smoother in her own head. Somewhere in the middle of the night she'd decided Mike's pride was wounded by whatever had happened at Houseman Pharmaceuticals. There was no way he was involved in anything illegal. He couldn't be.

The power was back on, so she found a towel and decided that even if she had to wear dirty clothes, she was going to shower. When she came out of the bathroom fifteen minutes later, she felt a hundred times better.

She went down to the first floor and still didn't see any sign of Mike. Poking her head out the back door, she heard a chainsaw whining in the distance. He was already out and attacking the fallen tree. She squashed a feeling of betrayal, certain he wanted her to leave as soon as possible.

Not much of a coffee drinker but in desperate need of a pick-me-up, she pulled out a caffeinated soda from the fridge and popped it open. Then she found eggs, cheese, and some lunch ham, good enough for an omelet. She made enough for a second one for Mike when he came in. They might be in a disagreement, but she never deprived anyone of food.

After cleaning up and with nothing else to do, Jennie decided she might as well look for house plans in the attic. She hoped Mike was enough of a professional he'd still let her archeology group come.

The attic was gloomy from the overcast day. She popped open the small window facing the road where Mike was working, allowing her to hear when he finished. Looking out, she could barely make out his shape in the clearing that marked the gravel driveway. The tree was no longer completely straddling the path, and large pieces of trunk lay piled in the brush.

For a moment she imagined going out and helping him, working next to him, watching his muscles strain with the effort. She dismissed the thought. Even if she had the appropriate clothes, she could not imagine Mike would be any more forgiving.

Instead she flipped open the large cedar trunk they had dragged over to the stairs last week. The lid bounced off the trunk's side with a thump and she remembered why they had put this one to the side. In addition to a few pieces of baby clothes, some folded linen, and other mementos were loose photos and photo albums. There were five albums: the one on top had photos dating from about the 1940s; the next two were from the 1920s and 1930s when the Garretson children were young; and the fourth album was of Caroline as a girl with her family.

The best album though was a small one about five-by-six inches filled with nineteenth century portraits, including some tintypes, small metal photos not bigger than three inches on one side. The photos were well-preserved, but the album itself was crumbling and difficult to handle. She carefully turned the pages until she got to one that read in delicate script: *Josef and Marie Houseman*, Mike's great, great grandparents, the builders of River Bluffs. They were young, possibly newly married, their unsmiling faces frozen to keep the picture from blurring as it was taken.

Even though these two were not her family, she was so tied up in their legacy at this point she felt like they were. It was this way whenever she researched someone's family history: first the name and dates that gave the person bones, then the documents that fleshed out the body, and finally the family traditions, history, and artifacts that gave the person character and life. Research took a person's name and turned him or her into a living, breathing human again, years after he or she had died. These two in this photo, they were significant even today. They were at least partly responsible for the Houseman secret. What would Josef say today if he could see what his actions had wrought?

The sound of water flowing through the house's ancient pipes broke her reverie. Mike was back and using the shower. Knowing it would only take her a couple of minutes to make the omelet she had waiting for him, she finished looking through the album. Then she found an old suitcase, gathered up the set of albums and loose photos, and placed them all in the case.

By the time Mike joined her downstairs, she had made him a three-egg omelet with ham and cheese and three slices of toast, poured him a glass of orange juice, and arranged the albums so he could look at them while eating. She questioned her sanity the whole time. What in the world was she doing?

For a moment, she thought Mike wasn't even going to come into the kitchen, as he'd come down the grand staircase and promptly headed into the library. But Zippy came to the rescue. He ran out into the hallway and yapped at Mike and ran back to the kitchen. He did this twice before she finally heard Mike say, "Okay! Okay! I'll come see what you want."

"Hey," Jennie said coolly as he strolled into the kitchen, not willing to find out if Mike thought this was a good morning. His hair was wet and tousled, and his T-shirt clung to a hard chest that wasn't quite dry. She kept her eyes on his face to quell the flutter in her stomach. "I made you an omelet. And I was looking for those house plans for the archeology visit when I found these photo albums upstairs in that trunk we set aside last week. There's an excellent photo of Josef and Marie Houseman."

He nodded. "Thanks."

Mike was not one to waste food and shoveled the omelet in quickly. At a loss as to what to do now, Jennie decided departure was her best bet. "Listen, I'd still like to see if I could find some house architectural plans, so I'm going to go back up in the attic for now. Sometime today, when it's convenient, I would like to go home and change out of these clothes. Since I'm not working for you anymore, I'll pack up your stuff and get it back to you."

She wanted him to take a hint and offer her to keep working.

"I cut up the tree. The drive is clear."

"Uh, thanks." So much for hinting. She stood a moment longer, deciding their conversation was over. "I'll be in the attic."

She wanted to be on friendlier terms again, but there was no way she could forget that kiss last night. Or that argument. She wanted to "unquit," but couldn't figure out how.

Back in the attic, she looked through the rest of the trunk, decided there was nothing else there of use to her, and shoved it to the end of the attic where they were putting the cleared things. After a half hour of fruitless searching, Zippy came upstairs, followed shortly by his owner.

Mike handed her a long leather tube. "Here. I found these in the library last winter. I'd forgotten they were there until you mentioned them."

She took the tube, tilting her head as she studied it, then undid the catch on the cylinder's top and slid out a roll of poster-size papers. Licking her lips in anticipation, she got down on her knees and unrolled the pages on the floor, pinning the corners down with a lamp and an ancient toaster.

"House plans," she whispered, carefully handling the pages.

The first page was the land plat and the layout of the house. And there, in the back, north of the carriage house, was the outhouse.

"Fantastic!" She stabbed a finger at the location. "There's the privy. This will make next week's archeology dig so much more successful. I can plot out the location."

"Later in the week, maybe. There are more storms heading this way," Mike said, walking over to the window she'd opened earlier and shutting it. "We're under a thunderstorm watch right now. I'd better drive you home."

His tone was back to the controlled, unrevealing voice of last week. She sighed inwardly. The archeology visit was still on, even if the job was done. She rolled up the plans again.

"Okay, then I suppose we should go."

Jennie led the way down the stairs, the precious tube under her arm. She hesitated in the kitchen, the suitcase of photos sitting on the table. Mike hadn't mentioned them. However, there could be useful information written on them for solving the family mystery.

Except she'd quit.

"Do you mind if I take these with me?" she asked. "Some of them would be perfect for use in my history classes. I'd scan and return them in a couple days."

He didn't answer immediately. Finally he

nodded and put them back in the old suitcase.

The drive back to her house was devoid of conversation, Mike turning on the radio to drown out the silence. When they reached her house, he opened the trunk and tried to hand her the suitcase of photos, obviously intent on going no further. However, she already had her backpack, briefcase, purse and the architectural plans filling her arms.

"Would you bring in the suitcase?" she was forced to ask. He grunted, and followed her to the door, where she fumbled with the keys before getting it open. He set the suitcase inside, and was heading back out almost before she could say anything.

But then he paused and turned, giving her an expressionless look that made Jennie's heart ache.

"By the way, just because you don't work for me anymore, doesn't mean you can talk about this. The year requirement still isn't up. Understand?"

Since she was still hoping to work on the case, even without Mike's knowledge, the thought had never occurred to her to tell anyone about it.

"Of course," she said. "But could you drop me an email when I can come out to plot out the dig location?"

"Yeah," Mike replied and shut the door.

For a moment, she stood there staring at the door, her teeth grinding in frustration. When she heard the car engine fade, she flipped on the TV and threw herself on the couch. It was only mid-morning on a Sunday and two-hundred cable stations had nothing worth watching. She ended up on the Weather channel, watching the storms moving into the area.

It took almost more energy than she had to carry the suitcase to the coffee table in front of the couch. Soon, she'd dragged her computer out and was comparing names to those she had in her database.

When she found a loose wedding photo of
Caroline and Frank Garretson, she decided she'd do
what she usually did with clients at the end of
project, give Mike something to remember the family
by. Usually, it was a bound book including research
and stories she'd discovered, whether it was the
history of a house, a city or a family. But since the
Houseman research would likely remain unfinished,
maybe she could do something else for Mike. She
found the photo of Josef and Marie Houseman,
scanned it at a high resolution, and saved it on a
flash drive. Snapping open an umbrella for the run
to her car, she headed to a photography store.

Chapter 17

Tanya Jefferson tossed a hand-designed purse on the couch as she dashed into her parents' dining room.

"Sorry I'm late." She gave Jennie a hopeful glance, said a quick prayer of thanks, and grabbed the nearest bowl of food.

Jennie hid a smile. No one showed up late for one of Mae Jefferson's Sunday dinners. Even she knew that, though she'd only been welcomed as part of the family for a couple of years. Tanya might have been studying or in the middle of a project. But that was no excuse to her mother, who had raised five children while working full time, or her father, who had worked two jobs to make sure they wanted for nothing.

Being welcomed into the Jeffersons' home had been an adjustment for Jennie. With a father who was often late or deployed, dinner was never much of a deal at her house. But dinner with the Jeffersons came dangerously close to some kind of clichéd television family, be there on time, elbows off the table, eat what you take, and absolutely no arguing.

As soon as her plate was full, the Jeffersons' youngest daughter brought up the subject Jennie had rather hoped to avoid. "So, Jennie, was my outfit a success at your event this weekend?"

Good. Neutral question. She could handle this. "Great. It worked perfectly. Your tastes were on target, as usual." She took a bite of mashed potato slathered in Mae's perfect, lumpless, brown gravy.

"Yeah? Darius saw you there. What were you

doing at the Housemans' family reunion anyway?"

Jennie inhaled abruptly, the potato heading down the wrong tube. She choked, eyes watering, as she tried to get a breath in. Mae was up in a heartbeat.

"Don't pound her back! That's a myth and it'll only lodge the food in further," Mae ordered, hovering near Jennie and gently rubbing her back. Not that anyone else was moving. Ben, Tanya's brother, had already cleared his plate and was calmly helping himself to seconds, and Russell Jefferson knew better than to get involved when his wife was in control.

Mae had a glass of water in hand when Jennie finally gasped for breath. She took the water and swallowed it in little bits, as her friend recommended.

"So, Tanya, what was Darius doing this weekend?" Mae asked as she slid back into her seat, still looking at Jennie.

"He was bartending for that caterer he works for sometimes. But I still want to know why Jennie was there. I mean, the Housemans are old, big money. I didn't know you knew any of them, Jennie."

"Just friends of a friend," she muttered. If she could have thought of anything to change the conversation, she would have. But her mind was stuck in first gear and digging a hole fast.

"She was there with Mike Garretson, weren't you, honey?" Mae's question only had Jennie sliding further into her seat, forcing the older woman into mother mode. "Don't slouch, dear. You'll get your hair in your food."

Jennie scooted back in her chair, evading Mae's piercing black eyes. If she looked, no doubt Mae would know everything, like some soothsayer.

"Did you know," announced Mae in a voice that said she was about to teach someone a thing or two, "that Mike Garretson's father and I were in band together in high school?"

Jennie's head shot up and she stared at Mae.

"Yes," continued Mae, "he even told me his grandmother had been born a Houseman. That must be why Jennie was there with Mike Garretson. And we have another connection too. Tell them, Russell, about when you worked at Houseman Pharmaceuticals."

Russell nodded, perking up to be included in his wife's curious conversation. "It's true. When we were newly married, I worked evenings cleaning the company. The company wasn't so big and powerful back then, so I met a couple of the Housemans when they worked late."

"You tell them, Russell," encouraged Mae.

"The most interesting night was after a weird week when this reporter from California had been poking around talking to people about the Housemans."

Jennie turned to stare at Russell. Was he talking about Sue McGregor?

Russell sat up a little straighter, clearly blossoming with the attention of someone who hadn't heard one of his stories. Mae was nodding enthusiastically, like she did when the minister got heated up with his sermon in church.

"Yep. She stopped me as I was going into work one evening, wanting to know if I knew anything about Fred Houseman being an imposter. Strangest question I ever heard. I guess she'd been asking everyone, getting into the old newspaper stories about the Housemans.

"Anyway, one night I'm doing my job, cleaning out one of the bathrooms in one of those executive offices of them Houseman brothers. There were three of them, and they all were in the office. I don't know if they didn't know I was there, or if they just didn't think about me being someone who would care, but they were talking about this reporter. They were talking about getting rid of her, and I don't mean firing her, since she didn't work for them. They were talking about protecting their father—that would be Fred Houseman—from her. Even said they ought to drown her in the Mississippi. Funny thing is, two days later, she drove off a bridge and did drown in the Mississippi."

"Which one?" Jennie practically whispered.

"Which bridge?" Russell asked, frowning. "Oh, which brother. I didn't see them, just heard them. Kind of didn't want to be noticed by that time. Thought it was in my best interest to pretend I wasn't there."

"Small world, isn't it?" Mae said, shaking her head. "Here we are, and we all have some connection to the Housemans. They really are all over the place, aren't they? This may not be a small town anymore, but if your roots are buried here, you don't escape your past. You got to be careful. Never know when something you do will come back and bite you." She was talking to the table in general, but Jennie knew the warning was for her.

Mae intentionally led the conversation in another direction, but Jennie was stuck on this new information. What else did Mae know? Jennie wanted to ask, but was afraid she'd violate Mike's rules.

He really needed to know about this. Now she had to figure out how to casually bring it up in conversation.

If she could get him to talk to her.

Chapter 18

Two days after dinner at the Jeffersons, Jennie was miserable. It was bad enough she was keeping secrets from her best friend and working on a research project behind her former client's back. But even worse, she could not get Mike out of her head.

If she hadn't been so overwhelmed by Paige Houseman's information, she might have remembered to tell Mike about Darius and his relationship to the Jeffersons. But she hadn't. No matter how she worked the conversation in her head, even if she added in Russell Jefferson's story about working at the drug company, she couldn't see Mike understanding the Jeffersons knowing she had worked on his family genealogy. She was caught and couldn't even turn to Mae to ask her how to get out of the situation.

Mae, at least, was sticking with Jennie's rules. She didn't mention Sunday's dinner conversation at school and did not so much as blink when the subject of baseball and the team's bid for regional championship came up at lunch one day. Jennie could only marvel at how the woman could manipulate a conversation like Sunday's to give her information, and then completely avoid it the next time they saw each other. Mae Jefferson knew more than she was saying, and Jennie didn't know what to think of that.

Instead, she threw herself into the job she'd quit, spending two evenings at the library looking up every mention of the Housemans in the newspaper archives, from social events they attended to the tragic deaths of Caroline Garretson's two infant brothers. By Tuesday night, she had a whole bunch of nothing useful.

Jennie desperately wanted to call Mike. While she knew he should know about Russell Jefferson's story, the reality was she missed him. She was stuck on how much fun she'd had talking with his family at his reunion and relaxing with him that night. And cleaning out the attic, talking about the research with him was unlike any other case she'd worked on. How often did she get to involve the client, especially someone smart and caring like Mike? Where there hadn't been enough hours in the days last week, this week time seemed to drag, even with all the extra work she was doing.

Tuesday evening, Jennie restlessly pulled out the architectural plans and spread them on her small dining room table. Stacking books to hold down the curling corners, she studied the hand-drawn sketch of the exterior landscaping and building orientation, making measurements and notes of what equipment they would need to dig up the privy's remains.

Having determined how she was going to rope off the area of the dig, she pulled back the first page to look at the plans for the rest of the house. The pages were fragile, crumbling a bit at the edges, so she carefully lay the top page face down on the floor. The second page was the cellar with its coal bin, heating plant, and little else. The third and fourth pages were more interesting, showing the first floor plans and details for bookcases, pantry cupboards and storage among other things. She carefully stacked the pages upside down on the floor.

There was something odd about the second floor plans. What she knew of the house did not match what was on the plans. Clearly, there was an extra room, seated between Mike's room and one of the other bedrooms. She didn't remember a room, so perhaps one of the bedrooms had been expanded. She peered closely at the tiny print with the house measurements on it. The room was at least five feet wide; the measurements on the rooms to either side seemed to be right for the size of the rooms today. Her eyes widened with excitement as she read more tiny print indicating the closet in the room Mike used should have a panel into the smaller room. An arrow to the side of the plan showed a close-up detail of a latch that was to be concealed in the large bedroom's closet.

She got up and did a little dance. "There's a secret room at River Bluffs!" she shouted to her empty house. This was it: her excuse to call Mike. She grabbed the phone and punched in his cell phone number. When there was no answer, she called his house phone.

The phone rang until the answering machine picked up. He had to be screening his calls.

"Mike, this is Jennie," she said, failing to keep the excitement from her voice. "Did you know River Bluffs has a secret room? It's on the second floor, right next to your bedroom. Call me." Just as she was about to hang up, she heard the telltale sound of someone picking up the call.

"Jennie?" Mike asked. "What did you say?"

She grinned at the sound of his voice. She had him. "The architectural plans show a secret room," she blurted out. She quickly told him about the room, waiting expectantly for his response.

"How significant do you think this is?"

She considered all the materials she'd been through in the last couple of days, realizing she could hardly tell him she was still working. "You have nothing to solve your mystery, Mike, and only ten days till your deadline. I'd say this is pretty dang significant." She paused. "I suggest you check it out soon. Tonight, if possible."

"All right. I'll meet you there. Can you find the house in the dark?"

She closed her eyes, punching a fist in the air. He wanted her there. He must—he could have asked for the plans. She looked outside; twilight was fading quickly. "For this I would clean the school bathrooms for a week," she said resolutely. "I'll bet my little Saturn can make those curves faster than your Mustang."

"Just get there alive," Mike said.

Maybe there was hope yet. All she had to do was get him to rehire her.

****

The lights were on in the house when she got there. Zippy bounced at her car door, going silent except for the whooshing of his tail when she rubbed his head. Mike loomed out of the parlor doors, the light behind him making him appear larger. Sucking in her bottom lip, she took a deep breath and grabbed the leather tube of house plans as she pushed herself out of the car. As she handed him the plans, she tried to read his mood from his eyes or his greeting. He didn't break into song, but he also didn't glare at her. Things were looking up.

"I brought a tape measure," she said. "Maybe it will help us find the room."

Mike took the front stairs two steps at a time with her behind him, barely keeping up with his long legs. Zippy dashed ahead, yapping excitedly. By the time Jennie reached Mike's bedroom, he had the tube top off and was unrolling the plans. After laying them on the foot of the bed, he peeled off three pages, one at a time, which she took and laid at the top of the bed.

"There," she pointed to the room, and then showed him the details. The lighting in the room was too dim to read them, so Jennie offered to get a flashlight from the kitchen. "Here," she said, handing him the measuring tape before heading downstairs. She hoped by giving him the lead to find the room, he would hire her back.

When she returned, he had the metal tape stretched from one side of the bedroom to the other. "It's exactly fifteen feet, eight inches, just as the plan indicates," he said, legs spread and hands on hips. "Let's check out the other room."

They hurried into the small bedroom on the other side, but there was no need to measure. It was obvious there was a hidden room, because there was a huge space between the two rooms.

After studying the plans some more, Mike went into the narrow closet to examine it. An uncovered bulb dangling in the tight confines gave brighter light than the small lamps in the bedrooms. Jennie hovered outside the closet, partly because it was too small for two people and also because she wanted him to find the room. Twice he came out to examine the plan. Finally, she heard a small snick. Zippy barked excitedly, squeezing in as the door swung inward. Jennie peered in, trying to see around Mike's body.

"The flashlight, please," he said, holding out his hand. She passed it to him and he moved slowly into the black room, brushing cobwebs out of the way. She edged in, watching Mike try to turn on an ancient lamp sitting on a small desk.

"Would you get one of the bulbs out of the lamp in the bedroom?"

Jennie ran over to the nightstand, burning her fingers on the bulb in her excitement. She pulled off a pillowcase to protect her fingers from the hot bulb. It cooled quickly though, and Mike was able to screw it into the lamp without her makeshift hot pad.

The light revealed completely blank walls, but the desk was another story. It had many nooks and crannies crammed with old papers. Jennie desperately wanted to take over, but stood back, again letting Mike make the discoveries.

This was it. There had to be something to push the case forward, something that would excite Mike enough to get her rehired. She clenched her fists, and leaned in.

****

As exciting as finding this secret room was, Mike found himself distracted by the smell of Jennie's hair. He resisted the urge to look at her. He'd missed her the last couple of days, and he resented that feeling as well.

Trying to ignore the shapely teacher breathing softly on his neck, he focused on the task at hand. River Bluffs constantly intrigued him, he thought as he picked through the desk material, most of it accounting paperwork, no more secretive than the books in the library. He had always thought he had an excellent sense in the three-dimensional realm, so it was a little annoying it took a historian to find what should have been obvious to him.

She was good at what she did. Why had he lost his temper over the stupid missing funds at HP? It was old news. But losing Jennie as his researcher was bad news. He'd tried to look for those wills she'd said they needed, Caroline Garretson and Fred Houseman. With the help of a clerk, he'd found them, but it'd taken abandoning his baseball team for an afternoon. He had to admit it was more interesting than he'd imagined to read something written by his great grandmother. But it hadn't helped him solve the mystery. He was moping around the house this evening, fairly certain River Bluffs was going on the auction block soon and Jennie would never speak to him again. He was even beginning to accept the reasoning it was a good thing their partnership was over, as he didn't need a female distraction. Then she'd found this room.

If he were wise, he'd forget about inheriting the house if she was his only hope. Apparently though, when it came to Jennie Foster, his wisdom reached amazingly low levels.

She was staying back, holding a flashlight to provide additional light. Having scanned the documents on the desk, he took a seat on the one wooden chair, and peered at the cramped handwriting on each document. He pulled at a narrow drawer. It stuck, so he had to wiggle the small brass knob before it opened. Inside the drawer were two letters and two black and white photos tied together with a bit of string. He loosened the string, and could feel Jennie move in closer, his own anticipation growing. The first photo was a young man dressed in an Army uniform, a cocky smile on his face. Written on it was Fred Houseman, 1918. The other was of a slightly older man, a much more hesitant expression on his face, but it too was labeled Fred Houseman, with the date of 1920.

He frowned. "They look like the same person to me," he said.

Jennie nodded in agreement. "It's no wonder Jacob couldn't get anyone to believe him when he said Fred wasn't who he said he was."

Mike set the photos down and opened one of the letters. It was dated January 20, 1918, and written in an uneven script.

Dear Uncle Josef,

I was pleased to get your letter. The family is fine. My father is doing better now that my sister Gretchen has married, and her husband Albert is helping with the crops. Albert excels at farming. My other sisters help too. Only Jacob gets away with little work. I am afraid we all spoil him since our mother died when he was so young.

As to your request that I join your business, I do

not know anything about medicine or drugs, but you already knew that. I do know how to run a farm and perhaps that is not much different than running a drug company. I would very much like to come to Illinois and see what help I can give you.

First I must see to the Germans though! As you can see from the enclosed photo, I have enlisted in the Army and will soon be leaving for Europe with the 2nd Division. I hope to finish off this war and return soon enough.

I will keep you in my thoughts while I am over there and look forward to meeting the rest of my family.

Your grateful nephew,
Frederick Houseman

"Wow," Jennie said in a hushed tone. "We're reading a letter from Fred Houseman."

"Yes. It's like seeing a ghost." He reread it, amazed at the connection he felt with this man, long since dead.

He unfolded the second letter. This one was typed, dated October 2, 1919.

Paris, France
Dear Josef Houseman,

My apologies for not writing sooner I have been in a hospital unit taking care of wounded. My own wounds were bad but I have recovered My unit is helping clear out the troops and taking care of prisoners. We will be leaving for New York soon I hope to come to Illinois soon after that do you still want me to come? There is no place for you to write so you will have to tell me to leaf when I get there if you do not need me

sincerely
Fred Houseman

Mike laid the two letters side by side. He was no expert, but these letters did not seem to come from the same person, even though the signatures were similar. The second letter's handwriting, limited to Fred's name, was shaky and less sure than the earlier one, but it could be excused due to his war injuries. The language, however, was another matter.

Jennie made the obvious comment first: "These are written by the same person? Not a chance."

Mike laid the photos next to the letters. "Josef had doubts," he said softly. "He hid these letters here and wondered if Jacob was right: the Fred Houseman Jacob knew as a boy was not the same Fred Houseman Josef knew as a man."

"But he looked at the pictures and saw the same man," she added, eyes glued on the photos.

Mike completed the search of the room, but the photos and letters remained the most significant find.

As he closed the door to the secret room, he thought Jennie might want to see the latch. "Do you want to see how it works?"

She smiled broadly, eyes lit with excitement. "Definitely."

She bent her head in next to his while he showed her the mechanism. Her hair smelled faintly of flowers and she'd left the red-brown mass out of its binder. He touched it as gently as possible so as to not let her know, closing his eyes in frustration. As he stood back to let her work the panel latch, he wondered if she'd skipped tying her hair back for him.

He waited for her in his bedroom. When she came out, her delight at the find wreathed her face. "That is so cool," she raved, and he found himself unable to resist a small smile.

"But, can you do anything with these?" he said, holding up the photos and letters.

She shook her head, frowning. "Not much. Historically, it places Fred in California in 1918, and someone who signed his name as Fred in France in 1919. It's great supporting evidence that 1919 Fred was not 1918 Fred, but I don't think there's a judge in the world that would rule in your favor with this." She sighed heavily. "It's great historical stuff, but worthless for our, uh, your purpose." Her cheeks grew pink in the dim light and she definitely slid him a look that made him wonder what was going through her mind.

"Oh, by the way, Jacob sent me an email saying his granddaughter was sending a package with the marriage records of Katrina and some notes of Sue McGregor's. Maybe that will help you. And there's still the Pennsylvania research. I'll pass it on to you when I get it."

Mike schooled his features to hide his emotions, but he was rather hoping she'd offer to keep working on the mystery. When she didn't, he swallowed his disappointment. He didn't feel it was his place to ask her back. She'd made clear her expectations. Full disclosure. He'd want her on his terms, and that would mean he got to choose what was relevant.

And now this, a secret room with as good a stuff as he'd ever seen and it wasn't enough. His expectations had been up and down too often already, and this one was hard to accept. Photos and letters of Fred Houseman were about as close to the subject as they would ever get. The secret room was a really interesting find, but would not be very useful to anyone when the house went on the auction block.

Oddly, Mike felt like he was letting Jennie down. He liked seeing her excitement and pleasure, and she definitely did not like this latest failure. However, she'd quit. He'd be damned before he begged her to take the job again.

"Well, okay. I guess I'll go," Jennie said, her face uncharacteristically drawn.

His heart was a leaden lump in his chest as he watched her drive away from River Bluffs. He should have said something. He should tell her about his time at HP, and then it wouldn't matter.

What was wrong with him anyway? It was a research project. He could hire someone else.

Yeah, right. As if there were a ton of great history researchers waiting to do his work with a week and a half to solve it.

"Dr. Jennie Foster," he muttered to himself as he watched her taillights disappear down the road, "you are messing with my mind."

Chapter 19

Though it was after midnight when Jennie crawled into bed, sleep wouldn't have been on her side anyway. School was in the last two weeks of preparations for finals and the pressure was on. All the teachers were cramming the last vital pieces of information the students would need to pass their classes. And, like the students, she would normally have been anticipating a summer of doing what she wanted.

She was unusually stressed this year. There was the upcoming archeology dig, but that was not a big deal in the scheme of things. She tried to deny the only remaining reason. But it appeared Mike was her problem. Acknowledging she had feelings for a man who didn't want anything to do with her hurt in a way she'd never experienced.

When she received an email from Mike on Wednesday, her heart leapt into her throat with wild imaginings of what he could be saying. Instead, it just suggested they meet at River Bluffs after baseball practice on Thursday so she could map out her dig for Saturday. She emailed him back to confirm the meeting, hoping maybe he wasn't as upset with her as she imagined. If he'd quit on *her*, she would certainly have considered canceling the archeology visit.

School, fortunately, was occupying a lot of her mind right now. She had projects due in her history classes. Students were required to write a two-page essay, complete a poster, and give a presentation on a person they admired that had lived in the twentieth century. With six classes of thirty students, her room was filling up with posters throughout the day. It would take the next three days to get through all the presentations, but most of the students liked this project. At least it beat note-taking and tests.

Flopping into her chair during her prep hour, she stared at her computer screen, which showed her email. She blinked and gasped as one came in from *robert.houseman@houseman.com*. She read the email quickly.

Jennie,

I found your email on the Swansea High School website. Though we hardly know each other, I am asking a favor of you. I have tried for some time now to get Mike Garretson to meet with me. Last Saturday's reunion was not the appropriate place for me to approach him, but it did remind me I have this unfinished business. I was hoping to call upon your friendship to get him to call me.

Would you mind meeting me briefly today, either after your school is out or sometime tonight? I would like to explain what I want to talk to him about. Perhaps you can speak with him on my behalf.

Thank you for considering my strange request.

Rob

After she recovered from the initial surprise of receiving an email from the president of a huge company who was also a murder suspect, she contemplated her options. By Paul Garretson's rules, she had not contacted Robert Houseman; he had contacted her. The subject didn't appear to be about the family genealogy. On those two scores she felt comfortable. What made her uncomfortable was Mike had specifically said to avoid Robert. On top of that, Veronica had wanted to know if George or Robert Houseman had tried to contact him. Was this some roundabout way to get to Mike?

Did it matter anyway, since she didn't work for him anymore?

She tapped her pen on her desk, considering her options. Someone at Houseman Pharmaceuticals was involved in this mystery. Russell Jefferson had confirmed that. Robert Houseman might have been involved in Susan McGregor's death, though he would have been very young at the time. It seemed unlikely an eighteen-year-old with a promising career ahead of him would murder someone. But maybe he was protecting his future, one that would dry up if his ancestral line was cut off from the Houseman fortune.

So, Rob *might* be a murderer. What was certain though, was meeting with him definitely meant she was going against Mike's conditions. He might believe what had happened to him at HP was irrelevant to his problem, but she was certain Mike was a piece in this puzzle. She had to know how he fit in. Rob could answer that question.

She had no idea what he wanted to talk to her about, but if it helped the research, she needed to do it. She'd already quit. What was one more black mark on her relationship with Mike anyway?

Decision reached, she sent a brief reply to Rob, suggesting they meet at a bookstore near the mall about four. His reply popped up later in the day, agreeing to the location and time, and thanking her profusely, even though she'd expressed doubt about how she could help him.

By the time she got through grading the posters that had been turned in, it was past time for her to leave for the store. She quickly packed up the essays needing to be graded. There wouldn't be any research tonight. If she didn't get through her school work this evening, she would be behind tomorrow. The meeting with Robert was not going to make her night any better—unless he confessed to murdering people or having proof of Fred Houseman being a fraud.

When she finally shoved the bookstore door open, she headed straight to the coffee bar at the side. Rob stood as she approached his table. He held out his hand and said, "Dr. Foster."

Matching his tone, she replied equally formally, "Mr. Houseman."

He smiled broadly. "First names okay with you?"

She nodded, returning his smile. If she didn't have Mike's opinion weighing heavily on her conscience, she would probably have liked Rob. At least as far as the president of a multi-million dollar company went, he was very personable. They sat down at a tiny café table.

"I wish I'd gotten more time to talk with you Saturday, but I suppose you got much of the family history from my father and uncle. They *are* the family history in any case. I'm rather a newcomer," he said depreciatingly. As he nervously twisted a cup of coffee in his hands, she was struck by his very unpresidential behavior. "Did they give you all you wanted to know?"

"Yes, wonderful family history," she said, intentionally cutting the small talk. "Rob, I don't mean to be rude, but I'm here without Mike's knowledge. To be blunt, he doesn't appear to like you very much. I really don't know what you think I can do for you. I'm not very close with him, more acquaintances than friends. In fact, I was at your reunion with ulterior motives." She let him assume she meant finding out about the family history.

Rob sighed. "Mike isn't close to anyone, except his family. And they surround him like a fortress. I can't get them to talk to him either. Did he tell you about why he left HP?"

"Not really." That was unfortunately the truth. He hadn't told her anything.

"I recruited Mike to our company. In his early years, I watched him grow up. My son, who is only four years younger, naturally idolized Mike. He was a great athlete, smart, and the girls fell over each other trying to get to him. When he chose chemistry for his college major, I waited until he graduated and hired him straight out of college to work in the company, even letting him pursue his baseball career at the same time. He was family, but more importantly, he was smart and sensible. I thought he'd go far.

"When he married Veronica I was a little surprised. Frankly, I still can't picture the two as a couple, but he doted on her. She certainly had him wrapped around her finger. I made sure they were in different divisions in the company to make sure their efforts didn't overlap. Veronica," he hesitated a moment, concentrating hard on his coffee, and then continued, "Veronica's management methods aren't mine. We disagree a lot. Of course, whenever she doesn't get her way, she goes to Uncle Joe, her grandfather, and I hear about it from my father. I'm sure you've heard about our melanoma vaccine research. Veronica's department is working on that. It's been our number one research effort for several years now." He paused, frowning slightly.

Jennie leaned in expectantly, hoping for clarity on Veronica's duplicity. Was the vaccine research good, or was it bad?

"I digress," he said, not answering her unasked question. "In any case, we had a little problem with some disappearing funds. Before I really got a chance to investigate the situation, Mike quit. This has been my deepest regret—I didn't even know he was leaving before he was gone. Sometimes senior management is the last to know things. If I could change one thing, I would have had him in my office shortly after the funds disappeared and told him I did not suspect him. I didn't think he was the problem then, and now I know it wasn't him.

"I've since learned there were plenty of rumors circulating that Mike was the culprit, none of which came from my office. In fact, I believe the man behind the funds problem may have committed suicide recently. At least the safety violation he committed that killed him was so basic as to be hardly believable he could have done it accidentally." Rob gave a small grunt. "It was suicide. That or it was murder, and I would find that harder to believe than an accident."

Murder. He was talking about that chemist Veronica had also said was murdered. And they agreed about his death. Jennie swallowed hard.

"So, what is it you want me to tell Mike?" she asked, her mind buzzing over the new information Rob had given her.

"Would you please tell him we want him back? I want him back?" Rob asked, his voice rising as he leaned toward her. "And even if doesn't want to come back, he should know that we—that I—have never thought he was involved in that fiasco. He was—is a brilliant chemist, and an even better leader. He'd go far at Houseman, or anywhere for that matter."

"Did you tell his family this?" She still didn't see how Rob could imagine she had any influence on Mike.

"I talked with Linda, Mike's mother, and she said Mike wouldn't even let her mention my name around him. She gets no further on the subject than I do."

"Why is this so important to you? You must be able to hire pretty much anyone you want with a successful company like yours. Why don't you just let it go?"

Robert leaned back in his chair and pursed his lips. "I have my reasons, which I would rather not get into now." He took a swig of his coffee, and gave her a pleading look. "Will you talk to him? Please?"

"Like you, I don't have much influence with Mike. But should the opportunity arise, I will tell him what you told me," she offered. She could hardly explain to this man that Mike was barely speaking to her right now.

"Thank you. That's all I ask."

As Rob left, she stared at his back. He was still on her suspect list, but he came across so sincere. He was either a great actor, or he was telling the truth. The way he treated her though, made her believe it was the latter. He was old enough to be her father, but he spoke with her as an equal, and in some ways, as a man who desperately wanted to correct a wrong.

She drove home dejected. First, the funds gossip from Paige. Then Russell Jefferson's story about Jacob Houseman's daughter, Sue McGregor. Now this meeting with Mike's enemy, who wanted *her* to talk to Mike.

Boy, had Mike picked the wrong person for his research. In fact, it was ironic she'd quit working based on Mike withholding information.

He was an amateur. The CIA would be hiring her soon at the rate she was keeping secrets.

****

When she got home, she found two packages in the mail, one from California and one from Pennsylvania. It was a welcome relief from the stress she was under. She opened them with contained anticipation.

Jacob's package had a marriage record right on top. It was for Katrina Houseman and Roger Daniels, married in Redlands, California in 1889. Roger's birth date was more than twenty years prior to Katrina's. That was a story in itself.

There was a note clipped to the top of the rest of

the papers. It was written in shaky handwriting.

Jennie—

Here is some information that Sue had gathered before going to Illinois in 1968. It got wet some years ago so I hope you can still use it.

Good luck and God bless.

Jacob Houseman

The papers were crunchy and obviously had soaked up a lot of water at some point. Trying to look at some of the pages, she discovered they stuck together. Not wanting to damage them further, she set them aside. With a pile of essays calling her, she didn't have time to take the care to separate them.

At least one thing was in her favor. Ken Capelli apparently had enough research material to send her a package already. Though it was not as thick as the one from Jacob, she expected more from it.

She flipped quickly through the papers and found the one piece she wanted most of all, the marriage certificate for Betsy Borders' first marriage, which was a modern certified copy printed from a computer. All she got from this was Betsy had married an Edward Clemment in 1917 in Washington County, Pennsylvania. Behind that page, however, was another record. Ken had written on a sticky note: *This is also in the county clerk's records. They don't make copies of these when you write them for certified copies, but I thought you might like a copy. I sweet-talked the clerk into it. An advantage of being old!—KC*

Unlike the certificate, this page had tons of information. It gave the couple's ages and birthplaces, a physical description of height, hair color and eye color, parents' names and birthplaces, marriage official, location of marriage, and witnesses and their relationship to the couple. Focused on eye color, she saw Betsy had hazel eyes, while Edward had brown eyes. While it didn't tell her anything useful, she hoped it would later.

There also was the *Washington County Journal* obituary on Edward Clemment.

COUNTY MOURNS LOSS OF SOLDIER
July 6, 1918

County officials received word earlier this week that Private Edward Clemment, son of Carl and Emma Clemment, was killed in a battle near Belleau, France last month. Private Clemment enlisted in the United States Army earlier this year.

Private Clemment leaves behind a wife, Betsy (nee Borders) Clemment. His parents preceded him in death and he had no children. He is also survived by his uncles, Gerald and Abraham Clemment and their wives.

There will be a memorial service Sunday at 4 p.m. at United Presbyterian Church in Washington.

She studied the information, recalling what she already had gathered on Betsy. It appeared she was a widow when she married Fred Houseman. However, it did not explain how she was living with him in New York before they were officially married. If Fred was in Europe from 1918 to late 1919, how did he meet Betsy? Was she a nurse or a volunteer during the war?

Too many questions and not enough time. She looked guiltily at the stack of essays she had to go through yet tonight.

The rest of Ken's material was on the Borders family, which she could leave for now, as she didn't believe the answer to Fred's identity was with Betsy's parents.

She pulled out a checkbook, filled out a check and stuck it in an envelope with a short letter to Ken.

If the proof had been in the research material, she would have had a reason to call Mike and talk to him.

But again, it was a dead end. Her shoulders slumping, she wished again she hadn't quit.

Back to earning her teacher's salary, she thought in frustration.

Chapter 20

Mae Jefferson stalked into Mike Garretson's classroom with fire in her eyes. He stood, happy the heavy lab desk was between him and the glaring librarian.

"Mike Garretson," she said between clenched teeth. "I do not know what in the world you are doing with Jennie Foster, but you sure as hell better stop it."

"What?" He'd met Jennie last night out at River Bluffs to rope off the dig locations. It had been another awkward meeting, but he hadn't done anything to her. "She was fine last night when I saw her."

"Fine? I don't think so. She's got purple circles under her eyes from lack of sleep, she's not eating, and she barely says anything at all." With each point, Mae tapped a manicured finger on the desk's black top.

"Why would you think this has anything to do with me?" Mike was truly baffled. She hadn't seemed any different last night. Well, maybe a little quiet. Not her usual cheerful self. But all teachers were tired this time of year.

"Let me tell you a little something about Jennie Foster. That girl has constantly had her heart ripped out of her. Her mother died when she was four. Her daddy was in the Army and every time she made a friend, they moved. Her grandmother died on her right after high school graduation. If you've given her any indication that you're a friend and then you did something to say otherwise, you're heading down the wrong road, son. She won't tell me about this stupid project you've got her working on, so I can't help her. You have got to talk with her. You will work it out with her." Though her voice's volume increased with the last comment, Mike did not take it as a question. He was pretty certain his mother had channeled Mae Jefferson.

"Uh, yes, ma'am."

Mae nodded curtly and trundled to the door, then stopped abruptly. "Oh, and Mike, good luck on regionals this afternoon. You may not be good for Jennie, but you're sure good with baseball." Then she winked and sashayed out the door.

Mike remained rooted in place for several minutes, analyzing what Mae had said. Jennie was upset? She was the one who had quit and even accused him of lying, hadn't she? No, she hadn't—just of withholding information, which was certainly true. He didn't know what he was supposed to do. If Veronica was any example, he stunk at relationships.

You've got to talk to her, Mae had said.

Okay, he could do that. Now he just had to figure out how and when.

****

Jennie had tried to bring up her meeting with Robert Houseman to Mike last night as they roped off the dig locations at River Bluffs. She was so tired though, she was worried they would end up in another argument. She couldn't handle that. She was afraid she'd screw things up worse than they already were. Mike had been solicitous in helping her, but that's where the mending had stalled.

Mike was probably preoccupied anyway. Swansea High School's baseball team had made it to the regional finals. If they won the game this afternoon, Mike and his team would be heading upstate for the state competition next week.

With few options, Jennie decided she was going to watch the game, maybe get a bit of Mike out of her system. At the very least, being around a bunch of fans would be more cheering than sitting in her house, pouring over her notes and trying to find something that wasn't there. She had to get back into River Bluffs to continue her efforts, but she didn't even know if she'd be allowed back.

Her classes finished their presentations early on Friday, so while the students worked on their review guides for the next week's test preparations, she hurriedly graded posters and as many essays as she could. Though Mike's team would leave for their game before school was out, the game wouldn't start until four. It was Friday, sunny, and a short drive to the playoff game, and the Swansea Skyhawks were favored to win. The fan base for the team had been swelling throughout the season, and today it would be at its peak. She could be in that crowd and leave as needed. Mike wouldn't even know she was there.

By four-thirty she was on her way to Belleville West High School for the game. After parking at a distant location, she squeezed into a seat next to some rabidly proud parents. The game was tied in the fourth inning, and the crowds were standing, loud, and enthusiastic.

They were down by a run in the seventh inning when Josh Kowalzski spotted her on his way back from the snack bar, a soda in one hand and nachos in the other. His face was painted gold on one side and blue on the other, and his shirt was bright gold.

"Dr. Foster!" he shouted. "Great game, isn't it?"

"Yes, Josh. I see you held back on your fan support," she said with a smile.

Josh laughed. "Hey, I've been this way for the last few games. You should come to games more often. If we win this one, I'm driving to Springfield with my friends. You should join us."

"Thanks for the invite, Josh. If I go, I'll get my own transportation." She let the sarcasm show she had no intention of joining a student at a game. He gave her a thumbs up as he headed past.

As the only child of an Army general, Jennie understood the basics of baseball, even if she didn't know much about baseball strategies, but the father of the right fielder sitting next to her assured her Mike had one. He was right, because by the last inning, the game was tied and the Skyhawks were up to bat last. If they scored, Swansea won; if they didn't, they would go into overtime because there had to be a winner.

Everyone in the stands was standing and shouting. She recognized the junior student up to bat. Thomas Harper was in her history class. Earlier in the year he had been in danger of flunking. It was only when he realized he would be kicked off the baseball team for low academic grades that he had come to Jennie for help. She'd spent many lunches and afternoons tutoring him to help him remember "boring history." He'd successfully brought his grade up to a "C," and was now starting as third baseman.

As he took his first strike, she quietly urged him, "C'mon, Tom. This is easier for you than the Civil War and you passed that."

He slammed the next ball straight out between right and center field, where the outfielders missed it. He drove in the runner on third and Mike signaled Tom to go home. They had already won and Tom deserved the chance to score as well. He rounded third before the ball from outfield hit the baseman's glove. Continuing his run, he dove head first into home plate, the catcher hovering over the plate, but an anxious overthrow from third base tipped the catcher's outstretched glove and allowed Tom to make the score 5-3.

Swansea fans jumped up and down, screaming

with excitement. Jennie watched the bleachers empty of blue and gold as the students headed down to the diamond to congratulate their classmates. Mike received the ultimate coaches' honor as two of his players dumped an ice cold cooler of water over his head. The normally stoic chemistry teacher was grinning from ear to ear as players ran up to him to shake his hand. One beefy student even managed to bear hug Mike, effortlessly lifting him into the air.

Satisfied, she decided to slip out and let the real fans enjoy themselves, but as she reached the bottom of the bleacher steps, Tom spied her.

"Dr. Foster!" he called. He dashed over to her with a hand held high for a high-five. "Dr. Foster, do you know if you hadn't gotten me through history, I wouldn't be playing today? How cool is that?"

She nodded, laughing, and returned his high-five. "That's *way* cool."

Suddenly she realized Mike was there. He must have heard Tom call her. His eyes were sparkling. Perhaps with this win under his wings, he was willing to forgive her for quitting. She stretched out her hand and shook Mike's hand.

"Congratulations, Coach. Nice game."

"I didn't know you were here," he said, still smiling.

She shrugged. "I wanted to see a winning coach at work." An awkward silence descended. "I should go. You need to dry off, and I think you have a team to celebrate with."

He nodded, gave her one last look over his shoulder, and went back into the crowd.

Jennie crawled into her car as her cell phone rang. She stared at the caller ID. It was Mike. "Hello?" she answered, puzzled.

"Hi," he replied. "I know you quit, but I really could still use your help. Do you suppose I could talk you out of quitting? Maybe talk about a few things that need to be cleared up?"

Jennie's throat suddenly choked up. She fought for control.

"Jennie?" Mike asked after a moment of silence.

"Yeah. I'd like to finish," she managed.

"So, uh, this weekend's our last chance to clear out that attic and check out all the other rooms too. If you want, you could use one of the other rooms and stay the night after your archeology dig. You know, to finish whatever we can before the deadline next Friday. I think we should maximize our time."

He was rambling, but she hardly noticed. Her heart thudded in her own ears. "Okay," she said, at a loss for any other comment.

"See you tomorrow then?"

"Sure. Bye," she answered, then snapped the phone shut.

She was welcome again. Now she needed to rebuild some bridges.

Chapter 21

Another rain had managed to dump on the area last night after the game, but Saturday morning dawned clear, a few white fluffy clouds dancing in the sky. Her archeological club members had been prompt arriving at the school and she'd led them out to River Bluffs, one of the students commenting they'd found the end of Illinois.

The ground rules were simple. Mike would stay inside the house, and would remain there since his association with Jennie and the house was not something he wanted these kids to know about. If they needed to talk, she was to call him.

After peeling off the sod to replace later, they had made sizeable holes in the ground. Her plan was to dig until they encountered something. Mike had helped her rope off four sections so there were three students on all but one, which Josh and Adam had claimed on seniority. She'd had to remind Kari Hanlon that the wastes deposited in a privy would have long since become compost. Kari was only in the club because she had a crush on Adam, and her reluctance to dig in the dirt supported Jennie's theory.

They had taken a break for lunch, but were now back at it, the noonday heat beating on the back of bare necks. Jennie had already ordered two of the guys to put back on their shirts, reminding them this was still a school event and she didn't want to explain to their mothers why they were sunburned.

Travis Conner made the first discovery, a broken piece of china. "Hey, check this out!" he called, and naturally the entire group came over.

"Great! That's exactly what we're looking for," Jennie said excitedly. "Where did you find it?" After a bit of renegotiating of the search areas, she soon had them digging nearer the broken china's location. Using small garden shovels and trowels, the students began to dig more gently in the dirt. Soon they had a tidy pile of buttons, a couple of bottles, broken porcelain, and rusted metal parts.

She was picking through the bits on a screen with two other students when Zippy dropped a long bone at her feet. She crouched down to pick it up, as the dirty mutt ran around her, wagging his tail so hard his rear should've fallen off.

"What's this, Zippy?" she asked, reaching a muddy hand to pick up the dirt-encrusted item. Intrigued, the nearby students left their dig. Except for Kari, who somehow had managed to keep the mud to her fingertips, they all looked like they had been mucking out pig pens. Zippy was thrilled with the attention and jumped more, with excited yips in between.

"Cool," said Travis with awe, stubby fingers caressing the bone. "That looks like a human bone."

The average person would have been quick to shed doubt on such a statement. However, anyone who knew Travis knew better. His family owned one of those grand nineteenth-century Gothic houses downtown that had long since been converted to a funeral home. Travis lived around human bodies.

Kari shuddered. "Are you sure?"

He eyed her with disdain. "I could be wrong. Maybe it's a squirrel skull," he said mockingly.

"Zippy," Jennie said to the excited dog, who happily bounced her way. His short wiry hair was caked with mud. "Zippy, can you show us where you found that bone?" she asked, waving in the direction he'd been exploring.

At first he just tilted his head, wagging his tail. So she stood and started walking in the direction he had come, and he shot off ahead of her, like a teenager filled with several energy drinks. Without exception, they dashed after him.

Keeping an eye on the group, she called Mike on her cell phone and told him what Zippy had found. Mike expressed doubt about the bone being human and she agreed with him. It could be a cow bone for all they knew. She told him she'd call him if they found anything else.

The ground was soggy and slippery from the record rains they'd had. They ran along the road for about a quarter of a mile, Jennie beginning to wonder about the likelihood of Zippy actually finding anything out here. But just as she was ready to call it quits, the dog took a sharp right into the woods, straight into the undergrowth. Unfortunately, they were all dressed for humidity, not for thorny bushes, and the brush did its best to rip off of their skin. On top of that, the bad weather of late had increased the number of ditches, making the group look like a bunch of keystone cops cursing and sliding after Zippy the criminal.

Stopping, the small dog jumped and yapped loudly. Faster and more nimble, Josh raced past Jennie, stopping short. They crowded into a small clearing behind him, gaping in silence. There in front of them was a human skull, half buried in mud, a single vacant eye socket staring blankly skyward. Zippy had promptly lain down as they arrived and watched them with big black eyes, his head propped up on his paws. At his feet, next to the remains of an arm, lay a small pistol.

Adam broke the silence with a curse word not normally heard between students and teachers. Her own words frozen in her mouth, Jennie forgot her educational duty of correcting his language.

Josh voiced one of his off-the-wall comments. "Whoa. Archeology just got way cool."

Flipping open her phone, Jennie dialed Mike again. "We have a problem."

Chapter 22

The archeological field trip turned into a day at the circus, the police doing their best to keep the teenagers corralled away from the grisly scene. Mike got Rick's blessing to call the police, though he had little choice. Jennie did everything to keep Mike's name out of the investigation. However, they quickly learned they had no control of the situation, except their location was rather difficult to find.

Detective Dave Hoffman took one look at the skeleton and announced his opinion. "He's been here a long time."

"Not him," Jennie said, grimacing as soon as she said it.

"What?" The detective glared at her.

"It's a 'her.' At least I think it is. There's an old legend associated with this place about a woman who disappeared back in the 1930s." Jennie was ad-libbing, still trying to keep Mike out of this disaster. "Her family thought she'd been shot by poachers, because the afternoon she disappeared they heard a gunshot in the woods."

Detective Hoffman flipped open a notepad and scribbled on it. "No poacher uses a pistol, I can tell you that. Do you know the woman's name? Her family's name?"

Jennie blew out air. A good detective would be able to find records on Betsy Houseman anyway. If she told him, she would move his investigation along faster. "Betsy Houseman. She was the wife of Fred Houseman."

Hoffman's eyebrows beetled together. "You

mean as in 'Houseman Pharmaceuticals'?"

Jennie nodded. Didn't it figure she'd get the detective who recognized the Houseman name. She hung around, waiting to hear something to confirm this was Betsy.

The medical examiner crawling around in the muck gave her the desired information as the team searched for bone pieces. He held up a sun-bleached clavicle. "Check this out, Detective."

Hoffman picked his way over to the ME.

"See this?" He pointed to a spot on the bone Jennie couldn't quite make out from the distance. "It's a bullet wound. Grazed the bone. And she had red hair too. Can't be too many red-headed women that died in these woods in the last century or so."

It was more than an hour later that Detective Hoffman came back to the mansion to announce they were finished. "The body was well-protected. We found all the pieces but one. A tibia. Your dog find it maybe?"

Jennie started to say Zippy wasn't her dog, but was caught by the memory of him bringing a large bone into the house. "Yes, actually. I think he did." She walked toward the house, flipping open her phone.

Mike met her at the door, the bone in hand. "How's it going out there?"

"Smooth as the ocean during a hurricane. I'll fill you in as soon as I get these kids home. They can't leave until the ME takes away the body, which I hope will be soon."

****

By the end of the day, the police, skeleton, and students gone, Jennie was relieved she did not have to drive home. She lay flat on her back on the floor of the parlor, still covered in dirt and sweat, but so tired she didn't think she could make it to the shower. She heard Mike come into the room softly, not realizing she was far from asleep.

She said with closed eyes, "I'm not asleep. I'm dead." She grimaced as she thought of the real dead person they'd found today, and then opened an eye a crack. "Sorry. Bad joke."

Mike held a plate as he watched her with a bemused expression.

"I thought you might like something to eat. I made you a sandwich."

"Thanks." She debated the points of lying on the floor all night over eating. Her stomach rumbled. "I smell like...Zippy." She struggled to a sitting position and took the plate Mike handed her.

"I hosed Zippy down outside. I'm sure he smells better than you."

"Great." Looking at her filthy hands, she decided she would have to get up anyway. Mike was there to help her. Dang him anyway. He was being nice again, and she hadn't told him about meeting Robert or Russell Jefferson's story. When she did, they would be right back where they were before.

She was trying to balance the sandwich and gracefully stand while clinging to Mike's grip. When she almost lost her balance, Mike grabbed her around the waist and pulled her much too close. Eye to eye with those soul-stealing green eyes, she was unable to breathe.

"You smell fine, like a farmer's wife, fresh dirt, a little hard-earned sweat. It's good."

She chuckled. "Darn Midwesterner. I need to wash my hands," she managed, afraid to break the tenuous truce.

"How about something to drink?"

"Tequila? Maybe vodka? Whiskey?" she said, dragging into the kitchen. "That's what I need to forget this day."

"How about a beer and some aspirin?"

"Fine. If that's the best you can do," she replied,

drying her hands and pulling a stool up to the table. She popped the pills, gratefully took the beer he offered her, and sucked down half of it. Mike sat down across from her, his face typically unreadable.

"You know," she said between bites of the sandwich, "the media are going to report a body was found out here. Anyone who knows River Bluffs, which may include our murderer, is going to know something's going on here."

He took a deep breath and ran his fingers through his hair. "There's not much we can do about it now. It's not as if we intentionally put that skeleton there."

"I managed to keep your name out of this, but Mae's going to guess things."

Mike snorted. "Mae should have been a detective or a psychic. She probably would have nailed down this mystery on the first day if I'd hired her."

"You know that would offend me if I didn't know Mae Jefferson so well." She hesitated, finishing her drink. Mike offered her a second beer. She took the bottled courage to help her bring up the topics she'd been avoiding.

"About Mae," she said, staring at the last couple bites of her sandwich.

She could feel Mike's eyes boring holes in the top of her head. "I forgot to mention something to you after the reunion last week. It slipped my mind when certain things kind of overwhelmed it." Like his unwillingness to talk. She took a long swallow of her beer, giving up on the sandwich. "The bartender at the family reunion was a friend of Mae's daughter. He recognized me. And he told Mae's daughter, who…"

"…Told Mae?" Mike finished, shaking his head.

"Essentially. But there's more." She repeated Russell Jefferson's story to Mike's amazement.

"Why didn't you tell me this sooner?"

"When would I have done that? I sort of, you know, quit."

"We were still talking," he protested, straightening his back righteously. "We found that secret room, and we set up the dig Thursday."

"There's talking, and there's tolerating. You were tolerating me. This sandwich," she held up the plate, "is the first sign I've seen from you that you aren't mad at me. As much."

"Fine. I was mad. You were prying into personal stuff."

"I was prying because I was upset to learn about how you left HP from a drunken congressman's wife. Contrary to what you believe, I think that little funds scandal has something to do with this whole mess. Someone was trying to get to you, or to your wife. It happened after you married Veronica, right?"

Mike tilted his head, his lips parted in surprise. "Yes, it did."

"Didn't you ever wonder why?"

"Constantly."

"Maybe Veronica's recent car accident is a continuation of the harassment."

Mike whistled. "Someone trying to get to her through me. I never considered that."

Jennie studied her beer bottle, finishing it while debating whether now was the time to tell him about Robert. Before she decided, Mike interrupted her thoughts.

"Jennie, there is one thing I'm worried about though. We know the media's going to pick up on this skeleton. It's too weird not to. We can now be certain a murder did occur since our victim today was shot. If our murderer puts together a few facts, like the existence of River Bluffs, you finding a skeleton, and us knowing each other, they're going to know we're hiding something."

"We're not in danger from a murder that occurred seventy-five years ago. Whoever did that could not possibly be alive today."

"What about Jacob Houseman?"

Jennie snorted and rolled her eyes. "He's ninety-seven years old. And what would have been his motive in shooting a woman he just met? Though, I must admit someone could be covering up what happened back then."

"I'm just saying this could be even more dangerous."

"If I'm in danger, so are you."

"That helps a lot," Mike said dryly. "Are you certain you want to keep working on this? I mean, I don't really need River Bluffs." His gaze wandered the room, the regret plain on his face. "Besides, you've done everything you can, except finish the attic."

She pursed her lips together stubbornly, shaking her head. "Oh, no. I haven't done everything. There are many places to search yet. I haven't gotten through all the material from the Pennsylvania genealogist or the notes from Susan McGregor's research. Not to mention we haven't finished the attic or found Caroline's missing journal. And I haven't gone to the courthouse to look up Caroline and Fred Houseman's wills."

"I did that."

Jennie stared at him. "You? You went to the courthouse?" Everything Mike had said and done indicated he hated researching historical material.

He shrugged and gave her half smile. "Guess my family history is all right. Kind of interesting when it's your own. At least the way you do research makes it interesting. And these people, my ancestors? They're like chemical elements. Mix them up differently and you change everything. Take Fred Houseman. He's the trace element that modifies the compound."

Jennie was trying not to let her mouth hang open. "I never thought of history like chemistry. But I suppose there are some similarities."

Mike was nodding, an eyebrow raised appreciatively. "I thought my family was a regular Midwestern family, nothing special. But it's anything but. I already know my great uncle and great grandmother were both right. Fred's a fake. We may never prove it absolutely, but I'm certain. And I'd never have guessed there's a murderer lurking in the family tree."

"A body in the woods isn't typical historical documentation, but it sure points to a murderer."

Mike leaned toward her, green eyes locked on hers. "Which brings me back to my original point. Consider this, Jennie: You found a dead person. Murdered. And it's probably Betsy and she sure as hell wasn't shot by a hunter. That changes the whole project. It's not about a house or a will or even proving the illegitimacy of a family line. It's about someone thinking murder is the solution to their problems."

"But I knew that when I started this research. The only difference is we have an actual gunshot wound showing it was murder." He couldn't cut her out of this now, not after just getting back on it. She had to finish.

Her cell phone rang from the parlor. She reluctantly wound her way past Mike and retrieved the annoying device. Curious, she thought, staring at the caller ID. It was another teacher from Swansea High, one she only occasionally spoke to. She pushed the button to send the call into voice mail and set the phone on the counter.

Mike stood and paced the kitchen. She watched him for a moment, set her jaw and stood in his path.

"Mike," she said, stopping his pacing with a

hand against his chest. "This is the most bizarre research case I've ever had. Frankly, you have weird relatives. And this house is the most incredible house I've ever been in. You are..." she hesitated, feeling his heartbeat under her fingers. "You are the most unique client I think I've ever had. I shouldn't have quit over something you considered outside my area. I still think the answer is out there. Your family tree is so interesting I don't even care if you pay me. Your best bet is to keep an eye on me to make sure I don't get us both in deeper trouble." Feeling the tension in him, she dropped her hand and turned away.

Mike caught her shoulder. As he turned her back around, he caressed her cheek. "Jennie." His voice was soft and dangerously seductive.

She swallowed. If she had quit last week because he had kept a secret from her, she did not want to be the cause of another fight now because she was keeping secrets from him. She needed drastic action.

"Before you shove me out the door, I have something for you." She dashed out to her car, rain beginning to tap on the roof. She grabbed her overnight bag and the paper-wrapped frame she'd placed in the back of her car after picking it up from Russell. He was an excellent framer. For the cost of supplies, he had framed her picture of the Housemans—without asking a whole bunch of questions.

"Here, this is for you," she said as she laid it on the kitchen table when she came back in. She rubbed at a spot on the table to avoid Mike's curious gaze. "It's nothing. Usually I give the client something at the end of the case. I know we're not done yet, but I wasn't certain." She lifted her gaze to his. "And I wanted you to know I never thought anything bad about you leaving HP. That wasn't at all what I was trying to say last week. I still suspect whoever killed your great grandmother might be tied up with the company as well."

She wanted to tell him about Rob right then, but the look in Mike's face undid her. Gone were the hard eyes and gritted teeth. Instead, he was tilting his head and looking at her as if he were seeing her for the first time. She felt ridiculously inadequate, reminding her of her first date.

"I need to take a shower, then you can tell me whether you want me to leave." She started up the stairs and then paused.

"My dad calls on Saturday night," she said, waving toward the cell phone still sitting on the counter. "Let it ring. I'll call him a bit later."

She hopped up the stairs, not waiting to hear a response. She'd tell him about the meeting with Rob when she felt better.

****

Mike considered Jennie's last remarks. He had thought some pretty awful things about her after their argument, but he'd gotten over it a lot faster than he'd thought he would. He'd already spent a considerable amount of time trying to get her out of his head, without success. During class, he'd write her emails he never sent. After practices, he'd check his phone for messages from her. He'd been relieved when she'd called about the secret room, and setting up the archeological site had been a good excuse to be near her.

All this distraction over a woman he thought had no more faith in him than his ex-wife.

Was he that wrong? Perhaps it was time to admit he might be touchy where females were concerned and maybe he had overreacted. Maybe Jennie was exactly as she seemed. He considered the idea thoughtfully.

Finally, he picked up the package Jennie had

left, peeling off the tape and brown paper. Beneath the paper was a portrait of Josef and Marie Houseman, the photo Jennie had found last week. It was a beautifully done historical picture of the couple that meant the most to River Bluffs. He ran his fingers over the elegant frame surrounding Josef and Marie.

Mike scowled at his own uncertainty. Jennie had taken some time to do this, when neither of them had much to spare. He realized she had taken the photo last Sunday, the day *after* she'd quit. He glanced up toward the ceiling, imagining her in the shower. He tried to fight down his growing desire and knew where Jennie was concerned, he was as sure of himself as a beginning T-ball player up to bat for his first time.

With expected regularity, the lights suddenly went out. Mike had forgotten Jennie had said it was raining. She hadn't taken a flashlight or candle, so he would have to take one to her. Blindly moving in the dimly lit room, he found a flashlight and used it to light some candles.

As he lit the candles, a phone rang. Briefly he touched his own phone before realizing it was Jennie's. He glanced at the glowing screen and saw the caller ID. His eyes narrowed and his heart hardened. The name read Robert Houseman.

Chapter 23

Halfway through washing her hair, the lights went out. Jennie barely blinked. She debated whether to get out and voted for finishing despite the dark. Finding the familiar shape of her conditioner, she squeezed some into her palm and rubbed it into her hair.

Pounding on the door startled her.

"Mike?"

"I brought you a flashlight," she heard Mike's muffled voice through the door. "And you got a call."

"Was it my dad?" She rinsed the conditioner out. She couldn't hear the answer and had to ask him to repeat.

His response sounded like a growl. "No, it wasn't your dad. It was Robert Houseman."

A few choice words rolled around in her head, but she managed to maintain a semblance of control.

"About that..." she said, stalling. She grabbed a towel and considered her options. The door was locked, so she could tell him through the door. That seemed cowardly. "Give me a minute to explain."

She wrapped the towel around her body, her hair still dripping on her shoulders. Taking a deep breath, she opened the bathroom door. The hallway was lit with a battery-operated lantern and the flashlight Mike wielded in his hand as he paced. He stopped as soon as she stuck her wet head out the door.

"Well?"

"It's your fault." The words burst out of her mouth. "If you hadn't been so damn prickly when we met Rob last week, I would have told you about my meeting with him a long time ago."

"Meeting?" he grumbled. "You met with that slimeball?"

"Yes, meeting. He wanted me to talk with you, because apparently you won't listen to your own mother and call him. He never suspected you in that stupid funds scandal and he would never have let you quit. He actually admires you, though God only knows why."

"Robert is a liar. He's the one who set me up. He was the only one who had motivation for getting me fired."

"That makes no sense," she said, waving an arm in the air. Her towel loosened and she grabbed at the slipping ends. "If he wanted to fire you, he would. He was the damned president of the company. He didn't have to set you up."

"He wanted to discredit me as well," Mike said, but his voice had dropped and doubt shadowed his words.

The cool hallway forced her to step back into the steamy bathroom. She caught Mike's hesitation outside the doorway, his gaze in the dim lighting trying to look anywhere but at the towel and the skin it didn't cover.

"Yeah, like the president of a half-billion dollar company couldn't call up a few buddies and have you blackballed from the industry. Rob had nothing but nice things to say about you and—whoops!"

Her train of thought derailed as she slipped on a puddle pooling the slick linoleum. With one hand still holding onto the towel, she flapped around uselessly with the other for something to grab onto. Peripherally she was aware of the Mike's flashlight falling to the ground. He cursed and reached out and she caught his hand just as her towel, still clasped against her chest, came unwound. "Mike!"

"Hold on!" In a last ditch attempt to save her from falling, he pulled her toward him, sandwiching the towel that now hung like a useless scarf between them. "You okay?" he asked, his lips nuzzled warmly near her ear and the suspicious sound of laughter tinting his words.

"I seem to have lost my dignity. It appears to be dangling between us." She grimaced as soon as the double entendre slipped out. "The *towel*, I mean."

This time his chest distinctly rumbled with a sound that shifted her awkward feeling.

"Did you *chuckle*? I cannot believe I am in this situation and you're laughing." She lightly thumped his chest, surprised to find herself smiling.

Until his hand dropped lower on her back. Her breath caught, willing his hand to slide lower. A curl of air slipped in the open window, touching wet skin that reacted to the cool breeze. Except the front of her body. Heat blazed with the touch of Mike's clothes, her nipples hard against his shirt.

Mike's cheek rested against her head. She felt him swallow hard, and she realized why. She could feel his erection pressing against her lower belly.

He kissed her head and groaned. "God, Jennie, I want you so bad."

She understood the feeling. She could hear his heart beating a rapid tattoo, feel the threads where her hand rested against his chest, smell his scent. She'd dated her last lover almost two years before they'd finally gone to bed. She wanted Mike with a desire that had turned her blood to white heat and she'd only known him two weeks.

"I can't do this," he said, with a heavy sigh.

What? Her mind rebelled. A man has a naked, willing woman in his arms, and he can't do something about it? If her face wasn't planted against his shoulder, her mouth would have dropped open in shock.

He tilted her head back far enough so she could
see his eyes, green jewels in the small light. "You're
the first woman I've wanted since my divorce. But
I'm not over my marriage. I screwed up so bad and I
don't know what I did wrong. I don't want that to
happen again."

"You're not interested in me," she threw out
flippantly. "That's okay." So this was what rejection
felt like. No wonder guys hated asking and being
turned down. It sucked.

Mike shook his head, running his hand down
her wet hair. "You misunderstand me. I have no
doubt—especially now—that you're sexy and
beautiful. I'm very interested. But you deserve a
whole person, not the unsure, suspicious, doubtful
man I've become. I practically chased you out of the
house last week when you brought up HP and those
missing funds. And look at how I reacted when
Robert called. Running up here to confront you.
Maybe he was calling you because he already heard
the news reports about the skeleton you found. But,
no. I assume you're up to something."

"Not that I'm defending you, but you were right.
I was up to something."

"And I definitely want the whole story. But you
have got to put some clothes on." He emphasized the
last sentence with a groan. "I'm familiar with the
kind of women who wants a man for sex. You are not
one of them."

She sighed, gathering up the towel to wrap it
around her body. He was right. She wanted him. But
the sex wouldn't be enough. The ache in her heart
gave her fair warning. Better to leave Mike alone.

She backed away and tucked in the towel.
"Straight-forward honesty in a man," she muttered.
Then she gave him a lopsided grin as she shut the
door. "Maybe I'll thank you some day, but not
tonight."

****

Mike waited for Jennie in the library.

When she walked in, he was once again overwhelmed with the desire flooding his veins. Unless he could get his head together, he'd be taking a cold shower tonight.

He stood and handed her some papers. "These are the wills I copied. Now, tell me why you were meeting with Robert Houseman." He tilted her chin up with a finger, melting in her warm gaze. As he asked the question, he realized it didn't matter why. If she'd felt she needed to meet with Robert, then she should have.

She frowned at his touch and moved away, then sat down in a chair, folding her bare legs under her. "He was probably calling to see if I'd talked to you. I said I'd try. He wants you back working at HP. He's a really nice man, Mike. I think you've misjudged him. Just as you misjudged me," she added, folding her arms across her chest. "The only reason I didn't tell you sooner about meeting him is because I thought I hurt you last week and I was afraid of hurting you again."

She thought *she* had hurt him? He closed his eyes, sighing heavily. "How is it you can make me feel like an ass by pointing out the obvious?" He dragged a chair around and dropped into it facing her. "You said Rob never blamed me for the funds disappearance?"

"No, in fact he said if he'd known you were going to quit, he would have had you in his office to tell you he didn't believe you were behind it."

"He could be lying. He might be our murderer, trying to throw me off."

"Maybe." Her voice was laced with doubt. "Would you at least think about talking with Rob? Your mother said you loved working at HP. He wants you working there."

Mike sighed. "I don't know who to trust."

"Trust your family. They all love you and would do anything for you. Do you think your mother would want you to talk to Rob if she thought he was up to something? But I get the feeling you've hidden yourself here at River Bluffs to avoid them."

He dropped his chin on his chest. He *was* hiding from his family, but not because of the HP scandal. Everyone in his family made their marriages work and he'd failed. What the hell did he know about family?

"Fine. I need some counseling," he grumbled. "But someone set me up at the company, and if it wasn't Robert, it had to be one of four other people, the only ones who knew my account information."

"Who else, besides Rob?"

"Three of the people in my division: my assistant, Gina Stevens; Jack Elliott..." His voice trailed off. He dropped his head into his hands.

"What?" She leaned forward and touched his arm.

He looked at her, horror creeping down his spine. "Jack's the chemist who died last week. He set me up, either on his own or at someone's request. Nobody may be able to prove it, but he was either murdered or killed himself out of regret."

"Oh, that's bad. But why target you? And if it was suicide, wouldn't he have told someone why he killed himself?"

"Murder, then." Mike shook his head, padding across the worn rug. "If he was murdered..." He ran his hand through his hair. Maybe it was just as well he avoided his family, at least the distant members.

"If it was murder, Mike, you need to tell Robert."

"No, Jennie, I can't. No matter what your opinion, Robert is still a suspect in the overall scheme of things. Let's assume all these murders are related. Betsy died in 1932: neither Robert nor

Veronica nor Charlotte was alive then. That leaves George, Joe and Jacob, of the people we know who are alive today.

"Sue McGregor died in 1968. Our previous three are still our most likely suspects, except it becomes unbelievable Jacob would kill his own daughter. But we can add a few sons and daughters of those three to the list, not the least of who are Robert, Geoffrey, and siblings Richard and Charlotte. Caroline died in 1991, which adds another entire generation of suspects, including Robert's children and Veronica, as well as both Richard and Charlotte's children. And now we have Jack Elliott, who had to have died from an inside job, which eliminates a whole lot of suspects while making this so much more complicated because he directly gains nothing from the company. Insiders are limited to George, Joe, Robert, and Veronica. Charlotte, though she's on the board, is doubtful."

"No, she's still in. She told me at the reunion she had spies in the company. 'Spies' was her term, not mine."

"In other words, we have the same five suspects we had at the beginning of this charade," he said, shaking his head. "The only difference is someone else has died, and we probably found Betsy, who was most likely murdered too."

"We're looking at this wrong, Mike. There's more than one murderer."

Mike stopped pacing, closing his eyes.

"One for Betsy, Sue and Caroline? Another for Jack?"

She shrugged. "Or any combination of the four. But why?"

"Fred Houseman? Would concealing his secret lead to all these people's deaths? We know almost for certain that's true for Sue and Caroline. But why Jack? And why Betsy?"

"Fred is our number one suspect for Betsy, if she found out he wasn't really Fred Houseman. And if Jack was setting you up to get to Veronica, it might be our current murderer has no relation to the imposter issue."

"I feel like we're playing Trivial Pursuit and none of the players can get any of the answers. We just keep going around and around." He walked over to the large window overlooking the expansive lawn, staring into the rainy darkness. He caught Jennie's reflection in the glass and remembered her first day out here. It seemed like he'd known her forever. Those few days she hadn't been around, time had crawled. With her back, the clock was moving again. He knew it would take a miracle to find evidence, even with Jennie on his side. The hunt had him caught, despite knowing he couldn't win.

He turned around. "If I could reverse the calendar a year, I'd call you right away and we could avoid this pressure to find a bunch of murderers running around metropolitan St. Louis."

"I don't think even with a year we would do any better than we're doing now," she said, sighing. "You were supposed to tell me if you were going to let me keep working on your project, with your permission, that is. Because I'll keep working on it one way or another."

"I think you had a very good point about keeping an eye on you. You're stubborn enough you'll keep stirring the pot, won't you?"

Jennie shrugged, a smile at the corner of her mouth.

"Fine. Keep searching. But you better tell me every move you make."

Jennie saluted. "Yes, sir!"

"That's more like it. Some respect." He grinned. "Now, about tonight. You can have my bed. It's the only one with a decent mattress. I'll take one of the other rooms."

"I slept on one of those other beds. You won't sleep a wink tonight. Why don't we share? If you're worried about your virtue, you can put a pillow between us."

His failed marriage had reduced to him to sleeping with a good-looking woman with no sex. Would he survive the night with Jennie next to him?

He buried his indecision. "We'll see."

Mike tromped up the stairs to the bathroom. The cold shower did not help him reach any momentous decisions. But when he walked into his bedroom half an hour later to retrieve a pillow fully intending to sleep somewhere else, he saw Jennie curled on her side, her face innocent in sleep.

Something inside him released and he knew he had to sleep next to her. He didn't need sex with her. He needed to smell her, feel her warmth next to him, know she was there for him.

Dragging an extra pillow from the closet shelf, he stared at the wisps of hair framing her face. He shook his head and tossed the pillow back in the closet, sliding under the blankets. He brushed a kiss on her cheek and wrapped an arm around her waist, before cocooning his body next to hers and drifting into a deep sleep.

Chapter 24

Stretching, Jennie sucked in a long breath. For the first time in a while she was well-rested. A warm body cuddled next to her. She knew Mike had slept in the same bed last night, his arm wrapped around her and the heat from his body keeping the chilly spring night at bay. Her insides melted at the memory. But this morning, he either had really bad whiskers or it was Zippy. She opened her eyes to the fuzzy dog, who happily slobbered all over her face.

Not quite the morning kiss she was looking for. She hugged the dog, scratching him behind the ears as he whined in satisfaction.

Sitting up quickly, she confirmed Mike had slept next to her. Dropping back into bed, she shook her head in confusion. He wasn't ready for a relationship, but he could sleep—platonically—with her?

She padded down to the bathroom to improve a bit on her morning image, then trudged down to the kitchen.

"Hi, beautiful. How are you feeling this morning?" Mike greeted her, a measuring cup in one hand and a bowl of pancake batter in the other.

"Hungry. And you?"

He grinned. "Slept like a log." He caught her around the waist and gave her a quick kiss. "Thanks. I needed last night."

She stared at him. "What? A bed warmer? We didn't do anything."

"No, for listening. And understanding. I know I'm not making this easy."

217

With her head in the refrigerator looking for something to drink, she muttered, "That's for sure."

"I heard that. Juice is on the table if that's what you're looking for."

Jennie's cell phone rang from where she'd left it last night. The ringing reminded her she would have to call Rob back at some point.

"Hi, Mae. What's up?"

"Jennie!" Mae's voice was loud enough Mike could hear her. "What in the world are you doing?"

Jennie looked at Mike, and shrugged. "I don't know, Mae. What am I doing?"

"You're in the paper, girl. You found a skeleton on that archeological field trip of yours. Why didn't you call me?"

Jennie winced. Under normal circumstances, she would have called Mae right away. But last night was not normal. "Uh, I didn't know you liked skeletons? What's the article say?"

Jennie put Mae on speaker phone while she read.

Field Trip Students Find Skeleton

Swansea High School Archeological Club students discovered a skeleton during a field trip yesterday.

Detective Dave Hoffman of the Caseyville Police Department said they received a call at 2:30 p.m. from Dr. Jennie Foster, a Swansea High School teacher and the club advisor, saying the group had found a skeleton and a gun.

"It's too early to speculate who this might be or why the person died," Detective Hoffman said. "We can't rule out accident, suicide or murder at this point. However, it does appear the body has been here for some time."

Students were practicing archeological skills on an estate in the Caseyville area.

Dr. Foster was unavailable for comment.

Jennie clicked off the speaker and wandered into the parlor to continue her conversation with Mae. "Sounds pretty factual. That's pretty much how it went, except they missed the part about all the mud, thorns, and bugs we had to navigate to get to the location."

"Did your students dig it up?"

"No. I had a friend's dog with me and he found it. He led us to the skeleton."

Mae was silent a moment, and Jennie had the eerie feeling Mae had reached another conclusion. She confirmed it soon enough. "Is the dog Mike's? What's this remote estate in Caseyville stuff anyway?"

"Mae, you're getting into murky territory."

"You can't tell me whose dog it was?"

"Fine. It's Mike's dog. But I can't tell you where we are." Jennie's eyes widened. "Uh, where we were."

"He's there with you, isn't he? Did you spend the night with him?"

"Mae!"

"Okay. But you be careful, girl. I worry about you."

"Thanks, Mae. But really, I'm fine."

Shutting her phone, Jennie found Mike eating the pancakes and bacon he'd made.

"Mae knows," she said, putting pancakes on a plate. Mike raised an eyebrow. "She told me she and your dad used to be in band together, and she knew your dad was a Houseman descendant."

"She just told you this?"

"No. That I learned last weekend when her husband talked about working at HP. But what I mean is I think she knows about River Bluffs."

"How would she know about River Bluffs? I don't even think my dad knows about this place."

"I don't know. Mae just *knows* things. Her

family is bigger and older than your family in this area. And she's a repository of information you can't believe."

"Do you think she would tell anyone?"

"Mae's like a sister to me, and sometimes a mother. She wouldn't intentionally do anything to hurt me. But she said 'be careful.' Why would she say that if she didn't suspect something?"

"She said something similar to me a few days ago."

"What? You were talking to Mae?"

"Apparently she's everywhere," Mike said dryly. "She's found me twice since I hired you for this job, mostly to make sure I was taking care of you."

Jennie laughed. "Mae and you. I wish I'd been there. The lion and the tiger meeting for a friendly chat."

He snorted. "Mae does not make me feel like a ferocious beast. More like a mouse about to be eaten."

****

They'd spent the day cleaning up the archeology site and working in the attic. While loading their supplies into the cars, Mike's cell phone rang.

"It's my mom," Mike said apologetically, and answered the phone.

"Oh, hi, Mom. Yes, that's the Jennie Foster I brought to the reunion last week. She's a history teacher, Mom. Archeology has a lot to do with history." He eyed Jennie with a cocky grin. "Why don't you ask her yourself? She's right here. I was helping her clean up her archeology dig."

Jennie took the phone Mike shoved at her, staring at him in disbelief.

"Jennie. Did you really find a skeleton yesterday?"

"Yes, Mrs. Garretson. Though we didn't dig it up. Mike's dog found it."

"Call me Linda. So Zippy, that funny little dog of Mike's, found it? Where were you doing this dig?"

"It's this old estate owned by a *friend* of mine," Jennie said, crinkling her nose at Mike. He tried to grab the phone, but she turned away. "You should meet this *friend*. You might like him, since he's into history too."

"I teach fifth grade, so we don't get to do interesting things like you high school teachers. If you ever go on another dig, call me, would you? That would be so exciting, and I'd love to meet your friend."

"I can always use another adult chaperone, so I'll take you up on that. Let me put Mike back on." She handed the phone back to him, smiling smugly.

"Okay. Love you. Bye." Mike ended the call and snapped the lid closed, failing to keep the annoyed look on his face. "What was that? A friend?"

"That was revenge for sticking me on the phone with your mom." Jennie cocked an eyebrow at Mike. "By the way, I'd like to be there when you tell her about this monster house. Ought to be a show and a half."

"Don't remind me. However, unless you can find me some proof, I won't have to tell her anything, since the house will never be mine."

She snorted. "A challenge just up my alley. I'll find that evidence, and take front seats to see you tell your mom you've been keeping secrets from her."

He wrapped his arm around her waist and pulled her in for a quick, chaste kiss on the lips. His touch left her knees weak.

"You find that evidence, and I'll invite the entire family for you to watch."

"Deal," she murmured, climbing into her car. But she'd rather have Mike's kisses than his family.

Chapter 25

"We're very proud our students at Swansea High School have wonderful education opportunities like Dr. Foster's archeology field trip," recited principal Ron Schuy. His well-modulated voice gave all the proper educational quotes for the TV crews.

Standing in a location well-removed from the cameras, Mike couldn't help but wonder how long it had taken his boss to memorize the statement. He could see Jennie waiting her turn before the cameras, wearing a forest green two-piece suit, while not the most stylish, that set off her red-brown hair, curling loosely around her shoulders. The lacy shirt underneath didn't quite dip far enough to reveal cleavage. Sighing, he reigned in his thoughts.

Turned out he'd only gotten one thing right about Dr. Jennie Foster. She was definitely the best researcher he could have hired. But he never would have guessed she was beautiful and sexy. His body was beginning to feel the stress of being around a woman he found hot. But he kept thinking of his failed marriage. Veronica had made his game record with commitment 0-1. Simple coaching strategy. He could practice, but he wasn't about to play again until he figured out how he'd lost the first round. And Jennie was not practice material.

Ron introduced Jennie, but rather than continue the principal's contrived press conference, she offered the three reporters an opportunity to talk to her and her students separately, a choice that was preferred over the mass questioning. She glided from one interview to the next, manipulating the interviews over to the students so quickly it was unlikely her face would even appear on the news.

Mike realized she had come up with the perfect method of avoiding the difficult questions. By splitting the interviews, she gave each TV crew less time with her, and by turning the interviews over to the students, the reporters couldn't get answers the students didn't have. He shook his head, amazed.

"That was brilliant," he whispered as he followed her out to her car.

She grinned. "Like it? When your dad's an Army general, you learn how to bend the truth through deflection, avoidance, and manipulation. Dealing with the media is much the same. In fact, that was way less scary than the interrogation I got after my first date."

"I'll remember that. I see you did a couple of interviews yesterday too."

She snorted. "My answering machine was packed with calls from newspapers, TV stations, friends, the principal, people I barely know, people I've talked with once, and archeologist Dr. Wilkie. He was really impressed. And I had to call my dad, in case he heard about it in Texas. Then I finally started answering the media calls. Let me tell you, phone interviews are easier than this media fiasco. They couldn't see the faces I was making as I contorted the truth into something I could tell them." She waved over her shoulder at the lingering crowd. "I had a hard time keeping a straight face for this circus."

"I'm impressed. I think you have a future in public relations if you decide not to teach anymore."

She shuddered. "I feel like a wet rag right now. I was so nervous. I can't imagine doing that on a regular basis."

"Even more reason to consider the field. You looked like a pro." He squeezed her hand reassuringly, and quickly dropped it. "What do you have on for tonight?"

"I have study guides to grade, but they're the students who are going for extra credit as the rest of the class won't turn theirs in until Wednesday. And I still have to get through that packet of Pennsylvania stuff and those notes Jacob sent me. I've been reluctant to start on them because they're all stuck together." As she finished her answer, she started to ask him a question. The look on his face made her pause. "That's not what you meant, is it?"

"Not really." Not at all. He had been thinking about her warm body next to his. The whole day was kind of fuzzy, since his mind seemed to be stuck on Saturday night's strange events. For a guy trying to keep his pants on, he was doing a lousy job.

"We could work together tonight," Jennie suggested. "You have ball practice. Want to come over afterward?"

"Sure." Relief flooded through him. For an instant, he thought his standoffish attitude might have scared her off. "You know I'm not going to be here Friday for the deadline. I'll be up in Springfield for the state championships."

"What if I find something at the last minute?"

Mike sighed. "As if that'll happen. But if fate suddenly favors me, I'll leave you with Rick's address and phone number."

"I'm still searching. I don't want you to lose River Bluffs either. It's a special house."

As they neared her car, they both stopped short, Jennie drawing in a shocked breath. The back window on the driver's side was smashed in. She let out a un-teacher like word.

"My briefcase is gone!" she cried, staring at the shattered glass littering her back seat. "We were barely out of sight of the parking lot and I was expecting to make a quick break for home after the media interviews. There were papers to grade and my laptop in that case. What am I going to do?"

Mike swallowed a sick feeling. "Didn't you have your work on the Housemans on there?" he choked.

"Yes. But I have that on back-up at home," she said. "But what am I going to do without my laptop, my email addresses, my schedule? And look at my car."

He sighed with relief, grabbing her face and kissing her hard on the lips. "That's easy. Your insurance will cover a new window and a new laptop, and you upload the back-up."

Jennie touched her lips, frowning. "Hey, what happened to low key?"

"I didn't account for you losing all your work. How did I find someone smart enough to back up her work, and beautiful enough to make Veronica jealous?"

"Veronica's jealous of me?" The surprised look on Jennie's face was classic. He kissed her again to reassure her she was equal to anything Veronica could put out.

"She did. She accused me of sleeping with you. Little does she know. C'mon. You need to get Officer Riley to come out here and I need to get to my practice. I think my assistant coaches are beginning to wonder if I'm still the coach."

"Go. But do you know anything about computers? I'll need it ASAP, and frankly, I know as much about computers as I do about cars."

"Sure. We'll go shopping for a new computer tonight and I'll hook it up for you."

****

"Jennie, you have a call." The front office administrator transferred the call to Jennie's classroom phone.

"Thanks," she said, and waited for the line to click over.

She hoped this wasn't an irate parent. After last night's binge computer buy, today had been rough. The students who had turned their review test guides in early, learned they were not getting them back, thanks to thieves. She'd hit them up with what she thought was a really easy quiz to make up for the missing grade. She'd almost had a mutiny. Just a typical school day.

She was rubbing her aching head when a deep, raspy voice said, "Dr. Foster?"

"Yes?" she replied, expecting an introduction.

"I have your laptop and I know what you've been doing."

She sat up straight, headache momentarily forgotten. "What are you talking about?" she tried to keep the alarm out of her voice.

"You're playing with fire. I know who killed Sue McGregor, and I know who killed Caroline Garretson."

"Who is this?" she asked, wishing she wasn't alone in her classroom.

"If you keep playing in the Houseman's family history, I know who will kill you. If you know what's good for you, stay away from Mike Garretson."

The phone went dead.

Chapter 26

Jennie dropped the phone in its cradle, staring at it with shock. Then her eyes narrowed and she glared at the phone, as if she could drag the caller into the room through the phone lines. Anger seeded her muscles.

"Coward," she said to the phone, her body trembling. She glanced at her closed classroom door.

Oh, come on, she chided herself. No one was sitting outside her classroom with an axe.

Mike was the only one she could talk to about the call and he was at baseball practice right now. Did she need to tell him right this minute? No. Although if someone really was threatening her, she could call in the police.

Breathe slowly. Don't panic. She willed herself to relax. It was a phone call. She could think this through.

The caller had admitted Sue and Caroline had been murdered. Who was this caller and how would he know who killed these people unless he did it?

She closed her eyes, rubbing at her forehead. The caller was her laptop thief. Someone knew she was researching the Houseman family. It had to be someone who knew about River Bluffs and who also had been at the reunion. Supposedly, the only people who knew of the house's existence would be George, Joe and Jacob, and maybe Robert or Charlotte. If she was going to go to extremes, Mae Jefferson was as suspect as anyone. Jennie wouldn't put it past Mae to have actually visited River Bluffs.

The voice on the phone did not sound like the

raspy voices of any of the elderly suspects, though it did sound disguised. Not to mention that picturing George or Joe beating out her car window at a high school filled with teenagers didn't fit. However, either of them could be paying to have their dirty work done.

To ease her mind, she tried to figure out what had changed with that call. The person knew Sue McGregor and Caroline Garretson had been murdered—but so did Jennie and Mike. The difference was this guy knew the murderer, or was the murderer.

She leaned back, digesting the information. Whoever it was, wasn't going to kill her at that moment. She might as well head home. She called Mike's cell phone and left a short message to call her when he was done with practice.

****

Jennie jumped when the doorbell rang, showing that her earlier bravado had faded. But when she peeked out the window and saw Mike holding the pizza he'd offered to bring, her stomach rumbled. She was more hungry than scared.

She opened the door and Mike leaned in to capture her lips in his.

"Pizza and a kiss? Are we dating?" she asked, paying as little attention as possible to the blood racing around her body.

Mike shrugged, a smile at the corners of his mouth. "Just a client-professional relationship. Isn't this how your other clients treat you?"

"I think you're thinking of some other kind of business."

"Maybe it's a new marketing technique you should consider." He set the pizza on the table. "So what's up?"

"It appears we are found out. Whoever took my laptop yesterday was not out for goods. He wanted

228

the information on it. He called me after school today."

"What?" All traces of humor vanished in the concern written on his face.

"I'm sure it's nothing. Well, maybe it's something." She repeated the mostly one-sided conversation to him.

As she told him the story, his mouth drew into a thin line and his eyes darkened. He ran a hand through his thick, dark brown hair.

"He also said I was to stay away from you."

"Damn it," he said with gritted teeth. He turned and walked to the front window of the living room.

"That's it. I'm going to Rick. We're shutting this down," Mike said.

"No, we're okay," she countered. "I've thought about this. The caller said he knew who had murdered Caroline and Sue, not that *he* murdered them. Maybe this was a friendly reminder. Besides, if we stop now, a murderer gets away. Someone tried to hurt you, someone tried to hurt Veronica, and now someone's threatening me. What if he had something to do with Jack Elliott's death? What if he kills again?"

Mike crossed the room and halted in front of her, catching her hand in his. His thumb caressed the inside of her palm. "Jennie, it's not about me. I don't want *you* getting hurt. The house is beautiful, it has wonderful history. But you're way more important."

A hard knot lodged in her throat. She licked her lips, concentrating on her reply instead of the thumb rubbing her palm. River Bluffs was important to Mike, in spite of what he said, and she wasn't going to let it go because of a phone call.

"You've only got until Friday. That's only four more days." She wrapped the fingers of her free hand around his wrist and locked her eyes on his.

"The caller never has to know I'm still looking. I've got research here, the Pennsylvania stuff and Sue McGregor's notes. As for the house, that place is so isolated, and with Zippy on patrol, we would know if someone besides ourselves was there. Not that we're going to get out there before Friday anyway."

Mike pulled out one of the table chairs, sat down heavily and dropped his head into his hand, rubbing his forehead. Jennie wrapped her arms around his neck, leaning over to press her cheek next to his. Her next suggestion nearly stuck in her throat.

"And we just don't see each other for the next few days." As she said it, she thought moving to another state would be easier.

He shifted in the chair and pulled her onto his lap. "Not see each other?" He hesitated, looking in her eyes. "Fine. I hope to hell I don't regret this. You'll call me if anything strange happens?"

He kissed her and she knew she was going to be sorry for her suggestion.

"I'll call you if I find the evidence too." She slid her hand down his muscled arm and he nestled his nose into her neck, planting a kiss that sent shivers down her spine.

She pulled back, wanting more and yet reluctant to go forward if Mike wasn't fully committed. "You know, for a guy who wants to remain celibate, you are pushing all the wrong buttons." She poked him in the chest. "Besides, I have a hundred and fifty quizzes to grade."

He sighed, reluctantly letting Jennie stand. "Finals can't be here soon enough. I have about the same number of study guides to go through. And I have to come up with a sub plan for Friday when we go to playoffs."

"That'll work good, because it will be another day we won't be together. You'll be in Springfield, won't you?" She opened the pizza box and placed two pieces on a plate for Mike and another for her.

"I was kind of hoping you'd come."

She stopped in mid-chew. "Really?" She didn't add the last thought, "As a date?" The idea spun around in her head because she was pretty sure that wasn't what Mike meant.

"You don't have to. I mean, I'm going up with the team early Friday morning so we can check out the fields, practice a bit. Game's not till evening. If we win, we'll stay overnight and play again Saturday morning in the semi-finals."

"You'll be in a hotel with the team Friday night?"

"If we win."

She watched him, realizing he wasn't putting the pieces together. She'd be somewhere in the stands during the game, somewhere else in Springfield if she stayed overnight. He'd be with the team—on a bus, at the game and at the hotel. Definitely not a date.

"How about I come up on Saturday if you make the semi-finals? Then I can take what we've got to that lawyer of yours on Friday, and spin it into a plausible case for keeping your house."

"You can do that?"

"We call it a preponderance of evidence in the research world. It's like building a case off circumstantial evidence. Lawyers do it all the time. Let's see if it works on the Houseman genealogy."

"Sounds like a plan. I'm worried about one other thing," Mike said. "Paul Garretson's will expires on Friday, right?"

Jennie nodded. She would have no reason to be around Mike after that. She had to find something for that lawyer. Mike had suggested she could help rebuild River Bluffs. But she had to find that evidence first.

"But Josef Houseman's will wasn't so limited. I

have no intention of keeping you on after Paul's will expires. But what if our caller, or the murderer, or whoever is interested in this research you're doing, doesn't know you've stopped? They think I've hired you because of Josef's will, not Paul's."

"Good question. I suppose we could take what we know to the police then. Let them deal with it."

He nodded in agreement. "The house goes on the auction block, the police come in and investigate, and there's nothing left to encourage more murders."

And she'd never see him again. "I guess that's one way of looking at it."

They finished up the pizza. Mike's cell phone rang as she took the pizza box out back to the garbage. When she came back in, his forehead was scrunched with concern. "That was George Houseman."

"What? Does he call you often?"

"No-o-o," he said, drawing out the word. "He's never called me. Even the reunion invites come through my mom. He wants to talk to me…and to you."

She stared at Mike. "Do you think this is a set up? Maybe he's involved in the laptop theft."

Mike shook his head. "I don't know what to make of it. He said he wanted to tell me—you—some family history. He said he had reason to believe you were working on the Houseman genealogy. He knows you have your own historical research business." He paused, giving Jennie a concerned look. "I can't be certain, Jennie, but he sounded worried."

"Worried about what? Us? Or someone else? He's a prime suspect," she said with irritation. She dropped onto her living room couch and gave out a heavy woof of air. "Well, one would presume the person who threatened me wasn't George, or he wouldn't be asking us to meet with him together."

"Or he's going to kill us as soon as we walk in the door. However, why warn us and then invite us for tea?" Mike remained standing with his phone still in his hand. "You said the caller mentioned Sue McGregor and Caroline?"

"Yes," she said, tilting her head, waiting to see where he was going.

"But he didn't say anything about Betsy or Jack, did he? We don't know for certain Jack was murdered. But Betsy..." Mike's voice trailed off. They were both silent a moment, running over the possibilities.

"Back to the two murderers possibility," Jennie said. "Betsy was most likely killed by the Fred Houseman imposter, so whoever killed Sue and Caroline might not even know about it. But all three were probably killed for knowing something about the imposter. But why would someone murder Jack Elliott? He couldn't have anything to do with the Houseman family history, could he?"

"You're right. Jack was killed for knowing something about the company, probably the melanoma research, if Veronica's to be believed. Which means he's working with the person who wanted my account sabotaged." Mike cursed softly, rubbing his eyes tiredly. "You know you were right."

She shook her head at him in confusion. "About?"

"When you accused me of withholding information from you about the missing funds." He sat down on the couch next to her. "I didn't think my work at HP had anything to do with the Houseman family. I thought it was a personal vendetta of Robert against me because I had married Veronica. I've been a real jackass," he said, throwing his head back against the couch.

Jennie patted his knee.

"Yes, you have," she agreed helpfully, smiling at

his epiphany. "So, we go see George?"

"We don't seem to have a choice," Mike said, shrugging. He looked at his watch and stood. "I'd better get going. School will still happen tomorrow morning. We'll meet George Thursday after my practice, about six. Can you manage the time?"

"Sure. I don't have a state-bound archeology club to tend to," she said, getting up also. Mike wrapped his arms around her and kissed her. She felt her blood heating up again. He was making it very difficult to keep her distance, not to mention her perspective.

"Lock this," he ordered, pointing at the door. She nodded, kissed him once more, and shut and locked the door behind him.

She watched him back out of her driveway from the living room window, giving him a wave as he drove down the street. Then she peered up and down the street, looking for that strange car. Nothing struck her as unusual.

That call had definitely shaken her up, but having Mike on her side was encouraging. They had a plan and she was comfortable with it until Saturday. She didn't want to think about losing River Bluffs and Mike both in the same day. Going to the baseball game would be one way of showing him she was interested in him, if he was ever ready to go the next step.

She plowed her way through the quizzes she'd given today, red pen flying. She still wanted to look at Sue McGregor's notes Jacob had sent her. About eight-thirty, she finished grading and picked up a letter knife, using it to gently peel apart the notes. She flipped on the early news, and continued the delicate work, reading each new page for anything useful.

A small movement in the corner of her eye caught her attention a short while later. She looked up at the picture window at the front of the house and swore she saw a face slide out of view. A reflection from the TV, or her imagination?

She walked over to the window, craning her neck to see. One of neighbors was getting her toddler out of a car seat a couple houses down. Encouraged, she opened the front door, standing on the stoop to scan the neighborhood.

"Hi, Kelly. Hey, Emma," she hollered to the mother and daughter. Kelly offered some reply that was lost in the sound of car passing on a nearby street.

As the neighbors vanished into their home, Jennie turned to go in—and spotted the masked face at the corner of her house.

"Hey, you!" Startled eyes blinked at her and then disappeared. Some kid playing a prank on her? Not unusual this close to the end of the year. She raced to the corner and caught sight of a short person running across her yard.

He was trying to scramble up the neighbor's fence.

"You'll get expelled if you do anything bad," she yelled at the kid, chasing after him.

He fell backward with a thump and Jennie was halfway across the yard before he stood and looked at her, his lips an "O" of panic in the black ring of the mask.

"Listen," Jennie lectured in her sternest teacher voice. "I don't want to know who you are. But you can't go around messing with teachers. There's only a week of school left. You don't want to get suspended or expelled now. Do you understand?"

He was only an inch or two shorter than her, but much stockier than she'd expect a teenager to be. He suddenly lunged for the ground, scooping up a broken tree branch and swinging it. Jennie had no time to react, the stick smashing against her head.

She dropped to her knees, stunned.

He cursed, dropping the stick and taking a step toward Jennie. "I'm sorry!" cried her attacker in a hoarse whisper. "I didn't want to hurt you. Stay away from Mike or he'll get hurt too."

Holding her head, Jennie caught his gaze before he sprinted off. In spite of the mask, his eyes looked sad.

She dropped back on her heels. Her attacker was the caller. He had to be. But what did he mean, he didn't want her hurt? He'd clobbered her with a stick. If he was trying to keep her from getting hurt, he was doing a lousy job of it.

She wobbled to her feet. She needed to call the police and call Mike. She stumbled around to the front door, still standing open. Closing it behind her, she leaned against it heavily and threw the deadbolt.

When she finally felt more stable on her feet, she called the police, who promised to send a squad car around. Like they were going to be able to do anything. What was she going to tell them? She was doing this historical research and someone wanted to kill her? They'd think she was a loony.

After taking some pain medication and filling a plastic bag with ice for her head, she dialed Mike's cell phone. It rang until she thought it would click over to voice mail, when a sultry female voice answered.

"Jennie Foster. How nice to be talking to you again," Veronica Houseman said sweetly.

Chapter 27

Mike flipped another chemistry study guide over, grimacing at the small handwriting on the next paper. Only a small stack of the papers remained, so it looked like he might get a decent night's sleep yet.

If he could get his mind off Jennie. Four days till the deadline. Maybe five till he could see her safely again. He stared at his cell phone sitting on the table next to him, not picking it up and calling Jennie like he wanted to. Besides, what was his fascination with her anyway? For someone who was supposed to be avoiding the female gender, his actions—and reaction—to her were out of character.

Zippy barked at the doorbell ringing. Mike frowned when he opened the door to find his ex-wife there for the second time in two weeks. Zippy immediately backed away, a low rumble issuing from his throat.

"Veronica," Mike finally said by way of acknowledgement. He did not invite her in, but she didn't let that bother her.

"I need to talk with you," she said, leaning forward and kissing Mike full on the lips. He remained impassive as she dragged a manicured fingernail down the side of his face. "Can I come in?" She didn't wait for his answer, pushing open the door and sliding past him.

"What is it now?" he asked, trying to keep the irritation out of his voice. "I have a lot of work to do. We have finals next week and I have a baseball tournament this weekend."

"I've been thinking about us," she said, pouting.

"We should never have divorced. I miss you so much." She rested a hand on his chest, her head down but with eyes looking pleadingly at him.

Mike pulled her hand, cold as ice, off his shirt. Crossing his arms, he tried to keep the anger from his voice. "It's over, Veronica. What do you really want?"

She sat down on the couch, so he took the armchair nearby. Nonplussed, she stood and sat down on the arm. Her knees butted up next to his. Mike pressed back as far away from her as he could, surprised at his own sudden intense dislike of this woman.

"It's HP," she said, her face twisted in distaste. "It's getting worse. You know Jack Elliott? Charlotte Wainwright called in the cops because she suspected Jack might have been murdered. Did you know Jack and Charlotte went to school together? They've been friends for years. And Robert has called in an independent investigation team to look at the melanoma research results. My whole department is up in arms." She drew in a sob. "Mike, Robert hates me! I swear he is behind all these horrible things going on at the company. Has he tried to talk to you? I think he'll use any method of getting to me, even through our relationship." She frowned, dabbing at her eye with a finger.

Jack and Charlotte? His mind buzzing, Mike used Veronica's dramatics as an excuse to extricate himself. "I'll get a tissue," he offered, pushing up out of the chair and nearly knocking her off. He found Veronica wanting when compared to a woman who looked good to him with mud all over her. He was nuts. Veronica had been his dream girl: blond, elegant, smart. So why was his brain thinking auburn hair, tall, and almost nerdy?

He handed Veronica the tissue. "Thank you," she whispered, standing when Mike did not sit down next to her again. She draped her arms around his shoulders, her head cradled against his chest. Mike patted her back unenthusiastically, doing his best to keep distance between them.

"Did you talk to Joe, like I suggested?" he asked her.

"Yes, of course," she said, pushing slightly back to look up at him. "But Grandpa is eighty years old, and he has less influence on the company than he should. Anytime he tries to help me, George reminds him he owns half the company. It's so awful there I've started thinking about going to another company. What do you think?"

"About you leaving HP?" Mike asked incredulously. Veronica lived for HP, an achievement that certainly wouldn't happen if she went to work elsewhere. "Don't you think another drug company would have problems hiring someone with the last name of Houseman, a known heir to Houseman Pharmaceuticals?"

"I know. I know," she said, sighing, sliding a hand down his shirt to fiddle with a button. "I don't know what to do. I'm a chemist. What else can I do?"

"You could teach," Mike said, realizing as soon as he said it that Veronica would not survive a day in a classroom. She was less a chemist than a dictator, at least according to her department coworkers.

She shook her silky hair. "No. You have the ability to get along with anyone. I am not so fortunate."

She was right there. Few people could tolerate her, especially Robert Houseman. Mike had always thought Rob was off-base when it came to Veronica. Jennie had opened his eyes to other possibilities.

Was Robert right about Veronica?

Mike managed to extricate himself from Veronica's arms, and this time retreated to his small dining area, where he sat down. Of course Veronica followed him, but short of sitting on his lap, she could not invade his space as easily.

"Veronica, I really don't have any suggestions," Mike said, aggravated. "I don't have any influence with Robert, and he certainly hasn't sought my advice." Mike hesitated, thinking of Jennie's unanswered call from Robert. Mike could call the company's president anytime he chose. But not for Veronica.

That thought was among his calculations on how to get Veronica out of his house when his phone rang. He automatically looked at the caller ID at the same time Veronica leaned over to read it as well.

Jennie Foster. Not good, not good at all.

"Aren't you going to answer it, Mike?" Veronica's calm tone was matched with a cool smile.

"No—" he started to say, but Veronica snapped up the phone and placed it to her ear.

"Jennie Foster. How nice to be talking to you again," Veronica said, her eyes holding Mike's in a dare. "It's me, Mike's wife, well, ex-wife, Veronica."

Mike snatched the phone out of Veronica's hand. "Uh, hi, Jennie," he said blankly. Two things ran through his mind: Jennie is not going to understand why Veronica is here, followed closely by Veronica is a Houseman and could pass this call on to someone who would really care.

"Did those notes I loaned you on Dmitri Mendeleev, inventor of the periodic table, help you?"

"Mike? Can we talk?" Jennie's voice was puzzled.

"No, no. Now's not a good time. You can bring the notes to my class tomorrow. I don't need them tonight." Would she understand what he was saying?

"She's listening, isn't she?"

"I'm sure." He threw Veronica a placating smile.

She was leaning against the kitchen bar, her stiletto heels crossed at the ankle.

"Okay. Then we'll talk later."

"You bet. See you tomorrow," he said cheerfully, closing the phone.

Veronica's brown eyes studied him intently.

"Listen, Veronica. I wish I could do more for you, but I'm not your best resource for help." All signs of the drama earlier were gone. Mike did not like the glint in her eyes that replaced the tears.

"Well," she said, picking up the purse she'd dropped earlier. "At least I got to see you, and talking has been such a relief. You don't know how much you've helped me tonight," she said leaning in again and giving him a cool kiss.

Mike breathed out in relief as she left, waiting until the sound her car engine faded. Then he opened his cell phone to call Jennie.

Chapter 28

The police arrived at the same time as her cell phone rang.

"Mike, the police just got here. Can you hold on?" Jennie asked, twisting the deadbolt.

"The police?"

She winced at the shock in his voice. "Wait. I'm telling this all wrong. I'm okay. Give me a second."

She welcomed the two officers and asked them for a second to talk on the phone.

"I've got to give a statement, so real quick. Here's the story. I thought some student was pranking my house, only it turned out to be the same guy that called earlier—at least I think it was, since his voice sounded the same. Anyway, he hit me with a stick when I chased him—"

"He hit you?"

"Yeah, I'm fine. It was just a bump, and now the police are here. I've got to tell them what happened."

"I'm coming over."

"No!" That was the last thing he should do. Her attacker might still be watching.

"Yes. I'm not leaving you alone one more minute."

She eyed the cops, who waited patiently on her couch. She wanted Mike here. Apparently it was just as dangerous to have him with her as it was to be alone.

"Okay. Come to the back door. Don't park on my street and don't let anyone see you. Call me when you get here so I know it's you."

"It's that bad?"

"I don't know, but I don't want to make it worse. If this guy's still hanging around, he can't see you."

"Okay. I'm on my way. You stay safe."

"I've got two cops in my living room. I'll be fine." And then it slipped out. "Why was Veronica at your house?"

Crap. She wasn't going to ask. It wasn't any of her business.

"Giving me more information about what's going on at HP. I'll explain when I get there."

Jennie had finished giving her statement and showing the officers where she'd been attacked when Mike called again.

"I'm just about done here. Can you wait a few more minutes?"

"Sure. I'm outside your kitchen door."

As soon as she'd locked her front door behind the police, she unlocked the back door and found Mike crouched against the wall, a lumpy duffel bag and Zippy beside him. Zippy gave her an enthusiastic greeting before Mike stood and pulled her into his arms.

"Are you all right? Did he hurt you?"

With his arms wrapped around her, she felt the tension roll off her shoulders. She hadn't even realized how stressed she was until he touched her.

"Just a bruise on the side my head." She led him and Zippy into the house, the dog off to examine the new smells.

Mike gently probed the wound when she showed it to him, his fingers delicately moving aside the mass of hair to find the bruise. Warm shivers slid along her skin.

He sighed. "Not even broken skin," he announced after the examination.

"This is going to sound weird, but I don't think he meant to hurt me. He said he was sorry the instant he hit me."

"He apologized?"

"Yes. And his wording was strange too. He didn't want us to be hurt, not that *he* would hurt us if we kept doing this."

Mike shook his head. "Odd. And why is he targeting you? Why not me? I'm the one who hired you."

She laughed, Mike raising an eyebrow in puzzlement. "He's my height, maybe an inch shorter, and a lot heavier. He might be afraid to take you on. I'm more his size."

"You should be more concerned about this. You mentioned knowing how to fire an M-16 rifle? Can you use it on him?"

"Yes. But, dang. I left mine at Dad's." She wrapped her arms around his waist and hugged him. "I think it's sweet you're so worried. And I know you weren't there, but this guy isn't the murderer. He's covering up for the murderer."

Mike grudgingly agreed she was right.

"What's in the duffel?" she asked.

"I'd like to stay, Jennie. I won't sleep if I know you're here alone. And if I can't stay, then you need to keep Zippy. He'll hear every movement for miles around. No one will get near you."

The part of her that her father had raised to be independent and strong balked. But the part of her missing her grandmother's hugs and kisses melted. He wanted to protect her. That was sweeter than anything a man had given her.

"I won't be a problem," he said, holding onto her hand and looking into her eyes. "I'll sleep on the couch, the floor, wherever you want me."

Wherever? This was not a good idea. She knew exactly where he could sleep, but there wouldn't be much sleeping going on.

"You'll have to leave pretty early in the morning, in case anyone's watching the house." It was the only excuse she could come up with to send him away.

"I was planning on it. I'll have to take Zippy home anyway."

"Then I guess it's settled." Her stomach flip-flopped. He wouldn't sleep if he wasn't with her, and she wasn't going to sleep with him here.

She gazed at her small couch and at Mike's six-foot-plus frame.

"You could share my bed."

"Is that reluctance I hear in that offer?" He leaned against the wall, his eyes lazily studying her. If she didn't already know he wasn't interested, she'd think he was checking her out.

"Yes, darn you." Her annoyance flared. "Maybe you're some god who can resist, but I'm no nun. And my bed's smaller than yours at River Bluffs. And my couch is too small for you."

She flounced down the hall to look for bedding. "I'll sleep on the damn couch and you can have the bed." She was acting like a spoiled child who wasn't getting her way. She couldn't help it.

When she reached up in the hall closet to grab a blanket, Mike's hands skimmed under her shirt and up her waist to her breasts. She froze.

"Or we could *share* the bed." The tone of his voice sizzled against her neck, raced down her spine and burst between her legs.

"I thought you were staying away from women." The argument came out a whisper, caught between fast breaths.

"I can't sleep at night." He pushed aside her hair and pressed his lips against her neck.

"My students and players think I've lost it, because half the time I'm not at practice and I lose my place when lecturing." His breath tickled against her ears.

"I'm sick of taking cold showers from being around you." His hand cupped her breast, finding the hardened pebble of her nipple under her bra. She leaned into his chest and felt his erection press into her butt.

"So you're sick and crazy and tired? And this is your solution?" She arched her head back against his shoulder.

He nibbled at her ear lobe. "My solution is to make love to you until we've both had enough or we collapse in exhaustion."

She turned around and molded her body to his. "I like your solution."

Chapter 29

George Houseman prided himself on his down-to-earth views. Few things got to him. Running a multi-million dollar company was easy if one was certain of his place in life.

Except George was haunted—or maybe he was so grounded because he was haunted. He could never tell. Now that he'd called Mike Garretson, he knew the ghosts from his past would visit. Long ago, when he'd told his brothers and sworn them to secrecy, the telling had actually eased the nightmares for the first time. He'd shared his burden and his brothers had taken the responsibility seriously.

Then he'd made the mistake of telling that reporter. She'd died, two days after he'd argued with Joe and John about killing her. Her grandfather, Jacob Houseman, had flown from California and confronted all of them, even their father, Fred. His gut twisted, even forty years later, with the knowledge that one of his brothers, or perhaps his father, had killed her.

The nightmares had returned. He should never have talked to the reporter. He shouldn't have told his brothers either. If only...

Now he was going to tell someone else. Mike Garretson could stop the cycle. This time, no one would be killed. George was making sure of that.

He put off going to bed as long as possible, avoiding the sleeping pill he knew would only heighten the effect of the dream. As he slid his legs under the covers, careful not to disturb his softly snoring wife, he held out hope his exhaustion would allow deep, dreamless sleep. Maybe the past would remain safely buried in the recesses of his mind.

It was not to be. The images came as always, the terrible day his mother had died.

****

George grabbed for his little brother John as his father slammed on the brakes of the new car, stalling it as he missed the clutch. George's arm was the only thing that kept his two-year-old brother from ending up on the floor. George couldn't help four-year-old Joe though. His skinny rump slid across the slick leather and he plopped onto the floor behind the driver's seat.

Dragging a whining Joe from the floor, George frowned in disgust. Mother and Father were arguing—again. As his mother struggled with the heavy passenger door, he knew this was going to be a bad fight.

"I am not riding in this car with you anymore," Mother said. She shoved open the door and pushed herself out, her yellow dress bright in the sunlight. George watched her stomp down the narrow road.

Too short at age twelve to see over the bench seat, he could still hear his father opening and slamming the glove compartment, growling, "The hell you're leaving me." The car shook with the slam of the door as he followed Mother.

"Stay here. I'm going to follow them to make sure they're all right," George whispered to his brothers. John nodded, but Joe complained while wiping a snotty nose against his sleeve.

Though Mother and Father disappeared into the woods, it wasn't hard to find them, their voices roaring like two angry lions. He caught sight of Mother's flying red hair as Father grabbed her upper arm. She stumbled in the undergrowth, nearly falling in a small ditch she was about to cross.

Peeking out from behind a tree, George gave a silent prayer of thanks that his father kept her from falling.

"No. You listen to me, Eddie," she was saying.

George frowned. His father's name was Fred. Who was this Eddie?

"I'm sick of these games. You and your girlfriends all over town. And I don't fit in here." Some of her normally perfect hair dangled in front of her face. She must be really mad to take no notice of her hair.

"Don't call me Eddie." Father's back was to George, but George could tell from his voice that his father was begging, not angry. "Betsy, we have a sweet life here. We're heirs, damn it! You tell Josef I'm not his precious nephew and we're done. No money, no place to live. These are hard times. We won't be just poor, we'll be run out of town on a rail. You don't want that, do you?"

George bit his lower lip. His father wasn't making sense. Uncle Josef wouldn't let them be poor, and Father had a great job at Houseman Pharmaceuticals.

"What I want is for you to leave me alone," Mother said, jerking her arm from Father's grip. She straightened her shoulders and caught the loose strand of hair and stuck it behind her ear. "You have the sweet life. I'm the 'little' wife shoved in the corner. Besides, you heard your so-called brother Jacob wondering how your eyes changed from green to brown. It's a matter of time before we're found out somehow. I've had enough."

"Jacob was only seven when he last saw Fred," Father said. "No one even listened to him today, not even Caroline."

"I don't care. I'm not living this lie anymore. Divorce me—let me go—or I tell Uncle Josef his real nephew died in the war."

"I can't let you do that, Betsy," Father said so

softly George almost didn't hear him. Father pulled something out of his pocket. A ray of sunlight bounced off metal. George stared at the pistol in Father's hand.

Mother was mad. "You wouldn't dare," she said, reaching for the gun. Father pulled away as she tried to reach the gun. Then, everything slowed down, like learning English on a sunny spring day. And the scene just played over and over in his head, a broken recording.

Father lifted the gun out of reach. Mother cursed and clawed at his chest as she stretched for the gun. She wrapped her hands around Father's wrist, trying to get to the gun. Shoving at Mother, Father staggered in the wet ground, losing his balance as Mother succeeded in bringing the gun down to her level.

A sudden explosion vibrated in George's ears. He reached out instinctively as Mother stumbled, her heel catching on thorny underbrush and soft soil. Her mouth was a small "O" of sound echoing forever in his head. The shiny gun slid silently to the ground. Father screamed Mother's name, clutching at air as he tried to stop her fall. But she tipped slowly toward the ground, one hand touching the yellow dress as if smoothing out a crease. But messing her beautiful dress was a spreading red stain beneath her hand. Her hip hit the ground first. George watched in frozen agony as her head hit a muddy rock. A stomach-sickening crunch of bone on rock echoed in the woods, as Mother's eyes, staring blankly skyward, closed slowly and did not open again.

George shut his own eyes, clutching at a thin tree as his chest squeezed painfully.

When he opened them again, Father was crouching beside his mother in the ditch, holding her limp hands in his. A tear fell into the red blotch on Mother's stained dress. George's knees buckled and he dropped, leaves crunching beneath him. Father gasped and turned with wide eyes towards the sound.

"George," he said, his voice sounding like a child. "It was an accident. You saw it, didn't you? The gun. I only meant to scare her. It was an accident."

Father looked at him, his pupils tiny black dots in his brown eyes. He gently laid Mother's hands on her chest. Then he straightened her body in the ravine's damp leaves, pulling her legs in so that she stretched the length of the ditch. She looked like an angel, asleep in the leaves and dirt.

"We have to cover her up. No one must know she's dead, George. If they do, we'll have to leave. You understand, right, George? You don't want to lose your Uncle Josef, do you?" Father talked without looking at George, throwing leaves, dirt, branches, the gun, anything his hands touched, on top of Mother's body.

Soon the yellow dress was no longer in sight, the blood concealed. Mother was completely hidden.

George rubbed his hands together, working to wipe off the feel of death. No luck. His memory was forever stained.

Chapter 30

Mike rolled his Mustang up the concealed driveway to George Houseman's mansion for the second time in two weeks. He glanced protectively over at his passenger, who was temporarily his secret roommate. They'd had to meet behind a strip mall to make sure Jennie wasn't observed getting into his car.

He was sneaking over to her house after dark and leaving before sunrise. It wasn't the best arrangement, but he had to be near Jennie to ensure she was safe. River Bluffs was low on his priorities lately. In fact, if he could somehow contact the murderer or Jennie's attacker, he would tell them he was done—and carry out his promise. But he feared Jennie's reasoning that someone thought they were doing the research because of Josef Houseman's will—leaving the ownership of Houseman Pharmaceuticals in doubt forever—was correct. Even with River Bluffs on the auction block, they might be in danger.

At least one good thing had happened in his life recently. The last two days—and nights—had left him oddly content. He was surprised to discover how natural it felt to have Jennie around. He couldn't help comparing his relationship with Veronica with this one. With Veronica, it had been the sex from the beginning. Only later had they started the process of getting to know each other. He'd thought they'd had so much in common: their work, their Midwestern backgrounds, a driving need to succeed. But it wasn't enough.

No question making love with Jennie was better than anything he'd experienced. But the thing he liked best was being with her. He loved talking with her, the way she picked apart things, watching her mind solve a puzzle. She challenged him, made him want to do better and to do what was right. He used to be like that until Veronica had tried to make him believe it wasn't how he reached his goal that mattered, but to reach his goal whatever the cost.

That was when his marriage had started to fall apart.

Stopping the car, Mike left the engine running as he studied the woman dozing in the bucket seat next to him. Long dark eyelashes brushed cheeks that bore little makeup. She was curled sideways in the seat, a tendril of hair curled against pink lips. He enjoyed lying next to her at night, holding her after her breath slowed with sleep. Hardly a surprise neither had gotten much sleep the last two nights. Unable to resist, he leaned over and kissed her.

"Hey, sleeping beauty, we're here."

Shifting into an upright position, Jennie opened her eyes and stretched. "Oh, that felt good. I needed that nap."

He walked around the car and opened her door. "Ready to see what George has in store for us?"

"Yeah, though this is more than a little odd," Jennie said as they climbed stone steps to the front door. "Of all the potential suspects, this is the man who has the most to lose if his father is proved an imposter."

Mike nodded. "Giving him the most motive."

A man in his twenties answered the door. "Mr. Garretson, Dr. Foster?" he asked politely. "Mr. Houseman is expecting you. I'm his assistant, Mitchell Whitaker. Please follow me."

Letting Jennie lead, Mike placed a reassuring hand against her back. He was glad Jennie was with him. If she wasn't going to stop researching, it was better having her safely in sight.

The assistant led them into George's home office, a huge room that would have housed a family of four comfortably. He was sitting at his desk, reading, and stood with difficulty as Mitchell announced them.

"Come in, come in!" he said warmly. "Have a seat over here. It will be much more comfortable. Mitch, can you bring us some drinks? Do you drink iced tea?" He rattled on, hardly taking a breath to hear their answers. Before long they were perched on the edge of a burgundy red leather couch, cold glasses in hand, and George had settled himself into an armchair. Mike resisted an urge to take Jennie's hand, instead settling for pressing his leg against hers.

"So I expect you are curious to know why I've asked you come here," he began.

Mike and Jennie exchanged glances and nodded.

"You'll be relieved to know I'm not going to ask you any questions. But I'm going to tell you a few things I hope will help you and maybe, finally, put my conscience at ease. You should know, though, I have been trying for a year to get that damn attorney of Paul Garretson's to tell me what was in his will without success. I think, Mike, you know what was in it."

Mike kept his expression bland but it disturbed him George not only knew who Paul Garretson's attorney was, but that he knew Mike knew something about it.

"But that's not why I have you here. Dr. Foster—Jennie—the news says you found that skeleton. It was at River Bluffs, wasn't it?" he asked, leaning forward in his chair and looking at her with sharp brown eyes.

Jennie didn't answer, throwing the ball into

Mike's court with a look. He shifted and sat back further on the couch. Crossing his arms, he said, "What makes you think that?"

"Because I know who it is." If George expected them to jump up with excitement, he was sadly disappointed. Neither Mike nor Jennie moved. "It's my mother."

Now that sounded strange. They suspected the skeleton was Betsy Houseman's, but hearing her called "mother" made it so much more real.

"I watched my father kill her seventy-five years ago and I've lived with it on my mind all these years. I want to tell you what happened now, before this goes any further."

"We know the family story." Jennie leaned forward with a hopeful expression on her face. "We'd like to hear your version."

He nodded. "My parents were star-crossed lovers. They loved each other terribly, and hated each other equally so. Until that day in 1932, I never had a clue why. They fought and made up; fought and made up."

He related what he knew of the day his mother died. They sat quietly when he finished, as he seemed to be lost in his own thoughts. Mike exchanged a curious look with Jennie.

"I'm sorry. So long ago, and yet so fresh in my mind." George's gaze caught Mike's. "The most important thing I remember though is Mother called him 'Eddie,' not Fred or Freddie, as she sometimes called him when she was trying to get him to do something for her, but Eddie. Father was upset when she called him that."

"I never went back to look for her. Hated driving that road every time we went out there. Later in life I pushed Frank and Caroline to add a more accessible entrance from below the bluff so I would never have to drive that back road again. And I didn't.

"I've lived most of my life knowing my father was a murderer and probably isn't even Fred Houseman. I tried once to do something about it, with tragic results. I think you can help me find out who my father really was. That's all I want to know."

Mike had leaned forward during the tale, his elbows on his legs, hands clasped together. "George, you do understand proving your father was not Fred Houseman means you would no longer be a Houseman—or associated with Houseman Pharmaceuticals?"

George nodded slightly, his loose jowls wobbling with the movement. "I've been expecting this for years. My kids won't be left suddenly penniless. I've expanded my financial portfolio into other areas. The company is important to me, but frankly, Rob doesn't have a flair for managing the company and it's doing poorly. Odd things have been going on there and he hasn't been able to control them. I'm too old to deal with them. Perhaps it is time to cut our losses and move on.

"Mike, I especially owe you an apology about that funds scandal," George said, placing a brown-speckled hand on Mike's hands. "First, Tori was incredibly rude to you at the reunion even bringing up the subject. However, that's my fault. When we completed the investigation into the funds debacle, we found someone had shifted them from your department to another. We still don't know who did it, though there were only a limited number of people who could and Rob has been watching them. Nothing new has happened in that area. We are having problems with what was promising research on the melanoma vaccine, and there are other things, but the company's problems are not what I brought you here for. The bottom line, son, is you were set up."

Mike stared at the hand of the most powerful man at Houseman Pharmaceuticals, and expected to feel different. He realized it didn't matter anymore. "You knew all along I hadn't taken the money?"

"Good Lord, yes. Poor Rob could never get you to talk to him to tell you that. You, my boy, carry one big chip on your shoulder."

Mike leaned back against the couch. He already guessed Rob hadn't set him up from what Jennie had said from meeting with him. But it didn't hurt to have a man he'd long admired confirm his knowledge.

Jennie took his hand and squeezed it. Mike squeezed back, smiling slightly. "I always thought he was jealous of me, especially after I married Veronica."

"Veronica? I suppose he could be jealous of Veronica. The company might do better under her leadership. Of course, she'd fire everyone who crossed her..." He frowned at his thoughts. "No. Rob's too damn nice is his problem. It's one of the reasons we'll probably need to find another president here soon. He's not firm enough. He wants to go into real estate development full time. Been dabbling in it for years. Tells me he has a replacement in mind but won't say who."

"Mr. Houseman," Jennie said, and corrected herself at George's urging. "George, did you ever tell anyone else about your suspicions about your family heritage?"

"Yes. Yes, I told Joe and John, my brothers. When Uncle Josef died, we all knew about his will and how it would take the company away from us if our father wasn't Fred. I told them so they would know how important it was to protect our father from potential scandal.

"Oh, I told one other person. She promised not to use it in her article, but she never got a chance to."

"You told Sue McGregor?" Jennie asked, startled.

George struggled to stand, and Mike got up to help him. "I know what you're thinking, Jennie." He said when he finally had his balance. He began slowly pacing the room. "After Sue's death, Caroline was adamant Sue had found something significant. She had, of course, since I told her. Caroline really got into the family research then. I know all about the stories that said Sue had been murdered, but I can't imagine anyone in my family doing anything like that. I know my father murdered my mother, but he spent his entire life making up for it. I can't believe he murdered again. And my brothers, they couldn't, could they?" The old man's face registered uncertainty as looked at Mike and Jennie.

"Would you be willing to go on record about what you saw in 1932?" Mike asked.

George paused in front of sliding glass doors overlooking the pool area. "I don't know if I'm ready yet," he replied quietly. He turned to face them, his stooped and tired shape silhouetted against the setting sun. "I'll think about it. God may be my final judge, but I still have to live here on earth, too. My family is prepared to face the consequences, but I don't know about Joe or Charlotte's families. I could hurt a lot of people with what I know."

They made some small talk as they walked to the front door. George put a hand on Mike's shoulder when they stopped for their farewells.

"I said I wouldn't ask you any questions, Mike. But let me ask one. Why are you researching the Houseman family history?"

Glancing over at Jennie, he debated what to say. "I can't tell you why. But I can tell you it has nothing to do with the Garretson branch getting some sort of late revenge for a wrong, if that's what you're thinking."

George grinned, wrinkles crinkling comfortably on his face. "Just what I needed to hear. You're a good man, Mike. I'm as proud of you as if you were my own grandson."

****

Mike had expected a visit to George Houseman would be unusual. But that it would be uplifting, he had not. Jennie sensed his mood. She was grinning as if it were she George had complimented.

"I like your Uncle George," she said, sliding into her seat. "He's off my suspect list."

"I agree. He's not behind these murders. He has everything to lose by telling us what he did, and nothing to gain."

"Ah. But he does have something to gain: peace of mind. And did you hear what he said about the funds scandal? Transferred to another account. Not even stolen. And they still don't know who did it."

Mike shook his head in disbelief. Two years he'd believed everyone thought him guilty. Why hadn't Veronica told him? She must have known. True, he hadn't encouraged her to keep in touch, but she knew how much the theft had hurt him. She could have mentioned it during one of their conversations in the last week.

And George counted him as a grandson. Now he recalled the Houseman patriarch's participation in his life. When they were growing up, Mike had played with George's real grandson, even though they were four years apart in age. He remembered outings hosted by George to Cardinals' games, a school chemistry field trip where George had made Mike out to be an important part of the Houseman clan, and graduation when George had proudly presented a company-sponsored scholarship to Mike, not because he was family, but because he'd earned it through academics and athletics. When had he forgotten those things?

When he'd met Veronica. She'd told him about how George had masterminded the buyout of Richard Houseman to be able to control her grandfather. She had complained about how she was excluded from family events because she had lived with her mother after her parents were divorced. Mike could think of a lot of wrongs Veronica had complained about, and he'd taken her side. She'd been his wife.

Mike spared a glance at Jennie, who was also wrapped up in her thoughts. "What are you thinking?"

"Trying to figure out what information George gave us that we can use. Like now we know how Betsy Houseman died. Killed by her husband in a fit of passionate anger."

"That skeleton you found, I don't think there's a doubt now it's Betsy."

"We could tell the police what we learned. They'd interview George and he'd have to tell them what happened."

Mike shook his head. "No. George spoke to us in confidence. If he wants to tell the police, let him go by himself."

Jennie touched his arm, nodding. "I agree. It's the right thing to do. You know, even if he's not related by blood, he's still family."

He wouldn't have been able to tell anyone why he felt the way he did about George, but Jennie got it. Other people would not be so understanding.

"There was one thing George said that might help our research. Friday's the last chance you can turn in proof to Rick Boston, right?"

"He notified me on May 20, which is Saturday, so Friday would be one year."

"Two days," she mumbled. "It's that name, 'Eddie.' Something familiar about it, but I need to see my notes." She tapped her fingers on the armrest. "Can't think what it is. Mike, since you're going off to Springfield Friday, I'd like to go back out to River Bluffs and keep trying to find something. I don't want to give up till I have to. I'll keep Zippy with me. And I do have a gun."

"I thought you said your dad had the gun?"

"That was a joke about an M-16 rifle, Mike." She rolled his eyes at him. "I have a very handy, licensed pistol, and unlike my first shooting lesson, I did learn how to shoot."

"You're amazing. But I'm still not comfortable about you staying at River Bluffs."

"Would you be more comfortable if I was staying at my house? Or maybe I could sneak into your room in Springfield?"

"I share with one of the assistant coaches." Besides, his players would have a field day finding their history teacher sleeping with the coach.

"So I'd be alone in another hotel, if I could get a room at this late date. I'm sure every parent in the state has already booked out the rooms."

He frowned. She was right. It didn't really matter where she was, he couldn't be there with her anyway.

"I guess the only place you've been attacked is at your house. And River Bluffs has been safe enough for me over the last year. You should be fine there."

She gave him a mischievous grin. "You could lose your game Friday and be back late Friday night. Then I wouldn't be alone at all."

For a moment, he was actually cheered by the thought. "You're right. We could lose and we'd come home right away."

Jennie's eyebrows rose in surprise. "Swansea High School's most-dedicated coach in history is okay with losing a baseball game? And you think *I'm* amazing."

Chapter 31

Mike had dropped Jennie off at her car and she'd hit up a fast food restaurant on the way home. He would join her at her house after the sun went down, stealing through the neighbors' yards to get to her kitchen door.

They hadn't talked about what would happen after the deadline passed. She imagined Mike would get on with his life and she would go on with hers. This was just a job that had developed a few side benefits, she reasoned in an effort to accept the inevitable. The similarity to her childhood friendships was too much. With moving every couple of years, she hadn't made deep friendships and she knew how to cut off the friends she had on a moment's notice. It was too exhausting maintaining old friendships from a distance while making new friends move after move.

Mike would be another old friend. She closed her eyes and hoped she could be happy with that. He'd said enough times he wasn't ready for a relationship. She'd known the ground rules, even before they'd slept together. She rubbed her eyes, already feeling the ache. It would fade. It always did.

Tonight was their last night together. She probably wouldn't see him tomorrow, unless the Skyhawks, who were ranked number two in the state, lost their first match. And by Saturday, they'd have no reason to see each other again. Realistically, he couldn't keep staying at her house, even if they *were* still threatened by some murderer wandering the countryside.

She would make tonight special for him, something she'd remember forever, and maybe he'd think about sometimes too.

If she found what she was looking for on her computer, tonight *would* be special, she thought as she hurried into her house and turned on her new laptop. She found Betsy Borders in the genealogy software index and called up her spouses. There was Fred Houseman, but before that marriage was the one to Edward Clemment.

She glared at the name on the screen. "There's the bastard who stole Fred Houseman's identity. How did he do it?"

When Mike arrived, tapping softly at the kitchen door, she opened it and planted a hot kiss on his lips.

"I got him. I know who stole Fred's identity. Remember George said his mother called his father 'Eddie,' which is short for Edward. Look at this," she said, pulling him into her office to look at the laptop they'd picked out the night before.

"Edward Clemment," he whispered. "Fred Houseman died in World War I and this guy took his place?"

"Wait. There's more," she said, calling up the American Battle Monuments Commission website she'd looked at two weeks ago, and just half an hour ago. She typed in Edward Clemment, and let Mike sit down in front of the computer to read the screen.

Edward Clemment
Private, U.S. Army
2nd Division
Entered the Service from: Pennsylvania
Died: June 6, 1918
Buried at: Plot A Row 6 Grave 61
Aisne-Marne American Cemetery
Belleau, France

"Incredible," Mike said with awe. "Didn't Fred's

letter to Josef Houseman say he was in the 2nd Division?"

He stood and allowed Jennie to open her computer directory. She searched through documents she'd scanned, a standard procedure she used with clients, and found the letter they'd discovered in the secret room.

"Yes, here it is," she said, opening it.

"You found him, Jennie. You found the imposter," Mike said, after reading the letter again over her shoulder. He pulled her of the chair, wrapped his arms around her waist and kissed her. "That's fantastic. But is it enough for Rick?"

"I can see if Clemment's draft registration exists. I'll call Sheila Armstrong tonight and see if she can get over to the Regional Archives tomorrow. That will have a physical description of him. If he has brown eyes, that helps. Combined with Jacob's statement, we might have enough. Given a little more time, I might be able to prove Eddie took Fred's identity, with signatures and other documentation. We've got a case with what we have. It's circumstantial, but lawyers have put criminals in prison on less evidence. I've got to talk Rick Boston into accepting this information."

Mike shook his head in disbelief. "I never thought I'd get this close to keeping River Bluffs. You're a helluva researcher."

She shrugged, not knowing a lot of people in her business and unwilling to compare.

"Even if this doesn't end with me keeping River Bluffs, Jennie, you have taken me on the ride of my life. I have learned so much." He kissed her slowly and liquid warmth ran through her veins. She loved being in his arms.

"Since tonight will be my last night working with you, I thought it should be something special." She traced a finger down his button-down shirt, stopping at each button and slipping it through the hole. When she reached his pants, she undid the snap, pleased to hear Mike's indrawn breath.

"I mean, after tomorrow, there's no reason for us to see each other again, is there?" She was trying to keep her voice even. Focusing on seducing Mike would make it less painful to confirm what she already thought. "We'll have one more fun night, I'll try to sell this evidence to Rick, and one way or another, this project is complete. Right?" She pulled down his zipper, feeling the bulge beneath the cloth.

"I suppose," he said breathily.

"And you thought I couldn't handle a one-night stand. Though I guess this is a three-night stand, isn't it?" She managed a low chuckle, but couldn't look him in the eye. But she'd said it. He was free. She wasn't going to do to Mike what Veronica had done to him. And she wasn't going to pine for him either.

"Jennie."

She pulled out his shirt tails and slipped his T-shirt over his head, stopping him from saying anything more. She ran kisses up his chest, whispering as she did.

"It's okay, Mike. I know you didn't want anything long term. Really. I've enjoyed our time together. Let's enjoy each other one more time."

Make it memorable. Don't let me forget you, Mike. Don't become the junk in my attic.

****

The warmth of Mike's caress lingered as he backed out of the driveway, a bare glow of Friday's morning light in the sky.

Last night had been spectacular. She'd gotten maybe two hours sleep. It didn't matter. She'd have the rest of her life to make up the sleep. But she'd never get Mike again. As expected, he hadn't said a single word about what happened after the project was complete.

Why should he? She was his employee and the work was finished.

The vice-like grip on her heart denied her words. He was moving on, like dozens of friends in her life, she reminded herself. She'd survived and built on her experience. Only one man would be gone out of her life this time. Much easier. Time to move on.

Get over it, Foster.

Drawing in a long breath of air, she shoved her concerns to the back of her mind. After all, today was the last day before final exams. And she had the package for Rick Boston to drop off after work before heading to River Bluffs, where at least she could enjoy the majesty of the home one last time.

The day had a surreal feel to it, with many students and teachers having traveled to the championship baseball games. Half of her thoughts were on Mike and the other half on what she might have missed about the Housemans that could save the house. That left very little attention left to focus on her students, who happily took what amounted to a free day.

"Are you coming for dinner Sunday?" Mae asked as she sat down next to Jennie for lunch in the faculty lounge. The discovery of the skeleton had monopolized faculty conversations earlier in the week, but was now old news. The topic of primary interest in the lounge today was the baseball championship, and, peripherally, finals.

Jennie wondered what she'd be doing Sunday with Mike's project no longer on her agenda. "Sure. My project will be completed and I'm guessing I'll be bored."

Mae snorted. "Then come over early and fill me in what you've been doing these last few weeks, besides digging up skeletons."

It occurred to Jennie she'd found more than one

skeleton during this project, though Betsy Houseman was the only real one. While chewing on a cafeteria burger, she looked at her cell phone, which she usually checked during lunches for client calls. Her message log had a call from Detective Hoffman. She murmured the name aloud.

"You mean the homicide detective? The one who did the interviews for the police?" Mae asked.

"That's the one," she said, tapping the call-back button on her phone.

"Detective Hoffman," he answered.

"Hi, it's Jennie Foster," she said. "You called?"

"Yes. Thought you would like to know about that skeleton you found. That family story matches up with the medical examiner's results. We also confirmed it with police records and newspaper accounts from the time. The body is a thirty- to forty-year-old woman with red hair. She's been lying there about seventy to eighty years. She was killed by trauma to the head. Basically, a crushed skull."

"She wasn't shot to death?" Jennie asked, surprised, then noticed Mae and a few of the closer teachers staring at her with wide eyes. "Just a moment, Detective." With a polite, vaguely embarrassed smile, Jennie stood and headed for a booth built in the teacher's lounge for private phone conversations.

"You were saying?" she asked, after she'd shut the door behind her.

"The ME says she hit a rock when she fell. There's no way of matching the gun to the bullet wound, but I would say it wasn't a hunter who shot her. We're ruling it an accidental death. It could be homicide if we knew for certain she'd been pushed. What we think happened is she shot herself, or someone shot her and she fell, cracking open her head. The mark on the clavicle caused by the bullet indicates the bullet would have gone through the muscle above the bone. Would have hurt like hell but it wouldn't have killed her."

"If someone shot her accidentally and then she fell and hit her head, how would that be ruled?"

"What do you mean 'accidentally'?"

"I mean she was fighting with someone over the gun and it went off accidentally."

"Is there something you're not telling me, Dr. Foster?"

"Um, just speculating." Another person she needed to talk to when this was all over. Ah, well. It was only a day. She'd call him tomorrow.

"Well then, it would be manslaughter, and depending on the person doing the shooting, would probably result in a short prison term or a suspended sentence. Covering up the death would be an extenuating circumstance that could get the person more time, but a good lawyer might get him or her out of that too."

"Thanks, Detective. I appreciate you calling me."

"If you hear any more 'speculation' with substance, give me a call, okay?"

"Of course." She flipped her phone closed, then paused before leaving the room. George was wrong. His father didn't kill his mother.

Mae was already moving toward her, her eyes firmly locked on Jennie's. "So, it was a woman. Was she shot?" she asked, keeping her voice low.

Jennie looked over Mae's shoulder, and was glad to see no one else was paying any outward attention to them. It didn't matter. What the detective told her would be public record anyway. Besides, in a few hours the will would kick in to sell River Bluffs and her research project would be over.

"The skeleton we found was a woman who was killed when she fell and hit her head on a rock or something. She had also been shot, but the bullet didn't kill her. The police are ruling it accidental homicide. Since it happened seventy to eighty years ago, they don't expect to find a witness or even the person that might have shot her."

"There's more, isn't there?"

Jennie shifted her stance, shrugging apologetically.

Mae let out a heavy sigh. "You're killing me here, girl. You said you could tell me about this on May 20. That's tomorrow. You calling me tonight?" she said, looking at Jennie from half-closed eyes.

"You staying up till midnight?" Jennie knew Mae went to bed around nine, because she liked to be up early Saturday to make a big breakfast for her family.

Mae huffed out a breath of air. "No. Call me tomorrow, at a reasonable hour."

"I'll be delighted to call you. You know I'm horrible at keeping secrets. This has been the longest month of my life, and I can safely say, the most amazing. What I can't help wondering is how much you already know."

As they returned to their lunches, Mae smiled, the kind that said she knew way more than Jennie guessed. "I'm sure I've guessed a few things. How are you and Mike getting along?"

Jennie frowned and ducked her head. "Fine. He's a good client."

"A good *client*? That's it?" Her black eyes were boring into Jennie's soul.

"Yes. He's a good person. I like him, but, you know, he's not my type."

"Oh, sweetie." Mae shook her head slowly and rubbed Jennie's arm, like she'd imagined her mother might have done. "He doesn't know he likes you yet. He'll figure it out."

Jennie bit into her burger to keep from saying something stupid. She had to keep chewing extra long because of the lump in her throat. Finally she took a drink and swallowed the combination down, nearly choking on it as she did.

She met Mae's eyes, keeping her face as expressionless as possible. "No, really. I'm fine. Mike and I, we're friends. I'm okay with that."

She hoped Mae didn't notice she couldn't finish her lunch.

Chapter 32

"It's good to meet you finally," Rick Boston said to Jennie, as he shook her hand before taking a seat behind his desk.

Sitting in the lawyer's office with the package on her lap, she studied Paul Garretson's attorney. He was in his mid-forties, a little on the thick side around the middle, and wearing a tie skewed to one side, as if he'd just tightened it. Paul had picked a lawyer who was not on the pricey end of the menu. Rick's office suite was nice, but not fancy, and the furniture was once quality, but worn from use.

"Mike asked me to give you these documents as he had to be in Springfield for the state baseball playoffs."

"Ah, yes. The Swansea Skyhawks," Rick said conversationally. "A friend of mine has a son on the team. I get to hear about them all the time."

She nodded politely, and handed Rick the folder she'd arranged for his benefit. It was thick with copies of material.

"Here's what I've got. Mike said he told you we talked with George Houseman and you wouldn't accept hearsay as evidence." She pulled out the documents on Edward Clemment, including the copy of the draft card Sheila had emailed her at work earlier.

"However, I believe there is sufficient evidence here to prove Fred Houseman was not who he said he was. With the draft card, the marriage licenses, the letters and their signatures, and the photos, I think we have proved post-war Fred Houseman was not the same as pre-war Fred Houseman." She put every ounce of confidence in her voice. She wanted Mike to keep River Bluffs.

Rick confirmed her worst fears as he flipped through the documents. "It looks good, but I don't know. It would help if you could get George to sign a statement."

"We asked. He's thinking about it," she said, still keeping her voice cheerful. "We tried to get Fred Houseman's World War I draft card, which I believe is what Caroline had requested before her untimely death. Unfortunately, though it was indexed, someone had stolen it. I would think the fact it was missing would be of significance as well."

Rick shook his head. "I want this as much as you. You know I benefit too if you can present evidence proving Fred Houseman was a fake. But I have to be on the side of the law. Without hard evidence, probate could go into litigation for years." He tapped a pen on his desk and leaned back in his chair. "You still have a little time," he said encouragingly. He took a business card out of the holder on his desk and wrote a number on it. "The office is closed tomorrow, but you can call me at home if you find something."

"I thought today was the last day. Mike said you notified him on May 20th," she said, taken aback.

"Yes, but it was one in the afternoon, so that gives you all morning tomorrow."

"Ah, swell," she said cynically.

****

Jennie couldn't decide if a reprieve of half a day was a good thing or not. Personally, she was glad she could still look for evidence. Professionally, she figured she was wasting her time. Leaning toward optimism, she plotted out her plan as she drove to her own home and packed a suitcase, threw some food and drinks into a cooler, and headed to Mike's house to pick up Zippy.

The white fuzzball was as thrilled as usual to see her and did a five-minute welcome dance, which gave her time to find the cable channel covering the high school baseball finals. Swansea was down by two runs. Jennie was of mixed emotions. Though she wanted her school team to win, she didn't want to be alone tonight. It was just as well River Bluffs didn't have a television. She could focus on research, not watching the game. She loaded Zippy into her car and drove to the mansion. Even with a miracle, this was her last visit. Mike wouldn't need her anymore after one tomorrow afternoon.

It was odd to go to the house with no one to greet her. Without Mike, the house seemed lonely. Zippy disappeared from the moment Jennie opened the car door, clearly anxious to check out all his usual spots. She turned on most of the lights downstairs after hauling in everything from the car, and carefully unpacked the Beretta she'd brought. She loaded it, made sure the safety was on, and laid it in the middle of the kitchen's metal table. Short of carrying it around with her, it was the best place she could think to leave it.

Mike was going to call her when the game was over, so that was her big appointment for the evening. She shoved her cell phone in the rear pocket of her jeans to make sure she didn't miss it. She had two things she wanted to do for her final attempt at research: finish taking apart Sue McGregor's notes and go through the last of the stuff in the attic. Sue's notes could be done in the library, but the attic job would be better tackled in the morning when she had more light.

She turned on a small radio Mike had in the library and sat down on a settee with her legs folded under her. For about half an hour she worked, sometimes humming with a song, but mostly letting her mind play around with the information she had on the Housemans. It seemed Rick was only going to take an eyewitness account or a government document. She couldn't see George giving them a statement before tomorrow afternoon, and she couldn't think of any historical documents she didn't already have.

She had been so involved in trying not to rip the page from Sue McGregor's notes she was working on that she didn't even look at what it was. When she read Fred Houseman's name on a three-by-four-inch rectangle, her heart leaped. It was a copy of a World War I draft registration card—and not just anyone's, but Fred's.

The front of the card was fairly legible, right down to the signature at the bottom, but the physical description would have been on the back. The copy of the front of the card was stuck to the next page. Hoping it was the back page, she carefully lifted the paper to peer between at the print underneath. She was thrilled to see it was the back page, but the writing near the top—where the physical description would be listed, was glued to the top page.

Moving out to the kitchen where the lights were brighter, she eyed a knife, trying to decide if it would be better at getting the pages apart. Having done almost twenty-five pages with the letter opener, she knew it wasn't the most effective tool, but it had kept most pages legible. What she needed was a historical conservator. Unfortunately, she doubted one could be found in suburban St. Louis on a Friday evening.

She opted for sticking with the letter opener and knelt down by the metal table, putting her eyes level with the pages. Then, holding her breath, she slowly began to work apart the pages.

Fifteen minutes later she stared in

disappointment at her efforts. The upper left corner of the copy was a torn mess. She could read Fred was slender, had brown hair, was not bald and was not missing any limbs. But the height, with selections of tall, medium or short, was missing and the eye color had only part of a letter and an "n," which meant it could be "green" or "brown."

Jennie hit the table with her fist, then rested her forehead against the cold metal. She'd had frustrating histories to research before, but this one took the prize. Making short work of separating the remaining three pages of notes, she headed back to the library to study Sue's notes again. Maybe she'd written about eye color somewhere in them. However, the notes were mostly directed toward relationships and information on the William Houseman side of the family.

In disgust, Jennie dropped the notes on the desk and decided to head to bed so she could wake up early to tackle the attic. Her phone rang in the middle of brushing her teeth. Checking the caller ID, she flipped it open. "Mike," she mumbled through the toothpaste, "just a minute." After her mouth was rinsed, she got back on the phone.

"Sure, I call with exciting news and I get spit," he protested with false hurt.

"You won?"

"Yes! 7-6, we're one of the top four finalists now. I'm calling now because I wanted to be in a quiet place, and it has not been quiet anywhere till I got to my room."

"Congratulations!" she said, pleased something in his life was going well. "When's your next game?"

"We play again at nine tomorrow morning. It was tough getting the players to go to their rooms. I hope they sleep, because I don't need a bunch of sleepy players on the field tomorrow. I told them anyone not playing up to par would be benched."

She laughed. "Scare any of them?"

"Probably not enough to make them go to bed early, but they'll monitor each other."

"I wish I had great news on my end, but it doesn't look like the material I gave Rick is going to meet his standards of proof."

Mike sighed. "I didn't give you enough time."

"But wait. I do have some good news. I have till one tomorrow afternoon."

"How?"

She explained Rick's reasoning. "But if I'm to keep working, I won't make it to Springfield tomorrow. I thought I'd tackle the attic. See if I can finish it up."

"Oh. I suppose a few more hours might pay off. Better than driving up here to see a baseball game."

Did she detect disappointment in his voice? She shook her head. Wishful thinking.

"It's not like you need me there, is it?"

"No."

Her heart sank. Move on. Just another friend along the road.

"What time are the finals?" she asked, compelled to give him one more chance.

"Two-thirty. You might make that." He yawned in the middle of his sentence. Jennie couldn't read anything in his tone. And the yawn?

"I'm sorry, Jennie. It's been a long day, and as you know, it was a short night. I'll call you after the semi-finals tomorrow. Find out how you're doing and tell you if there's a game to see."

"That'd be great. I hope you win. It'd be fun to see your team in the finals."

"Thanks. I should go. Wait! You got that gun with you?"

"Of course. It's sitting right in front of me. Shall I fire it for you?"

He laughed. "No, don't bring the cops out again.

Hey, you be careful, okay?"

She detected a note of concern. But that could be directed toward her as a friend.

"I will. You get some sleep and focus on your game tomorrow morning. Swansea's counting on you."

"Call me tonight if you need to. I'll keep my phone on."

After their farewells, she wondered about Mike's last comment. If she could have, she would have talked with him all night.

Chapter 33

Jennie shoved an old table to the "looked at" end of the attic, which was now the center of the attic. A natural morning person, she was seeing the last few weeks in a more positive light. Not only had she been able to explore this beautiful old house, but she'd also gotten to research the most incredible story.

And then there was Mike.

She would get over the house and put aside the Houseman family history, because she had to. She wished she'd kept her distance from Mike. Even now, sitting in this attic with the sun barely up, she missed him, wished he was here.

She sighed. Finishing the attic was about all she could do, if only because it was practically a pirate's chest of valuables. This morning as she looked over the chaos, she realized there had been a sort of dated organization to the mess. When they had started this project, a narrow aisle ran the length of the attic, enabling access to whatever it was the person was looking for. The farther back from the aisle stuff was, the older it was. So the newer items were near the stairs and the aisle; older objects were closer to the slanted roof and far from the stairs, exactly where she was looking this morning. Here was good substance: an atlas from the 1910s; National Geographic Magazines from the turn of the century; a dusty Native American pot from some trip to the Southwest.

Zippy had been her constant companion in the attic, especially pleased when she uncovered an area he hadn't smelled before. But with this last crate, filled with mason jars that hadn't seen preserves in years, she dropped spread-eagle on the floor.

"Well, Zippy. I guess that's it," she said, a historian's sadness descending on her. She'd never get an attic like this one again. At least there were thousands of dollars of antiques here. Mike would benefit from that.

She stared at the roof line, the old oak beams running from the peak down to the attic floor. She frowned as she stared at the base of the beam nearest the wall. Something black was wedged between it and the wall. She flipped over on hands and knees and crawled carefully into the corner.

It was a black wooden box, so dark with age that it was darker than the shadows. She scrunched down on her elbows and hooked the box between her hands, awkwardly sliding it back toward her. Still on her knees, she pulled off the lid. Staring up at her from the box was a photo of two grinning twins in matching World War I doughboy uniforms, their arms dangling over each other's shoulders. In blue ink at the bottom of the print was written, "Freddie and Eddie."

"Oh, my God. They're practically twins," she whispered faintly. Keeping the photo on her lap, she picked up the next item in the box. It was a folded and crumpled letter from Josef Houseman to Fred Houseman, asking him to come to Illinois. After reading the letter which corresponded to the one they had found in the secret room downstairs, she picked up a package of several letters, still in their envelopes, tied with a string. The envelopes were addressed to Fred Houseman from Betsy Clemment. She pulled open the first envelope and read:

August 20, 1918
Dear Fr(ed),
How odd to be writing my husband with a

different name. I will have to get used to this I suppose. At least it is far better than being the widow I thought I was when the government sent me notification that you were dead.

How are you and when will you be home? How is your leg healing? I have missed you terribly and it is difficult to pretend to be sad when I am so glad. I will be happy to leave here though. My father drinks too much lately and does not have a job. Mother is worn to the bone and I try to help, especially since we all have had to crowd into Robert and Margaret's tiny house.

Please come home soon. I will do whatever you want to have you back.

Your loving wife,
Betsy

A dozen letters detailed Betsy's miserable life at her brother's house, with her drunk father and an angry brother. Jennie barely breathed as she read the last letter in the bundle:

October 30, 1919
Dear Fred,

You have given me the best Christmas gift you could give me! I have received the money to meet you in New York. I will be there before your ship arrives November 16th. It has been a long wait for the Army to release you, though I am happy you are in such high demand as a soldier.

As you asked, I will find us an apartment to live in. And, yes, I will remember to sign my name as Mrs. Fred Houseman.

Hopefully you will receive this letter before you leave. I love you!

Your loving wife,
Mrs. Fred Houseman
P.S. See? I remembered!

Jennie let out a long whistle, catching up Zippy and rubbing his belly enthusiastically. "This is it,

Zippy! No one person, not the president himself, could deny this evidence."

Then she saw one more thing in the box. An envelope-size dark leather holder with ties was still sitting in the bottom of the box, matching the dark stain of the wood. She pulled it out and untied it, carefully folding back the leather. Inside were the service records for Fred Houseman. On top was a record of his discharge, clearly noting his eye color as brown. As she reached the last page of the documentation of his time in the service, she found a physical from his service entry medical exam. *Frederick Houseman, U.S. Army, Color—White; Height - 5' 11"; Weight—148 pounds; Hair color— brown; eye color—green...*

She stopped reading then and closed her eyes for a brief moment of thanks. She opened them again, and crowed, "Zippy! I have to pay a visit to a lawyer."

She was covered in dust, though she would have gone naked to get the papers to Rick. As she was racing down the stairs, she pulled out her phone. Then in the parlor she found her purse and the card with Rick's number.

"Rick," she said breathlessly. "I've got the proof. I've got Fred Houseman's medical records from his entry into the Army and they say he has green eyes."

"You're kidding? Can you get them to me?"

"Yes. Where are you? Give me directions and I'll be there ASAP."

"How about in an hour? I'm, uh, at the store right now."

Jennie agreed. Since it was mid-morning, she even had time for a shower, though it was the fastest she'd ever taken. Long before she needed to be ready, she was in her car, the precious box on the floor by the passenger seat. She patted Zippy on the head and asked him to guard the house. He gave a little yip of reassurance, and she was off.

Wishing she had Mike's Mustang, she drove her little Saturn as if she were in a race. At the chained entrance, she replaced the lock, and then, reminding herself she had hours until the deadline, took a deep breath and slowed down to acceptable speed limits.

Rick Boston's house was not anything like his office. It was elegant and tasteful in a respectable neighborhood in Collinsville. She parked behind a late model car that looked vaguely familiar. Rick answered the door.

"Jennie, come in," he said. "I can't wait to see what you found."

She told him where she'd found the box at River Bluffs, speculating either the imposter Fred Houseman or his wife Betsy had hid it there years ago. Rick looked through the material. Finally, he looked up, shaking his head and sighing heavily.

"Jennie, this is perfect, I'm afraid to say."

"What?" Jennie stood, staring at him. He acted as if her discovery was a bad thing. Her mouth open, but words lost in confusion, she felt the hairs on the back of her neck rise. Someone had entered the living room behind her. Rick's gaze had strayed to the person and Jennie was afraid to turn around. Her instincts screamed at her to run. This was a trap. She knew there was a murderer standing behind her. Maybe if she didn't look, it wouldn't be real.

"Too bad for you, Dr. Foster," said a very real, sultry voice.

Unable to resist, Jennie turned to stare at Veronica Houseman, looking as immaculate as she had at the reunion, except for one tiny blemish: the lethal-looking Glock in her hand. Jennie felt the blood drain out of her face.

"Veronica?" she managed to say, her mouth suddenly dry.

"You know that old joke that you can connect everyone through six people to a certain celebrity? Well, in this area, you can connect everyone to a Houseman. I believe you met my stepmother, Paige Houseman? Rick Boston is her brother."

Rick looked apologetic, but he only shrugged. "Paul only promised me five percent if Mike proved Fred Houseman was a fraud. Veronica promised me a half million if I made sure he didn't prove it. An easy job if you hadn't kept searching. Attorneys don't make what the public thinks they do. I could have a house like this. But I don't. It's Veronica's house, not mine."

Jennie felt the urge to say, "You won't get away with this," but her tongue had cleaved to the roof of her mouth. The murderer had always been a shadow with a big question mark in the middle of the face. She'd never really wanted to know who filled the silhouette.

"Where's Mike?" Veronica asked her.

Jennie swallowed hard and managed to choke out an answer. "He's in Springfield."

"What the hell is he doing there?"

Rick supplied the answer. "The Swansea Skyhawks are in the state baseball playoffs. They won last night and this morning they're playing in the semifinals."

Veronica scowled, wrinkling her perfect face. Long nails resting on her hip, she narrowed her eyes. Finally, she said, "I think it would be best if we kill the traitorous ex-husband and his cute little history doctor at the same time. Call him," she ordered Jennie.

Jennie's mouth dropped open in surprise. "Mike doesn't know about this. You don't need him." How many times had he tried to talk her out of continuing on this project for this reason? "He turns his cell phone off during games, so I couldn't tell him about the box."

Veronica strutted around the sofa, standing in front of Jennie, eyeing her from head to foot. Jennie was uncomfortably aware of her T-shirt, shorts and ratty tennis shoes.

"You're right. I don't need him. Not anymore thanks to you. You see, Mike was my ace in the hole. I figured if someone proved Fred Houseman was a fake, it wouldn't matter. I was married to the one descendant that would hold the greatest percentage in HP. I would still be able to control the company, whether my grandfather passed it to me as his heir, or as the wife of the largest shareholder. Then he messed things up by asking for a divorce. When Rick told me he was going to hire a researcher, I decided it was time to reel him back in. I planned on seducing him into marrying me again. Later, Mike would have a fatal accident, leaving his share of the company to me."

Jennie swallowed, too stunned to say anything. Veronica had been planning to murder Mike from the day she married him.

The blonde poked her in the chest. "Small problem. He wasn't interested anymore. Why? I asked Rick to find out, and he said it was you. I didn't believe it until you called him the other night. I don't understand what he sees in you."

Her cold eyes studied Jennie for a moment. "Call Mike. I want him here. He'll come running when you cry for help. I guarantee it."

"What do I tell him?" Jennie felt her ire rising. "Veronica, his ex-wife, the murderer, wants to see him? He's not going to leave his team for just any reason."

Veronica glared at her. Brown eyes, Jennie noticed. Not green, not even some blue color from another ancestor. Plain, old brown.

"I   can   make   your   final   hours   very

uncomfortable, darling. I suggest you be a good girl and I'll kill you first, so you don't have to watch Mike die."

Jennie blanched, eyes wide. She had no doubt it was exactly what Veronica would do.

"You will tell him you know who killed Sue McGregor. Say it's Joe Houseman and he's hired a killer to find you. Have him meet you at River Bluffs as soon as he can. Oh, and be sure to say you already called the police. We wouldn't want him calling in help."

Jennie fumbled with her purse, remembering she'd left her gun sitting on the kitchen table. Wouldn't it have been smart to put the damn thing in her purse? She pulled out the phone. Her mind was racing. She had to let Mike know something was wrong or he would walk right into a trap. Searching through her phone contacts, she remembered Josh Kowalzski saying he was going to the playoffs. Would he be there today? She had to take a chance.

She had not deleted any of the Archeology Club members' phone numbers from their recent field trip. They had exchanged numbers before the trip in case they got separated on the drive to River Bluffs. Now she found Josh's number in her directory and pressed dial. She prayed her volume was turned down low enough that if Josh answered, Veronica or Rick would not hear him. Holding the phone to her ear, she was relieved when no one answered.

When voice mail kicked in, she said as clearly and calmly as possible, "Mike, this is Jennie. You need to come to River Bluffs as soon as possible. I know who killed Sue McGregor. It's Joe Houseman. He's hired a professional killer and he's looking for me. I already called the cops. Please hurry." She shut the phone as soon as she finished talking.

"That was atrocious acting." Veronica snorted. "Ought to get him here that much faster. Give me your phone. Rick, get the duct tape from the kitchen, wrap her hands and put some over her mouth. I don't want her shouting at the neighbors. Then let's go."

Rick left, coming back with the gray tape. He silently wound it around her wrists held in front of her and pressed another piece to her face. Then Veronica, satisfied, waved her gun toward the door. "Get her keys and park her car in the garage. We'll get rid of it later. Now, let's see this mansion my grandfather is always talking about. It was dark the one time I visited it."

Rick wrapped a hand around her arm and led her to the car at the curb. As he helped her into the passenger seat of the car she'd noticed earlier, she groaned in realization.

She recognized the car because it had been parked on her street. The hiding man had been Rick. No wonder he didn't want to be seen. He was probably the prowler who had clobbered her as well.

Veronica took the back seat, briefly holding the cold metal of the gun against Jennie's cheek to remind her who was behind her.

Having only been to River Bluffs twice, Rick had to have directions.

Veronica ripped off the tape on Jennie's mouth, warning her she still had a gun pointed at her. About fifteen minutes into driving, Jennie's phone rang.

"Who's Josh Kowalzski?" Veronica said, slaughtering the pronunciation of the name she read on the caller ID.

Relief flooded Jennie. Josh had gotten her message. "He's one of my Archeology Club members," she said. "He was one of the students who found the skeleton last week."

"Hmmph. He won't be talking to you again." She dropped the phone back into Jennie's purse on the seat next to her.

Her only plan had kicked into action.

She hoped Josh knew enough to get in touch with Mike.

Chapter 34

In spite of his half-blue, half-yellow face, Josh Kowalzski prided himself on his deductive reasoning. So when he heard the strange message from Dr. Foster for "Mike" and she didn't answer him when he called back, he attacked the puzzle with enthusiasm. After all, his favorite teacher appeared to be in trouble.

He reasoned "Mike" was a common enough name that might apply to anyone Dr. Foster knew, friend, student, coworker. But, during the last few weeks, it was a well-known fact one popular history teacher had been seen covertly meeting and talking with one excellent baseball coach. That would be Coach Mike Garretson, the same coach who was currently giving a winning pep talk to one of his players.

Josh needed to get on the field so the coach could hear the message.

Security though, even at this high school game, was letting only authorized people onto the field. He had gone out of the stands to hear the phone message and now he ran back to his seat, stumbling over several other fans to get to Adam.

"Adam, let me borrow your camera," he said breathlessly.

Adam stared at him in disbelief. "No way! You trash everything you touch."

Josh tried to look hurt, though Adam was right. "Seriously, dude. I need your camera to get out on the playing field. I've got to talk to Coach Garretson. Here," he said, quickly calling his voice mail and replaying the message for Adam. Adam's eyes grew huge.

"Dude," he said, and, handed Josh his camera. Josh went back to the concession area, found a bathroom, and made a reasonably good effort at washing off the face paint. He was glad he hadn't gone with the hair spray as well. With Adam's camera hanging from his neck, he sauntered up to the security guard nearest the dugout, but far enough away from where he had been haranguing the umpire.

"I need to get out there to take photos for the school paper," he said casually. The guard looked bored. "What paper?" he asked.

"The Swansea Free Times, our school paper," Josh replied. "I'm late. I had car trouble and I had to have another photographer fill in for me. See? She's the girl taking a photo of the batter on deck." He pointed to the real school newspaper photographer.

The security guard made a face and then opened the gate to the field. Josh would have felt a sense of pride at his plan's success but there was more going on here than a game. He didn't even pause to talk to the photographer but headed straight for Coach Garretson.

****

The Skyhawks were up to bat, and Mike had sent his assistant coaches to first and third bases. The team was up by one point, so he was checking his batting lineup for a possible realignment. He looked up in surprise when he saw Josh pushing through the dugout with a cell phone in his hand.

"Coach, Dr. Foster called you on my cell," he blurted out, stumbling over bats, gloves and players' feet.

"What?" Mike said, certain he had misunderstood. Josh shoved his phone at Mike.

"Listen."

289

Mike held it to his ear and heard Jennie's controlled, flat voice. When the message finished, he had Josh replay it. As the message sunk in, Mike tensed, gripping the phone mercilessly.

Shoving Josh's phone back at the teenager, Mike pulled out his own. Turning it on, he checked messages. None. Why would Jennie call Josh? Unless...she knew he turned off his phone during the games. She was sending him a message by calling Josh. The only thing she gained by calling Josh rather than him was time. He got her message sooner. So, should he call her back?

"Josh, did you call Dr. Foster back?"

"Yeah. She didn't answer. That's when I figured you should hear the message."

"Call her again. Don't be surprised by anything she says." Josh redialed and waited. Dr. Foster's voice mail picked up.

"She didn't answer," Josh said as he flipped the phone closed. "But you know how voice mail comes right on when the phone is off? It didn't do that. Her phone is on."

Mike cursed, and looked around helplessly. "Josh, did you drive here?"

"Yeah, Coach, I did."

"Can I borrow your car?"

"Sure. But I'm coming with you."

"You can't," growled Mike. "It's too dangerous."

"Then find another car. I can't get stuck up here without a car. My parents would kill me."

"Fine, but I'm driving."

Mike called a time-out, startling both his team and the opposition, explained there was an emergency, and they would have to finish the game without him. He gave some last minute advice to his coaches and followed Josh off the field.

Josh waved Adam over as he passed the scowling security guard. "C'mon, we gotta go!"

Mike glared at Josh, but Josh raised his hands in defense. "What? He rode up with me. I can't leave him here!"

As they walked out of the stadium, Mike dug out the business card Jennie had given him from Detective Hoffman and dialed his cell phone.

"Detective Hoffman. I'm a friend of Dr. Jennie Foster. Did she call you today?"

"No. Should she?"

"She called and left a message she was in some kind of trouble. She said she called the police. Can you check to see if she called nine-one-one?"

"What kind of trouble?"

"I don't know. She left a message on a student's phone. She said Joe Houseman had killed Sue McGregor and had hired a killer to track her down."

"What? I know who Joe Houseman is, but who's Sue McGregor?"

"She's a reporter who died in the late 1960s. It's a long story. Would you check your nine-one-one calls first?"

"Sure, I'll call you back in a few minutes."

By the time Detective Hoffman called back, they were on the road, Josh riding shotgun in his mother's mini-van. Adam leaned in from the back to hear the detective's comments.

"I've got nothing on nine-one-one. I checked the duty desk as well. She might have called another police department. You know we have so many little towns around here, there's no telling where she would call. Should I be concerned?"

"Not yet, detective. But if I call you in couple of hours, do you know where the skeleton was found and could you find it again?"

"Of course. Do I need to head out there now?"

"I don't know. Probably a miscommunication between myself and Dr. Foster. I'm sure it will be all right."

"What about this murdered reporter?"

"Do you have some time? I'm driving from Springfield. I might as well fill you in on what Jennie and I have been researching. There are a couple of old murders in it, and maybe one new one. Guess you need to know sometime, and the will has expired."

Mike heard the detective's colorful response, raising the eyebrows of his two passengers. As he began his tale, he stepped on the gas and sped down the freeway for Caseyville.

Chapter 35

When they reached the chained entry to River Bluffs, Rick was the one to unlock the chain, since Miss Ice Princess of the World wasn't about to sully her perfect shoes. Jennie's hopes rose a bit as the lawyer climbed back in the car, not bothering with the chain again. It would serve as another clue for Mike to proceed with caution.

Zippy, unfortunately, was there to greet them when they drove up.

"Damn, it's that dog again," Veronica said disdainfully as the furry creature bounced outside the car door.

"That's Zippy," Jennie said. "He comes with the house." She didn't think there was anything she could say that would make Veronica like Zippy. In fact, she was embarrassed to admit she hadn't liked Zippy at first, putting Veronica and her in the same category. Now she wanted to protect him.

"Keep him away from me," Veronica warned.

"Then let me out so I can hold him."

Rick's pasty pale face didn't so much as twitch at Veronica's whining. "I'll let you out," he said to Jennie, as she was constrained by the tape around her wrists. "Stay put, Veronica, and we'll get rid of the dog."

"You better," she said.

To Jennie's amazement, Zippy instantly stopped barking when Rick got out of the car. She thought he loved everyone, remembering the dog's blissful greeting the first time she'd met him, even though she was a complete stranger. However, there must have been a short time after Paul's death that Rick had been responsible for the dog. Perhaps Zippy was predisposed to dislike Rick.

As soon as Jennie crawled out of the car, Zippy leaped into her arms. She somehow managed to keep from dropping him in spite of the tape. Veronica stepped out of the car, gun still clutched in her hand and steadily trained on Jennie.

"I'm not going to run, Veronica," Jennie said. Sarcasm probably wasn't her best choice of defense against an armed person, but it made her feel better, more in control. Zippy, held awkwardly against her chest, began to growl, a throaty noise that vibrated against her. Then his body tensed and he launched himself toward the blonde. In vain, Jennie tried to grab him with her taped hands.

He was at Veronica's ankles and nipping almost before Jennie could open her mouth to holler at him. Veronica was faster. She whipped the Glock around and fired.

Jennie screamed at the same time Zippy yelped, racing around the house. Veronica turned the gun on her, her perfect complexion marred by angry red spots and her eyes blazing fury.

"Get the hell inside!" the blonde shrieked.

Apparently used to sudden mood swings, Rick grabbed Jennie's arm and hauled her toward the house. While she waited for him to unlock the door, Jennie craned her neck to look for Zippy, but he had disappeared. Shaking, she let Rick push her onto the parlor sofa. Had Veronica shot Zippy? He had been nothing but a friend since she'd met him.

Cursing under her breath, Veronica had backed into the house, watching to make sure the dog didn't attack her from the rear. Rick wisely took a stance against the wall, removed from both women. With the door closed, Jennie felt the intensity of Veronica's glare.

"That dog will have to go as well," she hissed.

Veronica took several deep breaths to regain her composure. With her blonde hair brushed back out of her face, Jennie felt the woman's tension ease and her own mood veered crazily as Veronica's gun ended up pointing at Jennie again.

"Now we wait," Veronica announced.

Jennie's mind raced with nice, ordinary, safe things she could be doing instead of sitting here, like cleaning up the breakfast dishes. She flicked her gaze from Veronica to Rick, who was hiding in a corner.

"Why wait?" Jennie snorted, slumping against the couch. "Why don't you shoot me now and get Mike when he shows up?"

Veronica pursed her lips. "I could, but I like to play games. Especially ones where I win. This one's with Mike. You're just a pawn, though a really irritating one. It's Mike I want to see suffer."

Jennie matched Veronica's stare. "How about Jeopardy? I'll take Midwestern Murderers for $200."

"Cute," Veronica replied, with a humorless smile. "I think you'll have to offer way more than that for all the murderers in my family."

Jennie lifted her eyebrows. "Like your grandfather Joe?"

"Perhaps." Veronica was pacing, picking up the antiques decorating the room. "Is this Tiffany?" she asked, tapping on a lamp shade. Before receiving Jennie's amateur opinion, she continued, "The house is an eyesore, but it looks like old Josef Houseman had style." She glanced at her watch, sighing impatiently. "How long will it be before Mike gets here?" she asked Rick.

"I'd say maybe two this afternoon, earlier if the game finishes quickly. It's a two-hour drive from Springfield to here."

Veronica frowned. "This won't do," she decided.

"Find some rope and tie her up to a chair. I'm not going to hold this gun for hours."

Hurrying out of the parlor, Rick called from the library. "Veronica, you might want to come in here," he suggested. "It appears our girl was doing her research here."

"Get up," she commanded Jennie.

Before they entered the library, Jennie's phone began to ring again. Having dropped the purse in the parlor, Veronica retrieved the phone out of it.

"It's that Josh kid again. Does he have a crush on you or something?"

Hope filling her after Josh's second call, Jennie mumbled something about a special assignment. Veronica, tossing the phone onto the library's oak desk, did not appear to have heard. She waved Jennie into one of the needlepoint chairs, and Rick went in search of rope.

Checking out the mess on the desk, Veronica picked up some of the research Jennie had spread out last night. "You've been a busy little researcher," she said, flipping through the pages. "I was thinking of locking you in the basement to starve to death, but perhaps we will have to burn this place down. That'll make sure we get all this junk."

"It's about your family. It's history," Jennie protested.

With half-closed eyes, Veronica seemed to be contemplating Jennie's fate, something Jennie did not want her thinking about. Recognizing the document the blonde held, Jennie launched into a subject she hoped would distract Veronica. "The paper in your hand? That's a marriage record of Betsy Houseman's first marriage to Eddie Clemment. Eddie was the man who took Fred Houseman's identity."

"Really?" A thin eyebrow arched upward. "Explain. I don't know the details."

Relieved to find something that interested her captor, who was much easier to deal with when she was cold and calculating than when she was angry, Jennie plunged into the story she'd pieced together about Eddie, Fred and Betsy.

Rick returned with some rope he'd found somewhere. "Look what I found." He held Jennie's Beretta delicately between his thumb and index finger. Veronica's gaze shifted from Rick to Jennie.

"You know how to use that thing?"

Jennie shrugged. "I've had a couple lessons." Her dad had made sure she could shoot out the center of a target eighty percent of the time. If she got a chance to use it, she knew who she'd be shooting first.

Rick tried to drop it on the desk, but Veronica grabbed his wrist before he could leave.

"You use it. Stick it in your belt." She showed him the safety, flipping it off. "All you do is point and shoot. At close range, you don't even have to aim."

Rick's Adam's apple bobbed as he pushed the gun in the belt at his back. Then he returned to the rope he'd dropped and wrapped it around Jennie and the chair.

"So finish the story. Old Eddie killed his wife, didn't he?"

Jennie winced as Rick tightened the rope behind her. "No. The gun probably went off accidentally, but Betsy's head hit a rock as she fell, killing her instantly."

"Mmm," Veronica murmured, leaning back in the desk chair. "So great grandpa wasn't a murderer after all. Strike one for your Jeopardy game. I would have made Fred Houseman the five-hundred-dollar murderer. I heard he shot her because she was going to reveal his secret."

Jennie recalled the love in the letters from Betsy to her husband. "I think your great grandparents were very much in love. They got messed up in some bad stuff. He didn't mean to kill her, just threaten her."

"Makes you kind of wonder where we'd all be if she'd lived and spilled the beans, doesn't it?" Veronica said, standing and walking toward Jennie. "I wouldn't be at HP, because I wouldn't be a Houseman. What did you say my great grandfather's name was? Clemment." She shuddered at the name, and then sneered. "Mike would be a rich man, maybe even running the company. And you, you would never have met him."

Never have met Mike? Jennie swallowed, the unexpected pain in her chest making it hard to breathe.

Veronica's sneer turned into a thin smile, her mouth opening in surprise. "Oh, my God. You're in love. And worse, I think that idiot Mike is in love with you. Can you believe he passed up sex with me? Not once, but twice?" She strolled over to the window where Rick was trying to remain oblivious to Veronica. However, when she ran long fingernails down his face, neck and chest, Rick's eyes widened and his face reddened. With her other hand, she pulled Rick toward her by his shirt, pressing a thigh between his legs and sealing her mouth to his. The look on Rick's face was a cross between misery and heaven.

"See? Rick would never pass up sex with me. That is, if I offered it. Would you, Rick?" She shoved him backward, causing him to sit heavily on the wide windowsill. "Poor baby. Too bad he doesn't have anything I want." She turned back toward Jennie, her hips swinging provocatively.

Rick mumbled a weak apology and dashed from the room, Veronica's brittle laughter following him. "Men are so easy to manipulate. All they think about is sex. Even the hint you might give them some makes them slobbering slaves."

How had Mike fallen for this woman? Jennie was horrified to realize he had loved Veronica at one time. She wondered if she and Veronica had something in common, some personality quirk that attracted him to both of them.

The uncertainty must have shown on her face, because Veronica focused her attack back on Jennie. "So, when was the first time you two did it? You know. Had sex."

Jennie gritted her teeth, unwilling to reduce what she thought she had with Mike to Veronica's distorted level. But then she realized that was probably all it was to Mike. Just sex. "We have a client-business relationship," she said defensively, the words feeling thick on her tongue.

"Client-business? Oh, that's darling. Let me tell you about Mike. He probably loves your breasts. They're a nice size, perfect for his hands. He's likes a weighty pair. And your hair. He loves to run his fingers through it, doesn't he? Doesn't like it up, does he? And speaking of fingers, what hands that man has. Does he do the same things to you with those hands he did to me?"

Heat rising in her cheeks, Jennie stiffened her back in the chair. "That's sick."

Veronica strolled over to Jennie's taut body, grabbing her jaw and pulling her head back to look at her. She smiled. "Ah, good. The little teacher has some fire in her. I was beginning to wonder how Mike could have been interested in both of us."

Jennie wrenched her head out of Veronica's grasp. "You're disgusting. We're nothing alike. You tricked him, made him believe he was in love."

"I'm rather proud of that bit of acting. Mind you. It was easy to make out with Mike. He's one hot piece of meat. But you know that, don't you?" Returning to the chair behind the desk, she leaned back. "I kind of like you. I thought you'd be one of those nerdy researchers with no backbone. So, let's play your Jeopardy game. I'll give you the answer, you give me the question."

Jennie strained uselessly against the rope and tape, her nostrils flaring with anger. Words would not suffice for what she wanted to do to the blonde.

Veronica, still smirking and well aware she had the upper hand, continued. "Sue McGregor."

"What?" Jennie asked, not understanding what Veronica was doing.

"Jeopardy, dear. I give the answer, you have to guess the question. The answer is 'Sue McGregor.' Oh, let's make it for a hundred dollars. After all, I already gave you the answer."

It dawned on Jennie that Veronica was going to answer the questions she and Mike had been asking for the last three weeks. She recalled the message she'd been forced to leave for Mike. "Joe Houseman?"

"Oh, come on. You have to play the game right. You have to ask it like a question."

Jennie glared. "Fine. Who did Joe Houseman murder?"

Veronica made a dinging sound. "Right! Technically though, my grandfather didn't kill her. But he did hire the killers who doped her up with the drugs he supplied them. I don't think a court of law would recognize the difference. Now, how about the two-hundred dollar question? Caroline Garretson."

If Joe killed Sue, he must have killed Caroline as well. "Joe Houseman. I mean, who was the second person Joe Houseman killed?"

Sticking her tongue and making a raspberry sound, Veronica leaned forward excitedly. "Wrong. I killed Caroline Garretson."

"You? But you were a kid!"

"I was nearly nineteen and Grandpa instilled in

me an appreciation for what I would lose if Caroline proved our family line was illegitimate. Daddy was such a disappointment to him, didn't even want anything to do with HP. But HP is my baby."

Veronica locked her eyes on Jennie. "We Housemans worked hard to make HP what it is today. My great grandfather and grandfather put their lives into the company. And I've given everything I have to making sure it survives. It doesn't matter whose name is on it, it's ours. The Garretsons did nothing. They don't deserve any part of HP." Her eyes glowed with an intensity that chilled Jennie's soul.

"And George and his lot? They don't appreciate the business the way I do. Rob Houseman shouldn't be president. I should. I should be running HP. And I will. It won't be long now."

Veronica was mad, high on delusions of grandeur. Now Jennie could see how someone could murder.

Veronica's cold gaze bore into Jennie. "Besides, killing Caroline was easy. One nighttime visit to this old house and I shove some pills down an old lady's throat when she was already groggy. Easy."

Jennie shuddered. Killing Mike and her would undoubtedly be easy too.

"Next one. Jack Elliott."

Jennie felt sick. She knew the answer already and didn't want to say it. "You?" she said faintly.

"That's not proper format, but you're right!" Veronica said with false enthusiasm. "But for the big Double Jeopardy, do you know why?"

"It has something to do with Mike and the funds scandal and the melanoma vaccine." Her earlier bravado had evaporated.

"You are smart. They say you're the best in the area. Go on. I want to know what else you figured out."

Jennie hesitated, finally opting for keeping Veronica occupied. "Mike guessed Jack Elliott was behind the missing funds. He…we thought Jack was trying to get to you. Like the car accident with the brake lines. I thought it was someone else in the company working with Jack. Mike thought it was Rob Houseman."

Veronica stood up, clapping her hands lightly together. "Applause for me. First off, there was no accident. I made it up to get Mike to worry about me. And getting Mike to think it was Rob behind all HP's problems took a lot of time and effort on my part. Knowing Mike actually thought Rob was out to get him, that's priceless. Makes all my work worthwhile. The last thing I needed was those two to be buddies. Rob already suspected I was up to something, but he's too inept to run a place like HP. He couldn't figure out what was going on.

"Jack's job was to keep Rob chasing ghosts. He was supposed to be moving small amounts of money around. But he let his ego get involved when Mike was given the department's deputy position over him. I almost killed him two years ago when he made that mistake. Frankly though, I couldn't afford to lose Mike at the same time as Jack. So I held onto him for a couple more years. Unfortunately for Jack, I recently learned he was double-crossing me. He was feeding selected information to Charlotte Wainwright."

Having people talked about like they were pieces of Veronica's game was creepy. "And the melanoma vaccine?" Jennie prompted. "Is the research good or bad?"

Veronica smiled, raising an eyebrow questioningly.

Jennie sighed, closing her eyes. "You told Mike the research wasn't going well. You told your father it was going well. And you told Rob it wasn't. I would

say the research is on track and you had every
intention of using the misinformation to scare
Charlotte out of selling her shares."

She opened her eyes, cutting Veronica off as the
blonde began to speak. "There's more. You have done
the calculations on how the shares in HP will pan
out after your grandfather and George Houseman
die. You don't know what's in George's will, whether
he's leaving all his shares to Rob or splitting them
among his three children. However, together, they
would still have half the company. The only way you
could overcome their majority would be to buy out
Charlotte. And the only way she is going to sell is if
it appeared HP was about to sink."

"Oh. You are good. Really good. And you know I
have Charlotte sitting in the palm of my hand right
now. She's days from selling out. Poor naïve
Charlotte. Like Rob, whose daddy also didn't tell
him, she is completely clueless about Fred
Houseman being an imposter. I overheard my
grandfather and Uncle George arguing about it
when I was young. And then my grandfather told me
the whole story when I was fifteen. I convinced him I
wanted to run HP. The three of us are the only ones
who knew the family legend about Fred Houseman,
until you came along."

"You know about Josef Houseman's will," Jennie
said, guessing at another piece.

Veronica gave an exaggerated sigh. "Yes. The
idiot who screwed my whole family forever. You see,
that's why I had Rick keep you going, agreeing with
everything you wanted to do, even that archeology
dig. Who would've guessed you dig up my great
grandmother?

"But the point was that you would work as hard
as anyone to find evidence of Fred's crime, his
identity theft, as it were. And if the best researcher
in the area found anything, Rick just turned it over

to me, I sought out any originals, and destroyed it all."

"What about Fred Houseman's draft registration card?"

Veronica looked puzzled a moment, and then nodded. "Oh, yes. Grandfather took care of that. Flew down to Atlanta and picked up the card right out of the archives. I think he burned it."

"But that was irreplaceable history!"

Jennie's protest was met with Veronica's derisive snort. "Please. He had already killed one person. A piece of paper was nothing."

Jennie's shoulders slumped. How could she best this devil woman? She had more schemes than Jennie's imagination was capable of. For all her brains, she didn't have a single idea about how to get out of her ropes, the first step toward freedom.

Veronica yawned and looked at her watch. "This has been fun, but I could really use some water. Rick!" she called sharply, and the lawyer quickly appeared.

"Yes?"

"You sit here and watch our friend." She gave Jennie a glance and a flip of her shoulder. "I'd offer you something, but you have no hands to hold it with." She sashayed out of the room after getting directions to the kitchen from Rick.

Rick sat down in her vacant chair, pulling out Jennie's gun and playing with it nervously. He looked at her helplessly. "Really sorry about this," he said quietly.

"You're kidding, right?"

"No, really. I am sorry," he said. "I expected you would be unable to prove the relationship. I was counting on it, in fact. Then I would have earned a huge amount of money simply by keeping Veronica informed. When you found that skeleton, I got nervous. I stole your laptop, hoping that would slow you up. The spying and the phone call? Veronica wanted to frighten you, but I wanted you to stop. I'm sorry I hit you. Did I hurt you badly?"

"A small bump." Jennie eyed the empty foyer, and, keeping her voice low, said, "You don't have to do this, Rick. She's a murderer. You aren't. But you'll be at minimum an accessory if Mike and I are killed. Let me go and I'll speak for you."

He sighed. "I'm already an accessory because I helped with Jack Elliott's murder. I also knew about Sue McGregor's murder and Caroline Garretson's. Veronica wanted to make sure I was up to my eyeballs in it.

"I'm also the one who called you at the school. Veronica made me add that bit about Mike. She's extremely jealous of you, I think. She may not love Mike, but she considers him one of her possessions."

"Great," Jennie said, thinking Veronica had one more reason to want her dead. Closing her eyes, she tried to shift in her chair. She could only get a couple of millimeters movement. Giving up on being at all comfortable in her last hours, she had to keep working on Rick, the weak link.

"Veronica has every reason to kill you after this."

"I know. I've taken care of that. If I die, there's a whole bunch of evidence sitting in a safe deposit box that will be opened. There are certain advantages to being an attorney," he added.

"Oh, don't be so secretive, Rick. You've already told me about your evidence stash." Veronica strolled into the library with water in one of the hand-cut goblets from the butler's pantry. "These, I like," she said, holding up the crystal.

Veronica fiddled with the radio, cranked open the ancient windows and roamed the room. Rick took up a chair in the darkest corner, still trying to keep out of the blonde's way.

Jennie's phone rang as Rick's eyes began to droop. He popped up and picked it up, reading the caller ID. "Mae Jefferson?"

Veronica cleared the distance to the desk in an instant, looking at Jennie curiously. She stared at the phone. "How do you know Mrs. Jefferson?"

Jennie frowned, unsure of why Veronica was interested. "She's a close friend."

"Huh. You are an enigma. I can't believe you know Mrs. Jefferson. She's a powerhouse. A behind-the-scenes mover and shaker. My father, a congressman, practically worships her. She knows people, gets thing done, knows where donations can be found. Projects or people she doesn't support, fail. She's one scary woman. Daddy talks to Mae Jefferson all the time asking for advice." She tapped her lower lip. "I can't believe Mrs. Jefferson wastes her time with you. She'll barely give me the time of day."

Jennie's eyebrows rose with Veronica's description of Mae. She'd known Mae was an active woman, but she had influence with a congressman? Jennie couldn't speak for their friendship, but she knew Mae was a good judge of character. No doubt Veronica lacked any of the latter, making her uninteresting to Mae.

Jennie twisted her wrist to see her watch. It was nearing noon. She wondered if Josh had had the sense to take her message to Mike. If he hadn't, this was going to be a long wait, maybe even lasting into the evening. Miss Ice Princess would be a volcano of fury by that time. But between having Mike here or unaware, she preferred he didn't show up at all. That would mess up Veronica's schemes, even though Jennie knew her own life would be in question—as if it wasn't already.

Jennie's cell phone broke the silence again. This time Veronica picked it up and smiled.

"It's Mike," she said. "But we're going to pretend we didn't hear it, okay? That way he gets more worried."

When the phone stopped ringing, Jennie closed her eyes. Was he here? Did he just get her message at the game? She wanted to know what he was thinking, doing. Once this was over, seeing him at Swansea High School next year would be miserable. Not seeing him at all would be devastating. He had to live, that was all that mattered.

"He must be calling because his game is over," Rick noted. "It's about the right time."

"Then we still have another two hours," Veronica said, picking up her gun and playing with the clip in it.

Chapter 36

Having hung up on Detective Hoffman more than half an hour ago, Mike had patiently answered Josh and Adam's many startled questions. By the terms of Paul Garretson's will, he could tell everyone everything. He might as well get used to it.

When Josh and Adam ran out of questions, they all stared in silence at the road disappearing under their wheels. The van topped eighty miles per hour as they skimmed down the freeway.

Mike's chest hurt. He realized what he was feeling was nothing like what he'd had with Veronica. He'd mistaken the convenience of a companion with similar interests as love. In the five years he'd known Veronica, he'd never once been concerned for her well-being. If she had vanished one day, he would have easily survived the loss. It wasn't losing her that had bothered him these last couple of years, it'd been the failure of their marriage, the inability to repair their broken relationship. Competitive by nature, he'd compared his marriage to his parents' and could not understand how they had remained married for decades.

Now he understood. How could he fix the love between him and his wife when it had never existed to begin with?

Because he'd built a wall around himself, he was in danger of losing Jennie. She'd offered him everything and he'd mistaken her offer for lust.

Jennie wasn't Veronica. If he had the chance, he knew he would stay with her as long as she'd have him.

What if he'd blown it? She'd implied Thursday night was their last night together. Did she really think he was so shallow as to want her just for sex? But wasn't that exactly what he'd implied by telling her he wasn't ready for any commitments?

Let me make it up to her. Be okay, be alive.

Driving through the entrance to River Bluffs, he cursed at the chain lying on the ground. Jennie would never have left it lying there, so someone else had. Josh was eying him warily.

"You two have to get out here," Mike ordered. They protested, and Mike glared at them, the full force of his personality cowing them out of the car. "Call the police," he said. He found Detective Hoffman's phone number. "Call Detective Hoffman. There's trouble here."

"What do we tell him, Coach?" Adam asked, leaning in through the front window.

"He already knows everything. Tell him I'm going in to find out what's going on. That should get him moving." Before the boys could ask any more questions, Mike gunned the mini-van down the gravel road.

Out of sight of the house, he pulled the van over as far as he could, hoping the police would arrive soon. He had no idea what he was going to find, but if Joe had hired a professional killer, Mike knew he would be well out of his element. Surprise was his only weapon. He looked at his watch. The game in Springfield would be over by now. If she had faked calling Josh's phone, she was likely expecting Josh to contact him after the game. Maybe that was why she hadn't answered him when he'd called.

Still dressed in his baseball uniform, Mike picked his way through the undergrowth, aiming to get close enough to see what was going on and still keep his white baseball uniform out of sight.

The humidity within the forest of trees was climbing, sweat accumulating at the small of his back as he found a location with a side view of the house. He crouched down, scanning the still scene in front of him. Jennie's car was nowhere in sight, but a vaguely familiar older Buick sat under the porte-cochere. Rick Boston's car, he recalled from visiting River Bluffs with the lawyer last year.

What was Rick doing here? Mike resisted the urge to race to the house, fling open the door and yell for Jennie. If she was fine, a few more minutes of observation wouldn't hurt her. But if she was in trouble, he could only hope discretion was his best defense.

Several minutes passed quietly until Mike heard something moving in the woods near him. Distracted, he stared at the location of the sound and was surprised when Zippy raced silently up to him. His tail wagging as desperately as usual, the small dog made no more noise than a whimper, yet he seemed to be fine. Mike picked him up in his arms and scratched the dog's ears.

"I wish you could talk," he said, holding the animal close to his own head. "I'll bet you know what's going on in there." Zippy stared expectantly at Mike.

"It's you and me, buddy. Let's see what Jennie's up to, okay?"

Keeping low to the ground, Mike darted across the lawn, carefully climbing the stone steps to the porch with Zippy close at his heels. The dog's ears perked up and he gave a low growl, edging around toward the front of the house. Mike caught the sound of a radio playing as well, and followed Zippy.

The dog stopped short of the library's huge front window He crouched belly down and scooted back toward Mike, a low growl vibrating his body. The two side windows were cracked open, music drifting out. Getting down as low as he could, Mike eased himself next to the window. Holding his breath, he moved his head just enough to see into the room. Startled, he pulled back.

In his short observation, he'd seen Jennie tied to a chair and Veronica playing with a nasty-looking semi-automatic pistol. Veronica? Memories came back to him in a rush.

Veronica had been the one who had coerced him into marriage, her desire for him seemingly enough to make a marriage work. She also had laid out a tale of betrayal by George and Robert Houseman toward her branch of the family. She'd spoken often about how much better she would do running HP than Rob. Conversely though, she'd refused to let Mike address her complaints directly to Rob.

And now, here she was. A gun in her hand and the love of his life held captive in front of her. He wiped sweat from his brow. He ran scenarios through his mind. Offering himself up would only get them both killed quickly. The police had to be on their way. But if they came in sirens blaring, would Veronica shoot out of spite?

He was afraid she would. Veronica had a long history of doing things simply to satisfy herself. And if she was behind Jack Elliott's murder, Jennie's life was in serious danger.

****

In spite of the heat in the house and low-playing music on the radio, Jennie felt tight as a bowstring, ready to fire at the least provocation. So when her straying gaze caught a slight movement in the corner of the library's huge front window, she would have leaped out of her seat if she wasn't firmly attached to it.

Her father had accused Jennie of being a lousy poker player because her face gave away what she held in her hand. But this wasn't poker. Her heart racing, she quickly averted her gaze from the window, hoping Veronica hadn't seen what Jennie had seen—Mike's green eyes. She had to get one or both of these two to leave the room. Mike didn't have a chance against two guns, but one he might.

"There's a great view of St. Louis on the third floor. You can see the Mississippi and the arch too," she said.

A spark of interest lit Veronica's eyes. "Really? Is this place that high up? Rick, untie her. I want to see this view. Maybe after we burn this place down, I'll buy it and build a contemporary home, something with class."

Jennie had hoped Veronica would seek out the balcony on her own, leaving Rick for Mike to contend with. Having all three of them on the third floor was not going to make Mike's task easier.

Rick's face remained bland as he undid the ropes. Jennie, her hands numb under the duct tape, led them to the grand stairs, Rick trudging behind the two women. Veronica hesitated at the landing, wrapping her hand around Jennie's arm and pressing the gun against her neck.

"You stay down here, Rick. Go check around outside. I don't want anyone sneaking up on us. And find that damn dog. All we need is him barking his head off at the wrong moment."

Jennie's heart skipped a beat. Mike was outside. Had he heard Veronica? Worried she would hear whatever was about to happen on the porch, Jennie ignored the gun and energetically climbed the stairs, briskly taking on the second floor hallway to get to the back stairs and as far away from the first floor as possible. As they passed Mike's bedroom, she knew what she had to do. The secret room. If she could get to it, neither Veronica nor Rick would find her. If Mike had the same idea, they might be able to hold out until help arrived.

They reached the French doors leading to the third floor balcony and Veronica opened them since Jennie's fingers fumbled with the handle. Jennie preceded her through the doors, standing carefully off to one side, leaving the view for Veronica's appraisal.

Her gasp of delight was satisfying. Apparently even the cold Veronica Houseman enjoyed some pleasures. "Incredible," she cooed. "You can see the arch. Oh, I have to build something here. This would be a perfect location for entertaining, a beautiful deck for evening events." As Jennie had hoped, Veronica had edged toward the railing, though she still kept the gun pointed generally in her hostage's direction. Jennie didn't have full use of her hands, but she had arms and a fierce desire to live. Just as she was about to give the blonde a good, solid shove, a dog started barking somewhere down below.

Zippy?

The barking distracted Veronica, who turned her head enough that Jennie was out of sight. Jennie moved fast, pressing forward to drive her shoulder into her enemy. Veronica's head whirled at Jennie's movement. Though not the tumble over the railing Jennie hoped for, the push threw Veronica off balance, and the railing partially crumbled under her weight. With her free hand, Veronica snagged a post, her eyes coals of rage. She fired the gun as Jennie turned for the French doors.

Jennie felt a stinging in her arm, but didn't pause to contemplate what that meant. Instead, she ran: all the way across the third floor and down the narrow back steps, nearly losing her balance with her hands still encased in duct tape. Flinging herself into Mike's room, she used the crook of her elbow to twist the closet doorknob. She slid into the small space, and as quietly as possible, closed the door behind her.

Noisy heels clicking on the hardwood floor and a string of curses signaled Veronica's approach. Jennie ran her fingers over the wall, searching for the small latch without benefit of light, grateful that she'd had the chance to play around with it last week. Finally, a finger grazed the small groove and, holding her breath, she pushed. The door swung open. She slipped into the room and closed the door behind her. Seconds later she heard the closet door open and foul language spew from the princess's mouth.

"Rick!" she screamed. "God damn it! Rick! Get the hell up here. Find that bitch. She couldn't have gone far. I shot her."

Chapter 37

Mike caught his breath as he heard Jennie convince Veronica to go up to the third floor. He wasn't certain whether she had seen him or was trying to bond with the enemy. But with Rick coming his way, he was not going to waste an opportunity.

Zippy had his own agenda though. The instant the lawyer stepped outside, Zippy attacked with a ferocity Mike didn't know the dog possessed. He raced around the corner, catching Rick nervously trying to aim a gun at the snarling mutt, his teeth bared as he dove for the dancing lawyer's legs.

"I owe you, you lying bastard," Mike growled, planting his fist in Rick's face before the lawyer could shift the gun's focus. "That one's for lying to Paul Garretson."

Rick shrieked at the sound of his nose crunching. The gun clattered on the porch as he grabbed at his face. The second punch, sinking into Rick's soft abdomen, carried all Mike's anger. "This one's for putting Jennie in danger."

Dropping to his knees, Rick groaned. Mike didn't make a final blow. The sound of a gun firing froze the leg that was preparing to take on Rick's weak chin. Staring upward in shock, Mike cursed. He scooped up the gun and gave Rick a solid shove, toppling him like a broken tree.

With the gunshot ringing in his ears and adrenaline pumping through his body, Mike shoved open the parlor door and raced up the front stairs two at a time, Zippy panting along beside him. The warm metal of the gun did not comfort Mike. He'd fired a rifle as a kid, but nothing like this weapon. He found the safety as he paused on the stairs to listen. It was off. Rick would have shot to kill.

The thought of Jennie bleeding and needing help focused his efforts. He pressed against the wall at the top of the stairs. Veronica's cursing and calls for Rick echoed down the hall. Holding his breath, he realized she couldn't find Jennie. Jennie was hiding. Hopefully safe.

Veronica's voice retreated as she stomped up or down the back stairs, though Mike couldn't tell which. He slid around the corner, Zippy racing ahead and disappearing into Mike's bedroom. He followed, keeping the gun trained on the stairs. Mouth dry and heart racing, he pulled open the closet door, animal and owner slipping inside. Zippy whined softly, scratching at the panel. The barest sound of movement confirmed his guess of where Jennie was hiding. He found the notch that opened the door, and the panel swung in.

"Mike," she gasped, sobbing as he dropped to his knees next to her. With a rush of relief, he kissed her head, touching her face and arms.

Wrapping his arms around her, he noted she kept her arms pinned to her chest. "You're hurt."

She nodded against his shoulder. "It's my arm. She shot me, but didn't have a chance to aim. It's just a nick."

He peered at her forearm, feeling the stickiness slick against the tape still binding her wrists, nausea rolling in his stomach at Jennie being hurt. He worked off the tape. Pulling off his mostly synthetic baseball shirt, he ripped off his cotton T-shirt to wrap it clumsily around the wound.

"Did you see?" Jennie whispered while he worked. "It's Veronica. And Rick Boston. She murdered Caroline and Jack Elliott, and she paid off

Rick to keep her informed about our research."

Mike finished, showing Jennie where to apply pressure. She cradled the limb against her chest. Putting on his uniform shirt, he shook his head. "We'll worry about that later. We've got to get out of here. I've got Rick's gun. He's the worse for wear, but I don't think we're done with him."

"That's my gun. I'm sorry. I could have used it, but I left it at the house when I went to see Rick about the documents I found."

"Documents? The ones you turned into Rick yesterday?"

"No—"

He held a hand up to stop her from talking, the sounds of low voices and strange noises warning them. Mike wrapped an arm around Jennie's shoulder, the hand not holding her wounded arm clutching his hand. The closet was hot and stuffy, but they couldn't leave without knowing what Veronica and Rick were doing. He strained to hear a sound that would give it away.

He whispered into Jennie's ear, "The police should be on their way. Josh was supposed to call them. We can wait them out."

The noises stopped outside, worrying Mike more. Zippy whined.

"Do you smell smoke?" he said, shifting to see the door.

Jennie sucked in air. "Veronica said she'd burn down the house. She's doing it."

Smoke drifted under the doorway, filling the tiny room in minutes. Jennie coughed. They weren't going to be able to hold out. "I'm going out there," he said.

Jennie squeezed his hand painfully. "No, not without me. What if it's a trap?"

"Then I'll talk to Veronica. You've got to stay here. I've been blind for so long. I thought I needed

317

River Bluffs to get over my marriage. But what I needed was you. I don't care if I lost the house, because I got you. I win no matter what." He pulled her to him, and kissed her. "Sweetheart, I love you. Let me redeem myself by doing this."

She dug fingernails into his palm. "You don't have to redeem yourself. Stay here. Don't...leave...me," she said, carefully enunciating her words.

"Jennie, think this through. You're already bleeding. We're slowly dying for lack of oxygen. Let me go."

"Veronica wants you to suffer. I don't think she'd shoot you dead right away. She wants you to watch me die first."

He huffed out air, coughing as he did so. "Great, I think. At least she won't shoot to kill. That's in our favor. Then I'm going out, okay?"

"Fine, but anything goes wrong, I'm coming out after you. And you should know..."

He held a finger to her lips. "You hold that thought. Give me something to look forward to."

He ordered Zippy to stay, pulling open the door. The smoke was even thicker out of the closet, but he couldn't see any flames. He crawled on the ground, sliding the gun in front of him. Before he poked his head into the hallway, he edged up on his feet and held up the pistol, prepared for the worst.

On the floor stood a metal bucket, heavy, oily smoke pouring over the rim. Veronica, hidden beyond the doorframe, kicked his arm, the pistol flying into the air and clattering on the floor.

"That wasn't very nice what you did to Rick," she said, kicking viciously at his hand as he tried to recover Jennie's pistol. She fired a shot near his hand and he jerked back.

"Rick, get that bucket out of here. And open some windows. That stuff smells."

Sparing Mike a grimace, Rick seized the gun and grabbed the bucket using garden gloves Mike kept at the kitchen door.

"Where's your girlfriend?" Veronica demanded.

"What difference does it make? Your problem is with me." He remained crouching, his gaze glued on Veronica.

She frowned, marring her aristocratic features. "Oh, I definitely have a problem with you. And she's part of it. She's the one who found the evidence proving Fred was a fraud."

Mike's mouth parted in surprise. "What? I thought the evidence wasn't strong enough."

Rick returned, stumbling up the back stairs. "Jennie found proof this morning."

Veronica smirked. "Tell him what she found. Let him know how close he came to taking over Houseman Pharmaceuticals."

Rick outlined the facts, ending with Fred's physical. "The Army records, that's irrefutable proof. No judge will deny that," he finished.

Veronica gave a small laugh. "While you were off playing ball with your kids, she kept searching. Isn't it lovely? This house is all yours, Mike. For this moment, I'm the great granddaughter of an imposter. Too bad no one but Rick, Jennie, you and I know." She clicked her tongue. "And you and Jennie won't be around to talk about it. The burning bucket was a precursor. I *will* burn down this house."

Her eyes narrowed. "It's necessary for protecting my family's company. My company, Mike. The Garretsons did nothing to make Houseman Pharmaceuticals what it is today. I will stop you—and anyone else—from destroying my family's name and legacy."

The hint of madness glinted in her brown eyes. She shifted her stance slightly, leveling the black gun at his chest. "We're wasting time. Let's find

Jennie. Call her, Mike."

"The hell I will," he growled, glaring.

"Call her and I'll make sure her death is painless. She'll die in flames otherwise, a slow, agonizingly painful death. I can make sure the fire starts right here. I know she's in this room. You must have talked to her."

The evil emanating from his ex felt physical. She was as beautiful as she was mad. "Jennie!" he yelled. "Jennie, don't you dare come out!" Then he tucked and rolled into the hallway, intending to do his best to distract or delay whatever Veronica had planned.

Veronica hissed and fired, missing. Mike gained his feet, moving low and fast, trying to take out either of the pair. Two nearly simultaneous gunshots spelled the end to his flight. He rolled onto his back, hands up defensively, inches from Rick's feet.

Rick's timidity vanished with the first use of the weapon, his legs spread as he stood over Mike with the gun firmly pointed at his rival's head. Veronica edged toward the bedroom door.

"That was stupid," Veronica said, her lips pressed together angrily as she looked back at Mike's prone body. "What did you—?"

The sentence was left uncompleted as Zippy sailed out of the bedroom, teeth sinking into her ankle.

Jennie rounded the corner, as Veronica let out a string of curses and shifted the gun pointed at Mike to her small attacker. Smoke and Zippy's enthusiastic participation in the assault gave Jennie her opportunity. She launched herself at Veronica's hip and hit the well-toned body with her shoulder. The two women stumbled across the hallway.

Jennie tripped over Mike's legs in her tangle with Veronica, who somehow managed to twist and remain standing in spite of her three-inch stilettos.

Meanwhile Mike kicked the lawyer in the crotch and laid him flat with a sweeping leg. Jennie's gun dropped and spun.

With only one arm for balance, Jennie plowed into the wall, her wounded arm flinging outward to stop the fall, with excruciating results. She slid down the wall in a heap, clutching her arm with gritted teeth.

With a litany of foul language, Veronica fired a random shot. Mike scooped up the loose gun, as Rick regained his feet and threw himself at Zippy, grabbing him by the collar and dangling the snarling dog from an outstretched fist.

Veronica swung her gun at Jennie, rage and madness clear in her brown eyes. Mike's face hardened as he pointed Jennie's weapon at the blonde.

"Don't even think about it," he said, eyes narrowed dangerously.

Stillness settled on the scene, interrupted only by Zippy's persistent growl as he twisted in Rick's grip. Rick swayed none too steady on his knees, unable to do more than hold the squirming white dog away from him. Jennie held her breath, her gaze locked on Veronica.

"Standoff," Veronica said, her tongue snaking out along dry lips. Her breath was ragged and uneven. "What now?"

As if in answer, doors crashed open and boots thudded heavily across the floors downstairs. Veronica's face contorted. Backing quickly toward the grand staircase, she kept the gun on Jennie.

"This one's for you, Mike. Bye, bye, Dr. Foster," she said softly, her finger tightening on the trigger.

Like a scene from an old cartoon, Zippy wriggled out of his collar and dropped to the floor. He made a beeline for the blonde's already bloodied ankle. In response, she stepped back, her left heel catching on the loose board at the top of the stairs Mike hadn't repaired. Her finger automatically flexed on the gun as she tipped slowly backward, the sharp report of gunfire echoing in the hallway.

Mike fell on top of Jennie. She screamed his name in horror. While the clatter of a body tumbling downstairs continued, Veronica's curses abruptly ceased, leaving only Zippy's frantic barking and voices yelling at the bottom of the stairs.

Jennie shoved at Mike's body as footsteps clunked up the back stairs, more voices demanding, "Down on the ground!"

"Get that dog away from me," Rick pleaded, as Zippy turned his attention to the lawyer.

"Mike!" Jennie said again, her free hand rubbing his cheek.

"I'm fine," he said shortly. "Don't want to get shot by the good guys."

She drew in a sharp breath, choking on a sob as she wrapped her arm around his neck. "I thought you were dead."

Someone kicked Jennie's pistol away from the pair. "You two, move apart slowly," ordered someone in black boots. Mike slowly lifted himself off Jennie, keeping his hands in sight the whole time. As one of the black-clothed SWAT officers pushed him to the ground, a familiar voice stopped him.

"Not him," growled Detective Hoffman. "That's Coach Garretson, you moron. Don't you recognize the baseball uniform? And Dr. Foster. What the hell have you been up to?" Spotting Jennie's bloodied arm, he grabbed his radio and called for medical assistance, then turned his attention to Rick Boston.

"Are you all right?" Mike asked, helping her sit up.

She wrapped her good arm around his shoulder and pressed her face into his neck. "Now I am." Then she pushed back away from him, her gaze sweeping the dirty uniform for injury.

"I'm fine, Jennie." He nudged her chin up and brushed his lips against hers. Steady warmth replaced the hollow ache she'd felt when he was gone. She pulled herself closer to him.

"You two, don't leave. I have questions," Detective Hoffman said, taking Rick in handcuffs downstairs.

"Not a chance," Mike replied, wrapping both arms around Jennie.

"About that. Leaving." She angled her head back to see his green eyes. "I hate it when I have to leave my friends behind and I hate it when they leave me behind. You planning on going anywhere? Now, or for the next decade or few?"

His eyebrows rose and his smile tilted curiously. "The next decade or few?"

"Yes. Or longer. Because if I'm going to fall in love with you, I don't want you leaving. Understand?"

"If you're going to *fall* in love?"

"Fine. If I'm going to *stay* in love with you."

"What happens if I leave?" He ran the back of his fingers down her hair.

She felt her lips quiver at his touch. "Damn it. You'll break my heart. I don't ever want another person I love to leave me."

"Oh, Jennie." He rained kisses on her face till his lips found hers. "Then I'll never leave you."

****

They could have stayed cocooned like that for some time, but the medics arrived.

"Hey, you're Coach Garretson!" said the older medic. "You're my son's baseball coach. Tom Harper."

Mike's eyes widened slightly and she could feel his body tense. He gave her an apologetic look.

"Sure, Tom, third base."

Jennie grinned, guessing at Mike's unanswered question. "So how'd the game go? We've been kind of busy here. But despite that, I'm pretty certain the coach would like to know."

"Tom called me at the end of the semi-final match. They won! Man, I wish I could have been there." The man finished wrapping Jennie's arm. "And now I know where you went in the middle of the game. My wife said you left for an emergency. They're not going to believe me when I tell them someone was trying to kill you."

"Can you tell him I wish the team the best for the finals? Pass it on to the rest of team?"

"You bet, Coach," he agreed. "Give 'em something to dedicate the final match to."

As the medics worked, making sure Jennie's wound was the worst of the damage, Detective Hoffman returned with Rob Houseman trailing behind him.

"Thank God you're alive, Jennie," Rob said, letting out a heavy breath of air. "And Mike, you're okay too. When my father called, I was sure you'd be dead before we found you."

"What're you doing here?" asked Mike, surprised.

"I thought I was saving Jennie's life, but apparently you two took care of Veronica on your own. Dad has had private investigators tailing Veronica for some time. When they reported they'd seen Veronica and another man with a young woman bound in duct tape, he got the police involved. We would have been here sooner, but the investigator lost the car. We had no idea it was Jennie. Fortunately, Dad met with Detective Hoffman yesterday to tell him what he knew about Betsy Houseman."

"George met with you yesterday?" Jennie said to the detective, her mouth open in disbelief.

Detective Hoffman nodded, taking over the story. "Told me everything about Betsy, and that Fred Houseman was likely an imposter. So when George Houseman called me about a kidnapping, it was shortly after Garretson checked in looking to see if you'd called for police help. But the two messages didn't click for me until that kid, Josh Kowalzski, called me."

The medic interrupted them to ask them to move downstairs so she could be taken to the hospital. Jennie's wound would likely require a couple of stitches. Mike wrapped a supportive arm around Jennie's waist as they headed downstairs, Rob and the detective still on their heels.

"What happened to Veronica?" Jennie asked as they passed a broken pedestal on the landing.

The medic leading supplied the answer. "She has some serious head and facial trauma. Those stiletto heels should be outlawed."

Jennie shivered, exchanging a knowing look with Mike. Wasn't it these stairs the imposter Fred Houseman had fallen on one night, damaging a painting badly enough it had to be replaced with a new one? One that showed the startlingly green eyes of the Houseman descendants?

"You going to tell me what's going on here?" Detective Houseman asked as they reached the front porch. "Mike filled me in on what he knew on his drive. I need the rest of the details."

Jennie recounted the last few hours while the detective took notes. Mike interrupted nearly as often as the detective. He hadn't heard the new material either.

"Four murders. You two have been busy, haven't you?"

"You haven't heard the half of it," Jennie said, reaching out to trap Mike's hand in hers. "When you search Veronica's house, please recover a small brown box with a leather case in it. That's evidence that is going to shake up Houseman Pharmaceuticals big time." She looked at Rob apologetically.

HP's president smiled benignly, patting hers and Mike's clasped hands. "I know where you're going, Jennie. Don't feel guilty." He turned toward Mike. "However, you owe me, Mike."

Mike frowned slightly. "After today, yes, but..."

"No buts, Mike," the older man interrupted. "I had big plans years ago and, frankly, a less sure man would have given up on you. But I knew you were the one then, and I still think you are. I'd like you with me in HP's executive management."

Mike's stunned face was Jennie's delight. "That's what you wanted to talk to him about?" she asked, nearly laughing.

"Yes. Even as the missing funds were being investigated, I already knew I wanted him as my chief operating officer. You might have lost the biggest funds out of your department, but you weren't the first with the problem and you weren't the last. I never once considered you responsible for it. But COO might not be enough. You tell me, Jennie. What was in that box? Did you find the proof that my great grandfather stole Fred Houseman's identity?"

Mike was still staring at Rob as if he'd grown a horn out of the middle of his forehead. Squeezing Mike's hand, Jennie explained to Rob and Detective Hoffman the significance of her morning discovery, since they'd been unaware of Paul Garretson's will. Then she told them how Josef Houseman's will could affect the drug company.

Detective Hoffman had forgotten to write in his notebook, his jaw dangling as he stared at Rob Houseman. "Let me get this straight. You're not a Houseman." He pointed at Rob, and then at Mike.

"And you are?"

Mike shrugged. "Guess that sums it up."

"I'm a little confused myself, Rob," Jennie said. "You just learned you're probably going to lose your job and your inheritance in HP and you're acting, well, pleased? Excited, even?"

"Don't spread this around, but I hate my job," he said, leaning in. "I've always wanted to build things, majored in architecture in college. But when your family business is making drugs, you go into the business. However, I'm pretty certain Joe Houseman and Charlotte Wainwright are not going to take this lying down."

Detective Hoffman grunted, scribbling a few more notes and then flipping the notebook cover closed. "Don't worry too much about Joe Houseman. He's got a few questions to answer that could put him behind bars with his granddaughter." He nodded his head toward the medical helicopter coming in to land. "That is, if she makes it."

Chapter 38

"Reunion," Jennie said, taking her eyes from the laptop balanced on a tray on her lap. She and Mike were stretched out on new lounge chairs on the porch of River Bluffs, Mike tossing a beat-up toy for Zippy in the late evening sunset.

"What?" Mike's long legs were draped on either side of the ten-dollar chair he'd splurged on. Despite his sudden wealth, he still had the decorating desires of an average male. Fortunately, with Jennie's advice, Mike had several contractors ready to provide professional help in renovating the old house.

"You've got to have the next reunion here. You know, sort of in honor of Caroline. Invite both the California and Illinois descendants."

Mike hmm'd, quite happy with the addition of one resident to River Bluffs, but not sure about inviting a whole slew of new people here. Without air conditioning, the house wasn't ready for permanent residents, so the couple spent their time split between Jennie's house and Mike's new acquisition. This June day had been all about cleaning out trash, including old carpet and lumpy mattresses.

"It's not as if George Houseman can host the Houseman reunion now, can he?" Jennie continued. "I know he's been extremely accommodating under the circumstances, but he's not genetically a Houseman anymore."

"Why don't we see how the renovations go and how the legal situation with HP works out. Lots of big 'ifs' still to overcome."

Jennie leaned over, catching his hand in hers. "Are you excited? I mean, excited to be going back to HP, but as its chief operating officer?"

Excited? Yes. Anxious, sad and happy. His ex-wife was still in the hospital under police guard. She'd been arrested on murder charges with no bail, along with Joe Houseman. His baseball team had won the state championship and River Bluffs was all his. He had an incredibly passionate and loving woman sitting next to him, and he could not get his fill of her. Tomorrow's reentry into the business world was one more step out of the hole he'd fallen into when he met Veronica Houseman.

"Nah," he replied, squeezing her hand, a smile on his lips. "Same old, same old."

"Yeah, right," Jennie said, rolling her eyes at him, then turned back to working on the Houseman genealogy. George Houseman, though ready to turn the company over to the real heirs to the drug company, still had to contend with Charlotte Wainwright, who had decided not to go down without a fight. Poor Geoff Houseman, a politician sandwiched between his murdering father and daughter, wanted nothing to do with the company, but you couldn't tell the media that. In the meantime, Jennie was on HP's payroll to find all the heirs to Josef Houseman's legacy.

Between Jacob's enthusiastic support of the project and Jennie's research on the Garretson family tree, two-thirds of the family's pedigree was completed. Now she had to determine where Josef's sister, Katrina, had disappeared to and if she had any descendants.

Her left arm ached a little while typing, but the hunt demanded her attention. She stared at the information she had typed into the computer. Katrina Houseman had married Roger Daniels. The name clicked in back of her mind. Abruptly she sat up, throwing her legs to the either side of her lounge chair and setting the laptop in the space in between. Leaning over the computer, she searched the index, finding five more Danielses.

She threw a hand over her mouth when a chuckle escaped. Mike raised his left eyebrow, staring at her.

"You are not going to believe this," she gasped, bouncing up and down in the plastic chair. "Roger Daniels was the older man Katrina married in California. She bore him a son they named Robert. Later, in Pennsylvania, we have Betsy Borders' mother living with Robert Daniels and his family."

Mike's bewilderment grew. He stood up to look at Jennie's computer screen, staring at the chart she had on screen.

"Katrina's first husband, Roger, died in 1895 in Pennsylvania, where they'd settled. Katrina remarried a man named Charles Borders. Katrina bore him four more sons and a daughter, whom she named Elizabeth."

Jennie paused, watching Mike's face change from confusion to dawning realization. "Names a hundred years ago changed frequently, sometimes misspelled, sometimes because people didn't know other people's real names. You see, Kate is a nickname for Katrina. Katrina Houseman was both Kate Daniels and Kate Borders, the mother of Elizabeth 'Betsy' Borders and the mother-in-law of Eddie Clemment, the man who stole Fred Houseman's identity."

Mike was speechless, eyes wide in disbelief. He grabbed Jennie's hand and pulled her up out of the chair, holding her at arm's length.

"You're telling me George and Robert Houseman are still Houseman descendants?"

"Through Betsy Houseman. Charlotte's the one

fighting Josef Houseman's will. Wonder what she'll do when she discovers she's still a Houseman and she's fighting herself?" Jennie asked, grinning.

Mike raised an eyebrow, tilting Jennie's head back to kiss her. "She'll be happy I have superb instincts in hiring the best researcher in town."

About the author...

After living all over the United States and in two other countries, AJ Brower now considers the Midwest home and will never, ever move to another state. While she loves to take trips through her writing, she has to travel, just to make sure she doesn't move. Her husband willingly participates in the travel, and tries very hard not look bored when his wife talks about romance.

Along for the journey are her two teenagers, often providing current cultural and comedic references for her books. Left to enthusiastically greet the family coming home, when both virtual and real trips are completed, are a German shepherd and two cats.

For more information, go to www.ajbrower.com

Thank you for purchasing
this Wild Rose Press publication.
For other wonderful stories of romance,
please visit our on-line bookstore at
www.thewildrosepress.com

For questions or more information,
contact us at
info@thewildrosepress.com

The Wild Rose Press
www.TheWildRosePress.com

Other suspense-filled Roses to enjoy from The Wild Rose Press

DON'T CALL ME DARLIN' by Fleeta Cunningham. Texas, 1957: Carole faces not only censorship but mysterious threats and a fire-setting assailant. Will the County Judge who's dating her protect or accuse her?

~from Vintage Rose (historical 1900s)

SECRETS IN THE SHADOWS by Sheridon Smythe. Lovely widow Lacy had taken in two young children—and the rambunctious little angels wasted no time getting her into trouble with Shadow City's new sheriff...

~from Cactus Rose (historical Western)

SOLDIER FOR LOVE by Brenda Gale. An award-winning novel set on a lush Caribbean island. As CO of the American peacekeeping force, Julie has her hands full dealing with voodoo signs and a handsome subordinate.

~from Last Rose of Summer (older heroines)

TASMANIAN RAINBOW by Pinkie Paranya. A concert violinist grapples with remote ranch life, intrigue and the mystery of a missing diary, the peril of a flood in which all could be lost, and the undeniable attraction of the man who would do anything to protect his son.

~from Champagne Rose (contemporary)

THAT MONTANA SUMMER by Sloan Seymour. Samantha has everything but love. Dalton has only one thing on his mind: land. Neither wants to be a summer fling or be stalked by a mysterious attacker.

~from Yellow Rose (contemporary Western)

A CHANGE OF HEART by Marianne Arkins. Jake Langley returns to Wyoming to find more than changes at the family ranch. Discovery of a well-kept secret sets duty against heart's desire, changing hearts and lives forever.

~from Yellow Rose (contemporary Western)

DRAKE'S RETREAT, by Wendy Davy. Maggie needs a place to hide. Drake's Retreat, deep in the Sierra Nevada Mountains, is the perfect solution. But she has to convince the intimidating resort owner to let her stay.

~from White Rose (inspirational)

Breinigsville, PA USA
13 November 2009
227539BV00003B/3/P